Striking a Match, Book 1

Embers of Love

Tracie Peterson

Bethany House Publishers

Minneapolis, Minnesota

Embers of Love

Cover design by Jennifer Parker
Cover photography by Kevin White Photography, Minneapolis

Scripture quotations are from the King James Version of the Bible.

Published by Bethany House Publishers
11400 Hampshire Avenue South
Bloomington, Minnesota 55438

Bethany House Publishers is a division of
Baker Publishing Group, Grand Rapids, Michigan.

Printed in the United States of America

Library of Congress Cataloging-in-Publication Data

Peterson, Tracie.
Embers of love / Tracie Peterson.
p. cm. — (Striking a match ; bk. 1)
ISBN 978-0-7642-0819-5 (hardcover : alk. paper) — ISBN 978-0-7642-0612-2 (pbk.) — ISBN 978-0-7642-0820-1 (pbk. large-print)
I. Title.
PS3566.E7717E48 2010
813'.54—dc22

2010015874

In keeping with biblical principles of creation stewardship, Baker Publishing Group advocates the responsible use of our natural resources. As a member of the Green Press Initiative, our company uses recycled paper when possible. The text paper of this book is comprised of 30% post-consumer waste.

To Judy Miller

Your friendship has blessed me
in so many ways.
I pray God gives you strength
to manage the days to come.

Books by Tracie Peterson

www.traciepeterson.com

A Slender Thread • *What She Left for Me* • *Where My Heart Belongs*

Song of Alaska

Dawn's Prelude • *Morning's Refrain* • *Twilight's Serenade*

Alaskan Quest

Summer of the Midnight Sun
Under the Northern Lights • *Whispers of Winter*
Alaskan Quest (3 in 1)

Brides of Gallatin County

A Promise to Believe In • *A Love to Last Forever*
A Dream to Call My Own

The Broadmoor Legacy*

A Daughter's Inheritance • *An Unexpected Love*
A Surrendered Heart

Bells of Lowell*

Daughter of the Loom • *A Fragile Design* • *These Tangled Threads*

Lights of Lowell*

A Tapestry of Hope • *A Love Woven True* • *The Pattern of Her Heart*

Desert Roses

Shadows of the Canyon • *Across the Years* • *Beneath a Harvest Sky*

Heirs of Montana

Land of My Heart • *The Coming Storm*
To Dream Anew • *The Hope Within*

Ladies of Liberty

A Lady of High Regard • *A Lady of Hidden Intent*
A Lady of Secret Devotion

Ribbons of Steel**

Distant Dreams • *A Hope Beyond* • *A Promise for Tomorrow*

Westward Chronicles

A Shelter of Hope • *Hidden in a Whisper* • *A Veiled Reflection*

Yukon Quest

Treasures of the North • *Ashes and Ice* • *Rivers of Gold*

*with Judith Miller **with Judith Pella

TRACIE PETERSON is the author of over eighty novels, both historical and contemporary. Her avid research resonates in her stories, as seen in her bestselling HEIRS OF MONTANA and ALASKAN QUEST series. Tracie and her family make their home in Montana.

Visit Tracie's Web site at *www.traciepeterson.com.*
Visit Tracie's blog at *www.writespassage.blogspot.com.*

Chapter 1

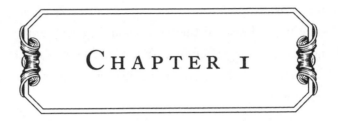

Philadelphia—June 1885

"I won't let you go through with this," Deborah Vandermark declared. She clasped her best friend's gloved hands. "Even something this drastic will not win your mother's respect, and it certainly won't soften her heart with love."

Elizabeth Decker—known as Lizzie to her dearest friends—shook her head. "You don't understand. If I don't go through with this, I'll have to return home with her."

"Nonsense," Deborah replied. "You can come home with me. My brother is waiting at the train station—or will be in another half hour. There's no reason to remain here. You're of age, and my guess is that even your father will approve."

"Simply one more thing my mother would blame him for."

Deborah squeezed her friend's hand. "Lizzie, your parents are divorced and your father is capable of dealing with this. They live in different towns. They needn't ever speak to each other again—and even if they do, it won't change how you feel about Stuart. Don't let your concerns about everyone else be the reason you go into a loveless marriage."

Lizzie walked over to the window and gently removed her wedding veil, revealing carefully coiffed blond hair. With that one simple action, Deborah took hope that her friend was finally starting to see reason.

"Oh, Deborah, how I can stop things *now*? Everyone is seated and waiting for a wedding. And what of Stuart? He doesn't deserve such ill treatment."

"Stuart doesn't love you any more than you love him. This is all some sort of game to him. You are simply a beautiful ornament for him to add to his life."

"Just as my mother has always said. Men do not marry because of love."

"That isn't entirely true, and you know it," Deborah countered. "Many men marry for love. My father, for one."

"But if I walk away, then Mother wins this battle." Lizzie shook her head. "I can't believe I'm saying these things . . . and after I fought so hard for this day."

"Marriage and romance isn't a war—at least it shouldn't be," Deborah replied. "You speak of the fight to get to the altar, not of the hope, joy, and love that should have brought you there. You don't want to marry Stuart Albright. You're only doing this to upset your mother."

Lizzie bit her lip. "It's not just that. I have to prove to her that I can make my own choices. She's so steeped in her battles for women's rights. She cares about the treatment of every woman in America—except for me."

Deborah joined her friend at the window. "Perhaps that's true, but I care about you, Lizzie. And it's not too late to stop this marriage. You can walk away—run away. You can leave now with me."

"I can't. If I don't marry Stuart, Mother will expect me to return home with her and involve myself in the suffragette fight. She'll drag me from one rally to another. Not only that, but I'll have to offer some sort of explanation to Stuart and his family—to my parents—to Jael and the rest of the congregation."

"Jael knows you're making a mistake. She's the only other friend we have here in Philadelphia. She'll be back any minute and we'll simply explain that you've come to your senses."

"How is running away from a promise coming to my senses?"

Deborah wanted to shake Lizzie until some semblance of reason formed in her brain. Instead, she took hold of her slender shoulders. "It is when the promise was falsely made. You don't continue with a lie just because you were the one who started it. Your mother's love will not be won this way. Your mother doesn't understand what she has lost. She doesn't see your value for who you are. You don't have to go home with her. As I've already said, you can come with me."

Lizzie looked at her oddly. "What would I do in Texas?"

Deborah tapped the side of her cheek considering the question. "There's plenty to do. You can stay with my family. We don't have the luxuries that we've known here in Philadelphia, but there's no reason we can't make the best of it. You can share my room, just like we did while attending college."

"But how would I explain this to my family—to the guests?"

Joy surged through Deborah. Now it was just a matter of helping Lizzie reason through the details. "We'll let your father handle it. He will understand completely."

"But I've already signed the church records."

"No vows have been said. The preacher has not officiated any ceremony."

"And what of Stuart?"

Stuart Albright had a reputation for getting what he wanted. He had been seeking Lizzie's hand for the past two years, and in order to spite her suffragette mother, Lizzie had finally agreed to the wedding. Deborah knew he wouldn't take kindly to being publicly humiliated, but on the other hand, she honestly didn't believe he loved Lizzie.

"Perhaps your father will have an idea. Let me get him." The church bells chimed the hour, and Deborah knew their time was up. "I'll be right back."

Carefully maneuvering in her cream and pink silk gown, Deborah made her way into the hall. Just then Jael Longstreet returned, her red curls bouncing very nearly to her waist.

"The church is full and everyone is waiting. Why is Lizzie not ready?"

"Because she's not going through with it," Deborah announced.

Jael's eyes widened and she clapped her gloved hands together. "Oh, won't this make for a scandal."

"Don't take such joy in it, Jael. This has been very hard for Lizzie. I'm going to take her to Texas with me. You go wait with her. I'm going to find her father."

Near the church's foyer she spied Mr. Decker. He was pacing rather nervously, tugging at the starched cuff of his sleeve. When he caught sight of Deborah, he halted and squared his shoulders.

"Are we ready?" he asked, beaming a smile.

"Not exactly." Deborah cautiously looked past him toward the church sanctuary. "Would you please follow me?"

"Of course. Is there a problem?"

Deborah waited to speak until they were back in the tiny room where Lizzie was waiting with Jael. "Something was wrong, but now we are trying to make it right." Deborah left Mr. Decker's side and went to Lizzie. "Your daughter doesn't want to go through with this wedding."

They had no way of knowing how Mr. Decker would take the news, but his broad smile was not at all what Deborah had expected.

"I'm so glad, Lizzie. I know you don't love him, and it gave me real concern."

Lizzie took several halting steps toward her father. "How did you know?"

"It was quite evident that you were doing this only to assert yourself. I could clearly tell during our supper last night that you and Stuart shared little affection for each other. Then after he left and your mother began railing at you regarding the marriage, you never once mentioned love."

"Stuart has pursued me quite diligently," Lizzie said. "He has lavished me with gifts and attention. I'm sure he must care for me, but I do not love him. That much is true."

"Oh, my sweet girl, that man does not love you," her father said, taking her small hands into his. "I believe he has been using you as much as you have been using him."

"How, Father?"

Decker shrugged. "He likely believes you would benefit his political and business ambitions. A beautiful wife who possesses all the social graces always does."

"Then he will not willingly let me go," Lizzie said.

"Oh, don't worry about him," Jael interjected. "He'll survive."

"But I feel cruel."

The sorrow in Lizzie's tone only strengthened Deborah's resolve. "Mr. Decker, my brother G. W. is waiting at the train station for me to join him as soon as the wedding has concluded. We are to journey back to Texas, as I believe I told you last night."

He nodded. "I remember."

"My thought—that is, if you approve—is to take Lizzie with me. My brother will not mind, and my mother will relish having another young lady in the household. Lizzie can stay with us as long as she likes."

"That would be a good solution, Lizzie," Mr. Decker said, turning back to his daughter. "Texas will put enough distance between you and the Albrights so that I can smooth things over. Your mother will be upset that you didn't tell her good-bye, but I suggest you two slip out of the church right now." He reached into his vest pocket and pulled out a leather wallet. "I will give you all the money I have on me. It should be enough to see you through for quite a while. If you need more, simply write to me."

Lizzie took the money he handed her. "But, Father, what if—"

He put his finger to her lips. "There is no time for further questioning. Leave now, and I will explain to the congregation that you have taken ill and we are postponing the ceremony. Once I've had an opportunity to speak to Mr. Albright and your mother privately, I will explain that the wedding is permanently canceled."

Deborah reached out for her friend's hand. "Come on. We can slip out the back door."

"But what of my clothes? I can hardly remain in my wedding satin."

Deborah considered the situation. "We are the same size and we shared our clothes all the time while attending university. There's no need for much finery where we're headed, so I'm sure to have suitable attire for us both."

"Besides, your steamers are packed for the wedding trip. I can simply have them forwarded to you when the time is right," her father added.

Deborah smiled. "There, it's resolved."

Lizzie's father leaned forward and kissed her soundly on the cheek. "Go. Go quickly. Miss Longstreet and I will stall for as long as we can." He looked to Deborah. "Where can I write to Lizzie?"

"Address letters to her in care of Deborah Vandermark in Perkinsville, Texas. There will be no problem in receiving correspondence there. It's a tiny town. Once she arrives, everyone will know her."

G. W. Vandermark was uncertain what to think when his sister and a satin-clad bride approached him at the train station. Nearly everyone in the depot stared at the two as they approached.

An older woman behind him commented to her friend, "How ridiculous. What bride wears her gown for such a trip? Why, it will be covered with soot in no time." She came alongside G. W. and looked at him. "Do you know them?" she asked as the girls walked toward him.

"I reckon I do," he replied. "At least I know the dark-haired one." He stepped forward, ignoring the old woman's grunt of disapproval.

Deborah put down a small carpetbag before throwing herself into G. W.'s arms. "I've missed you so much."

"Looks like you grew up while you were away. I can see I'm gonna have to beat the boys off to keep them from hangin' all over you."

"Oh, nonsense. You're the one to worry over. Just look at you, all duded up." She pulled back with a grin. "Come meet my dear friend."

G. W. glanced to where the young bride waited and tipped his hat. "Lookin' for a wedding?" he asked in a lazy drawl. He'd never seen anything like her; she was the prettiest gal he'd ever laid sight on. Her blue-eyed gaze locked onto his face and G. W. could not look away. She was like one of those fancy store-bought dolls with gold curls and smooth white skin.

"Lizzie, this is my brother G. W. Vandermark. G. W., this is Miss Elizabeth Decker."

G. W. tipped his hat again. "Howdy."

"We have a problem. Lizzie—Miss Decker—needs to travel west with us. She cannot go through with the wedding."

"Is that a fact?" His mind raced with thoughts of all the complications that had just been created. It was typical of his little sister to stir up a nest of hornets.

"I suggested she come to Texas with us. Her father is even now explaining the situation to her mother and Mr. Albright."

G. W. checked his watch. He had a hundred questions but knew they would have to board the train now or wait for the next one. Unable to figure out what he should do, he pulled at his tie. He hated dressing up, but for the trip east to retrieve his sister, he had promised his mother he'd wear the new store-bought clothes. Unfortunately, the black wool sack suit was layered with a stiff long-sleeved shirt, and the June heat was nearly unbearable. Not to mention the collar was about to strangle him. G. W. was tempted to remove the offending pieces, but noted the gentlemen around him were wearing theirs. It was a good thing he'd decided against wearing the waistcoat.

"I don't guess I understand, but I suppose you ought to give me your bag," he said, trying to figure out what they should do. "Oh, wait. Miss Decker's gonna need a ticket."

The young woman reached into her reticule and pulled out a

wad of cash. G. W. smiled, took several bills, and handed the rest back to her.

"This'll be enough," he said and made his way to the ticket agent. What in the world had Deborah gotten herself into this time? Showing up at a train station with a woman in her bridal gown was unusual, even for his sister. There were bound to be further consequences, but trouble seemed to follow his sister. Well, maybe not trouble so much as . . . disruption. As he made his way back, he could see that the folks around were still gawking and pointing at the young bride-to-be.

"I have all our tickets now," G. W. announced. "So you wanna tell me what this is about?"

"Look, G. W., I can explain once we're on our way," Deborah said, pushing him and Lizzie forward. "Now, help Lizzie onto the train. This dress is cumbersome, and she may well fall on her face if you don't assist her. I can get my own bag."

G. W. shrugged and picked up his case, then took Lizzie's arm. "Miss Decker, it's this way." He didn't wait for her comment, but instead headed to the platform and the waiting train.

"Congratulations," the conductor offered as G. W. and Lizzie approached. "My, but you two make a handsome couple."

G. W. looked to Lizzie, who was blushing red. He thought to offer the man an explanation, then just nodded and helped Lizzie up the steps to the passenger car.

They showed their tickets to a waiting porter. "Bettin' it was a mighty fine weddin'," the porter declared, taking the bag from Deborah. He bore a smile that ran from ear to ear. His dark skin appeared even darker against his white coat.

"It was the best I've been to in a long time," Deborah told him. The man nodded and secured their bags just as the conductor called the final board.

Once they were settled in, G. W. couldn't help but notice that all heads had turned to watch them. Smiles were plastered on every face, and without warning, one man began to applaud. This caused the entire car to begin clapping.

"I wish I could melt under the seat," Lizzie said, tucking her head. "I'm so sorry."

"It can't be helped," Deborah said, patting Lizzie's hand. "Once we make our first stop for the night, you can change clothes."

G. W. felt sorry for her. No doubt she was completely offended at the idea of being married to a backwoods bumpkin who could barely read, even if he was wearing a thirty-dollar suit bought in Houston. He offered her a smile, but she couldn't see it since her gaze was fixed on the floor.

"So why don't you tell me what's goin' on and why you two showed up at the station in your weddin' duds," he said as the train pulled out.

"It's a truly complicated story, but we have a long trip ahead of us, so here goes," Deborah began. "Elizabeth—you can call her Lizzie, as she hates the name Elizabeth." She looked to her friend as if for confirmation. Lizzie nodded. "Lizzie had to escape."

G. W. felt a sense of confusion. "Escape? From what?"

"Well, you see, she was only doing this . . ." Deborah gestured toward the bridal gown. "That is, she wasn't in love." G. W. would have laughed had she not remained fixed with a serious expression.

Deborah stopped short and shook her head. She sat back and folded her hands. "Wait. Maybe I should start from the beginning."

"That's generally best," G. W. said.

"Elizabeth and I attended classes together at the university in Philadelphia and shared lodging. She's been my closest confidante for these last few years. I'm sure you remember me telling you about her when I was home for the summer two years ago."

"Sure I do," G. W. replied, though he was sure she never mentioned how beautiful this woman was.

"Well, Lizzie's like family to me. She has a sad past—a tragic one."

"Oh, Deborah, do not make it sound so melodramatic." Lizzie gave a quick glance around as if to see who else might be listening. "Our appearance is bad enough. Let us keep it simple." She looked directly at G. W. "My parents divorced some years ago. My father has remarried and my mother is working for the cause of women's rights and feels men are unnecessary in her life."

"And because of that," Deborah went on, "Lizzie found herself at odds with her mother's plans for her future. One thing led to another, and she began a courtship with Stuart Albright."

G. W. listened to his sister go on about the sorry state of Lizzie's relationship with Mr. Albright. Apparently the man was a bore and not the least bit in love with the golden-haired beauty. But how he could keep from loving her was beyond G. W.'s ability to reason. She looked like an angel. Who wouldn't want her for a wife?

"Though she didn't love Mr. Albright, Lizzie felt she had no recourse but to go through with the wedding. That is, until just a little while ago, when she finally admitted that she didn't want to be married. Her father agreed with her and with my idea that she should come to Texas with us."

"And what of your groom?"

"I didn't feel that I could . . ." Lizzie began to offer before Deborah could speak again. "Well . . . you see . . . he's not one to take bad news easily. I was, quite frankly, afraid. Call me a coward if you must, but that's the simple truth."

G. W. shook his head. "I wouldn't be one to call you a coward, Miss Lizzie. I don't rightly know you well enough."

"Well, she's no coward," Deborah announced. "She's very brave, in fact, to put an end to this farce before it became final."

"So she's just gonna live with us?" G. W. asked.

Lizzie blushed again and looked out the window. Deborah nodded. "She needs time and distance so she can better think of what she'd like to do next. Her father will be in touch with her."

"Don't seem like her father will be the problem," G. W. said. "What about that mother of hers? What about her groom? He don't seem like the kind of guy to take to this kind of thing."

"Maybe not, but he won't know where she is." Deborah turned to Lizzie. "Once you're settled in with us, we'll see to it that no one can harm you. Never fear."

"It may be a moot point to worry ourselves anyway," Lizzie replied. "After all, what man would want to chase after a woman who has clearly rejected him?"

G. W. laughed. "If she looked like you, I know I wouldn't let her get away."

Lizzie's mouth dropped open. G. W. might have roared in laughter, but he felt pretty sure it would only serve to offend her further. Leaning back in his seat, he pushed his hat down over his eyes. He needed to have a think, and it would be just as well if the ladies thought him to be sleeping.

Of course, he'd much rather spend his time looking at Lizzie Decker. My, but she was a fine figure of a woman. She was all genteel-like. In fact, she reminded him of the stories his ma had told about the Georgian women before the war. Ma had been every bit as genteel before going west with their pa. She said Texas took the elegance right out of a lady, but Pa always said she was still the most elegant woman he knew.

G. W. frowned at the thought of his pa. Three years had passed since the logging accident that took Rutger Vandermark's life. G. W. had been right there when a huge pine log had crushed his father. The memory never faded. It was only made worse by the fact that G. W. blamed himself for the accident.

G. W. had relived the day of the accident over and over at least a thousand times. The guilt ate him alive and, try as he might, he couldn't shake off the horror of his father's mangled body. He'd been killed instantly by the two thousand–pound log, so at least there had been no suffering. But neither was there time for good-byes or to tell him how much G. W. loved him—how he needed him to live.

There was just no time.

Chapter 2

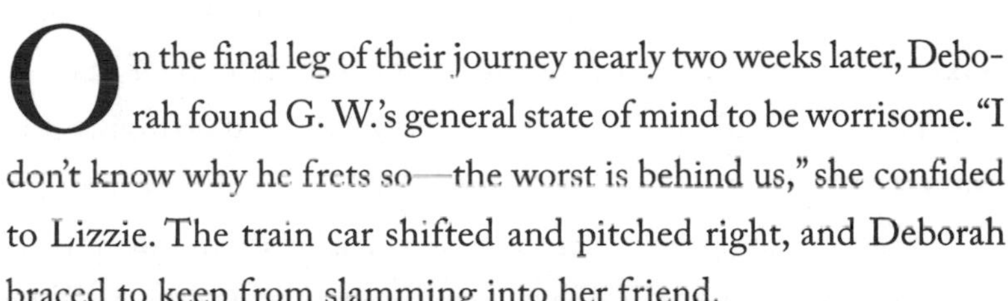

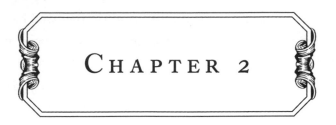

On the final leg of their journey nearly two weeks later, Deborah found G. W.'s general state of mind to be worrisome. "I don't know why he frets so—the worst is behind us," she confided to Lizzie. The train car shifted and pitched right, and Deborah braced to keep from slamming into her friend.

The Houston East and West Texas train, affectionately called "the Rabbit" because of its tendency to jump the narrow gauge track, was not at all a pleasant experience. Having connected from another line in Nacogdoches, they were riding the Rabbit into the heart of the Piney Woods. Deborah would have just as soon ridden horseback, but she knew Lizzie was not experienced.

Paul Bremond, well known among Houston businessmen, had a vision to create a rail line from Houston to Shreveport, Louisiana, and the HE&WT was the reality of that dream. Poor Mr. Bremond had died just the month before, unable to live long enough to see his railroad completed. Folks had chided him for the narrow gauge creation, telling him he would rue the day, as standard gauge lines were bound to take over the country. But Mr. Bremond had continued with the line and now it was rumored that by next year, it would be complete.

Deborah thought it sad that the man had worked so hard for his dream, only to die before it was ever realized. Of course, sometimes she felt the same might happen to her. The only problem was, she wasn't entirely sure what her dream might truly be.

"This train ride is so uncomfortable," Lizzie declared, squirming. "I can't imagine people using this as a main means of transportation."

A smile crossed Deborah's face. "They don't. Well, that's not exactly right. The railroad is the main means for bringing supplies into the Piney Woods region. However, it is expensive and most folks never travel more than twenty miles from home—if that."

"I can certainly understand why," she replied, gripping the armrest.

"Most would stay whether the train was a luxurious ride or not." Deborah looked at her brother's empty seat and continued. "Take G. W., for example. He loves Texas, and the only reason he ventured out was to escort me back and forth. Oh, he goes occasionally to Houston or Lufkin for supplies, but he has no desire to leave the area. He loves his forest and the people here."

Lizzie shook her head. "Seems a mundane existence."

"I suppose to some." Deborah looked out the window and noticed several dilapidated houses. "Some don't get a chance to choose. Folks here are far from rich. Most work for sawmill or logging companies. Some raise cattle and cotton, others farm. But the war was very hard on the South, you must remember."

Her friend turned and put her hand on Deborah's arm. "I'm sorry. I didn't mean to offend."

"Oh, Lizzie, you could never offend me. But you must prepare yourself for somewhat of a shock. Perkinsville is not Philadelphia. Many of the people who will be your neighbors have had very little education. They can't read and write much. They really don't understand why it's important, but my hope is to show them. I truly want to encourage education in our area."

"Is there no school?"

Deborah thought of the tiny school. "There is, but education is not valued—hard work is. The important things of life take on a different appearance in Perkinsville. Here, folks count themselves lucky to have a roof over their heads—never mind a floor."

"What do you mean?" Lizzie appeared to forget about the roughness of their ride.

"Many folks have only dirt for floors—although it's the cleanest dirt you will find." She laughed. "It's always strange to see women sweeping their earthen floors. Mama told me that she used to do the same until Papa put in a wood floor for her. She said my uncle and father worked day and night for months to put together enough scrap lumber. She cherished it until they moved into the new house shortly before Papa died."

"What happened to your father, Deborah?"

"He was killed when a log rolled onto him."

"A log? How could that kill a man?"

Deborah pointed at the passing trees. "See those? They're shortleaf pines. They are much like the pines we saw in the East. We log longleaf pine."

"Isn't one pine tree pretty much like another?"

The question was innocent enough, but Deborah laughed. "Hardly. Stick around for a while, and you'll learn the difference soon enough."

"But what happened to your father?"

"G. W. and my brother Rob were helping Father bring the week's harvest to the rail. They were pole rolling logs onto the train cars. That's where they hook the mules up on one side of the railcar and run a series of chains and cables to the log they are bringing up on the other side. Several sturdy poles are positioned so that when the mules are driven forward, the log rolls up onto the train car. Usually it works very well, but this time the chain snapped and the log rolled back onto my father. It weighed about a ton, and he couldn't get out of the way in time."

"A ton? That's hard to imagine."

"This particular log was a huge butt log—one taken from the very base of the tree." Deborah looked once again to the passing scenery. She hadn't been home when her father was killed. Word came to her through her beloved Aunt Wilhelmina—the same woman who was responsible for seeing that Deborah received an education.

"My father's skull was crushed, and he died immediately. Mama said he knew the dangers and would have wanted it that way. A quick death was always desired over a painful lingering. . . . I was traveling with my aunt at the time, and we didn't get word until nearly a month after the accident. By the time I learned of his death, school was nearly ready to begin again, and my father was long past buried."

Lizzie nodded. "That was the year we met."

"Yes. And what a godsend that was."

"But, Deborah, you've never talked much about this before. Why?"

She considered Lizzie's question for a moment. "I suppose because of the pain in remembering. But I also learned that G. W. blamed himself for our father's death, and I suppose I buried it deep within to hide from both his pain and my own."

"I'm so sorry, Deborah." Lizzie frowned. "And what of your other brother—Rob? Does he blame himself, as well?"

"No. Rob was injured. The mules pulling the logs got scared when the chain whipped back. They took off, out of control. Rob got a good beating as they dragged him. G. W. blames himself for the accident because he couldn't hold the log back. He felt he should have added more support. Mama said it could have happened to anyone. Others agreed—after all, they weren't working alone. By this time, Papa and Uncle Arjan had hired another five men to help them."

"Were they hurt, too?"

"No, just Papa and Rob."

"I hardly see why G. W. would blame himself—especially if even your mother doesn't."

"I can blame myself without anyone else needin' to help me," G. W. said from behind them.

Deborah watched Lizzie look away in embarrassment. "Yes, but it still doesn't make you right," she told her brother. She was never one to keep such thoughts to herself.

"Doesn't make me wrong, either," he answered, taking his seat across from Lizzie. He folded his arms against his chest and fixed his gaze on Deborah.

She could see the pain in his blue eyes. "No, it just makes you stubborn."

"Deborah!" Lizzie gasped. "Don't be so harsh."

G. W. seemed surprised by her sudden support. He nodded with a smug look of satisfaction. "Yeah, don't be so harsh."

Deborah rolled her eyes and shook her head. "I'm not about to coddle him, Lizzie, and don't you dare, either. He doesn't need that from us. The accident wasn't his fault, and if he's too bullheaded to see the truth for himself, then I say it's our job to help convince him." Silence descended like a heavy mantle over them. No one seemed willing to challenge Deborah's comment or to continue with the conversation.

After several moments, G. W. finally spoke up. "We'll be stopping in about twenty minutes." He cast a quick look outside. "Unless the Rabbit jumps the tracks."

"Oh, you don't really think it would, do you?" Lizzie asked, her hand going to her throat.

He shrugged. "It's been known to happen, but it shouldn't. Not the way we're pokin' along. I swear I could have walked from Nacogdoches faster."

And with that, the tension broke and G. W. seemed to relax. Deborah closed her eyes and whispered a prayer for him. Her mother had said very little about his continued sadness, but Deborah hoped she could find time when they could be alone so that she could talk to him. She had to convince him to let go of this guilt.

In her no-nonsense way, Deborah added such matters mentally to the list of things she already planned to see to once they returned home. She was soon to take the helm as bookkeeper and manager of the Vandermark Logging Company. It was her obligation, now that she'd completed her education. She had made a promise to her family—a promise driven by her love of learning. She remembered long talks with her father.

"I'm going to learn all that I can to help the family," she'd told him. *"I want to make things easier for you. I can't very well log, but I can handle the books."*

She could very nearly recollect her father's smile and feel his pride in her. *"You do that, darlin'. You'll be mighty helpful to me."*

Deborah had studied as hard as possible, always keeping the image of her family before her. She might not have the stamina for heavy labor, but anything that required reasoning was right in keeping with her abilities. Her family needed her, and it was for that reason she felt she could put aside her own desires. More important—she didn't allow for any desire that wouldn't benefit her kin. It would only muddy the waters, and Deborah needed to stay clear on what her duties were.

She kept her eyes closed, pondering the future and pushing aside her concerns. She found bookkeeping hopelessly boring. Truth be told, she had preferred her biology and botany classes.

If she'd had her choice, Deborah would have remained in school for a time longer. She gave a sigh. What possible good could come from fretting over it now? Women were not expected to attend college, nor were they truly accepted as scholars. But her love of knowledge was something no one could take from her. Deborah cherished reading new books, exploring new worlds and cultures. Her intellect, however, was nothing to wear as a badge of honor. Men were offended by her, and women, intimidated. In truth, she believed it was more that the men felt stupid and the women were afraid to admit that they, too, would like to learn. But it didn't matter. Her family needed her now, and there was some comfort in that. Well, maybe not exactly comfort.

Father God, she prayed silently, *I don't know why you made me just this way. Is it wrong that I long for something more?*

Perkinsville had been built alongside the railroad to accommodate the loading of lumber and unloading of supplies. It was,

Deborah said, a typical sawmill company town—whatever that meant. Lizzie wasn't at all familiar with such a thing and definitely didn't know what to expect. Everything, in her eyes, looked hopelessly dirty. The day was unbearably warm, and Lizzie was glad that she'd listened to Deborah regarding her attire. They had stopped at a secondhand shop in Nacogdoches and purchased lightweight blouses and skirts. G. W. had long ago replaced his wool suit with a simple shirt and trousers, and Lizzie thought he seemed far more relaxed, although he carried a coat with him and donned it as propriety demanded.

Lizzie dabbed at her forehead with her handkerchief as Deborah showed her about the town. Philadelphia could be hot and humid, as well, but it lacked the same heaviness she felt here in the South. She longed for a bath, or perhaps a quick plunge—clothes and all—into the nearby pond. When she mentioned this Deborah laughed.

"That's the mill pond. We used to swim there on occasion, but now it's much too busy and Mr. Perkins has asked folks to keep their children out for their own safety. The mill is dependent upon the pond." Lizzie followed Deborah's gaze. "They unload the logs from the train and dump them there. Later they use a series of conveyors and chains called a jack ladder to pull the logs into the sawmill."

Lizzie spotted the smoke belching from the stacks. "With the damp air and thick smoke, I can't imagine living here."

"Usually there's a breeze to move it out. We arrived on a still day, and that tends to make things worse."

"My mother would say it serves me right," Lizzie murmured.

"That's really the first time you've mentioned her since leaving the wedding." Deborah eyed her thoughtfully for a moment. "I haven't wanted to pry, but how are you feeling toward her?"

"To be honest, I've actually found myself concerned for Mother. I know she had great plans for me prior to my wedding announcement and, no doubt, had figured out some way to use me for her purposes even after I married Stuart."

"And what of Stuart?"

Lizzie grew thoughtful. "I feel guilty for having embarrassed him so publicly." She paused for a moment. "My main thoughts are for Mother, however. I suppose now that we've arrived, I should send her a letter. She must surely be worried. Is there a post office here?"

"Of course, right over here." Deborah continued the tour. "Then this is the depot and commissary. There are many things housed under this one roof," Deborah explained. "The pharmacy is here, the post office and paymaster for the sawmill, plus it is the main source of supplies. The commissary itself is quite large and contains most everything you could ever need." She smiled. "Yet like I said before, it's hardly Philadelphia." She glanced around. "I can't imagine what's keeping Rob and G. W."

G. W. had gone off looking for their brother. Rob was supposed to meet them at the station with the wagon, but so far he'd not shown himself. Lizzie hoped he'd arrive soon. She wasn't sure how much of the heat she could stand. She looked at the unpainted buildings and dirt roads. *What in the world have I gotten myself into?*

Deborah chatted on as if the heat didn't bother her in the least. "Across the street just there is the boardinghouse for whites. On the other side of the tracks is the black boardinghouse and quarters where the blacks live. In the South, you will find that the color of your skin determines a great deal. Folks around here try to be tolerant, but many cannot put the issue aside. And it's not just in dealing with the blacks. Mr. Perkins hates Mexicans and Indians. He won't even allow them to live or work here."

"And why is that?"

"Something to do with the past and his family. I believe they were injured or killed by people of those races. Folks around here always have a reason for hating others—that way it seems more acceptable to them."

"I suppose it isn't easy. Being a different color isn't exactly something you can hide," Lizzie commented. "The town is so small," she said, casting her gaze back to the commissary. "Is this the only store?"

"Very nearly. This is a company town, owned and operated by the Perkins family. They own the sawmill and arranged for most everything you see. Mr. Perkins is a very nice man, so folks here count themselves blessed. Some towns suffer at the hands of cruel masters. Here the people are treated quite well. Prices are not overly inflated and people can be paid in cash upon proof of an emergency. Oh, and they pay out cash at Christmas and Texas Independence Day—March the second. Some folks are suggesting it be changed to America's Independence Day, but like I said, many of the citizens are still feeling rather hostile toward the northern states."

"I'm not sure I understand what you said regarding money. Aren't the people otherwise paid?"

Deborah smiled. "Not in cash. They're paid with company tokens that they can exchange for goods. Payment for rent and medical needs is taken out of their salaries. They even tithe in tokens."

Lizzie had never heard of such a thing. "But how then can they save up money or invest for their future?"

Her friend shook her head. "They can't. They have no future but this town. They are essentially owned by the company."

"But that's slavery, and Mr. Lincoln abolished that during the war."

"Don't talk about Mr. Lincoln too loud down here. Folks won't take too kindly to it." Deborah motioned to the commissary. "Let's step inside. It's much too warm to stand out here in the sun. G. W. will know where to find us."

Lizzie followed her up the wooden steps, avoiding the splintered rail. Three large dogs were resting near the door and looked up only long enough to ascertain whether Deborah and Lizzie were a threat before putting their heads back down.

The screen door moaned as Deborah pulled it open. Lizzie stepped inside, taking a moment to allow her eyes to adjust to the darker interior. The walls were stacked to the ceiling with shelved goods. Rows of tables and display cases offered everything from razors to shoes to writing paper. Across the store in the far corner were shelves lined with canned goods and sacks of rice, beans, and cornmeal. Each was clearly stamped, along with the weight.

"Let's see if they have anything cold to drink. Mr. Perkins brings ice in from time to time." They made their way across the rough-hewn floor to the counter, where an older man was busy folding fabric.

"Mr. Greeley, it's good to see you again," Deborah began.

The man looked up and studied the two women for a moment. "Miss Deborah?"

"It's me," she replied, laughing. "All grown up, as Mama would say."

He put aside his material and gave them his full attention. "I knew you were expected. Your mama has been tellin' everyone about you comin' home."

"Just came in on the train. G. W.'s gone to find Rob. He was supposed to be here with the wagon since we didn't want to wait for the log train."

"Are you home for good?" He looked at Lizzie. "Oh, where are my manners? Introduce me to your friend."

"This is Miss Elizabeth Decker. We attended school together. She will be staying with us for a while."

"Miss Decker, you are like a ray of sunshine. Menfolk down here will be happy to see another female. It's a pleasure to make your acquaintance."

"Likewise," she said, uncertain if the nod of her head was the proper greeting.

Deborah didn't give her time to consider the matter further. "We were hoping you might have something cold to drink."

"I surely do. Mrs. Greeley made two pitchers of lemonade, as well as some sweet tea. Which do you prefer?"

"Oh, lemonade would surely be perfect," Deborah declared.

"Why don't you two have a seat, and I'll bring it right out to you."

Deborah nodded and led Lizzie to an area just beyond the counter, where several small tables and chairs had been positioned. "The men often gather here for coffee and checkers. Sometimes they even have a meeting or two."

Lizzie took a seat on the obviously handmade chair. She worried that the unfinished wood would snag her skirt, but noted that Deborah seemed to give it little thought. Deborah had been right; this was quite different from what she had known back East.

"As you can see, the store has an ample supply of cloth goods, foods, and household supplies. My mother wrote to tell me that they recently opened a hardware store across the street to handle some of the larger tools and building materials. Down the street is the church and school. There's a livery and blacksmith, as well as a new doctor's office and infirmary. According to my mother, Mrs. Perkins finally convinced Mr. Perkins to hire a quality doctor since a great many women have died from childbed fever or in childbirth itself."

“How sad that they should have died when such progress has been made. Remember the lecture we heard just before graduation? Mrs. Lyman was the speaker.”

Deborah nodded. “Yes, I know she was especially encouraged that medicine was making abundant improvements, especially in women’s needs. But a doctor will be very valuable to the men in this community, as well. There are frequent accidents. A doctor will be a blessing.”

“Here you go, ladies.” Mr. Greeley reappeared with two glasses of lemonade.

Lizzie immediately sampled hers and smiled. It was just right—not too tart. “It’s very good.”

“Mrs. Greeley will be pleased to know you enjoyed it.”

“Just put it on our account, please,” Deborah instructed.

“Oh no, Miss Deborah. This one is on the house. We’re just pleased as can be to have you home. Bet your mama is fairly dancin’ a jig. She’s talked of nothing but your return.”

Lizzie marveled at the easy manner in which they fell into conversation. There were no formalities, yet there was a certain genteel respect that she found rather comforting.

“I finally found him,” G. W. declared as he and another man bounded into the commissary. Lizzie looked up just as Rob Vandermark caught sight of her. He grinned from ear to ear and stepped forward in three bold strides to take hold of her hand. Bowing low, he drew her fingers to his lips.

“Why, if you aren’t the purtiest gal! Hair the color of corn silk and eyes bluer than a summer sky.”

“This is my brother Rob,” Deborah announced. “He’s the poet in the family.”

Lizzie nodded, but found herself at a loss for words. Rob seemed more than a little delighted as he turned to face his sister.

"For once you've brought me somethin' worth my time," he declared, then looked back at Lizzie and gave her a wink.

G. W. frowned and Deborah shook her head. "Rob is also the Romeo of the family."

"She calls me that all the time," Rob said, laughing. He tucked his thumbs in his suspenders. "Guess she can't help it, what with havin' such a handsome brother. Can't fault me for lookin' for my Juliet."

Lizzie could scarcely take it all in at once. Rob was rather like a whirlwind compared to G. W.'s soft-spoken, easygoing manner.

"Rob, this is Miss Elizabeth Decker. Lizzie to her friends."

"Miss Lizzie," he said, turning back to her with a beaming smile. "I certainly hope we will be very good friends."

Chapter 3

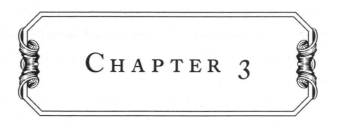

Deborah found her homecoming bittersweet. The longing for home and family had nearly consumed her in Philadelphia, mixed with an equal measure of regret. Well, maybe not so much regret as concern.

And yet that wasn't exactly right, either.

A fear of things changing—of losing something precious.

Education had been an escape from the loneliness and isolation she'd known in childhood. It had given her purpose and a sense of being able to help those she loved. But because no one else in her family desired an education, Deborah felt alone.

Living miles from any real town, Deborah had grown up with only her mother and their cook, Sissy, for female company. Later, she had a girlfriend or two at school, but they never thought or felt the same way she did. Their idea of fun was sharing new quilt patterns or parading around, vying for the attention of boys. Deborah wanted to talk about books she'd read or what was going on in the world. Unfortunately, the only ones talking about current events were the men, and they had no interest in discussing the news with the female gender. Truth be told, the men paid her little attention until she blossomed into a teenager, and by then, her heart was far more desirous of learning than loving.

"Mama!" Deborah cried, jumping from the wagon as G. W. drew it to a stop. She ran the distance to her mother's open arms. Two big hounds bayed a greeting and dashed across the porch to welcome her.

"Jasper! Decatur!" Deborah lavished attention on the dogs before turning to her mother. "Where's Lula?"

"She's had another litter of pups." Her mother motioned her to turn around in a circle. "Oh, just look at you," her mother whispered. Taking hold of Deborah's face, she shook her head. "You are even prettier than you were the last time I saw you. I'll bet you have the tiniest waist in the county." She gave a quick glance past Deborah. "You boys will have your hands full keeping order with the men who come a-callin'."

"Mama, I missed you so much." Deborah hugged her mother close. It wasn't a lie. If she could have had her mother with her back East, she would have done so. "So tell me what has changed."

Her mother laughed. "I'm older and a little more gray, and the house is a little more worn. Guess we both are."

Euphanel Vandermark was not known for her great beauty, although Deborah thought her a pretty woman. She was instead known for her strength, honesty, and integrity. People knew when they made an arrangement with Mrs. Vandermark that she would keep her word.

Standing several inches shorter than Deborah's five-foot-six-inch frame, Euphanel Vandermark was a petite but formidable force. Uncle Arjan often teased her about being a hurricane, but Mama took no offense at such a statement. Since their father's death, Deborah and her brothers had seen their mother triple her efforts at efficiency and productivity, but never at the expense of her beliefs. Her faith in God was her mainstay, and from that foundation, she would never be moved.

"You don't look a bit older," Deborah declared. "Papa used to say you never grew older, just more beautiful."

Her mother's expression softened. "He did say that quite a bit, didn't he?"

"And with good reason." Deborah turned and motioned to Lizzie. "I have someone for you to meet, Mama. I hope you won't mind, but I've brought a friend home with me." Deborah reached out to Lizzie. "This is Elizabeth Decker. Call her Lizzie. She's the young woman I roomed with—the one I often wrote you about." Jasper and Decatur sniffed around the stranger as if to ascertain her acceptability.

"I would recognize her anywhere," Mother said. "You are just as beautiful as Deborah described. We'll be pleased to have your company."

"Thank you." Lizzie exchanged a look with Deborah, then turned back to the older woman. "I hope I might be useful to you."

Deborah's mother laughed heartily. "You are a guest, and you needn't be anything else. Come along inside. I'm sure you want to freshen up. Deborah, take Lizzie on upstairs. I'll bring warm water to your room. The boys will carry up your trunks, and later, when you're ready, I'll make sure you get a bite to eat."

"Mother, we're hardly invalids. We can join the family for supper."

"I know how exhausting that trip can be," Mother replied. "I wouldn't want you to feel that you had to sit at the table and share conversation with the rest of us."

"There's plenty of time to wash up and rest a bit before supper," Deborah assured her. "I've been looking forward to sitting down to a family meal; please don't deny me that privilege."

"That makes two of us. No one cooks like you and Sissy," G. W. said as he passed by with one of Deborah's trunks hoisted on his shoulder. "What in the world do you have packed in here, little sister? More friends? It weighs a ton."

She grinned. "You could say that. It's full of books."

He shook his head. "Most females would be fillin' their steamers with gowns and pretty doodads, but not my sister. She brings back books."

Deborah waited until Rob followed after with two of the suitcases before turning to her mother. "Mama, there's a heaviness about G. W., and I'm not speaking of the books. From time to time, we managed to get him to smile, but he's just not his old self."

"If you got him to smile at all, I'd say that was a great accomplishment. He's changed since your father died, and though I've tried to talk to him, I think he worries that if he says too much to me, it will only serve to bring me sorrow."

Deborah looked to her friend. "We shall do what we can to encourage him, won't we, Lizzie?"

The blonde seemed taken by surprise, but nodded. "Of course."

After a supper of corn bread, beans with thick pieces of pork, and spicy rice and tomatoes, Deborah settled into a porch rocker alongside her mother. She was glad that Lizzie had chosen to retire early and that the boys were elsewhere discussing business with Uncle Arjan.

"I hadn't realized how much I missed your cooking."

Mother smiled. "I'm sure you had fancier meals back East."

"Maybe fancier—but not better. We certainly had more beef than we eat here. People were absolutely amazed that we should eat so little beef when our state is known for its cattle."

"Known for it because we ship them north and east," Euphanel said with a chuckle. "Still, if they were here to see this place for themselves, they would understand. It's hard enough to keep other things, much less beef, from spoiling."

"That's what I would tell them. I explained about the large number of wild hogs and how much easier it is to salt and cure, or even smoke pork, than it is with beef."

Silence descended and Deborah shifted uneasily in her chair. How was it that she could be so happy to be somewhere, and so miserable at the same time?

"So you want to tell me what's wrong?" her mother asked.

The night air was full of sounds, magnified by the heaviness of the air. "Nothing is wrong," Deborah replied.

When her mother didn't say anything more, Deborah turned. "I suppose I'm worried about G. W. He blames himself for Papa's death."

Mother swatted at a mosquito on her arm. "He does. I've talked to that boy until my throat was raw, but he still won't listen. Arjan says that in time he'll come to accept that the accident wasn't his fault. I can only hope he's right."

"Me too." Deborah glanced at her mother with a grin. "Maybe Lizzie can help him."

"Don't you be matchmakin' for your brother," her mother warned. "Nothing good ever comes out of putting your nose in other folks' business. If the good Lord intends those two to fall for each other, He'll work out the details."

"But if G. W. could strike a match, it would take his mind off of Papa."

"Let G. W. determine that matter. The only matches you need to strike are ones for the kerosene lamps." Her mother's tone was firm, but not harsh.

"Yes, ma'am," Deborah said, reverting to childhood politeness.

"Now, tell me what else is goin' on in that head of yours. You seemed mighty preoccupied tonight at supper."

"Well, I am tired. The trip is not for the faint of heart, to be certain. I'm also anxious to get started with the bookkeeping and such. I know Uncle Arjan said it's going to take some time to get things recorded properly. A lot of what I need to put down on paper is registered only in his head."

Mother gave a light laugh. "Arjan has a good mind for such things, but I keep sayin' that if something happens to him, we won't none of us know what's going on. I think he's more relieved than I am to have you take over the office."

Deborah looked out across the darkness. Occasionally fireflies winked their light, but otherwise the velvety blackness remained unbroken. "It feels strange—coming home after being gone so long."

"You're no longer a child." Euphanel gazed at her daughter. "Something happens to us when we cross that threshold to womanhood."

Deborah considered that a moment. "Everything seems different, and yet nothing has changed."

"You've changed."

She startled at her mother's words. "I'm still the same old Deborah."

Her mother shook her head. "Hardly that. You are a woman now. While many would have called you one before, there can be no doubt about it now. You have tasted the world and its delights—traveled to see so many exciting things. You walked beyond your own gate, as my mother would say. It opens your heart and mind to so much that you didn't know before."

"I suppose so," Deborah admitted.

"It was what made life so difficult for me when I first came to Texas as a young bride," her mother continued. "I had walked beyond my gate, and I knew what the world could offer. Your father brought me here in 1858. His dreams fueled his desire for a new life here, but my dreams were wrapped up in him. Texas seemed a terrible desolation to me—at least until your grandma and grandpa came west during the war. I kept thinking of all that I'd known in Georgia. Now you will think of all that you knew back East."

Deborah shrugged. "But while I was back East, all I could think about was Texas. I honestly missed my family and home. But . . ."

"But?"

She heaved a heavy sigh and looked at her mother. "I almost feel like a stranger in returning. Does that sound odd to you?"

"Not at all. I remember when I accompanied my parents back to Georgia just before my grandmother passed on. Let me think now . . . you were just a little girl of eight—maybe nine."

"I was nine and heartbroken that you left me to accompany them," Deborah said. "I was afraid you might never return."

"It was hard to leave you here—the boys, too—but I knew it would be a hard trip for a child to endure. The South had suffered so much during the war and frankly I was afraid of what we might face." She paused for a long pregnant silence. "I was right to be afraid. Nothing was the same. It broke my heart to see the changes, and I was glad to return to Texas. That's when I realized, however, that my heart had changed—this was home now. There was something bittersweet in that realization."

"I think I'm going to miss my classes a great deal, but not the city. I prefer the quiet, easygoing pace I find here. There is a frantic spirit in the East that seems to devour everyone in its path. I will miss hours of reading and educating myself to new cultures and ideas, but I will be happy for the peace. And for the comfort that comes in knowing that people know you, recognize you, have a history with you."

"You needn't stop learning just because you're back in Angelina County," her mother chided.

Deborah couldn't suppress a yawn. "I suppose you're right."

"I'm also right in suggesting that you need to go to bed. I want you and Lizzie to sleep as long as you can in the morning. Don't you even think about getting out of bed before eight."

"Yes, ma'am." She grinned. "I doubt you could rouse me before then." Deborah got to her feet. "At least it's cooled off enough for sleeping."

"Oh, I forgot to mention that Mr. and Mrs. Perkins are coming to dinner tomorrow night. There's some sort of business to discuss with Arjan, so you'll probably want to be available for that. The girls are coming, too, so you can introduce Lizzie to them."

"Maybe with all the ladies at the table, G. W. will have more to think of than his misplaced guilt."

Her mother nodded and slapped at another mosquito. "Perhaps, but you let G. W. make his own choices. Nothing's worse than being thrown into the arms of a person you'd just as soon avoid. From what you've told me, your friend Lizzie's situation should have proven that, if nothing else. G. W.'s heart will lead him to love when the time is right."

"I just hope he's not too focused on what isn't true, and misses what is."

Her mother got to her feet and embraced Deborah. "Then we'll just have to pray that his mind is clear."

ꕥ

Lizzie studied the small room from the edge of her bed. Deborah had warned her that things would be different, but it felt as if she'd stepped into another world completely. The walls had been papered with a delicate print of violet sprigs entwined with white ribbons, while a simple braided rug adorned the oak floor between the two iron-framed beds. Homemade muslin curtains hung at the windows and decidedly feminine quilts covered the beds.

The door slowly opened and Deborah peered around it into the room. "Oh, I was afraid you were already asleep."

"I thought about it," Lizzie admitted. "I'm very tired, but I wanted to make sure everything was all right with your family. I mean, what with me coming unannounced."

Deborah entered the room and closed the door behind her. "Of course it's all right. Mother is delighted to have you here." She began to undress. "I wouldn't be surprised, however, if she doesn't have you canning and working in the garden before noon tomorrow. I told her you wanted to learn how to be more self-sufficient, domestically speaking."

Lizzie smiled. "I'm glad. Do you know that I've never had to cook for myself? I can honestly say that I would like to learn."

"Then you've come to the right place. My mother is a wonderful cook and a superb teacher. She learned a lot from Sissy, and I'm sure together they will be more than delighted to help you."

"Was Sissy a slave?"

Deborah nodded and pulled pins from her long dark hair. "She was, but she and Mother were close and she came here when my grandparents came to stay with us during the war. My mother hired her on to work at our house when my grandparents went back to Georgia after the war. I doubt Mama would have hired anyone, but Sissy was sickly and needed help. She was too proud for charity, so my mother suggested Sissy teach her to cook. That way, Mother did a lot of the work, while Sissy recovered her health. It worked well."

"Your mother is such a gracious lady. She seems so innocent at times—yet so knowledgeable."

"She's not highly educated. She attended school until she married my father when she was sixteen. But she always loved learning and regretted to a degree that she could not continue her education. Of course, women were even less encouraged to seek out schooling back then than they are now."

"Still, she seems very happy with her house and family. I wish my own mother might have shared such thinking. I can't help but imagine what life might have been like had she enjoyed her domestic duties."

Deborah discarded her blouse and skirt and stretched before releasing the hooks on her corset. "But perhaps you wouldn't be the dear woman I know and love now. Mother always says there's no sense fretting over what might have been, since it can't ever be."

"She's no doubt right about that," Lizzie admitted. "Your mother seems very wise."

"It's a wisdom borne of experience." Deborah pulled a nightgown over her head.

Lizzie said nothing for several minutes, then gave a sigh. "I suppose then, in time, it shall come to each of us."

Deborah looked at her oddly as she came to her bedside. "What shall?"

"Wisdom," Lizzie answered. "Wisdom borne of experience."

"I suppose it shall, but it will have to wait until I get some sleep. Mother said she didn't even want to hear us rousing before eight. I assured her I could very easily yield to her request."

Lizzie laughed. "What a chore! But as a guest, I suppose I have no choice." She eased back onto the bed. "Tomorrow I shall begin my new life as an East Texas woman."

Deborah laughed. "Then Texas be warned."

Chapter 4

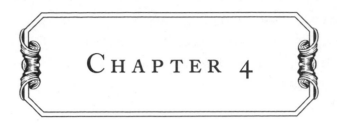

Rachel and Zed Perkins arrived the following evening with daughters Annabeth and Maybelle. Both shared their father's fair complexion and red hair. They were pretty girls, with trim waists and lovely blue eyes, but Deborah found their general silliness overwhelmed their virtues.

The real treat of the evening was the unexpected guest that Zed and Rachel introduced as the new company doctor. Christopher Clayton was a handsome and witty man who hailed from Kansas City, but he had studied medicine at Bellevue Hospital Medical College in New York City.

"Dr. Clayton, we are certainly happy to have you join the community," Deborah's mother declared as Sissy placed a large platter on the table. A succulent ham, complete with a molasses glaze, wafted a tantalizing aroma into the air. She hurried back to the kitchen and brought out another platter with two large baked chickens.

"Sissy, come join us and meet the new doctor."

The woman smiled. "I gots too much to do, but I's pleased to make your acquaintance."

Dr. Clayton nodded. "As am I, to make yours."

Sissy gave a little curtsy that she reserved for strangers and headed back to the kitchen. Mother lost little time explaining to the doctor. "Sissy's a good friend, and I hired her to work so she could help her family."

He seemed to understand her discomfort. "You needn't explain to me, Mrs. Vandermark. I'm just grateful to share such fine company and food."

"You haven't even tasted it yet," Deborah teased.

He studied her for a moment, as if appraising her features. His scrutiny made Deborah feel uncomfortable.

"I think I shall enjoy living here," Dr. Clayton replied. He glanced around the table. "Beautiful ladies for company, delectable food for nourishment, and intelligent conversation with the gentlemen. Who could ask for more?"

Deborah frowned. "Perhaps you could have intelligent conversations with the ladies, and the men could be admired for their beauty."

Rob laughed out loud and the Perkins girls giggled uncontrollably. Dr. Clayton, however, nodded in agreement. "Why not?"

She could see the response was not offered in jest. Dr. Clayton seemed to genuinely agree that the idea was possible. Deborah couldn't help but throw him a smile.

"Do you have a family, Doctor?" Deborah's mother asked.

"If you mean am I married, then the answer is no. I do have a family, however. I am the oldest of fifteen children. My mother and father reside in Kansas City."

"Fifteen children," Mrs. Perkins said, shaking her head. "Goodness! And I thought my five were plenty to keep a woman busy."

"My mother is indeed a busy woman. She was made even more so, I'm sorry to say, when my father was left crippled after an accident in the rail yard."

"How tragic," the woman replied. "I often worry after Zed at the sawmill, although he's not nearly so busy with the day-to-day running as he used to be. But I am concerned for my sons. Injuries happen all the time."

"Well, that's why we brought in a doctor, Mrs. Perkins," Zed told his wife. "So you would stop fretting so much."

Everyone chuckled at this. Sissy placed the last bowl of food on the table and stood aside with folded hands as was her traditional signal that it was time to pray. Deborah bowed her head, finding even this simple reminder of home to be a blessing.

Grace was offered by Uncle Arjan and conversation was put aside to focus instead on fried okra, rice and beans, and of course the promise of dessert. Deborah smiled appreciatively at the sight of her mother's buttermilk biscuits. How she'd missed the food of her childhood.

The conversation picked up a bit after the eating began. Once their initial hunger had abated, folks began to discuss the issues of the day between bites. Deborah listened with great interest as Mrs. Perkins addressed her desire for a larger school.

"I believe with the growing number of children in our community, it would serve us well to build a school separate from the church. I've been after Mr. Perkins for some time now to consider the matter. The schoolmaster agrees it is a much needed project."

"I think that would be grand," Euphanel Vandermark replied.

Deborah knew her mother's longtime friendship with Rachel Perkins often had the women seeing eye-to-eye on town matters. "Education has long suffered in this area."

"Too many folks associate free school with the Reconstructionists and their impositions on our society," Mr. Perkins stated.

Mrs. Perkins nodded. "People are inclined to cut off their noses to spite their faces. Still, I think if we offered a nicely built school with quality desks and good books, educating children through the eighth grade would be no problem at all."

"Rachel is good about spending my money before I make it," Zed Perkins said, laughing.

"Aren't all women?" Rob questioned with a wink at Lizzie. "It's because they're so pretty, though, that we don't seem to mind too much." He smiled at the Perkins sisters, causing them to flush and giggle all the more.

"Why not take them beyond eighth grade?" Deborah asked.

Everyone looked at her for a moment, and then Annabeth shrugged. "Not many folks are even interested in education beyond that point."

Mrs. Perkins nodded and looked to Deborah. "It's true. I doubt there's much of an interest. It's hard enough to get the people around here to spare their children for six years of education, much less eight. I'm hopeful, however, that we can make it more appealing."

Deborah held her tongue. No sense in appearing too confrontational on her first full day back. If the last four years away had taught her anything, it was that sometimes it was best to watch and listen. Popping a piece of buttered biscuit into her mouth, Deborah closed her eyes and savored the flavor. It was just as good as she remembered.

"Miss Vandermark, you have an expression that suggests pure euphoria."

Deborah's eyes snapped open to find Dr. Clayton watching her. Actually, everyone was now watching her. Apparently Dr. Clayton's comment had interested them all. She fought her embarrassment and swallowed.

"My mother makes the best biscuits in the county—probably even the state, although I've not attempted to verify that fact."

Dr. Clayton grinned. "I would agree." He turned toward Deborah's mother. "I've never eaten anything quite so delectable. If my mother had made biscuits half so well, I might never have left home."

"Why, aren't you just the kindest man to say so," her mother declared. "I shall have to make sure you get an extra large piece of pie for dessert."

"Hey, just hold on a second. You know I love your biscuits, Ma. I tell you all the time," Rob threw out from the opposite end of the table. Everyone laughed at this, and Euphanel nodded.

"You shall have a large piece of pie, as well. I happen to know it's your favorite—egg custard."

Rob grinned and pushed his plate back. "Why didn't you say so? I could have just skipped the rest of this food and started there."

His mother laughed. "That is exactly why I didn't tell you about the pie."

The meal passed amicably with conversations about the locals and even some of the concerns in areas around the county. Deborah enjoyed it, although she found herself more an observer than participant. She wasn't exactly sure why, but a sense of reflection seemed to hold her captive.

With each absence from home, Deborah had found the differences more noticeable. But she also found the precious things more poignant, as well. Little things, like the creaking sound of her mother's rocker on the porch as she snapped beans; the warmth of a dog curled up at the foot of her bed; even the wonderful scent of the pines mingled with woodsmoke. Each memory could bring a smile to her face. Deborah was bound to her birthplace in a way that she couldn't quite explain. She had once tried to write about it for a school paper but found herself doing a poor job. Her teacher had chided her for being "dreamy and childish" in her declaration that, "Nothing will ever comfort me quite as much as the scents of my mother's lavender sachet, strong coffee brewing, and freshly cut wood." Deborah felt sorry for the professor. He would never understand the way she felt.

She couldn't help but notice G. W.'s silence. He focused on his meal, nodded in acknowledgment from time to time, but otherwise shared very little of his thoughts. Deborah had hoped that one of the young women might have attracted his attention, but upon reacquainting herself with nineteen-year-old Annabeth and seventeen-year-old Maybelle, Deborah was just as happy that G. W. was preoccupied. What ninnies those two turned out to be! One minute they were giggling and blushing, the next they were staring wide-eyed at the handsome doctor.

Lizzie seemed to be enjoying herself. Mrs. Perkins had very nearly assaulted Deborah's friend with questions about her background and how the two women had met. Lizzie didn't seem to mind, however, and took each question in stride.

"So you were both attending university in Philadelphia?" Dr. Clayton asked.

Deborah nodded, but it was Lizzie who answered. "Deborah was my dearest friend and always shall be. She kept me from giving up when our studies turned difficult."

"And what studies were those?" he asked.

"It was that wretched biology class," Lizzie said with a shudder. "Seems like just yesterday. I spent more time confused than in understanding. I had fully planned to give up my attempts to understand cells, but Deborah began tutoring me, and before I knew it, the class was concluded and I had managed to get a passing grade. But just barely."

Dr. Clayton smiled and turned to Deborah. "And what of you? Did you enjoy the class?"

Again Lizzie jumped in. "She most certainly did. One of the professors tried to interest her in the women's medical school."

Deborah found all eyes turned to her and gave a weak laugh. "Then I could have opened an infirmary in the logging office."

Her mother's gaze seemed fixed upon her, and Deborah felt the need to move the conversation elsewhere. "Lizzie is quite gifted in the arts. She plays piano and sings, and has the most amazing talent with watercolors."

"All very useless skills for real life," Lizzie added.

"Not at all, Miss Decker!" Rachel Perkins's excitement got the best of her. "We suffer for entertainment in these parts. It would be marvelous to plan an evening where you could sing and play for us." She turned to her husband. "Don't you think such an event would be popular? Why, the folks would simply love it."

"I believe she's right," Zed Perkins replied. "We will depend upon you, Miss Decker."

Lizzie threw Deborah a rather panicked look, but Deborah was simply glad to have the conversation turned elsewhere. The last thing she wanted to do was answer any more questions regarding her own interests.

After pie was served and praise issued with the devouring, the men wandered outside to the porch to discuss business. Mrs. Perkins and the girls settled in the living room with Lizzie, while Deborah helped her mother serve coffee. She could hear the men's muffled discussion through the open windows but paid it little attention.

To think too long on such matters only made Deborah wish for the classrooms she'd left behind. She enjoyed a rousing discussion of politics and business. Too bad a woman would be considered out of place to position herself with the men rather than to gossip with the ladies.

"I do wish we could have taken a stroll," Annabeth declared. "It seems the perfect night for such a thing. The moon is nearly full."

Mother shook her head. "I'm afraid it would be dangerous. We've had trouble with the Piney Woods rooters."

Lizzie looked at Deborah for an explanation. Deborah leaned closer. "Wild hogs."

"Very dangerous animals indeed," Mrs. Perkins said as she lifted her coffee cup. "Many a man has been desperately wounded by those beasts."

"By a pig?" Lizzie asked.

The Perkins sisters burst into laughter. "Oh my dear," their mother interjected, "they aren't merely pigs. These are feral animals—razorbacks that roam the woods at night. They are smart and can outthink a normal man. They are mean and ill-tempered, with fierce tusks that can tear you to ribbons."

Deborah could see that Lizzie was notably impressed. "There are a great many dangers no matter where you live. We had our share of desperate beasts in Philadelphia, as well," Deborah offered. "Most were two legged and wore trousers, however."

Mother met her gaze and smiled. "I'm sure your experience here helped to keep you safer back there. However, I'm very glad to have you home now."

"Have you a beau, Miss Vandermark?" Annabeth asked innocently.

For a moment, the question took Deborah by surprise. "I hadn't the time for such things. I needed to get my education so that I could come back to Perkinsville and help my family. It was what my father wished for." Deborah saw Mother frown, but continued. "As I understand from Uncle Arjan, we need to totally modernize our methods of doing business. I'm going to see to it that this happens in an orderly fashion."

"Oh, I would hate to have to work," Maybelle said, fanning herself furiously. "Just the thought of trying to add up numbers and keep track of orders . . . Goodness, but you are more—oh, what's the word I want? Well, I suppose *industrious* would do. You're more industrious than I, what with your interests in things related to business."

Deborah knew that the comment was a veiled insult. What Maybelle really seemed to be inferring was that Deborah was less womanly—more masculine in her concerns. But again, Deborah held back. There was certainly nothing positive to be gained by cutting Maybelle Perkins down a peg or two.

"Oh, we simply must tell them about the new gowns we have ordered," Annabeth said, as if to cover up for her sister's indiscretion. "Mother ordered us new dresses from France. Isn't that exciting?"

"To be certain," Lizzie answered with a sympathetic glance at Deborah. "Of course, there aren't quite as many grand occasions to wear them as we enjoyed in Philadelphia, I suppose."

Deborah appreciated her friend's effort, but didn't wish for the Perkinses to dislike Lizzie. She smiled and patted her friend's hand. "I hope we shall see your new gowns at the Christmas dance, perhaps?"

The girls tried unsuccessfully to suppress their excitement. "That is our desire, as well. Mother was assured they will reach us in plenty of time." Annabeth's volume was increasing with her enthusiasm. "My gown is lavender, and Maybelle has one of iced blue. I am positively delirious at the thought of actually wearing the gown for the first time."

Mother lifted the china pot. "I'm sure it will be an occasion to remember. Now, would anyone care for more coffee?"

"None for me," Mrs. Perkins replied. "In fact, I'm afraid the hour has slipped Mr. Perkins's attention. We should be making our way back. I've so enjoyed our evening."

Deborah watched her mother replace the pot and offer Mrs. Perkins a gracious smile. "As have we. I'm so glad you were able to talk Mr. Perkins into bringing us a doctor. The community will benefit from such generosity."

"Well, there's still Mrs. Foster to deal with," Rachel Perkins said in a conspiratorial tone.

Deborah's mother nodded. "She's served the area as healer and midwife for a very long time. She will, no doubt, be put off at such modernizing."

"But with all of the deaths we've suffered over the last few years—especially with our women," Mrs. Perkins replied, "I hardly think we can do anything else. Perhaps it's her age, but Margaret Foster is clearly unable to deal with the needs of our town." The two Perkins girls bobbed their heads in agreement. When their mother got to her feet, the sisters followed suit.

"Do come see me when you are next in town," Mrs. Perkins told Deborah's mother. She turned then to Deborah and Lizzie. "You are also welcome. It's so pleasant to have good friends drop by for a visit."

"Thank you, Rachel. I'm sure we will take you up on the offer very soon," Mother replied.

They departed, and Deborah was relieved to see them go. She thought the nonsensical Perkins sisters absolutely exhausting. "And to think I considered encouraging G. W. to take up with one of them."

"What was that?" Lizzie asked.

Deborah shook her head. "Nothing much. Just glad to see this evening come to an end. Did you enjoy yourself?"

"I found it all very fascinating." Lizzie looped her arm through Deborah's. "Your family all seem to genuinely enjoy one another's company. What a concept."

Deborah laughed and squeezed Lizzie's arm. "At times we are less congenial, but for the most part we are quite companionable."

"I wish I might have known the same in my family."

Her wistful tone caused Deborah to stop. "You can be a part of my family now. We shall love you as our own. And who knows—maybe one day you will truly be a part of it. I do, after all, have two unmarried brothers."

Lizzie laughed and playfully nudged Deborah with her elbow. "Yes, and one seems to constantly notice my every move like a child with a new puppy, while the other has no interest whatsoever. Hardly encouraging."

Deborah joined in her friend's laughter. "Well, take heart, Miss Decker. Your visit has only begun. Who is to say what will happen in the days to come?"

Chapter 5

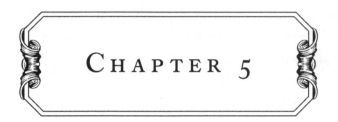

Christopher Clayton frowned as he caught sight of the unpacked crates. He felt he'd been unloading supplies all morning. When Zed Perkins hired him to be the new company doctor, Christopher had given him a long list of things that would be needed for a proper medical facility. As far as he could tell, Mr. Perkins had purchased everything he'd requested. Now it was his job to find a place for each article.

Another task would be to figure out how to keep the dust and soot from coating everything. Christopher was a firm believer that fresh air was healthy and helped to promote healing; however, the air quality in this town would not always be beneficial. If the wind was blowing just right, it appeared that Perkinsville could escape the worst of it. But if the day was calm, folks just had to endure the smoke and soot put out by the sawmill chimneys.

He ran a finger along the windowsill and shook his head at the collection of blackened dirt. He would have to figure out something that could be done. Perhaps if he tacked up material across the windows? It would have to have a very fine weave to hold out the damaging elements while still allowing fresh air. Wiping his finger on his already dirt-stained trousers, Christopher turned back to the job at hand.

He was generally pleased with the arrangements Mr. Perkins had made. The man had built the facility to the doctor's suggested specifications. While most of the houses here were of unfinished wood, the new doctor's office and infirmary was a stark white. Christopher had made a firm requirement that everything be whitewashed for easy cleaning. It stood out in the tiny town just as Christopher had hoped it would.

The front door opened into a small waiting area, and behind that was a private office that led into the examination room. Beyond the examination room was the infirmary. There were four cots and a washstand in this room, with a back entrance that allowed for easy access from the mill. The thought had been that should a terrible accident arise, it would allow for a wounded man to be brought in without making a scene.

A side door off the infirmary led to Dr. Clayton's private quarters. There he had a small kitchen, living room, and bedroom. It was nothing fancy, but neither did it need to be. Christopher was quite content.

"Hello?" A knock followed the female voice.

"I'm in the back," he called in reply. He hoped fervently that it wouldn't be a patient in need, for he wasn't ready to set up shop just yet.

Deborah Vandermark marched through the doorway with a plate extended in front of her. She looked rather like one of the wise men presenting his treasure to the Christ child. "I have come bearing a gift," she announced.

He smiled. "I can see that."

She returned his smile, and he very much liked the way it seemed to spark a fire in her dark brown eyes. "Mother made fresh doughnuts and instructed me to bring you a batch straightaway. I rode the train into town when they brought a load of wood."

He took the plate from her and put it on a nearby table. "Well, that was most kind of you. You will have to thank your mother for me."

"I will. It looks like I caught you at a bad time," she said, glancing around the messy room. "Might I help? The train won't be heading back for another hour."

"I couldn't let you spend your day laboring over this mess." He reached absentmindedly for one of the doughnuts and had it in his mouth almost before he realized it. The pastry practically melted on his tongue. "Oh, this is delicious."

Deborah turned and smiled. "My mother makes the best in the county."

"Along with biscuits?"

She laughed. "And many other things. So what is all of this? If you don't mind my asking."

"Not at all." He moved to where she stood. "This box has medical supplies. I ordered them from Mr. Perkins. The next crate holds many of my personal books and medical journals, and the others . . . well, I haven't opened them yet so I'm not exactly sure what they hold."

"I presume you will have an office?"

He nodded. "The small room you came through on your way

back here—the one with the bookshelves—will be my office. This is the examination room. Through that door over there is the infirmary, where I can care for long-term patients. Mr. Perkins had the entire structure built according to my suggestions."

"And are you pleased?"

"Very much so. Mr. Perkins also ordered the equipment I asked for. I was rather surprised to find most everything waiting and ready. He even managed to get this examination table for me." Christopher put his hand to the metal table.

Deborah reached into the crate of books. "Why don't I start by putting the books on the shelves? You can organize them at a later date, but at least it will get them out of the box."

"Thank you. It's most kind of you to help."

"I'm just nosy, that's all," she said in a teasing tone. "I love to read. Books are simply irresistible to me. I think I shall miss the libraries back East most of all."

"I gather your love of literature is rather unusual around here."

Deborah took up several large books. "Sadly, that is true. Folks leave school at an early age in order to work or marry. Reading is a luxury and books are a novelty. So, too, is having a doctor. You do realize that you might not be well received at first." She didn't wait for an answer but trotted the books to the office.

When she returned Christopher couldn't help but ask, "Why is that?"

"Margaret Foster has taken care of folks around here for as long as I can remember. She's a widow with three grown sons."

Again she headed off with more books, then quickly returned. Christopher admired her petite form as she bent to pick up additional medical tomes. "And she's the reason I won't be accepted?"

"Partly. People can be very odd. Mrs. Foster is superstitious, and she's convinced a lot of other folks to see things the way she does."

Deborah straightened and smiled. "But she didn't have to try that hard. Superstition walks hand in hand with ignorance."

"I've found that to be true," he replied, nodding. "But somehow I don't think that's a concern with you."

"Hardly."

Christopher laughed. "So what is a concern of yours?"

She shrugged and stopped to consider his question. "There are a great many things that concern me. My family's welfare is probably at the top of the list. Helping the people of this community is another."

"I heard someone say that your father passed away a few years ago."

"Nearly three. He was killed in a logging accident." Her expression sobered. "It was very hard on my family. We were all extremely close. We still are."

"I can well imagine. My own father was injured . . . in an accident." He hesitated. "It nearly claimed his life, but instead left him crippled and my mother struggling to support my siblings."

"Oh my, and you're the oldest of fifteen," Deborah said, shifting the books. "How in the world does she do it?"

He was touched by her concern. "Only the five youngest are still at home. The rest of us do what we can to help." The conversation suddenly made him feel self-conscious. "It seems your family is good about helping one another."

"Oh, they are. Uncle Arjan and my father were brothers, and when Papa died, my uncle felt it was important to see to Mama's needs. The boys inherited Papa's land and business—that's the way the law works down here. Everyone agreed, however, that Mama will never want."

"How was it that you ended up going to college?"

"The blessings of a wealthy aunt—one of my mother's sisters.

My folks needed me to learn what I could in order to help the business. My brothers weren't interested in an education. You'll see that about most folks. However, I hope that will change around here. I believe most people are ignorant of the possibilities."

"And you intend to show them?"

"I hope to. I want them to see how beneficial an education can be. There are some very hardworking people in this community. Education simply hasn't been something that was valued."

"How do you propose to help them change their minds?" he asked, intrigued by this little powerhouse of a woman.

"Mainly by example, I suppose. I'd like to show them how pleasant it can be to simply enjoy a good book—to be able to read the Bible for themselves. To better understand science, medicine. If they understand what you are able to do for them, Dr. Clayton, they will be more open to accepting you." She headed back to the office once more with an armload of books.

Christopher picked up several books and followed her. He waited until she'd secured the books on the shelf. "You really don't have to keep doing this." He placed his books beside hers.

She eyed him intently for a moment. "Are you too proud to accept help?"

He rubbed his bearded chin. "Not at all."

"Then what?"

He liked her spunk. "The books can wait, actually. If you truly want to be useful, I need to get the examination office set up first."

Deborah dusted off her hands and headed back to the other room. "Very well. Let's get to work. They'll sound the whistle when the train is ready to head back up the line."

Helping Dr. Clayton set up his examination office was a great diversion for Deborah. She found it fascinating to unpack his medical equipment and listen to his reasons for placement. When she came upon a collection of medical journals, Deborah couldn't help but thumb through a couple of them.

"These look quite interesting."

"If you're of a mind to read them, be my guest. Just bring them back."

She looked up to see if he was serious. His expression assured her he was. "I would like that very much."

"You may feel free to borrow any of my books, as well."

Deborah hugged the journals to her breast. "Do you always lend your books?"

"Never," he said, turning back to a crate he'd been emptying.

Deborah thought about this for several seconds and was about to extend an invitation to him to utilize her book collection when someone called out from the open back door.

"Doc, you in there?"

"I am," Dr. Clayton announced. He moved to the door and welcomed in a man and woman.

Deborah didn't know the couple, but she knew their type. They were dirt poor, ill-kempt, and probably had no more than six years of education between them. The woman looked tired and was clearly with child. Her face was edged with lines and her hair was stringy and dirty. Neither the man nor woman looked as if they'd had a bath in a week of Sundays.

"I'm Dr. Clayton. What can I do for you?"

The man held up his hand. "I'm John. My wife here wanted me to see you. My hand is hurtin' me something fierce."

"What did you do to it?" Dr. Clayton led the man to the examination table and drew up a chair. "Just sit here and rest your hand on the table."

The doctor went to a bowl of water and washed his hands.

Deborah saw him pour something onto his hands before taking up a clean towel. He then took up a brown bottle and another clean towel.

Deborah could see the man's hand had swollen to nearly double the normal size and was clearly inflamed. A jagged cut oozed green-tinged fluid. She watched as Dr. Clayton took the matter in stride.

"How did you injure your hand?"

"Cut it at work. Didn't seem that bad. Miz Foster put a poultice on it, but it don't seem to be any better."

The doctor continued his exam. "When was that?"

Deborah couldn't help drawing closer to see what was happening. The woman stepped forward, as well. "He cut it near a week ago. Ain't been right since. Cain't work with it like that."

"Now, Sally," he said, throwing her a grin. "You stop your frettin'. I came here like you asked."

"And it's a good thing," Dr. Clayton announced. "You'll be lucky if you don't lose that hand."

"What?" The man was clearly stunned.

"It's desperately infected. I'm afraid this will be quite painful. Miss Vandermark, would you please bring over a basin and my scalpel set?"

Deborah didn't even question him. She hurried to do his bidding, rather excited to be of some help. The procedure that followed was not at all pleasant. Without so much as an injection of morphine to kill the pain, Dr. Clayton cleaned the hand and applied the knife. The infection shot from the wound, filling the room with a hideous smell.

Unmoved by the situation, Deborah continued to follow the doctor's instructions, handing him the supplies he needed to treat the infected hand.

"This town doesn't seem to overly concern itself with cleanliness. You cannot have a wound of this magnitude and not pay heed to keeping it clean."

The man and woman exchanged a look. The woman frowned. "Miz Foster said to keep the poultice on. She told us not to wash it at all—said the herbs would draw it until the moon was full. It was a full moon last night, and we took off the bandages."

"Well, apparently she was wrong," Dr. Clayton said. He looked to Deborah. "Is this some of that superstitious nonsense you told me about?"

She nodded as the doctor continued to clean the hand. The man was clearly in horrible pain, but though his face paled, he said nothing. She fanned away the flies that hovered and prayed that God would intercede to heal the wound.

"I'll need to see you first thing in the morning," Dr. Clayton told the man.

"Cain't." He barely breathed the word. "Gotta be at the mill."

Dr. Clayton straightened. "If you do what I tell you to, I might be able to save your hand. If you don't, I can guarantee you that you will lose it."

"John, you cain't lose your hand." The woman's voice was edged with hysteria. "You cain't work without a hand."

Deborah reached out to touch the woman's arm. "Dr. Clayton is a good man. He'll do what he can, but you have to be willing to do your part. Mr. Perkins trusts him, and you should, too." She knew that most everyone thought fondly of the sawmill owner. "He looked far and wide to find a doctor as well trained as Dr. Clayton. He wouldn't allow your care to just anyone."

"She's right, Sally." A fine line of perspiration edged the man's upper lip. "Doc, will you let Mr. Perkins know that you told me to come here in the morning?"

"I will speak with him as soon as we've finished. Now this wound needs to drain." He instructed Sally as to what she needed to do. "Do exactly as I've told you, understand?"

She nodded. Deborah felt sorry for the woman and patted her hand. "You did the right thing in coming here. Dr. Clayton will do everything he can."

Once the couple was gone, Dr. Clayton turned to Deborah. "You handled that well."

She shrugged. "I just wanted to help."

"You definitely did that."

The train whistle sounded in the distance and Deborah realized she would need to go. She quickly washed her hands. "Things are starting to look a whole lot better in here, but I need to go. Thanks for the loan of the journals." She gathered up the three magazines that she'd set aside to take with her. "I'll have them back soon."

"Please thank your mother for the doughnuts."

"I'm sure there will be other offerings as people get used to the idea of having a regular doctor. You'll find folks around here can be very friendly once they feel safe with you."

She wanted to tell him how much she admired his skills but held back. Instead, she just smiled and headed for the door. "Mama also wanted you to know that you're always welcome at the house. Come anytime for supper—or any other meal, for that matter."

Deborah didn't wait for an answer but headed out across the dirt road and made her way to where the little engine waited.

"Come on up," the fireman said, extending his hand.

Deborah gathered her skirts, careful not to damage the journals, and made the stretch to reach the first step. She grabbed the grimy rail and pulled herself up. George steadied her as she finally made it into the engine compartment. The engineer, an older man named Jack, tipped a finger to his cap and gave the whistle another short blast.

"I figured you'd come back with all sorts of girly geegaws," George told her. "Told Jack we probably wouldn't have room for it all."

She smiled. "I'm not much of a shopper, George." She held up the journals. "More of a reader."

"Never learned myself." He turned back to his job of loading the firebox as Jack put the train in motion. "Never saw a need. Guess you can read enough for all of us."

Deborah shook her head. "You ought to learn, George. You'd be surprised how much fun it can be. I could even help you if you'd like."

He laughed. "Won't help in gettin' the steam up, so I don't reckon I need it."

She looked out the window and sighed. Ignorance seemed the answer to all things uncomfortable or challenging.

Lord, she prayed, *I know you brought me back here to help my family. I want to help them. I love them. But there's so much more out there, beyond my little world in Perkinsville, Texas. . . .*

Chapter 6

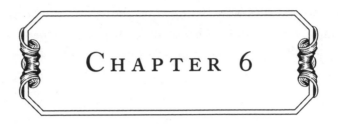

After church on Sunday, the congregation gathered outside under the shady box elders and hickories and held a picnic lunch. Everyone brought something to share, and soon the atmosphere was quite merry. Lizzie had never experienced anything like it. Gone were the pretenses and worries of social status. Even the Perkins family blended with the lowliest mill worker and his family.

The contrast in clothing was evident. The members of the poorer families were dressed simply in garments that had seen a great deal of wear. Many of the outfits bore patches and stains, but it was the best they could offer. People from more affluent families wore stylish outfits that looked store-bought and new, compared to the outfits of their less wealthy neighbors. The Vandermarks fell in between, neither too fashionable nor too unkempt. Lizzie now understood why Deborah had traded most of her beautiful gowns for simpler fare at the secondhand shop in Nacogdoches. Yet even now, as Deborah approached in a lovely gown with yellow flowers set against a cream-colored background, she looked radiant—almost elegant. Everyone seemed happy to see her and stopped her frequently to bid her welcome home or to ask about her travels.

At last Deborah managed to separate herself and closed the distance to Lizzie, who was filling her plate. "G. W. is all alone, and I want you to help me keep him from stewing and fretting."

Lizzie met Deborah's determined expression. "What can I do?" She turned back to the table and took a piece of corn bread.

"Just go talk to him. He tends to get moody at these gatherings because he doesn't want to have to talk to anyone about anything. Just sit with him and keep him from thinking on Papa's death."

Lizzie took up a piece of fried chicken and looked to her friend in confusion. "And how am I supposed to do that? I can hardly keep a man from thinking about what he chooses."

"If you talk to him about other things, he'll have to keep his mind elsewhere." Deborah took hold of Lizzie's arm and pulled her in the direction of the creek. "He's over here."

Barely keeping her plate balanced, Lizzie fought to keep up with Deborah. She didn't think this was a good idea, but it didn't appear she had a choice in the matter.

"G. W., Lizzie doesn't have anyone to talk to. I told her she could come sit with you," Deborah said, releasing her friend as they approached G. W.

He sat with his back to a tree, a plate of food uneaten in his lap. Lizzie could tell that he wasn't in a mood for company, but he was too much of a gentleman to say so.

"I can go if it's too much of a bother," she said softly.

He shook his head. "That's all right."

Deborah smiled. "I told you it would be fine." She lifted her skirt and whirled off in the opposite direction. "I'll be back after a bit."

"I really am sorry," Lizzie told him.

G. W. shrugged. "I know what she's up to. So long as you know it, too, then we won't be duped."

She looked at the ground and then to her plate, wondering how she was going to sit without dumping her food. G. W. seemed to understand her predicament and put his own plate aside. He was on his feet assisting her before Lizzie could ask for help.

"Thank you. I was rather perplexed for the moment." She smiled and settled the plate of food on her lap.

They sat in silence for several minutes. Lizzie nibbled at her chicken while G. W. stared out at the muddy waters, lost in thought. She couldn't help but wonder what was going through his mind. How could she possibly impose her own interests upon him? Whether Deborah liked it or not, Lizzie knew there was only one topic of conversation that would help G. W.

"If I'm not causing you even more pain, I wonder if you might tell me about your father's accident. Deborah tells me the anniversary of his death is coming up."

G. W. looked at her in surprise. For a moment, Lizzie wasn't at all sure he would even remain at her side, much less speak. Finally, however, he exhaled a long breath.

"Three years next month," he said as if she'd asked for confirmation. "But it seems like just yesterday." He started at the beginning and filled in the details that Lizzie hadn't known.

"The work is unpredictable," he told her after reliving the accident in detail. "Any time you combine sharp tools, animals, and human error, you're bound to have trouble."

"It sounds like logging is a very dangerous industry," Lizzie said. "Did your father realize just how dangerous it was when he started this business?"

G. W. gave a brief laugh. "He knew. He'd been around it in Georgia. My father and uncle had honestly planned to come here and plant cotton, but loggin' seemed a necessary way to start."

"Why?"

"The good farmin' ground was taken by the time they arrived. The land they were able to get was all wooded. They figured they could log the forests, get the lumber to the nearby towns, and clear their land at the same time. They were fixin' to clear out enough of the forest to plant cotton, but it never worked out that way. The loggin' proved to be a valuable means of gainin' an income. Pretty soon they were buyin' more forest land, and Vandermark Logging became a permanent operation. It was actually my father's pride and joy. He loved the work he did."

"So they chose their profession, even knowing the dangers. That's true bravery, in my mind," Lizzie said casually. "It amazes me that a man, knowing the possibility of death lingered just around the corner, would continue to put his hand to a task."

"It was Pa's way of earning a livin' for his family. He always said he got along well with the Piney Woods. I reckon he could have done something else. He was a smart enough man."

"Obviously. Just as you are. Look at how successful the logging industry has proven to be. Why, I heard Deborah say that eastern investors are all over the place looking for land to buy so they can be a part of this success. Your father had great insight."

G. W. nodded. "I suppose you could say that. He knew the yellow pine was good wood, even though a lot of folks didn't care for it. He had a way of doin' the right thing, at the right time. Too bad I didn't."

"Why do you say that?" Lizzie watched the play of emotions in his expression.

"If I had been like him—knowin' what to do at the right time—Pa might be alive today."

"Maybe he should have trained you better," she suggested.

"There's no call to say that. Pa was a good teacher. Like I said, he was smart. He taught me and Rob real good."

"Well, I suppose I'm confused." She gave him an innocent smile, hoping he wouldn't realize the trap she'd put in place. "If your father was smart and trained you well, and if he knew all of the dangers about the business, but continued to log anyway—how can his death possibly be your fault?"

G. W. opened his mouth to speak, then closed it. He looked at her for a moment and shook his head. "You book-learned women sure have a way of confusin' a guy."

"Maybe it's not as confusing as you think. I'm just suggesting that accidents have a way of happening, no matter how smart or careful people might be. You know the risks in your job. Your uncle and brother know them, too, yet all of you go out to work every day. Your father knew the risks and even had a choice to do something else. He chose to stay with logging." She smiled. "I think maybe it's time to consider that his death was simply one of those risks he was willing to take."

"Well, here you are," Rob declared as he joined the twosome. "I've been lookin' pert-near everywhere for you."

Lizzie held G. W.'s gaze for a moment longer, then cast a glance toward his brother. "Your sister brought me here, and it's so much cooler here in the shade that I couldn't help but linger. I'm afraid I've been talking your brother's ear off."

Rob plopped down on the ground in front of Lizzie. "You can

talk my ear off anytime you like." He grinned. "I reckon that would suit me just fine."

Deborah saw Rob heading over to join G. W. and Lizzie and frowned, wishing it were her instead. She'd been swarmed by people all afternoon. Most folks wanted to welcome her back, but others were would-be suitors who seemed quite bold in rekindling previous acquaintances.

"Miss Deborah, I wonder iffen you'd like to take a walk with me," Sam Huebner asked.

She looked up at the tall, lanky man. She'd known Sam for just about as long as anyone. His folks had been good friends with hers. "Hello, Sam. How are you?"

His smile broadened. "So you remember me."

"Of course I remember you. You've hung around my brothers and worked for my family nigh on forever." She noticed his brother working to spark an interest with one of the Perkins girls and nodded in that direction. "Looks like Stephen is sweet on Annabeth Perkins."

Sam followed her gaze. "He's got rocks for brains. Ain't no chance of courtin' her, and he knows it."

"Well, I suppose a man can dream." She turned back to Sam. "What of you? Have you settled down and married?"

He turned red and shook his head. "No, ma'am. Wouldn't be here talkin' to you iffen I had."

Deborah spied her mother approaching from behind Sam. "Well, don't worry, Sam," she said, moving to the side. "One of these days the right gal will come along. If you'll excuse me now, it looks like my mother needs me."

She was glad to hurry away before he could say anything else.

When she reached her mother, Deborah couldn't help but grin. "You saved my life."

"What in the world are you talking about?"

Linking their arms, Deborah walked with her mother toward the tables of food. "Sam just asked me to take a walk with him. I needed an excuse not to go."

"But why? Sam's a nice boy. You might have enjoyed a walk."

Deborah shook her head. "I don't think so. He can't even read."

"You would reject a man's love because he couldn't read? Your father couldn't read very well, and yet I loved him."

Deborah felt chastised. "I'm sorry, Mama. I didn't mean it to sound like that." She let go of her mother's arm. "I just . . . well, it's so hard sometimes." She looked around the gathering of people. "I wish I could explain it."

Her mother smiled and reached out to smooth back an errant strand of hair from Deborah's face. "Why don't you try?"

"I'm glad to be home—truly I am."

"But . . ."

"But . . . I don't really know. Things feel different, yet they're the same. I feel different, yet I'm the same."

Mother shook her head. "Nothing stays the same. It might have some of the same appearances, but changes are always taking place. The town's grown a bit. There are new buildings and people. The mill has expanded. You're older and, hopefully, wiser. You're more educated and have experienced more than you had two years ago."

"I know, and maybe that's part of the problem," she said, feeling like such a snob for even continuing. "Mama, I loved learning. I love reading and writing. I love books that teach me new things.

I want to discuss those things with others, but this isn't exactly the place to find someone of a like mind."

"Oh, sweetheart, I completely understand."

"Do you really? Because I'm not sure I do. I feel horrible for it. It sounds like I think myself better than others, but that's not it at all."

"Of course not," her mother agreed. "Just because you have one interest and someone else has another doesn't mean either one of you is better. Zed Perkins knows how to run a sawmill. Jack knows how to engineer a train. You can't drive a train. Does that make Jack better than you—worse than you?"

Deborah shook her head. "But I'm afraid that when it comes to courting, it will be a problem. Not that I have time for that." She ignored her mother's frown. "Mama, when Sam suggested a walk all I could think about was how I could never marry someone like him. I know that's horrible, and I'm sorry." She looked at her mother in desperation. "Please don't hate me, but I'm not sure I could fall in love with a man who didn't have an education."

Her mother reached out to pat her cheek. "Darling, when the right man comes along all of these things will fall into place. Don't fret over it. No one is asking you to marry Sam. The important thing to keep in mind is whether or not you're like-minded when it comes to God. Being unequally yoked can certainly pertain to other things, but spiritually, it is a never-ending battle that no married couple should have to endure. You need a man who first and foremost loves God."

"A man who loves God and is intelligent," Deborah said. "Of course, he should be thoughtful and kind, as well."

Her mother laughed. "And it wouldn't hurt if he was handsome, too. Maybe even well off."

Deborah grinned. "Well, if we're making a list, we might as well add it all."

Mother gave her a hug and released her. "I'm glad you're home. I missed your sense of humor and open frankness. Just don't fret over what you can't change. Folks here are just glad to be working and have a roof over their heads. Reading and writing isn't something they miss."

"Maybe not, but maybe that's only because they never had it to begin with," Deborah replied. "They don't know what they're missing."

Her mother nodded. "Sometimes that's the best way to get by. I find it a lot easier to be content when I'm not pondering the things I miss."

"Like Papa?"

"Yes," her mother said with a sigh. "He was my best friend, and it's hard to lose that. I know he's in a better place, but sometimes I'm lonely."

Deborah didn't know what to say. She longed to be able to say something that would give her mother just the right sense of assurance, but truth be told, Deborah felt completely unable to help. What did she know of losing a mate—a best friend of nearly thirty years?

Finally she put her arm around her mother's shoulders and simply held her close. Sometimes, words simply had no power to help.

Chapter 7

July 1885

The weeks of June slipped into July, and as the heat grew more intense, Deborah's efforts to set up the Vandermark Logging office did, too. She had decided the best way to get organized was to actually have an office. In the past, Uncle Arjan had just carried a ledger around with him to the logging site and then back to his small cabin just a few yards behind the main house. Now, however, Deborah believed the size of their organization merited a place for everything and everything in its place.

There was a sewing room on the ground floor of the Vandermark house that would work quite well. With her mother's enthusiastic encouragement, Deborah arranged for her brothers to move the sewing things upstairs to the storage room, where she and Lizzie could fix it up properly. There would always be mending and sewing to see to, but Mother said they could tend to it on the second floor as well as on the first.

Still, Deborah knew it was a sacrifice. The upstairs was much warmer in the summer, and while they saved most of their major sewing projects for the cooler winter months, it would still be less than ideal. Maybe in the future she could encourage her uncle and brothers to build a separate cabin for the office.

With Lizzie's help, the office took shape quickly. Deborah arranged a small desk, several chairs, and bookshelves, along with other things she would need. Now that she was settled, the trick was to interpret her uncle's chicken-scratch notes. Often she found a few figures and a name without any other comment. Deborah was hard-pressed to know exactly what they meant, but she gradually began to recognize his style.

She was just finishing tallies on May's figures when her uncle and Mr. Perkins showed up at the door of the office. Uncle Arjan looked rather perplexed.

"Sorry to bother you, Deborah, but Mr. Perkins has some papers for us to look over."

"Good to see you, Mr. Perkins. Come in," Deborah said, putting down her pen. "Pull up a chair and tell me what you need."

"I told Arjan that I wanted someone in the family to read over this contract. One copy is for you and one's for me. I need to have it signed to take with me when I go to Houston on Friday."

"A contract?" Most everything related to the business had always been done on a handshake. Contracts had never been needed among friends.

Mr. Perkins looked rather embarrassed as he handed her the papers. "I know what you're thinking, but it's not my idea. The bank wants me to give them proof that I have a steady supply of logs pledged for production at the sawmill. I'm getting signatures from all my major providers."

Deborah began reading over the contract. "But why?" she asked without thinking. She glanced up and smiled. "If you don't mind my asking."

The older man shook his head. "Not at all. Like I said, I know this comes as a surprise. Here's the situation: I want to double the size of the mill."

"Double?" She looked at her uncle. "Would that mean we would have to double our output, and double the number of employees, as well?"

"It would definitely mean adding people," her uncle replied.

Mr. Perkins moved forward. "See, I need to get a pledge of so many logs so I can project our board feet. This becomes a sort of collateral for the bank. They will see the contract agreements as a promise of production and your agreement to sell only to me, and in turn they can feel safe in loaning me the money I need for the expansion."

Deborah couldn't begin to imagine what that would do to the size of their small community. "I suppose you will have to bring in additional stores and housing for the workers, as well."

"Yes indeed. I'll be adding at least another ten houses right away, with plans for twenty more. Now that we have the new doctor—not that folks will go see him—" he muttered under his breath, "the missus wants me to think about bringing in a full-time preacher and maybe build a regular icehouse."

"All of those things would be very nice, especially with additional workers." Deborah looked at the papers again, and then to her uncle. "Has Mr. Perkins gone over the numbers with you?"

Uncle Arjan nodded. "He did."

"And are you in agreement with that number?" She glanced

down to look at the figures once more. "It says here that you'll provide logs with a potential of ten thousand board feet a day until the mill's first phase of additions is complete. After that, you'll increase to fifteen thousand, and after phase two and the completion of all additions, you'll increase to at least twenty thousand board feet a day, with bonuses paid if you go over your quota. Oh, and it's all to be paid in cash rather than script."

"Yes, that's always been our agreement. As for the amount of wood, I think we can do that, so long as we get in a good crew of workers," Uncle Arjan told her.

"And you'll have a few months to get them trained," Mr. Perkins added. "Once I get my loan, I intend to see the work completed by Christmas at the latest. That will give you a full five months to hire and train your men."

"I'm comfortable with that," Uncle Arjan declared.

Deborah worked some figures on paper for a moment. "So eventually you will need to provide something like between twenty-seven and thirty-five trees a day by the time the mill is doubled. Is that correct?"

Uncle Arjan laughed. "I told you she was the smart one in the family."

"What about these figures on what you'll pay Vandermark Logging?" Deborah asked Mr. Perkins. "Shouldn't there be an allowance for escalation, should the price of lumber go up?"

"She is the smart one," Mr. Perkins agreed. "I'm sorry I didn't think of that myself. Shows that my mind was purely on my own gain, and for that, I apologize. Why don't we figure a percentage that will be acceptable to both of us?"

"A figure based on increases of more than five percent in finished lumber prices could trigger the escalation clause. If the prices bottom out, we would revert to the original base price. That base price, however, could not be allowed to drop—at least not without new negotiations. If we have to pledge to provide a specific amount of board feet and take penalties if we fail to meet our quota, then you must, in turn, pledge to pay for the wood even if the market suffers. There should also be a clause that allows for acts of God—fire, hurricanes, and such."

"That's only fair," Mr. Perkins granted. "Write that in. I'll sign off on it."

They haggled over figures for another few minutes before Deborah was finally satisfied. Mr. Perkins reached out to shake her hand. "Your family will benefit greatly from you handling their affairs." He turned to Uncle Arjan. "Don't let her get away from you."

"I don't intend to," her uncle agreed.

She felt a mixture of emotions at his words. It wasn't that she didn't want to benefit her family, but with each passing day, Deborah had the distinct feeling that she had backed herself into a corner. She remembered one of her professors once saying, "Be careful of making yourself irreplaceable and indispensable, lest you find that you are."

"You'll be providing half my supply." Mr. Perkins patted her shoulder. "Your pa sure would have been proud."

Deborah nodded. "He would have been." She finished adjusting the terms of the document on one set of papers and handed the paper to her uncle. Dipping her pen in the ink, she passed that to him, as well. "You should both initial where each of the changes are listed and sign on the last page."

Uncle Arjan took the pen and did just that. He let Deborah blot the signature then handed the contract back to Mr. Perkins. "Looks like I'd better hire me some men."

Mr. Perkins initialed and signed while Deborah adjusted the

second copy of the contract. Once all of the signatures were in place, Zed Perkins handed Arjan his copy. "I'll be in touch as soon as I get back from Houston. I don't think we're going to have any problem now. I have four other small operations agreeing to provide wood, so the bankers can easily see that I'll have the wherewithal to furnish what I say I can. It was good to do business with you, Miss Deborah."

She smiled. "Likewise."

Uncle Arjan left momentarily to walk Mr. Perkins to the door, then returned to the office. Deborah looked up and smiled. "Guess you have your work cut out for you now."

"Well, my first order of business is to assign you a salary. You earned your keep today."

She shook her head. "I didn't take on this job expecting to be paid. Father wanted me to do this job. I benefit from the prosperity of the company—same as you. I don't need a salary."

"I can't say that I ever recall your father thinkin' you needed to work at anything. Leastwise, he never told me."

"That can't be right. We used to talk about it all the time. He knew I couldn't very well log, but he said many times that everyone in the family needed to pull their weight. So he allowed me to go to school."

"I don't suppose I know about that. Your pa talked about how proud he was of your ability to think—especially for a woman."

She grinned. "That sounds like him."

"And he loved to indulge you. But, anyway, everyone needs some spending money," Uncle Arjan countered. "What say you let me pay you a dollar a day? If you find you need more money than that—say you want to buy something special—just come and see me. Agreed?"

Deborah considered it for a moment and nodded. "Very well."

She got up and kissed her uncle on the cheek. "You are awfully good to me—to Mama, too. I want you to know how much I appreciate that."

His face reddened slightly. "You and your mama mean the world to me—the boys, too. Wouldn't expect anyone else to take care of you."

"Even so, I'm grateful. Mama's peace of mind is important to me. I know she's come to depend on you and the boys a great deal. Hopefully, by taking this job, I can pay you back in a small way."

He laughed and gave her shoulders a squeeze. "Little gal, you are more than payin' me back by what you did here today. You know how this business works, and you know how the world works because of all that schoolin'. You benefited us all today, and I'm right proud of you. Just wait until I tell your brothers. They'll be dancing a jig."

"I doubt G. W. will dance a jig anytime soon." She frowned and looked up at her uncle. "Have you ever talked to him about Papa's death?"

Uncle Arjan grew thoughtful. "I've tried. He knows I don't hold him responsible. Doesn't change the fact that the boy holds himself in that place."

"I know. Mama said she worries about him for that very reason. I keep praying for him, but I sure wish I could do something to encourage him—get his mind off the fact that the anniversary of the accident is coming up."

"He's got to come through this himself, Deborah. You can't force a man to make peace with his own self. Give him time. He'll come around sooner or later."

But Deborah wasn't at all convinced that he would.

Lizzie brought Deborah a glass of lemonade and plopped down on a chair opposite her. "Goodness, but it's hot down here."

Deborah laughed. "Yes, and this is only July. Just wait for August."

"I can't imagine it getting any worse." Lizzie dabbed her damp forehead with the edge of her apron.

"I suppose Mama had you busy in the garden all morning?"

"Only for a little while. She was worried about me and the heat, so she wouldn't let me work for long. I tell you, I feel positively useless to you all. I really shouldn't have come."

Sampling the lemonade, Deborah nearly choked. "What? Why are you saying that?"

Lizzie shrugged. "It's just that everyone has their duties and tasks—everyone but me, that is. I'm just living here and eating your food and doing nothing. Your mother wouldn't even take money from me for my keep."

"I'm sure she wouldn't," Deborah replied with a grin. "Goodness, but she would never want it said that she charged a guest."

"But I wasn't thinking of it that way. I just wanted to help out."

"Don't fret about it. Mother is glad you came. She said there is nothing she can imagine worse than marrying a man you do not love. One of her sisters did that and it proved to be nothing but misery. Mama often uses Aunt Alva as an example."

"Why did she marry a man she didn't love?"

"To help the family. Her husband was from Holland and had a great deal of wealth. When he told her they would live there instead of America, she was very unhappy. Mama says her letters are always full of sorrow."

"How sad."

"Exactly so. Which is why it's good that you are here and not back in Philadelphia, playing the role of Mrs. Stuart Albright and sending *me* letters full of sorrow."

Lizzie shuddered at the thought. "Even the Texas heat is worth enduring to avoid that. I do wish, however, that Father would write. I can't help but wonder how Mother took the news. I'd imagine she was quite humiliated."

"Or extremely happy," Deborah offered. "After all, she's the one who believes women needn't marry or otherwise have a man in their affairs. She might have been miffed at first, but she's probably greatly satisfied by now."

"I just hope she isn't too mad. You know how awful she can be when she gets spiteful. Her tirades can be worse than a child's. I'm glad to have the distance between us." Lizzie watched as Deborah downed the lemonade. "Would you like more?" she asked.

"No, I'm fine. I need to get back to work on these ledgers. Some of this," she waved to a pile of papers, "is quite confusing. I feel I should have schooled in some foreign language just to interpret it, but I don't know which one might have helped."

Lizzie smiled. "Well, before you get back to work, maybe you can help me with this problem of feeling useless. Might there be some sort of job I could take on? Something I could do to benefit the family?"

"Goodness, no," Deborah said. "They really don't look highly on women working in these parts. It's different for me because this is my family. For you, however, it would be scandalous."

"I know my talents are few, but there must be something. What about taking in washing?"

"And see men's unmentionables?" Deborah asked in mock horror. "We'd get six weeks of sermons on women of low character from the Bible, only to be punctuated by the preacher standing at the front of the congregation letting a bit of salt run through his hands to remind us of poor Lot's wife. I can just hear it now." Deborah cleared her throat and lowered the timbre of her voice:

" 'Women are to be protected and sheltered from the unpleasant things of life. When they stray from such protection, they give themselves over to the influence of Jezebel, Delilah, and Sapphira. Let us remember this, and tremble.' "

Lizzie couldn't help giggling. "You really do that quite well. Perhaps you should take up preaching."

Deborah rolled her eyes. "That is a whole other set of sermons. Truth be told," she said, settling her gaze on Lizzie, "I agree for the most part. I think that in fighting against the boundaries set before us, often we forsake the good that could be had. I rather like the idea of being sheltered and protected from certain things. Other things . . . well, I suppose I would like to see some matters changed. But I don't want it enough to raise the ruckus your mother does."

"Me either," Lizzie agreed. "The very thought of going to jail for something like the cause of women voting is appalling."

"Well, I don't think you'll have to worry about that down here—at least not for a while. Anyway, I wouldn't worry about having nothing to do. My mother is good about keeping folks busy. I heard her mention that the Texas blacks are just about ready for picking."

"Texas blacks?"

"Grapes. You'll find that every month there is something new to harvest around here, and my mother has recipes for it all. I wouldn't fret about being idle. Once you get accustomed to the heat, you'll be busy enough."

Lizzie reached to take the glass. "Are you sure you won't have another?"

Deborah shook her head. "No. I'd probably just spill it all over everything, and then all my hard work would be for naught. Please tell Mama thanks for me."

"I will."

Lizzie bounded out the door just in time to run headlong into G. W. He reached out to take hold of her, but Lizzie still managed to fall against his chest and step on his foot. He continued to hold on to her as she regained her balance.

"I'm so sorry, G. W. I wasn't expecting anyone to be here. Your mother was out in the garden and . . . well, I just didn't think."

"No harm done. Are you all right?"

"I'm fine." She looked up and smiled. "How about you? Did I crush your foot?"

"A little bitty thing like you?" His drawl was thick and more pronounced.

She laughed. "If I keep eating fried green tomatoes and ham steaks, I won't be little for long. Gracious, but your Mama can cook."

"She sure can. I'm sure if you ask, she'll learn ya."

"When I was in town, Mrs. Greeley told me a girl has to be able to cook a decent meal in order to catch a decent man," Lizzie said without thinking.

G. W. surprised her by laughing out loud. "Miss Lizzie, you could do nothing but burn water and still catch a man."

Deborah appeared in the doorway. "What's all the fuss? A person can't even hear themselves think with all this noise."

Lizzie felt her face grow hot. "I . . . well . . . I came rushing out the door . . . and . . ."

"She threw herself at me—plain and simple," G. W. said, still grinning.

Deborah shrugged. "Well, it's about time someone did. You need a wife, G. W. Now, if you'll both excuse me, I have work to do.

Maybe you two could take your courting outside." She closed the door, leaving G. W. and Lizzie to stare in stunned silence.

Finally, Lizzie gathered her wits and hurried away. *After all this time*, she thought, *you would think I'd be used to Deborah's outspoken ways. But just when I think she can't surprise me any more, she goes and says something like that.*

Chapter 8

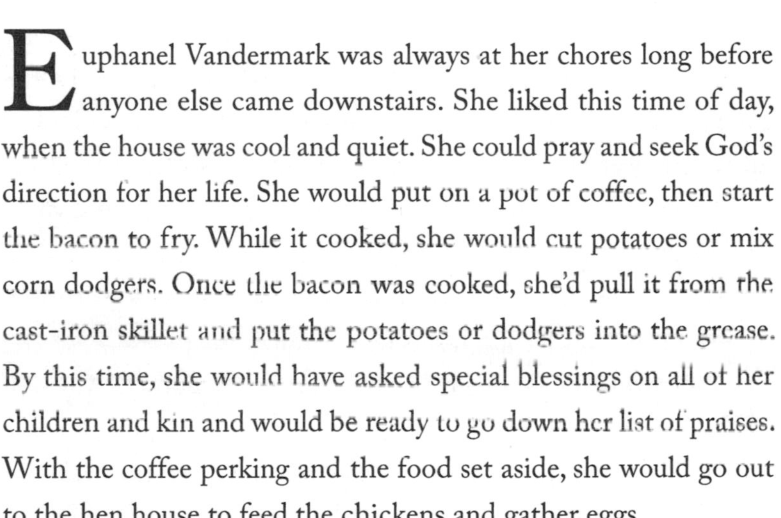

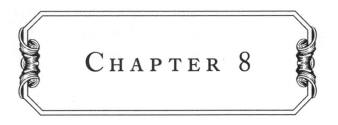

Euphanel Vandermark was always at her chores long before anyone else came downstairs. She liked this time of day, when the house was cool and quiet. She could pray and seek God's direction for her life. She would put on a pot of coffee, then start the bacon to fry. While it cooked, she would cut potatoes or mix corn dodgers. Once the bacon was cooked, she'd pull it from the cast-iron skillet and put the potatoes or dodgers into the grease. By this time, she would have asked special blessings on all of her children and kin and would be ready to go down her list of praises. With the coffee perking and the food set aside, she would go out to the hen house to feed the chickens and gather eggs.

It was the way she'd lived her life most every morning for the last twenty-some years. At forty-three, she felt well seasoned in the duties of motherhood and keeping house. Having married at sixteen, Euphanel had spent far more of her life married with children of her own than alone. She supposed that's why it was so hard now to be a widow with children who no longer needed her as they once had. Oh, they still enjoyed her cooking and were grateful to have the cleaning done, but there were no bedtime stories with little ones or moments of lingering in the arms of her man.

She pushed aside the sad thoughts and opened the gate to the chicken yard. She threw out some feed as she called, "Chick, chick, chick. Come along, little chicks."

With the hens and their broods busy eating, Euphanel could quickly gather the eggs—what there were to gather. The hens were laying light, no doubt because of the heat. She made her way toward the house with Decatur and Jasper now at her side. Dottie, the larger of the two milk cows, lowed miserably as if to remind her that she was in need of Euphanel's attention even if no one else was.

"Don't you worry, Dottie girl. Sissy will be here soon." This drew the attention of the other cow, which seemed to think it necessary to join in. Euphanel laughed. "Now, Dorothy, you just keep Dottie company, and we'll see you both in a few minutes." The dogs looked up hopefully at the sound of her voice. Euphanel shifted her basket and leaned down to give Jasper a rub behind the ears. "Yes, you'll be taken care of, as well."

By the time she arrived in the kitchen, Euphanel was surprised to find Lizzie and Deborah setting the table.

"Boys will be right down," Deborah told her mother. "Any sign of Uncle Arjan?"

"I didn't even think to look," she replied, putting the basket of eggs on the counter. "Guess my mind was otherwise occupied."

"I'm sure he'll be here soon," Deborah said. "He'll smell the coffee and bacon and that will bring him running."

Euphanel laughed. "It always has in the past."

"Can I do something?" Lizzie questioned, looking ever so hopeful.

"Absolutely. Come on over here. You wipe off these eggs and I'll go get the few we had left from yesterday. We'll fry up a batch for breakfast and then mix up some flapjacks."

Lizzie began the cleaning process while Euphanel fetched the additional eggs. How merry it was to have the girls with her in the kitchen. In a few moments, the boys had joined them, and by the time the flapjacks were done and the eggs fried, Arjan had made his way to the house, as well.

"We have a lot of work to do today, boys," he declared. "Better pack us a big lunch, Nel."

Arjan was the only one besides Rutger who had ever called her by the nickname. She smiled and placed a platter of flapjacks in front of him. "Don't I always?"

He grinned up at her. "I thought yesterday's was just a mite on the small side."

Euphanel met his teasing expression and cocked a brow. "I thought you looked like you were wasting away."

He laughed and leaned back to pat his ample but well-muscled midsection. "Glad you noticed."

They all chuckled at this as Euphanel took her place at the table for prayer. Bowing, she couldn't help but remember when Rutger had started the tradition. Shortly after they'd arrived in Texas, he'd gathered her and his brother to the breakfast table one morning and announced that it was about time they got their priorities straight.

"We need to be startin' and endin' the day in His presence," her husband had begun, *"and we need to be mindful of our heavenly Father*

throughout the day. It's the only way to get through, and I'm convinced we've been rather poor in this."

No one had questioned Rutger's decision. Euphanel smiled to herself. Her broad-shouldered husband had a way of commanding respect without ever raising his voice. She'd only seen him mad twice in his life, and both times were more than justified—once when a feisty mule had kicked him square in the head, and the other when a wild hog had cornered her. Rutger had seen red both times, but once the trouble was behind them, he had calmed down just as quick.

"Gotta get glad in the same clothes I got mad in," he used to say. *"Might as well be quick about it."*

"Mother?" Deborah called.

Euphanel looked up rather sheepishly as she realized the prayer had ended. "Amen."

She was about to offer some excuse when Sissy bustled into the dining room. "It be a glorious day. The Lord is good and the world rightly declares it."

"The Lord is good," Euphanel replied. "Good to see you feeling so fit this morning. I was worried about your hip."

"Bah, my hip ain't gonna stop me." The older woman gave her leg a slap. "I'm too ornery to let the devil catch hold of me."

Euphanel added food to her plate. "I'll be out to help you in just a few minutes."

"You take yor time, Miz Euphanel. Ain't no bother to me," Sissy declared. "I heard Miz Dottie and Miz Dorothy callin' for me." She chuckled and took up the clean milk pails. "We'll have ourselves a little time of praisin' the good Lord."

"You do that," Euphanel said. "The girls love to hear you sing."

The black woman made her way outside, leaving everyone

in the room feeling more lighthearted. Deborah was the first to comment.

"I swear that woman is the best medicine. If you could bottle her and sell her to people, you'd make a fortune."

Her daughter was right, Euphanel thought. Sissy always had a way of making folks feel better. It was almost impossible to stay troubled or discouraged when she was around.

Euphanel ate her breakfast quickly and made a mental list of all that she wanted to accomplish that day. She had plenty of gardening to tend to and canning to do. She had laundry and mending, meals to fix, and she still hoped to get some cleaning done upstairs.

First, however, the cows needed milking. Sissy would have already started with Dottie, but poor Dorothy would be beside herself if Euphanel didn't make haste.

"Mother, Lizzie and I can fix the lunches," Deborah offered as Euphanel got to her feet.

"That would be a great help to me," she said. "That way I can get right out to help milk."

"Could I learn how to milk the cow?" Lizzie asked.

"You sure you want to learn?" Rob asked in disbelief.

Lizzie nodded and looked to Euphanel for an answer. "I need to start learning useful skills. I might know about art and music, but I haven't had an opportunity to use my knowledge here."

Euphanel smiled. "Of course you can come and learn how to milk a cow. I'll be happy to teach you most anything. Just remember, though, when the heat of the day is upon us, I want you to take it easy."

"I promise I will." Lizzie set aside her napkin and got up from the table. Looking to Deborah, she asked, "Can you handle packing the lunches by yourself?"

"Of course. Go on and enjoy your new experience."

"And don't get yourself stepped on—Dorothy's real bad about that," Rob declared.

G. W. nodded and added, "And watch the bucket—she likes to kick it over."

Euphanel held out her hand to Lizzie. "Come along. I'll show you all the tricks."

ꕥ

Several hours later, after seeing her friend busily occupied with Mother and Sissy in the kitchen, Deborah announced she was going to Perkinsville.

"I have some journals to return to Dr. Clayton," she told her mother. "Is there anything I can bring back from the store?"

"Sissy can go with you and get the supplies we talked about," her mother replied. "I don't like you going all that way by yourself."

Deborah didn't argue with her mother. It wouldn't have done any good. It was probably best that her mother never know about the many times she'd walked unescorted through the city streets of Philadelphia. Probably wise, too, that she not mention the times she'd attended evening functions unaccompanied.

"I'll hitch the wagon," Sissy said, pulling off her apron.

It was also wise not to argue with Sissy. The woman might be fifty years old and shorter than Deborah, but she was a powerful opponent if the situation arose.

"I'll be back soon, Lizzie. Is there anything in particular I can bring you?"

"A letter from my father would be nice," Lizzie said, looking up from a bowl of green beans.

Deborah knew her friend longed for news. It had already been several weeks, and still no word. "I'll do what I can," she promised.

Sissy had the team harnessed and ready to go in no time at all.

Matthew and Mark were two of the sweetest Morgans ever trained. Their temperament even allowed for them to be ridden from time to time, although it was usually bareback.

Deborah climbed up on the wagon and sat down beside Sissy. "You wanna take the reins?" Sissy asked.

"It's been awhile, but there's no time like the present to get back in practice." She clucked her tongue. "Walk on, Matthew. Walk on, Mark."

The day was warm, and the building clouds threatened of storms to come. Deborah hadn't noticed them until they were nearly to Perkinsville or she might have stayed home. Texas thunderstorms were not to be ignored.

"Looks like we may have rain," she told Sissy.

"Yes, Miz Deborah, I do believe we will. Guess we'll get a soakin' on our way back."

"Unless we wait it out here," Deborah said. "You've got friends to visit, don't you?"

"Shore I do, but yor mama don't pay me to visit."

Deborah laughed as a loud rumble of thunder sounded. "I don't think Mama would want us out in this storm. I have things to do myself. I'll meet you back here at the store after the storm has passed." She handed the reins to Sissy and stepped down from the wagon. "Why don't you go visit first, and then when the storm lets up, you can get our shopping done. That way, we won't have supplies getting wet in the wagon."

"I reckon that be best," Sissy said.

Deborah smiled. "I'm sure it is." She hurried off in the direction of the doctor's office, careful to keep the journals close in case it started to rain. She'd just reached the door of the office waiting room when the first large drops started to fall.

Opening the door, she called out. "Hello? Are you here, Dr. Clayton?"

He immediately appeared from the opposite doorway. "Well, hello. What brings you here today?"

Lightning flashed and Deborah hurried to close the door behind her. "I brought back your journals."

"And did you enjoy them?" he asked with a smile.

"Actually, I did. I was hoping to maybe borrow another." She held out the collection.

He took them and motioned her to step into the office. "Help yourself, but I have to ask: Was there anything in particular that you found appealing?"

Deborah headed to the stack of journals on the bookshelf. "I was rather fascinated by the article on Dr. Robert Koch."

The doctor's face lit up. "He discovered the tuberculosis bacillus, and his work on cholera has been highly discussed."

"Yes. That's the very man," Deborah replied, quite excited. She jumped at the boom of thunder. "The storm caught me by surprise. Our cook, Sissy, came with me to town, and I'm afraid we'll be stuck here until the storm passes."

"Well, why don't you wait here with me? We can discuss the article."

"I wouldn't want to keep you from your work . . . and folks might think it strange for me to be here." She considered leaving, then shook her head. "Let them think what they will."

He chuckled and rubbed his bearded chin. "By all means, have a seat. Free time is all I seem to have." He motioned for her to take a chair.

She frowned. "Why do you say that?"

"Because it's true." He sat at his desk and leaned back to stretch his arms behind his head. "I have all the time in the world—it's patients I don't have. Not one person this week, and only one in the weeks before."

"I was hopeful that word would get around regarding your good work with John Stevens. His hand is healing well."

"It would seem Mrs. Foster's word holds more weight. She's got the town stirred up, believing that if they come to me for help, it's going to offend the spirits or some such nonsense. Mr. Perkins is quite beside himself. He's hired me and pays me a good salary, and here I sit idle."

"Give them time," Deborah advised. "I'll be sure to say good things about you and encourage others to do the same. Many of the folks here are uneducated and steeped in superstitions and traditions. It's always a headache for the preacher, too."

"I suppose I was expecting folks to be grateful to have a doctor."

"Maybe they're afraid they can't afford it," she offered.

"Mr. Perkins takes fees out of the mill workers' wages each week for their doctor and hospital needs. They're entitled to my services."

She shrugged. "Like I said, it will most likely take time. The people around here have to come to terms with change. It's always hard for them. In the meanwhile, Mr. Perkins is doubling the size of his mill and hiring a great many new people. Maybe they'll be able to bring in folks from outside the area who won't be so superstitious."

Dr. Clayton looked unconvinced. "I have no patience for ignorance."

"Neither do I, but I find that often the only way to get folks to see things right is to give them an example. John's hand is a good one. In time, word will get around that it was your handiwork, and not Mrs. Foster's poultice, that did the trick."

Rain hitting the window drew her attention and a brilliant flash of lightning filled the room. The boom of the thunder came nearly on top of it. "I do hope the men working outside got to safety."

"Seems we can use the rain," Dr. Clayton offered.

"Yes, I suppose we should be grateful for that." She brushed imaginary lint from her brown skirt. "Dr. Clayton . . ."

"Call me Christopher," he suggested. "We are friends after all."

She looked at him for a moment and saw a glint of amusement in his expression. "It would be scandalous if I were to do so. You're new to the community. I didn't grow up with you around. And you're my elder."

"I'm not that old. I've yet to start using a cane, and I still hear quite well."

Deborah giggled. "It would be inappropriate. I can just hear the reprimands. Why, the preacher would probably be informed on his next visit, and I'd be called before the congregation to repent of my sinful ways."

He leaned forward and crossed his arms. "Well, I suppose I can't have that. Still, couldn't you call me Christopher in private?"

"I don't think it would be wise. I might become too comfortable and blurt it out accidentally." She sobered. "There are a lot of rules for young women—for any woman, actually. I wouldn't want to stir up trouble after just arriving home. To be honest, I think people are looking for something they can point at."

"What do you mean?" he asked.

Deborah went to the window. The rumble of thunder seemed to be growing less frequent. "I know I'm being watched carefully by those who knew me before. They will want to see that I didn't pick up any bad habits while attending school in the East. They don't really value education."

"Why is that?"

"No one can afford the luxury of it," she replied. "Children are needed to help earn a living, so school for them is usually done by the eighth grade—if they get to attend that long. Adults have no time for pleasures like reading. Even so, few can read—especially among the men. When I went off to school, folks were mixed on how they felt about it. Some thought I was lucky and wished me well. Others frowned on it and said I was sure to be ruined by the ways of the world."

"You don't look too ruined to me," he said with a chuckle.

Deborah studied him and found she liked the way tiny lines formed at his eyes when he laughed. He was a handsome man—perhaps Dr. Clayton would find a woman here in Perkinsville and marry. Maybe it would even be one of Mr. Perkins's daughters. They had certainly enjoyed his company when they'd been at the Vandermark house for supper.

She put aside such thoughts. "It will be scandal enough that I'm here. Of course, the storm will be my excuse. I brought back your periodicals and took refuge until the rain let up."

"What of when you brought me doughnuts?"

"I was doing the good Christian thing in greeting a new neighbor. I stayed to help, because anyone would have done likewise. But mark my words: Someone will have seen me come here today and make a comment about it later. Hopefully it won't cause harm to your reputation."

He laughed and shook his head. "I doubt anything could harm it more than Mrs. Foster's warnings."

Margaret Foster was raising a ruckus when Deborah entered the store a short time later. The rain had let up and folks had started to come out again. The store was the most common gathering spot; even the men would come after their shifts to hear the latest gossip and news.

"He ain't got no right to be forcing a doctor on this town. I've been doctoring folks for thirty years," Mrs. Foster railed. "A good many of those right here."

Deborah spotted Sissy and made her way across the store. Deborah could only hope the supplies were paid for and Sissy was ready to go. The last thing she wanted was to get into a confrontation with Mrs. Foster herself. The woman had never approved of Deborah.

"She been like this since I got here," Sissy whispered. "Been tellin' the world—leastwise, the part that will listen—that Perkinsville got no need of no doctor."

Deborah watched Mrs. Foster corner Helen Greeley and Olivia Huebner. "That book-learned man ain't gonna know how to treat the ailments we got here in Texas. He ain't even from Texas."

Leaning toward Sissy, Deborah asked, "Are you finished with the shopping?"

"Shore 'nuf. I got myself over here soon as the storm passed. Everything's sittin' on the porch, waitin' to be loaded. Mr. Greeley said he'd come put it in the wagon."

"Maybe we could just do that ourselves. He seems busy with—"

"Deborah Vandermark! What sort of rudeness did you learn back East that you stand over there whisperin'?"

She forced a smile. "Why hello, Mrs. Foster. How are you?"

The woman scowled as she made her way across the room. She pointed a crooked finger at Deborah. "I heard tell you was there when that man commenced to cuttin' on poor John Stevens' hand."

"I was, indeed," Deborah replied, nodding. Mrs. Huebner and Mrs. Greeley made themselves scarce as they hurried into the back room. "The hand was horribly infected."

"It were healin'," Mrs. Foster countered. "It didn't need to be cut open."

"It was swollen to twice the normal size."

"'Course it were. The poisons were gatherin'. They woulda burst out and drained if it'd been left alone."

"Nevertheless, it was hurting him, and the doctor did a fine job of cleaning out the infection. I hear that John is able to use it again."

The older woman screwed up her face. "Ain't 'cause of that doctor. You'd do well to steer clear of him. He's gonna be nothin' but trouble, and them that keeps company with him ain't gonna have nothin' but bad luck."

"I don't believe in luck, bad or good, Mrs. Foster. I only count on the Lord for my well-being. He's more than able to see me through." With that, Deborah took hold of Sissy's arm. "We'd best get the purchases back to Mama. She'll be waiting for us."

Chapter 9

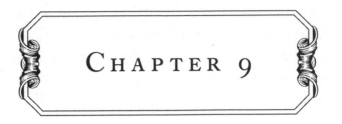

To everyone's delight, the fierce heat of summer cooled a bit, making the days much more bearable. Lizzie adjusted easily to life in Texas. The world of logging yellow pine fascinated her. It wasn't long before she was identifying a variety of trees and vegetation, not to mention snakes and insects. She would have happily done without the latter, but the Vandermarks assured her she'd be better off for knowing what was poisonous and what wasn't.

The days seemed to pass quickly as Lizzie immersed herself in household chores. She liked learning to work with her hands and was becoming a fair cook. She found baking to be her favorite. The men in the family particularly seemed to enjoy those treats, so she supposed the attention she got added to her pleasure in the task. How very different this family was from the one she'd grown up with. Here, folks didn't mind teasing or being challenged on habits or thoughts. The Vandermarks seemed quite open, in fact, to discussing most anything. In Lizzie's experience, families rarely spoke about anything except the causes of the day. She had vague recollections of conversations with her father, but the years and distance between them had faded the memories.

There was still no word from her father and that discouraged her. Lizzie just told herself he would write when he could. At least she hoped he would. He had told her that he'd hated not being a part of her life.

"If you hated it so much," she had asked him the night before her wedding, "then why didn't you come back?"

He had looked so troubled by her question that Lizzie immediately wanted to take her words back. But she didn't. His response was a feeble attempt to rectify the matter.

"I didn't want to make life more difficult for you," he had replied.

He needn't have worried. Her mother made it difficult enough for all of them. Lizzie had felt like a burden—a strange but unique possession that had to be maintained but wasn't really desired. It wasn't until she got older that her mother actually began to see some value in her. She had great plans for Lizzie to get an education and show the world that women could accomplish important things. Lizzie, however, had little interest in school. She had barely passed her classes at the university.

Lizzie found her true calling being with the Vandermarks and learning how to run a household. *This is how life should have been,* she thought. She bent over the washtub and began scrubbing at one of Euphanel's blouses. Perhaps if she'd had siblings and parents who'd remained together, it might have been this way for her. Instead, there had been nothing but fighting and misery in her youth. Her mother had left Lizzie to an indifferent upbringing by nannies while she went out to save the world. At night, she would return to rant and regale Lizzie and her father with a list of injustices that women were forced to suffer. Lizzie had followed her father's example and learned to say little in response.

A dull ache in her neck caused Lizzie to abandon the wash for a moment. She stretched and tried to work out the knot in her tired muscles. She wasn't having much luck when, to her surprise, G. W. appeared.

"Can I help with that?" He didn't wait for her response, but brushed her hands aside and began to massage her shoulders.

Lizzie didn't know what to think for a moment. The warmth of his hands seemed to permeate the thin cotton of her blouse. Ordinarily, she would never have allowed a man to touch her so intimately.

"Is this helping?" he asked softly.

She gave the slightest nod, certain that if she opened her mouth to speak she would make a fool of herself. Lizzie felt mesmerized by the rhythmic kneading of his hands on her shoulders and neck. She felt her stomach do a flip and her pulse quicken as the strokes softened to a gentle rub.

She pulled away rather abruptly and turned to face him. "Thank you. What are you doing home at this hour?"

He stared at her for a moment, and Lizzie almost felt as if she couldn't breathe. What was happening to her? Maybe she was working too hard and the heat was worse than she thought.

"I had to come pick up another ax. We broke two today."

She could see that for some odd reason, he was perplexed. Maybe touching her had also affected him. The idea rather pleased her, and she didn't want to say anything to change the feeling of the moment.

"I want to tell you that I've been thinkin' on what you said the day of the church social. About Pa knowin' the risks and takin' 'em anyway. I know you're right, 'cause like you said, I do the same." He shook his head and looked toward the sky. "I reckon I couldn't have stopped the accident—not if God said it was Pa's time to go home."

Lizzie nodded. "No one could."

"And a single man couldn't very well hold back a log that size—not with the chain broke and all."

"I'm glad you can see the truth of it," she whispered.

He cast his gaze back on her face. "You're a right smart gal, Miss Lizzie. I think maybe now I can start puttin' Pa's death behind me."

She smiled and without thinking, reached out to touch his arm. "I do hope so. I know your family has been very concerned for you. I've been concerned, as well."

"You have?"

"Yes."

He put his hand on top of hers and held it in place for a moment. Lizzie's knees trembled, and when G. W. brought her hand up to his lips, she thought she might well faint. "Thank you for caring about me."

She could only nod. As he released her and turned to head off toward the barn, Lizzie let out the breath she hadn't even known she'd been holding. For a moment she felt as if the blood rushed to her head as she gulped in another breath. She wasn't entirely sure what had just happened, but there was little doubt that it was important.

Later that evening after supper, G. W. sought Lizzie out once again. She was alone in the dining room, repositioning the tablecloth and lamps, when he found her. He couldn't begin to understand the way she made him feel. He'd been sweet on girls before, but this was the first time he'd actually thought about spending the rest of his life with someone.

"I was wonderin' if you'd like to sit with me on the porch before it gets too dark."

Lizzie seemed startled by his question. Her blue eyes seemed to grow the size of saucers and her mouth was open, but no words were coming out.

"I suppose that was a little bit forward of me," he said, trying to think of how to smooth the awkwardness over.

She shook her head and put aside the lamp. "I'd like it very much."

G. W. couldn't help but grin. "I would, too."

They made their way out to the porch. G. W. had no idea where the others had gone. Sissy had returned to her home just before supper, and he knew Uncle Arjan had gone back to his cabin. Otherwise, there was no telling. No one was here on the porch at the moment, and that was really all he cared about.

Taking a seat in one of the rockers, Lizzie appeared a picture of the prim and proper lady. In the soft twilight, G. W. thought she looked almost angelic, with her pretty blond hair fixed just so atop her head.

For a moment he stood rather nervously, not knowing what to do. Finally, he cleared his throat and took a seat beside her. "I thought . . . well, that is . . . I was hopin' you might tell me about yourself."

Lizzie focused on her folded hands. "There really isn't a lot to tell. I'm an only child, and my parents divorced when I was eleven."

"That must have been really hard," he said, trying hard to weigh each word before he spoke.

"It was," she said in a wistful manner. "My parents' relationship had always been strained, but to see them divided . . . well, it was heartbreaking for me. I used to cry myself to sleep every night."

"I'm sorry," he said, almost regretting that he'd brought up the subject. "I shouldn't have asked about something so unpleasant."

She looked at him and a slight smile touched her lips. "I believe I could tell you most anything, Mr. Vandermark."

"G. W. Please call me G. W."

"What does that stand for?"

It was his turn to be uncomfortable. "Promise you won't laugh?"

"I would never laugh at a person's name."

"My people are from Holland. I got named traditional-like. As a firstborn son, I was named for my father's father. His name was Gijsbert Willem Vandermark. Folks called him Gijs."

"Keys?"

"It's spelled with a G. I didn't like it much, so I made folks call me G. W."

"I think it's a fine name, and quite wonderful that you were named after your grandfather," she assured him. "I was named after one of my mother's women's suffrage heroines. Elizabeth Cady Stanton. I actually hate the name—hence the use of Lizzie."

"I like Lizzie better," he agreed. "So why did your folks divorce?"

She grew thoughtful, and for a moment, G. W. worried that she wouldn't answer him. Had he asked too intimate a question? Maybe she never spoke to anyone about such matters. He'd never thought to ask Deborah.

"My mother was always swayed by causes. She loved the temperance movement and it just seemed to flow naturally into women's suffrage. I seldom saw her, but I loved her fiercely. Maybe I loved her more because she was so absent in my life. I could pretend she was the mother I wanted her to be, even if she wasn't present. I was raised by a long list of nannies who would endure Mother's rantings for only so long, then leave the job. Eventually, she arranged for me to attend boarding school—but that was after the divorce."

"What about your pa?"

"When I was little, my father would come to see me every evening after I'd been given supper. He would read me a story and ask me about my day. Sometimes he would even dance with me." She smiled sadly. "I cherish the memories—what few I have. Until the day before the wedding, I hadn't seen him for nearly a decade."

"Why not?"

"Mother. She became so obsessed with her cause, she felt he corrupted her by marrying her. Funny . . . most women would have felt just the opposite. After a great deal of fighting, he finally left. I didn't see him again because my mother refused to allow him to visit. Once I asked if I might go see him, as he and his new wife had moved to another state by that time. She was livid and accused me of being a traitor to her. Her anger kept me from ever mentioning it again."

"I'm sure sorry for what you went through."

Lizzie glanced back at her hands. "I'm sorry that you had to witness my shameful attempt to get back at her. I didn't really want to marry Stuart, as much as I wanted to prove to my mother that I could make my own decisions. It was terrible of me, and I can only hope he will forgive me."

"So you really didn't love him?" G. W. knew this was what Deborah had said, but he was never quite certain of Lizzie's feelings.

"No, I didn't love him. He was everything I knew my mother would hate. He was overbearing and particular about what I could do and where I should go. He was quite opinionated about politics and deeply resented the women's movement. Oh, he was charming, but I knew he only wanted to marry me because of my appearance and what it would mean to his political career."

G. W. shook his head. "Seems like he owns as much shame for that weddin' as you."

"I suppose so. But my own guilt keeps me from thinking about his responsibility in the matter."

"A man ought not act in such a way."

"Neither should a woman." Lizzie looked up rather hesitantly. "I let the wounds of the past keep me from good judgment. I don't intend to make that mistake again."

He was about to comment when Rob came flying out the front door calling his name.

"I'm right here. You don't have to be yellin'." He got to his feet. "What's wrong?"

Rob turned abruptly, nearly falling off the porch. "Well, I didn't see you there. Nothin' wrong. Uncle Arjan sent me to fetch you. He wants to go over some plans for tomorra."

Lizzie stood. "I should go inside anyway. I'm afraid the mosquitoes are having quite a feast on me."

G. W. nodded, regretful that their conversation should end so soon. "Thank you for speakin' with me."

She smiled, then turned to head into the house. "Any time, G. W."

He felt awash in pure joy at the sound of his name on her lips. Feeling just a little taller, he punched Rob on the arm and grinned. "You heard her. Any time."

Chapter 10

August 1885

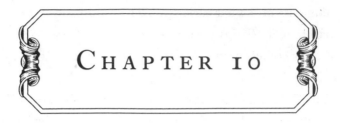

After being in Perkinsville for almost two months, strolling among the houses and people as he was doing just now, Christopher Clayton had come to an understanding of why the community had lost so many women to childbed fever. The answer was quite simple: Margaret Foster. The woman was the driving force behind healing and medicinal treatments, yet she had no use for soap and water or any other means of fighting bacteria. She went from patient to patient without ever washing her hands, much less her instruments. She was passionate about her cures and tonics, but again, he doubted they were prepared with cleanliness in mind.

He had tried to approach the woman, hoping to explain and offer at least some small bit of advice to combat the dangerous situation. "You know, they are making great strides in medicine,"

Christopher said one morning after coming face-to-face with the midwife at the commissary. "With the discovery of various bacteria and how they cause illness, we've learned that keeping our hands and instruments clean is of the utmost importance."

Margaret Foster's lips curled into what could only be described as a snarl to reply, "I ain't got no use for city medicine."

"But it's not just useful for the city," he countered with a smile. It was hard to maintain a civil attitude with such hatred staring him in the face, but Christopher put his best skills to work. "Mrs. Foster, I respect what you have been able to do for the community. But the truth is, it's been documented that childbed fever decreases considerably with proper cleaning techniques. I would be happy to discuss the matter with you, as a colleague."

"I ain't no colleague," she nearly growled. "Whatever that is. I don't need your book learnin' to heal folks around here. You'd do well to leave this town before someone—like me—puts a curse on you."

It was there that Christopher did the wrong thing. He laughed. Apparently no one had ever laughed at Margaret Foster's threat of a curse. "Madam, I do not believe in curses."

"You'll believe it soon enough," she said. She muttered a string of words so quickly that Christopher had to strain to make sense of them. It was something to do with bad luck following him like a wounded hound or some such nonsense. She stormed off then, leaving him to wonder why she held him in such contempt. He wondered still.

Crossing Third Street, he saw Deborah Vandermark exit the commissary. Christopher couldn't help but call out to her. Perhaps she was in town to borrow additional medical journals. He'd recently received several in a package from his mother.

"Miss Vandermark!"

Deborah looked across the street and saw him. He waved and she did likewise. "I have new journals," he declared, closing the distance between them.

"How tempting," she replied. "I will have to keep that in mind for my next trip into town. Right now, I'm afraid the workload at home is more than I can keep up with. There's been no time for pleasure reading."

"Just know that they are available whenever you'd like to borrow them."

"So are you coming from a house call?" she asked, nodding toward his medical bag.

Christopher had decided to carry the bag with him when he went for his walks around town. That way people would get used to seeing him with it and perhaps realize he was the doctor. As it was, he doubted that he'd been able to meet more than a handful of citizens. He was a stranger to most.

"No, I just always take it with me in case there is a need."

"I suppose that makes good sense."

He chuckled. "Not really. Folks around here still don't want anything to do with me. I suppose they all know that Mrs. Foster put a curse on me."

Deborah laughed. "There aren't many who haven't had one of Mrs. Foster's curses imposed on their peace of mind."

"You?" he asked.

She nodded. "Once when I was quite young, I took some papaws from her yard. She ran after me with a broom yelling for all the world that with the setting sun, I would bear the thief's curse. Of course, I never knew exactly what that was. Mama heard about the situation and made me return with a batch of cookies and an apology. Mrs. Foster took the curse off and that was the end of that. I've avoided messing with Mrs. Foster ever since."

"That's no doubt for the best. Still, it seems most folks around here are afraid of her."

Deborah looked past him toward the row of houses. "People fear what they don't understand. In your case, medicine is a great mystery. Talk of things like bacteria and internal disorders makes no sense to them. You might as well be speaking a foreign language."

"But there's so much good that could be done. Women needn't die in childbirth. Men needn't die from injuries. Poor Mr. Perkins is beside himself. Here he is, taking money from the workers and giving me a good salary, and I'm doing nothing."

Deborah put her hand up to block the sun. "It's not for a lack of trying, though. Mr. Perkins knows you've made yourself available. He knows that you are willing to work at the task he's hired you to do. You must hold on to the belief that time will change things."

With the sun bearing down on them, Christopher motioned to the shade of the commissary porch. "Perhaps you'd be more comfortable if we got out of the sun."

Deborah glanced around and nodded. "I'm actually waiting for my mother. She's gathering the mail and seeing the paymaster."

They made their way to the porch bench, where Deborah took a seat while Christopher remained standing. Her simple blue calico gown accentuated her trim waist and black hair, but it was her intelligence that continued to draw his admiration.

"So I presume your family is of Dutch ancestry with a name like Vandermark," Christopher began. "Yet you have ebony hair and dark eyes."

She glanced around and leaned toward him as if to share a great secret. "My mother's side of the family had Spanish ancestry, as well as Dutch. I'm told that I take after my mother's grandmother." She eased back and grinned. "I just don't say that too openly around here. There is still a fair amount of negativity toward Mexico and Spain."

"Yet I've noticed that Mr. Perkins hires people of color for the sawmill work."

"You will find that to be true in most of the mills around here. Workers are workers. If the men can be trained and prove capable, they are kept on. A lot of former slaves came here to work because Mr. Perkins has a reputation for being fair. My family has also hired former slaves for the logging business."

"And what of your cook, Sissy? Was she also a slave?"

Deborah nodded. "She was with my mother's family from birth. When the war came my grandparents thought to remain in Georgia. Things just got worse, however, and when the Emancipation was issued, my mother's family took the matter seriously, much to their neighbor's displeasure. Grandma and Grandpa told their slaves they were free to go. Someone set fire to their fields the next night. It nearly took down the house. They were worried about how much worse things would get, so they decided to board up the house and come stay with Mama and Papa.

"Sissy loved my mother and asked my grandparents if they might consider letting her accompany them to Texas. They did, and Sissy has been with Mother ever since."

"And does she live with you?"

"No," Deborah said, trying to adjust the ribbon in her hair. "She fell in love and married a man named George Jackson who works for us as a logger. They have a family and their oldest son, David, works for my family, as well. They have a house just north of town."

The ribbon came free and Deborah's black hair rippled down across her shoulder. "Goodness, but my hair can be a nuisance. Sometimes I think I should cut it all off."

"No!" he responded rather enthusiastically. Deborah looked up in surprise, and Christopher laughed nervously to cover his excited reply. "I would hate to see you do that. I once treated a woman who needed to cut her hair following weeks of sickness and fever. The hair was hopelessly matted and falling out anyway, so she had it cut short. She was so miserable."

"Well, it can be wretched with a mass of hair to contend with, too." She managed to adjust the ribbon and pull the hair back up off her neck. "Especially in the heat."

For a few minutes, neither one said anything else. Christopher thought of asking Deborah about the work she was doing for her family or maybe about her schooling back East, but he suddenly felt self-conscious as two young women made their way up the porch steps to the commissary. One was Mrs. Stevens; the other, he didn't recognize.

"Hello, Sally," Deborah called out. "Dinah." She turned to Christopher. "You both know Dr. Clayton—don't you?" The women turned rather shyly and nodded toward Christopher.

"Afternoon ladies," he said. "How are you feeling, Mrs. Stevens?"

"Tired," she replied. "Guess I've got about another month before the baby gets here." She put a hand to her belly and nodded to the girl at her side. She couldn't have been more than seventeen or eighteen. "We're both tired."

Deborah turned to Christopher. "This is Dinah Wolcott."

He smiled. "Are you expecting, as well?"

The sallow-faced girl nodded and pushed stringy blond hair from her face. "Gonna have a young'un, come next year."

"Well, congratulations. I'm sure your husband is delighted."

Deborah turned to Christopher. "Her husband works for Vandermark Logging." She smiled back at the young woman. "I'm sure Dr. Clayton will be able to help you when your time comes."

The two young women exchanged a look. "Mrs. Foster's been seeing to us," Sally Stevens replied. "She said . . . well, that men got no good reason to be tendin' women in a family way."

"Bah," Deborah said. "Women back East have men deliver their babies all the time. You know, there have been quite a few cases of childbed deaths in this area. Mrs. Perkins was quite upset at the number of young women passing on during delivery. That was one of the biggest reasons she brought in Dr. Clayton."

Sally's eyes widened. "You don't suppose there's a curse on this town—do you?"

Deborah shook her head. "I don't believe God works that way. The Bible says Jesus became a curse for us—it also says that by His stripes we are healed. I think God has better plans for us than cursing us with dead babies and mamas. Just think about it. I know having a new doctor can be rather frightening, but I assure you Dr. Clayton is a knowledgeable man. Of course, I don't have to tell you, Mrs. Stevens, since he saved your husband's hand."

She looked at the wood planks of the porch floor. "Miz Foster says it were her poultice that did the cure."

Christopher started to comment, but Deborah got to her feet. "Mrs. Foster would, no doubt, say that, but you know as well as I do that your husband was in great pain when he came to the doctor. We both saw that hand. It wasn't getting better—it was much worse than when Mrs. Foster began treating it. Wasn't it?"

Sally Stevens nodded very slowly. "I reckon it was. I don't rightly know what to believe. Mrs. Foster said my John could have lost his hand what with the doctor cuttin' on it and all."

"Mrs. Foster is just afraid that word will get around that her poultice didn't help. I mean no disrespect to the woman, but you two must understand that for all her experience, she's just a human being and she will make mistakes. Doctors make them too, but they have so much more training and understanding of the human body. I want you to really think about it, Sally. You too, Dinah. The lives of your babies, as well as your own life, might very well depend upon such reasoning. Don't be afraid."

The women murmured something Christopher couldn't quite make out, then nodded toward him and Deborah and hurried into the store. He looked at Deborah, who was fussing with her rolled-up sleeves by this time.

"I appreciate your support," he said softly.

Deborah glanced up and shook her head. "I hope they'll listen. I would certainly hate to see more deaths in childbirth."

"If Mrs. Foster would just listen to reason and sterilize her equipment and wash before and after tending to patients, it would help a great deal. I'm not opposed to herbal treatments and using nature for medicinal purposes, but it's well-founded that thorough cleaning can terminate the growth of bacteria and save lives."

"Well, I'm sure word will get around of what I said and I'll receive another curse," Deborah said with a grin.

He chuckled at the delight in her expression. "I'm still scandalized to know that you would steal from anyone."

"I learned my lesson, Dr. Clayton. I haven't stolen since. A green switch to my backside sealed the deal for me. I'm living a completely righteous existence now."

Mrs. Vandermark came from the commissary just then, carrying several letters and a basket containing a variety of articles. Dr. Clayton offered to take the basket, but she waved him off.

"Thank you, but we have to get on home and the wagon is just over there in the shade. It's good to see you again, Dr. Clayton. Do you think you could join us this evening for dinner? I figure if I don't ask, you won't just show up."

"It hardly seems right to just drop by unannounced."

"Around here, we don't stand on such concerns," Mrs. Vandermark replied. "I told you we wanted to see you joining us regularly, yet you haven't been out since nearly a month ago. So will you join us this evening?"

He couldn't think of anything he'd like better. "I would love to. May I bring something to help with the feast?"

She laughed. "Nothing but yourself."

Deborah reached past him to take the basket from her mother. "We'll see you tonight then, Dr. Clayton. I'll take this now, Mother. Goodness, but it must weigh twenty pounds. What all do you have in here?"

Her mother laughed. "Only a small portion of what I needed. They're bringing the rest by train when the supplies come in. Good day, Dr. Clayton. Dinner will be on at six."

He watched them leave and felt a genuine loss in their going. The Vandermarks were among his few friends in Perkinsville. He especially enjoyed his conversations with Deborah, but knew it was probably just as well that she lived well out of reach. He had to remain focused. If he strayed from his purpose, others would suffer.

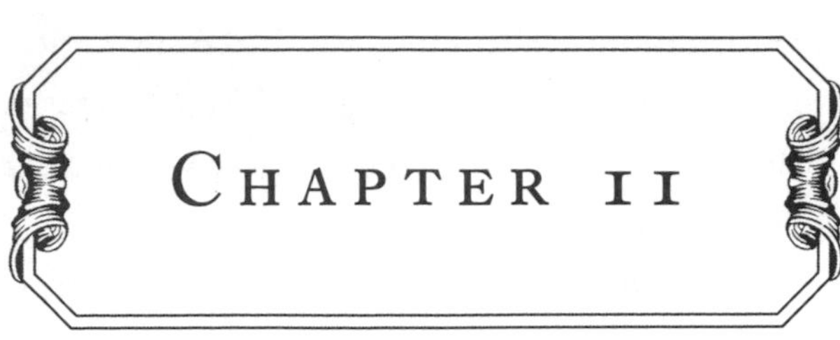

CHAPTER II

Lizzie had never expected to see Stuart Albright again, yet here he was standing in the Vandermark living room. He pinned her with a stare that might have withered her had Deborah and G. W. not been standing at her side. A few feet away from Stuart, her mother, Harriet Decker, was conversing with Euphanel. It was all like a very bad dream.

Rob sauntered into the room casually after bringing the two visitors by wagon from Perkinsville. He just happened to be in town on one of his many Saturday evening courtships when someone from the boardinghouse had announced there were folks looking for the Vandermarks.

"It's wonderful to get to meet you," Euphanel told Harriet Decker. "Your daughter has spoken of you on many occasions."

"Elizabeth is a thoughtless young woman," her mother replied. "She has left us these many weeks worrying after her well-being." With a quick glance around the simple room, the woman added, "And I see for myself it was with good cause."

"Mother, there is no need for rudeness," Lizzie interjected, trying her best to ignore Stuart's continued glare. "Mrs. Vandermark and her family have been quite good to me. I have very much enjoyed living here with them."

"Oh, the pleasure's been ours, Lizzie. You are a great help to us," Euphanel said.

"And you are an incredible teacher. Did you know, Mother, that Mrs. Vandermark has won awards for her canned goods? She's been teaching me, and I find it all so very fascinating."

"Well, that's enough of that," her mother replied. "We've come to take you home."

Lizzie stiffened and looked to Deborah first and then G. W. "But I'm perfectly happy here."

"But you have a husband who is not perfectly happy for you to remain here," her mother said as she crossed the distance to where Lizzie stood. "You shamed this family by running away as you did. We were able to cover it up with the excuse that you were ill and needed to come west to take the cure, but now you need to return home."

Lizzie shook her head. "No. I'm of age, and I choose to remain in Texas. And I hardly know why you call Mr. Albright my husband. We are not married. As you recall, I left before the ceremony."

"But not before signing the papers," Stuart declared. "It matters not that the traditions of religiosity were not performed. You are, by law, my wife."

She would have laughed had Stuart's expression not silenced her with its intensity. Married? How could it be? She had of course signed the papers given to her prior to the ceremony. They had been witnessed, and the minister had said that . . . that . . . Oh, what was it he had said? Something about it not being official until he joined them in the sight of God and man. Deborah and her father had both been convinced she wasn't bound in any legal manner.

"I can see we've taken you by surprise," her mother remarked. "See there, Mr. Albright. She didn't run away as your wife. She simply had bridal nerves and thought herself still free to do as she pleased." Her mother looked back to where Lizzie stood. "You know how I feel about marriage. I didn't want you to marry in the first place. I saw no use in it. However, you're married now, and that changes everything."

Lizzie stumbled backward and might have fallen had G. W. not shot out his hand to take hold of her. Stuart's eyes narrowed. He had always been very possessive of her—it was one of the things that drove her mother into fits and one of the reasons Lizzie had chosen to marry him.

"I cannot be married to you," she said in a barely audible voice. "I made no vow."

"Your vow was your signature. Now we must return to Philadelphia. I have work to do. My father is also quite anxious that I assist him with his legislative affairs, as well as our family investments."

"I won't go," she said, shaking her head slowly. She looked at Euphanel and then Deborah. "I don't want to go."

"You needn't go if you do not want to," Deborah said matter-of-factly. "Honestly, this is the most preposterous thing I've ever heard." She stepped in front of Stuart. "Why would you wish to be married to a woman who doesn't love you?"

He laughed and Lizzie felt her knees grow weak. "Frankly, I have no love for her, either. In time, she will grow comfortable with my presence, and I shall enjoy being seen with her on my arm." He sobered slightly. "In time I might even become fond of her."

"And this is the life you want for your daughter, Mrs. Decker?" Deborah asked. "You would desire her to live in misery—to be used as ornamentation by this man?"

Lizzie saw her mother's face contort. "As women, we will always be used by men. We might as well be the ones to decide who that man will be. My daughter gave her word. I care far more about her keeping her word than about whether or not she made a poor choice of masters."

Lizzie could bear it no longer. "I can hardly believe that you, of all people, would say such a thing. I thought you believed women superior to men! I thought you said women had no need to be chained to a husband—they needed only to expand their minds with education and use them, in turn, to better their lives."

Mrs. Decker looked taken aback for a moment, but it was Stuart who spoke. "I believe the choice was already made. This argument is a moot point. You are my wife, and you will return with me to Philadelphia."

Deborah's mother stepped forward in an attempt to calm the waters. "Why don't we have some coffee or tea? We can all think better if we sit down and try to relax a bit. No doubt you two are very tired. You've been traveling for days, and we know how uncomfortable the train trip here can be."

"I have no desire to take coffee or tea," Stuart replied.

"Then you can return to Perkinsville," G. W. said casually. "I'll escort you back."

Stuart looked at him in disgust. "Excuse me?"

"My brother is offering to take you back to the boardinghouse in Perkinsville," Deborah interjected. "That way Mrs. Decker and Lizzie can have a bit of a discussion over coffee."

"Elizabeth doesn't drink coffee," her mother declared.

"Oh, yes I do," Lizzie said, feeling ever so daring to voice her new vice. It made her feel only marginally back in control. "Furthermore, I'm tired. I had no idea that you would be here. I've been up since four this morning helping with chores and making jam. I am ready now to retire for the evening. I'm sorry if this is a problem for either of you, but I will speak to you more about it tomorrow."

With that she turned and left, hoping—really praying—that no one would try to stop her. When she reached the stairs, she felt a surge of triumph. Deborah and Euphanel were busily commenting on how Stuart and Mrs. Decker could return in the morning as early as they liked, or perhaps prefer to meet at church.

"We always attend church, if possible. We'd be happy to have you here for dinner afterward," Euphanel told them.

Lizzie shook her head and continued to make good her escape. She could scarcely draw a breath. How could it be that she'd had no word of warning from her father? Perhaps he didn't know her mother's plans—after all, they were no longer civil to each other and didn't even live in the same state.

Throwing herself across the small bed, Lizzie wanted to cry. What if Stuart spoke the truth? What if she truly was married to the man? The very thought chilled her to the bone. He'd make her miserable for leaving him at the altar.

The door to the room opened and Deborah stepped inside. Her expression was a mixture of sympathy and determination. "Are you all right, Lizzie?"

"How can I be?" She made the effort to sit up, but what she really wanted was to crawl under the bed instead. "I cannot believe he followed me here. I can't believe Mother came here, either. What is happening? Has the world come to an end and someone failed to notify me?"

Deborah sat opposite Lizzie on the edge of her own quilt-covered bed. "Mother has managed to ease tensions for the moment. She invited them to join us here after church tomorrow. That will give us time to consider what is to be done."

"But what *is* to be done? Stuart says that I'm legally wed to him. I don't see how that can possibly be."

"I don't, either," Deborah said thoughtfully. "I don't know a great deal about the law, but perhaps I can speak with Dr. Clayton before church tomorrow. He might have some knowledge."

"If only my father were here, we could ask him," Lizzie said sadly. "Oh, and my life was just starting to settle into place. I was actually happy."

Deborah nodded. "So was G. W. I don't think this will brook well with him at all. Did you see the way Mr. Albright looked at him when he kept you from falling backward?"

"I did. That's Stuart's way. He cannot tolerate any other man touching me or speaking to me overly long. Oh, Deborah, I simply cannot bear this. Why is this happening?"

"I don't know, but I firmly believe all things happen for a reason."

"Yes, but this is for a very bad reason. Of that, I'm sure." Lizzie got up and began pulling pins from her blond hair. "I don't wish Stuart ill—I never did. I'm sure that Father would have made that clear to him."

"It's not your father who puzzles me," Deborah said, following Lizzie's example. She crossed the room to where they shared the simple dressing table and placed her hairpins in a decorative ebony box. "What is your mother doing here? She should have been quite happy that you didn't marry. It would have given her a great story to tell her suffragette friends. She could have gone on and on about how you finally came to your senses, realizing no woman needs a man to make her complete."

Lizzie picked up her brush and began to run it through the long waves of hair. "That's right. I cannot imagine her caring one whit about Stuart's feelings, and obviously she doesn't care about mine." She grew thoughtful. "What is she doing here?"

"We shall have to figure that out." Deborah picked up her own brush. "But in the meantime, I don't think you should fret. Let's send a telegram to your father. Perhaps with his connections he can advise you best on the matter."

Lizzie gave a heavy sigh. "I certainly hope he can. I don't want to find myself Mrs. Stuart Albright."

ꙮ

Sunday dinner at the Vandermark house was an unusually serious event. Rob and Uncle Arjan sat on either side of Stuart and occasionally made comments to him, while Deborah made sure that Lizzie was sandwiched between herself and Uncle Arjan.

A last-minute addition was Dr. Clayton. Deborah had thought it a good idea to include him. It gave their side a man of learning to balance against Stuart Albright. At least that was her thought on the situation.

Lizzie was too nervous to eat and pushed her food around the plate so much that Deborah wanted to take away her fork and spoon. Instead, she launched into comments about the sermon that day, hoping it would draw the focus away from the underlying tension in the room.

"I am quite frustrated with the sermon this morning," Deborah began. "I know the preacher meant for us to take away the lesson of what God's people can do when they come together, but I think there are serious issues with the story that did not get discussed."

"Such as what?" her mother asked, immediately realizing Deborah's intent.

"Well, in reading through chapter nineteen of Judges, I found myself completely at odds with the entire matter. You have a man who is a Levite. That was supposed to mean great things in those days. They were faithful when the rest of Israel fell down to worship the golden calf during Moses' absence. They were blessed because of it. They were appointed to be rabbis and teachers of Israel. The Lord was their inheritance, rather than lands and properties."

She could see from their expressions that Stuart and Lizzie's mother had no more understanding of the topic than did the dogs sleeping on the front porch.

"So you have this Levite and he has a concubine, which in those days was, if I understand correctly, an acceptable position as a second wife. Although she couldn't be endowed, so her children couldn't inherit. At least, I think that's what the rabbi told me."

"You spoke with a rabbi? But you aren't Jewish," Harriet Decker said in surprise.

"Our Deborah believes it's important to get to the heart of the matter and understand a situation—or in this case, a Bible story—from all angles," her uncle explained.

Deborah nodded. "I went to a synagogue in Philadelphia after reading this book the first time. The rabbi, a very forward-thinking man, explained several things to me. In fact, he was the one who taught me about the Levites. Anyway, so you have this man and his wife and she plays the harlot or, as the rabbi told me, the Hebrew word is *zanah*. And while its primary definition is whore or participating as a whore, it can also mean to dislike—to hate. He said it is entirely possible that the woman hadn't committed adultery but had merely fought with her husband. They could simply have had a fight, and she went home to her father's house. This could explain why the husband doesn't require her to be stoned. It would also allow for why her father let her stay with him—he surely wouldn't have done so if she were an adulterous woman." Deborah tapped her finger to her chin.

Dr. Clayton joined in. "The fact that the man goes after her, yet stays to eat, drink, and make merry with her father suggests to me that he was not at all in ill spirits. The fact that, as you say, he did not go there to have her put to death says to me that he was of a mind to put the matter behind him. I tend to think there's great possibility in your thoughts on *zanah*, meaning that there was some sort of fight and they were angry with each other."

Deborah nodded. "Even so, here's this man—this Levite. He's supposed to be knowledgeable and a strong man of God. So let's say she was at her worst and he did the honorable thing by forgiving her. As far as I can see, that's where his merits end."

"How so, Deborah?" her mother questioned.

It was almost comical the way Harriet Decker stared at them while Stuart kept his gaze on the plate in front of him. He said nothing, but his irritation was evident by the way he mutilated his food.

"The Levite has so little regard for the safety and well-being of his wife. Even if he did consider her nothing more than property, as many did, you would have thought he would want to protect his property."

"That's right," Dr. Clayton said. "Yet he leaves late in the day and heads into territory that he knows will be a problem. He has made no provision for their lodging."

"Oh, but he has food for the donkeys and for the people," G. W. interjected. "I remember the preacher saying that."

"Yes, he had food," Deborah agreed. "But he made no other provision. Not for safety, not for lodging, and certainly not for the welfare of his wife. So an old man finally shows up, well after they'd given up hope of finding a place to stay, and he takes them in. The Bible says they were 'making their hearts merry' when these horrible men show up at the door demanding to have carnal knowledge of the Levite."

"I say, this is the most inappropriate conversation I've ever been forced to endure," Stuart Albright declared. "I would never allow a young woman of my family to speak as you do." He looked to Arjan. "Is this how women act in Texas? If so, I'm glad to get my wife out of here before she can be further corrupted."

Arjan looked at him hard. "Deborah is sharing Scripture and talkin' about understanding God's Word. There's nothin' wrong with that, as far as I can see."

"It's completely unacceptable." Stuart threw down his napkin. "She's talking of adultery and men . . . well, I will not repeat the matter. Suffice it to say I cannot and will not sit by and allow my wife to be a part of such conversation. Elizabeth, go pack your things."

Deborah had never seen Uncle Arjan truly angry, but the muscles in his neck tightened and his eyes narrowed over Stuart Albright's outburst.

"Son," Uncle Arjan began slowly, "this is the Vandermark house. My sister-in-law is the lady of the house, and it's entirely up to her to say who stays and who goes. But to my way of thinkin', you're the one who should leave. Unless, of course, you can make yourself civil."

For a moment, no one said anything. To her surprise, it was Lizzie's mother who defused the situation. "Mr. Albright, I must say it is the height of rudeness that we should chastise our hostess and her family for the topic of conversation that they choose. In fact, I find the subject quite interesting."

Stuart looked at her strangely for a moment, but Harriet simply patted his hand. Deborah, too, found her behavior confusing.

"Would anyone care for dessert?" Deborah's mother asked. "I find difficult questions go down better when accompanied by pecan pie."

"Sure sounds good to me," G. W. replied.

Rob and Uncle Arjan nodded, while Dr. Clayton patted his stomach. "I think I can find room," he declared.

Stuart said nothing. He fixed Deborah with an icy stare, made only more chilling by the blue of his eyes. He was cold and harsh. His stare told her clearly that he did not approve of her or her intellectual discussion of the Bible. It was almost as if he were trying to will her into silence.

Better men than you have tried, Mr. Albright. The thought made her smile.

"So now, what was your question, little gal?" Uncle Arjan asked.

Deborah met her uncle's amused expression. It was almost as if he could read her thoughts. "The men come with their demands of . . . unmentionable evil." She looked at Stuart. "Is my word choice better?"

He refused to answer but instead folded his arms against his chest. Deborah smiled sweetly. "I suppose I can understand how disturbing the Bible can be." She turned back to her uncle. "The men want their way, and the host and the Levite, wanting no part of that evil, offer instead the man's virgin—Oh, should I not use that word?" She again looked to Stuart for an answer.

Lizzie gave an unladylike snort that she quickly covered with a coughing fit. G. W. offered her a glass of water, further irritating Mr. Albright. Deborah decided she was being too difficult and drew a deep breath. "I do apologize, Mr. Albright. I tend to let my temper get the best of me from time to time, but there is no call for me to take it out on you. Now, where was I?"

"You were about to mention that the host offered his virginal daughter and the Levite's concubine to the evil men instead," Dr. Clayton threw out.

Deborah gave him a smile. "Of course. So for whatever reason, they reject the virgin and take the concubine. They do all manner of evil to her throughout the night. God alone knows what that poor woman must have had to suffer. And the story doesn't stop there."

"It does give a person a mite to ponder," Uncle Arjan said between bites of pie.

"You should ask the preacher about it," G. W. suggested.

"I did," Deborah said, looking hard at Stuart Albright. "He said my mind was a wonder, and that for a woman I thought entirely too much. He said that God knew what He was doing by putting it in the Bible, and that men of God would understand it, and women needn't worry about it."

Dr. Clayton managed to draw her gaze from the smug expression of Mr. Albright. "I'm a man of God, and I don't believe I understand it."

"Neither do I," her uncle agreed. "Seems to me it's a hard story to understand."

"If your own minister will not reveal its mysteries," Mrs. Decker began, "then perhaps it is best we leave it as an example of the thoughtlessness of men toward women. I will definitely remember this story and use it as an example of how women have been treated throughout the ages."

"I hardly believe that was God's purpose in the story, Mother." Lizzie said, much to Stuart's displeasure.

"You can hardly know what God was thinking," Stuart said

firmly. "Now, if you don't mind, and with your permission, Mrs. Vandermark, I would like for my wife to pack her things so that we can make our way to Philadelphia."

Deborah started to comment, but her mother spoke instead. "Mr. Albright, I am a woman of reason. It is my understanding that Lizzie is of age and capable of making her own decisions. She is of the belief that the marriage did not take place, and therefore she is not your wife." Albright started to speak, but Mother held up her hand. "However, even if she is your wife, and I'm not saying that she is, she is still able to decide for herself if she will continue being your bride. There are alternatives that would rectify the situation either way."

"Of all the nonsense." Stuart got to his feet. "Mrs. Decker, let us speak with the legal officials in town. I'm certain we can accomplish more there than here."

Mrs. Decker nodded and got to her feet. "I believe you may be right in that. Elizabeth, I want you to come to town and stay with us that we might be able to speak with you privately."

"There's nothing anyone can say to me that I would not allow these good people to hear," Lizzie replied.

"Well, there is much I would say to you, and frankly, I believe it very rude to bring strangers into such intimate conversation. It only serves to make both parties uncomfortable."

"I doubt anyone would be all that uncomfortable, Mother. And these are not strangers to me." She exchanged a smile with Deborah's mother.

Deborah was proud of Lizzie. It took a great deal of courage to stand her ground in the face of her mother's demands.

"Very well. Perhaps we shall speak of it tomorrow."

Deborah's mother walked out with Mr. Albright and Mrs. Decker, leaving the others to consider all that had just happened.

"I'm so sorry," Lizzie said. "I never meant to bring this on you all."

"Y'all," G. W. said with a smile. "If you're gonna be a Texan, you ought to learn to speak like one."

This brought chuckles from the table, but to Deborah's surprise, Dr. Clayton's expression remained serious.

"Are you all right? Is something wrong?" she asked.

He nodded. "I'm fine, and yes, something is wrong. I'm afraid I shall be thinking long and hard about Judges nineteen and twenty." He smiled. "And I agree with the preacher—at least in part. Your mind is a wonder."

Deborah didn't even think before elbowing him soundly as she might have done one of her brothers. Realizing what she'd done, she covered her mouth with her hands. Her uncle and brothers dissolved into laughter, while Dr. Clayton looked at her in surprise.

"You have to watch yourself with her," Rob warned. "That's why we won't sit beside her. We've had sore ribs too many times."

Deborah shook her head and lowered her hands. "I'm so very sorry. I never meant—"

He put a finger to her lips and grinned. "You are forgiven, but you really should learn to control that temper of yours."

Her eyes widened, but she said nothing. Instead she put the Bible aside and picked up her fork as Dr. Clayton went back to eating.

"We should definitely keep him around," G. W. said, smiling. "I've never seen anybody be able to shut her up like that."

Chapter 12

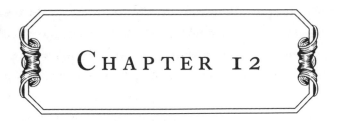

A week later, Mr. Perkins stood at the front of the small church with preacher Artemus Shattuck at his side. "As you know," he began, "Brother Shattuck has been riding the circuit to speak to us every other Sunday. I'm happy to announce that he has agreed to become our regular minister and move here to Perkinsville."

The congregation murmured and nodded approvingly. Brother Shattuck smiled and bobbed his head in return. G. W. thought it a fine idea to have a regular preacher, although he couldn't help but wonder how Deborah would feel. She had often commented that Brother Shattuck had admonished her on more than one occasion that she should marry, saying her husband would explain the biblical things she didn't understand.

"Let's pray and be dismissed," Brother Shattuck announced after shaking hands with Mr. Perkins.

G. W. bowed his head and found that his focus of prayer was once again for Lizzie's safety and security. He had unexpectedly fallen hard for this young woman. She had been a quiet strength in his life these past few weeks, for when he needed to talk about his father and the accident, she was there for him. Little by little, he had found that his memories had lost their power and God was healing his pain.

He also found himself praying that God would take Stuart Albright and Mrs. Decker back to Philadelphia or any place but Perkinsville, Texas. He didn't like Albright, his bossy way of dealing with folks, and the claim he had on Lizzie.

"Amen. Now go with the Lord's blessings," Brother Shattuck declared.

Casting a quick side glance, G. W. saw Deborah slip away, leaving Lizzie to remain in the family pew. He wasn't about to desert her and leave her to the likes of Albright, so he offered her his arm as they exited their seats. Lizzie took hold of him and smiled. "I thought the sermon quite interesting today."

G. W. nodded. "Preacher definitely gets all fired up for the Lord. That's a good way to be."

"I agree. Although I'm not sure what Deborah will think about him becoming the regular pastor."

"She'll get used to it. It's him I feel sorry for," G. W. said with a grin. "My sister isn't likely to let him off easily."

Lizzie laughed softly. "No. I'm sure she won't."

They shook hands with Brother Shattuck and G. W. thanked him for answering God's call. They were just making their way down the steps when Mr. Perkins approached with a couple of strangers.

"Excuse me, G. W., but I want you to meet Mr. Wright and Mr. Bishop of Buffalo, New York. These gentlemen have come to Perkinsville to observe our logging and milling industry."

Lizzie patted G. W.'s arm. "I'm going to go speak with Mrs. Greeley for a moment."

He reluctantly watched her go, then turned his attention back to the trio. The men extended their hands and G. W. obliged with a firm shake. "G. W. Vandermark," he declared. "Glad to meet you." But he eyed them cautiously.

Lately, there had been more and more visitors from the East showing up to buy property and start new sawmills. Logging in East Texas was becoming something akin to a gold rush of sorts. Where once yellow pine had been considered too full of resin for practical use, it now was finding more public approval. Especially as eastern white pine became scarcer. Eastern investors were like bloodhounds, sniffing out a profit to be made.

"I was hoping I might persuade you to take these gentlemen with you for a visit around some of the logging sites. I know you have a decent camp where they might stay and learn about the industry."

"I don't know. That takes me away from my work," G. W. answered. The last thing he wanted to do was play nursemaid to a couple of society fellas.

The man introduced as Mr. Wright spoke up. "I assure you, Mr. Vandermark, we won't be any problem. We are quite happy to sleep outdoors and enjoy God's nature. We aren't without our own skills in the woods. We both grew up in forested areas. What we'd like to do is see how your operation differs from those we've been a part of in the past."

G. W. could see that Mr. Perkins had his mind made up that he should somehow be the one to show these men around. He decided to oblige him, for Perkins was his family's oldest and dearest friend in the area.

"I suppose they can come along. They can ride the train out and back."

"I had in mind that you might actually show them the full extent of your property and operations. They'll even hire out some of the livery horses," Perkins explained. "And, of course, you will be subsidized for the time away from production."

"That's quite right. We are prepared to pay you a fee for acting as our guide and informant. We truly seek to learn all that we can from this trip," Mr. Bishop said. A quick glance to his companion had both men nodding.

G. W. felt there was no choice. "Have 'em come in the mornin'. We'll leave after breakfast and ride north to where we're cuttin'. I hope you fellas brought a sturdy pair of shoes. You'll need 'em."

"We have, indeed," Mr. Wright answered.

G. W. caught sight of Lizzie. Mrs. Greeley was bidding her good-bye, and Stuart Albright had maneuvered beside her, no doubt to harass her about leaving Perkinsville with him. The very thought that she might actually be married to the man gave G. W. a sick feeling in his gut. Surely it wasn't true. He didn't want to be pining over a married woman.

He thought of Lizzie declaring to all of them that she didn't consider herself married—that she'd made no pledge to God and therefore the signed paper meant nothing. But the law of the land could say otherwise, he supposed. He couldn't help but hope Lizzie's father would write soon to tell them the matter was resolved in her favor. She and Deborah had sent Mr. Decker a telegram immediately after Stuart had arrived, and then they had followed that up with a letter supplying all the details of the situation. They were all anxiously awaiting a response.

A thought came to mind as Perkins and the gentlemen turned to go. G. W. couldn't help but be concerned about the problems that might occur in his absence. "Mr. Perkins, I think it might be a right friendly gesture if you were to include Mr. Albright. He's a fella from Philadelphia who also invests," he offered as explanation to the two strangers. "Let me call him over." G. W. turned. "Mr. Albright."

Stuart Albright looked up, none too pleased at the disruption. Lizzie quickly slipped away and G. W. motioned the man forward. "Join us. Mr. Perkins has something to say."

Albright closed the distance, a scowl edging his face. "Mr. Perkins, gentlemen," he said with a brief nod of his head.

"Mr. Albright, these are two business associates from Buffalo, New York," Zed began. "They've come to investigate the logging industry, and G. W. plans to take them along tomorrow to see the Vandermark operations. We thought you might like to go along."

"No, I have other business," Albright answered.

"You aren't by any chance related to Garrison Albright, the legislator and railroad baron?" Mr. Wright questioned.

Stuart seemed to take interest in the man. "I am his son."

"Well, this is indeed a pleasure, and how fortuitous!" Mr. Wright said, looking to Mr. Bishop. "We are working even now on an arrangement that will include your father's interests, as well as your family friend, President Cleveland. You should definitely join us, as we hope to convince them both to invest in Texas lumber."

Albright considered this new information for a moment while Mr. Bishop jumped in with additional news. "We have already toured several operations around Orange and saw the mills at Beaumont. We are happy to say we've bought several parcels of forested acreage at very reasonable prices and hope to do so in this area, as well."

G. W. was none too happy to hear that but held his tongue. He thought Albright looked rather uncomfortable at this open conversation, as he seemed to hurry its conclusion. "Thank you for the offer. I will be happy to go," he agreed. "How long will we be?"

"Plan on several days—maybe a week," G. W. replied. He hadn't thought to take the men out for more than a few days, but keeping Albright away from Lizzie was uppermost in his mind. He looked to Zed Perkins. "You may need to outfit Mr. Albright. I doubt he brought anything but dress shoes and suits."

Zed patted Stuart on the back. "Not to worry. We've got everything you need at the commissary. We can just slip in the back door and take the supplies you'll need since you'll be leaving quite early tomorrow morning." He looked to G. W. for confirmation. "I think the Lord will understand, and since no money will change hands, we won't be guilty of commerce on the Lord's Day."

G. W. took that moment to exit the conversation while Mr. Perkins continued to speak to the trio of Eastern investors. He wasn't entirely sure why Perkins felt so compelled to accommodate the men.

"Unless he's thinkin' to sell out," G. W. muttered. But no, the man had been working with the bank in Houston to arrange a loan. Expansion was already taking place. He wouldn't sell out now—there was no reason for it. Still, he seemed awfully happy to attend to strangers who could very well prove to be his competition.

"Why, hello there, G. W." Annabeth Perkins practically gasped the words, trying overly hard to play the prim and proper southern belle. "I do declare it's a hot day, don't you think? Even with the rain threatenin', it hasn't cooled." She batted her eyelashes and opened her fan. Waving it back and forth in a lazy, unhurried manner, she smiled. "You aren't too warm, are you?"

"I'm just fine. Thanks for askin'."

"How do you like my new dress?" she asked.

He glanced at the blue-and-white-striped arrangement. "It's nice."

She frowned. "It's silk. Don't you think it's beautiful?"

He fingered his collar where it rubbed him just as wrong as Annabeth Perkins did. "I don't think much on such things. I'll bet my sister would discuss it with you."

"Your sister is much too unconventional." Annabeth simpered. "Honestly, you would think she didn't enjoy the company of her own gender. I swear she spends more time in discussion with the town doctor than anyone. She isn't sick, is she?"

"Of course not. They just have a lot in common, what with their book learnin'."

"That's my point exactly. She's not acting very ladylike. Going away to finishing school would have been one thing—but she attended the university. That's entirely another matter."

G. W. frowned. "Why don't you talk to her about it? Maybe she can help you understand. Now, if you'll excuse me." Before she could stop him, G. W. hurried around the corner of the church and made his way to the wagon. He paused as he approached the back of the church and heard recognizable voices.

"I think it's a good thing you're going along," Harriet Decker was saying. "You can get information and keep an eye on that ghastly bumpkin. If he's with you, he won't be attempting to woo my daughter."

"You mean, my wife."

"Call her what you will. I'll have better luck working on Elizabeth if he's out of the picture. She'll come to her senses in time."

"And what if she doesn't?" Stuart Albright questioned.

G. W. frowned as Mrs. Decker answered. "Just leave it to me. She'll do what she's told, and then everyone will benefit."

"I hope you're right. We've already wasted a lot of time down here. I'm anxious to return to Philadelphia."

"As am I. I have no desire to spend my days in this backwoods town. There isn't a decent meal to be had. Goodness, but if I see one more piece of ham or pork, I might very well throw the entire thing across the room. Come along now. Let us return to the boardinghouse before it starts to rain."

Backing away slowly, G. W. considered what he'd heard. He waited for several minutes before he approached the back of the church. Albright and Mrs. Decker were gone, much to his relief.

He made his way to the wagon and found his uncle already preparing for the trip home. "You look like you've been suckin' on a sour persimmon," Arjan declared.

"I overheard something that gave me concern," G. W. replied, climbing up to sit beside his uncle for a moment. "Zed Perkins wants me to take some investors out tomorrow to the campsite and then escort them around the area—maybe for as long as a week. I didn't want to do it, but he didn't give me much choice. And they're payin' for it."

Uncle Arjan nodded. "Guess we can make it through. I just arranged to hire a couple of new men."

"I convinced Mr. Perkins to include Stuart Albright so I could keep him away from Lizzie for a time. Turns out, he knows the men who've come. They're actually workin' with his pa and the President of the United States."

"And that's what you overheard?"

"No. They said that much outright." G. W. leaned closer. "I just heard Mrs. Decker talkin' to Albright, though. She was sayin' something about how she was gonna work on Lizzie to convince her to leave with 'em. Said it would benefit them all."

"That's a curious thing," his uncle replied.

"It concerns me somethin' fierce. I cain't hardly be in two places at one time, but I'm hopin' folks at home will look out for Lizzie. Her ma don't seem to hold much affection for her, and I worry about what she has planned."

"You'd do well to share your thoughts with Deborah. She'll see to Lizzie. She'll get your ma's help and Sissy's, too, if need be. They won't allow Miz Decker to take liberties, even if Lizzie is her daughter."

"Seems to me some folks treat their kin worse than they do strangers," G. W. said, shaking his head. "Just don't seem right."

"It ain't, to be sure," Uncle Arjan agreed. "Here come our ladies."

G. W. jumped down from the wagon and assisted his mother up to Uncle Arjan. By the time he got to the back of the wagon, Rob was handing up Lizzie and telling her how pretty she looked and saying something about her being brighter than the sun.

Deborah rolled her eyes to the heavens and settled her gaze on G. W. "You look tired. Are you all right?"

"I reckon I am," he replied and then helped her into the wagon. He leaned close and whispered, "I wouldn't mind a few words in private with you later on."

Deborah turned to eye him curiously but said nothing. She gave him a nod and turned her attention to Lizzie and Rob. G. W. admired his little sister greatly. She was very smart when it came to seeing beyond the surface of things. He hoped she would have some idea of what was going on with Albright and Mrs. Decker.

༄

Later that night, after hearing G. W.'s concerns regarding Stuart and Mrs. Decker, Deborah returned to her bedroom and confronted Lizzie.

"Do you have any idea what it might mean?"

Lizzie shook her head. "I honestly don't. Mother can be quite manipulative when she has something to gain. There must be some benefit, but for the life of me, I can't imagine what it is. And then there's Stuart. I can't see Mother having anything that would help him. His family is wealthy and well connected."

"Well, despite that, it sounds as though your mother plans to impose herself upon us and make certain you listen to her every thought on the matter. I will do what I can to help you, but I'm not entirely sure what you need me to do."

Lizzie shrugged. "I'm not sure I know myself. I suppose it would be good if you could help me to avoid being alone with her overly much. I know she'll want some privacy with me, and that's fine. I can tolerate her haranguing me for a short while, but then I simply lose my patience. I don't want to make this matter worse than it already is."

Deborah considered her words for a moment. "If you were to leave first thing in the morning with my mother and go grape picking, then you wouldn't be available to your mother."

"We can hardly go pick grapes every day until my mother leaves," Lizzie countered.

Laughing, Deborah pulled down the quilt and sheet and slipped into her bed. "You don't know my mother very well. She'll find something for you to be picking for as long as you need."

Lizzie sat down on the edge of her bed. "I can't avoid my mother forever. I shall simply have to stand up to her and be the brave and strong woman she raised me to be. It's not like she can force me to leave. Your brothers and uncle would never allow for that."

"Especially not G. W." She paused. "I think you've completely won his heart."

Her friend flushed. "I think he's won mine, as well, but this matter of whether or not I'm legally married to Stuart is a problem we cannot ignore. Oh, I do wish Father would write."

"Don't worry. In time, he will. Until then, we shall simply do what we can to avoid confrontation. If that means picking grapes, pecans, papaws, or any number of other things, then that's what we'll do." Deborah smiled. "You have the advantage here."

"And what would that advantage be?"

"We have time and the Lord. Both will be to our benefit."

Chapter 13

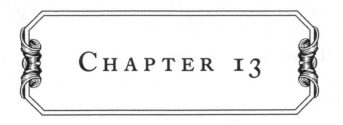

Harriet Decker sat prim and regal as if she were a queen holding court. Dressed from head to toe in a severely cut navy blue suit, she looked every bit the righteous matriarch. Deborah could see why she intimidated her daughter. Lizzie's nature was far more lighthearted compared to the stout woman whose serious expression demanded solemnity.

Sipping the tea Deborah's mother had served, Mrs. Decker finally got to the point of her visit. "I do not pretend to be happy about my journey here. However, I found it most necessary, given the legalities of the matter at hand."

"And what legalities are those, Mother? Did you ask Father to check into the situation, or are we relying solely on the word of Stuart?"

Her mother frowned. "Your father has no need to be consulted in this matter. I was aghast to have him make an appearance at the wedding. It was an embarrassment."

Deborah watched Lizzie fix her mother with an emotionless stare. "He's my father. He had as much right to be there as you did."

"He had nothing to do with your upbringing. There was no reason for him to be there, although I'm sure he enjoyed making me feel uncomfortable."

Lizzie put down her cup and turned to Deborah and then to Euphanel. "At my mother's insistence, my father had little in the way of visitation. Those few times he did attempt to see me, she was cruel and made the situation quite difficult."

"How dare you lie? And with me sitting right here. I was not cruel or difficult. Your father wasn't interested in visiting you. He found another woman with whom to take his comfort and had little to do with either of us after that."

"You drove him away and then faulted him for taking comfort with someone else. I hardly consider that fair."

Mrs. Decker stiffened. "I can see that you understand nothing of what really happened."

"It would seem that the past is not nearly as important as the present," Deborah's mother interjected with a smile. She picked up the tray of grape tarts and extended them toward Harriet Decker. "Would you care for another?"

For a moment, Deborah thought Mrs. Decker would refuse, but from the woman's expression, she'd very much enjoyed the first two. She reached for the tart and continued. "I completely agree with Mrs. Vandermark. It is the present that holds the key to your future, and your future is with Stuart Albright."

"I'm sorry, but I don't feel the same way," Lizzie replied. "I do not love him, Mother, and realize now I was only marrying him to prove to you once and for all that I could make my own choices. Now I'm doing that again. I'm making my choice not to become his wife."

"But you are already his wife—at least on paper."

"I spoke with Dr. Clayton, who is a learned man," Deborah interjected. "He suggests that if Lizzie's signature does indeed bind her in marriage, an annulment would be quite easy to secure, given that the marriage was never consummated."

"But Stuart does not wish for an annulment. He is quite willing to forgive your flight and move forward in the marriage. The Albright family represents the very best in society and politics. They are dear friends of President Grover Cleveland and can offer Elizabeth introduction into the best places in society."

Lizzie frowned. "But none of that interests me. Honestly, Mother, until I came here to Angelina County, I wasn't sure what did interest me. Now I know. This place is exactly what I was searching for all along."

"You are better than this place." Mrs. Decker looked to Deborah's mother. "I have no issue with the fact that you have chosen this way of living for yourself, but my daughter was hardly raised to do menial labor. Why, look at her hands! They're horribly stained."

"We all have stained hands," Euphanel replied. "We've been pickin' grapes and puttin' up jam. Stains are just an unfortunate part of the process. Getting dirty is a part of life here in Texas."

"Which is exactly my point. Your daughter may have been raised to such an existence, but mine was not. Elizabeth was raised to see the value in being an independent woman—in thinking for herself."

"Yet you condemn me for that very thing, Mother. How is it

you can speak of such qualities as admirable and valuable in one breath and fault me for them in another?"

Mrs. Decker eyed her daughter for a moment and tried her best to soften her stern expression. "Elizabeth, I do not fault you for wanting to stand on your own two feet, but you hardly have the skills needed to do so in this land."

"I beg to differ with you," Deborah's mother said. "Lizzie is quite capable. She has eased my work load considerably. Whatever else might be true, Lizzie lacking skill is not an issue here. She learns quickly and seems to genuinely enjoy working with her hands."

"I do," Lizzie agreed. "I find this work to be satisfying. There is something quite noble—and dare I say it matches perfectly with your suffragette beliefs of providing for one's self and family. The average woman here in East Texas must be mistress of many skills. Not only is she needed to serve alongside the men, but she is primarily responsible for the benefit and well-being of her family. She must plant gardens and reap the harvest. She must prepare foods that can last through the year so that her family will not be in need. She must tend to the sewing and mending."

"These are hardly duties that will make a difference in the world," Mrs. Decker said rather haughtily. "I raised you for something better."

Lizzie shook her head. "I thought you raised me to be a good woman—to make choices that would make me happy no matter what society said. You once told me, 'While society may scorn me for my decision, my conscience rewards me in full.' Well, Mother, my conscience rewards me for making this choice."

Mrs. Decker turned red, and Deborah briefly wondered if the woman had stopped breathing. She looked quite angry and turned to Deborah's mother. "I do wonder if you would excuse me to speak in private with my daughter."

"I have no desire to speak with you in private, Mother. Not if you have come to harangue me. I will not be Stuart's wife, and I will not return to Philadelphia. The matter is settled. You cannot convince me to do otherwise."

"I have never been so insulted. You are in such a state of mind that you cannot even be civil with your own mother."

Lizzie got to her feet. "I have been nothing but civil. You and Stuart arrived here uninvited and proceeded to argue against what I want in life. You tell me I'm a rebel and a disappointment, all the while insulting the things I've come to love. Furthermore, I fail to understand why you are suddenly in support of my marrying Stuart. You have no respect for marriage—you've said so on many occasions."

"That was before," Mrs. Decker replied, seeming to regain control of her emotions. "You are the type of young woman who needs a man to help guide her. You are not as self-sufficient as you would like to believe. Your mind simply does not work in the same way as a woman of more worldly understanding."

"Excuse me?" Lizzie looked at her mother in disbelief. "You have long told me women are not only equal to men but superior in many ways. Now you tell me that I am the exception? That I need a man because my mind is too frail to possibly retain concepts important to living on my own? Well, perhaps you are right, but understand this: I will not be wife to Stuart Albright. I might very well take a husband, but it will not be anyone's choice but my own."

With that, she stormed off, leaving her mother to stare after her in gape-mouthed surprise. Without warning, Mrs. Decker turned to Deborah. "I blame you for this. Elizabeth would never have done this without your encouragement."

Deborah nodded. "I think perhaps you might be right, and for that, I congratulate myself. Lizzie would have been most miserable married to Stuart Albright. She deserves to find true love and happiness, and I believe perhaps here she has done exactly that."

"With that backwoods bumpkin brother of yours?" Mrs. Decker asked, her voice rising ever so slightly to emphasize the insulting words. "You can hardly expect me to be overjoyed at the prospect of that."

"Mrs. Decker." Euphanel put aside her cup and saucer. "I cannot allow you to come into my home and insult my son. G. W. is a good man with a loving heart and strong work ethic. Your daughter could do far worse."

"Equally, she could do far better. I do not say these things to insult your family but rather to point out the truth. My daughter is educated and refined."

"But you also said she needed a man to guide her," Euphanel countered. "It seems to me you have different standards for different women. Either we are all intelligent and capable or we are not."

Mrs. Decker was momentarily taken aback. After a long silence she regained control. "Elizabeth was not born to this life of hard work and sorrows. She would never be able to withstand this difficult environment, nor could she possibly respect a man such as your son."

Deborah sipped her tea to avoid betraying the way Mrs. Decker's words reminded her of her own heart. She had said and thought similar things. She knew that an uneducated man—a man who couldn't read or understand the concepts of science and world history—would never be of interest to her.

"I don't believe your daughter is that shallow," Deborah's mother replied, furthering Deborah's own guilt. "A good woman would look beyond the surface of things that could easily be changed and reflect instead upon the heart. A good woman would be far more interested in whether her husband loves her and is willing to treat her with the same love and respect as Christ had for the church. I believe Lizzie understands a great deal. She is hardly the kind of person who would refuse a man simply because he lacked education or social standing."

Deborah wanted to agree, but the words stuck in her throat. She felt strongly about the very things her mother spoke out against. What kind of woman did that make her? She wanted—no, needed—to have a man to match her intelligence and love of learning. She needed to know that he valued education and that he would want to see their children educated.

East Texas was full of people who were smart enough in the ways of everyday life. There were truly good, admirable people who had no more than a few years of home education. There were loving, kind, gentle folks who couldn't read more than a few words, who would never write letters or read a variety of literature. Deborah loved many people who fit that description. Most of her family would definitely fall into that category. But when it came to considering a husband—someone with whom she would spend every day of her life—Deborah knew she longed for something more.

Her heart sank. Maybe she was destined to spend the rest of her life alone.

"I don't expect either of you to understand the problems that this can cause," Mrs. Decker stated, drawing Deborah's attention once more. "The Albrights are powerful people. They could cause a great many problems for Elizabeth if she refuses to honor her word. They will not appreciate their son being shamed in this way."

"Do you suggest they mean to harm her?" Deborah asked.

Mrs. Decker met her gaze. "It is possible."

"Then Stuart can't possibly love her."

"Love is not the only thing of importance here," Mrs. Decker replied. "As I said, I don't expect you to understand, but I do. I know what this could mean to Elizabeth's future—perhaps even to mine. I will not see my causes suffer simply because my daughter could not keep her word."

Deborah didn't know how to respond. She supposed it was possible that powerful people like the Albrights could cause harm to Lizzie. She didn't know to what extent they could reach her here in Texas under the protection of G. W. and the rest of the family, but she wasn't a fool. Stuart Albright already struck her as a man to keep under a careful watch. Perhaps there was more at stake here than she'd first thought.

ᔓᔕ

G. W. introduced the work crew to the visitors he'd brought. Rob was busy harnessing the mules but took a moment to shake hands with Mr. Wright and Mr. Bishop. He nodded to Stuart Albright, then turned to his brother. "We've got more damaged seedlings. Looks like the rooters were at it again."

"The rooters?" Mr. Bishop asked.

"Feral hogs," G. W. explained. "They have a particular fondness for the pine when it's in a young state. He pointed to a tree that had gone undamaged. "Over there, you'll see what I'm talkin' about."

He crossed to where the new pine stood. Long grasslike needles had showered down to settle around the seedling stem that was only some twenty inches tall. It looked rather like a clump of grass from afar. "These young trees are quite tender, and apparently very tasty. We are trying to save 'em so that we'll always have trees to harvest. They can stay in this small state for seven or so years. During that time, they're quite vulnerable."

"Can't something be done to corral or kill the beasts? What about fencing?" Mr. Bishop asked.

"Folks around here don't take well to fences. As you probably saw on your ride out here, animals pretty much run where they will. They graze on the forest grass at will. If we were to put in a fence or even set up traps, it would cause a lot of hard feelings in the community."

"It hardly matters what other people want," Albright piped up. "This is your land, is it not?"

"It's ours alright, but we try to be good neighbors, as well. Open grazin' is the law of the land."

"It really isn't all that critical," Mr. Bishop added. "The point of logging this area is to bring in the wood and move on."

"Cut out and get out," G. W. muttered.

"That's right. There's no concern to us about replanting. It simply takes too much effort to cultivate and care for a new crop of trees, as proven by your comment regarding these wild hogs. The cost would not be worth the effort," Mr. Wright declared. Mr. Bishop nodded.

"Well," G. W. said in a slow drawl, "isn't that part of the reason you've come west for your lumber? You've stripped out the forests back East and now find that there's little there to profit you?"

Albright narrowed his eyes. "That seems a rather opinionated thing to say."

"It's true, isn't it? I've heard that over and over. Nobody wanted yellow pine for the longest time. It wasn't until after the war that folks outside of Texas even started givin' it much of a look. Now with shortages of other woods, they're suddenly interested. I'm not tryin' to be overly opinionated, as you suggest. Just statin' the facts."

"It is true that the forests in the East and around the Great Lakes are seeing a great depletion," Mr. Bishop said thoughtfully. "But by coming here and utilizing the yellow pine, we can give those forests a chance to grow again. I hardly see a problem in that. By the time we are able to harvest the Texas wood, it may well be time to start to work again on the white pine."

"Well, I happen to believe that God called us to be good stewards of the land," G. W. replied. "My father told me that it was important to cultivate it and allow for the replenishin' of what we took from it. So that's why it's important to me to see these seedlings protected." He squared his shoulders and looked each man in the eye. "Now if you'll follow me, I'll show you some of the work we're doing today."

Chapter 14

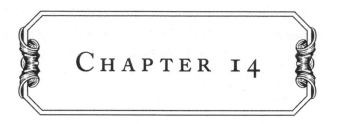

Deborah drove Mrs. Decker back to Perkinsville with a reluctant Lizzie at her side. The day was uncomfortably hot, and word had come that severe storms on the coast might be headed their way. With the heaviness of the afternoon, Deborah thought the rain might actually benefit them—release the tension. Too bad there wasn't something equally beneficial to relieve the tension of Lizzie's situation.

"I would appreciate it if you would at least grant me the decency of accompanying me to the boardinghouse," Lizzie's mother stated as Deborah pulled the wagon to a stop near the commissary. "There are a few things I'd like to speak to you about—in private."

Lizzie sighed. "I suppose if I refuse, you'll just continue to nag me about it." She got down from the wagon and looked back up to Deborah. "I'm sorry about this. Do you mind waiting?"

Mrs. Decker gave a huff and looked away. It was clear she didn't like her daughter seeking someone else's approval before agreeing to see her mother alone.

"Not at all. Mother sent some grape tarts for Dr. Clayton. I'll just go deliver them. I'll meet you back here at the wagon." Deborah took her brown skirt in one hand and secured a hold on the wagon with the other as she climbed down. Together, she and Lizzie assisted Mrs. Decker from her perch.

"I won't be long," Lizzie promised.

Deborah lifted the basket of tarts from the wagon and made her way down the dirt street to the doctor's quarters. The air was thick with soot from the mill. With very little wind, the smoke seemed to blanket everything. It only added to her anxiety.

Knocking at the waiting room door, Deborah felt a sense of relief when Dr. Clayton opened it. He smiled and stepped back. "Well, this is a pleasant surprise."

"More so than you know. Mother has sent her black grape tarts," Deborah said, holding up the basket. "They are quite delicious."

He closed the door. "I must say were it not for your mother, I might never get a decent meal." He paused for a moment and shook his head. "No, that isn't exactly true. Mrs. Perkins has me to the house at least once a week. The preacher and I share their table and hear all of the latest gossip about the town. Annabeth and Maybelle Perkins are better than having a newspaper's society page."

Deborah nodded. "I know that to be true." She pulled the plate of cloth-covered tarts from the basket and placed them on a small table by the door.

Dr. Clayton seemed to immediately sense her mood. "Something is wrong."

She met his gaze. "That's putting it mildly."

"Does this have to do with Mr. Albright and Lizzie's mother?"

"Mostly it has to do with Mrs. Decker. She has no consideration for Lizzie's desires whatsoever. She came to visit and went on and on all morning. Even at lunch, which Mother graciously invited her to, Mrs. Decker made everyone miserable. I couldn't wait until I could suggest I drive her back to town.

"Lizzie accompanied me and on our journey here, her mother berated us both until I very nearly thought I'd push her from the wagon bench." Deborah looked away. "I wouldn't really have done it, of course, but she just keeps insisting that Lizzie is married to Stuart Albright and that she should remain so! Furthermore, she's insisting that Lizzie leave with them when Stuart returns from observing the logging operations with G. W."

The doctor motioned to one of the chairs. "Why don't you sit and tell me all about it? Did you mention to Lizzie the possibility of getting an annulment?"

"I did. She said that if her father finds out that she truly is legally married, then she will journey to Houston or wherever necessary and arrange an annulment."

"So why this degree of contention?"

"I can't really put my finger on the exact problem. Mrs. Decker is clearly up to something, but I can't figure out what that might be. Lizzie is quite clueless, as well. There seems to be some reason Mrs. Decker stands behind this marriage—even though she's divorced herself. But I'm ranting, and that's hardly fair." She forced a smile. "How are things coming along for you here?"

"Miserably. I have managed to see one patient, but otherwise, it's remained as quiet as a graveyard."

Just then the door burst open, nearly startling Deborah out of her skin. She saw the worried expression of Jeren Perkins and knew something must be horribly wrong.

"They're bringing an injured man from the mill. There was an accident with one of the saws. He's nearly cut off his arm, and he's bleeding profusely."

Dr. Clayton got to his feet and motioned to the exam room. "Tell them to bring him through the side door. It will be quicker that way. Miss Vandermark, I'd appreciate your help. You know where everything is in the exam room, and I'll need someone who can work fast to help me."

"Of course," she said, feeling a surge of excitement.

The doctor went immediately to wash up, and Deborah opened the side door to admit the men. She had presumed Jeren had exaggerated the degree of injury, but as the men rushed into the examination room, she could see for herself that he had not.

Butch Foster's clothes were drenched in blood, despite the fact that someone had thought to tie a tourniquet just above where the arm had been cut. The man was pale and unconscious, not offering so much as a moan when the men placed him on the metal table.

Dr. Clayton motioned Deborah to his side. "Hold his arm."

Deborah frowned. "But I haven't washed."

"We can't save that part anyway. Hold on to it while I cut away the remaining piece. All we can hope to do is stop the bleeding and keep the man from infection." He worked quickly, freeing the arm from the man's body. Deborah stood rather dumbstruck for a moment, not knowing what to do. She looked down at the arm, then back to Dr. Clayton.

"Put it in the spare washbasin," Dr. Clayton instructed.

She did as he told her, washed up, and hurried back to the table to see what she might do to help. The men who had brought Mr. Foster in had backed away from the scene, keeping their distance from the injured man. Dr. Clayton was already busy examining the oozing stump and cleaning out pieces of debris. Time seemed to stand still, yet Deborah knew the minutes were flashing by. When

Lizzie called out from the front room, Deborah had nearly forgotten all about her. The medical emergency had consumed her focus. She glanced at the clock and realized it had already been an hour.

"I'm in here helping the doctor, Lizzie."

Her friend came to the entrance. "What's happened?"

"Mr. Foster lost an arm at the mill. The doctor's trying to get the wound cleaned and cauterized so that he won't bleed to death."

Dr. Clayton stopped and looked at Deborah with a frown. "Mr. Foster? As in a relative of Mrs. Margaret Foster—the very one who cursed me?"

"The same. This is one of her sons."

He shook his head and went back to work.

"Lizzie, if you don't mind—I'm going to be a while. Why don't you take the train back? They'll be returning shortly, and you can hitch a ride in the engine. Let Mother know what's happened and tell her I'll be home later."

Her friend hesitated but finally nodded. "I'll do that."

The train whistle blasted and Deborah motioned her toward the door. "Hurry or you'll miss your ride."

As Lizzie left, Mr. Perkins showed up, anxious to know of Butch's status. "Will he live?" he asked.

"I don't know," Dr. Clayton replied. "He's lost a lot of blood and infection is bound to set in. I'll do what I can to ward it off, but there's no guarantee."

Mr. Perkins nodded and then seemed to notice Deborah. "This is no place for you! Why are you here?"

"I asked her to stay," Dr. Clayton told him. "She helped me set up the examination room and knew where my instruments were. She also has proven herself to have a strong stomach and stable nature in the face of such matters."

Mr. Perkins looked to the men who'd brought Butch to the

doctor. "Why don't you men get on back to the mill? You too, Jeren. I'll stay and see what happens."

"Do you want me to go find Mrs. Foster?" Jeren asked.

"No," Dr. Clayton replied before Mr. Perkins could speak. "Not yet. I don't need to have a distraught mother hanging over my shoulder. She has little use for me as it is."

"You heard him. Go on with you now." Mr. Perkins inclined his head. "See to things at the mill."

Jeren nodded and took the two men with him as he left. Deborah couldn't help but wonder what would happen when Mrs. Foster did learn of her son's condition. If Dr. Clayton could save him, this might turn out to be the very thing that would change Mrs. Foster's mind about him. Mother always said that God worked in mysterious ways, and Deborah supposed losing an arm might well be one of the strangest she'd seen.

"He was a good man," Mr. Perkins said, coming alongside the table. "Hard worker. I hate to see this happen to him."

"If he lives, he'll have a long recovery," Dr. Clayton told Perkins. "He'll have to learn to do for himself all over again—this time without two hands. He certainly won't be able to work at the mill."

"No, I don't suppose so. Not unless I could find something for him to do that required only one arm."

"His balance will be off, and the pain will be excruciating for a long time. Of course, that's only if he can somehow recover from the blood loss." Dr. Clayton stood back and eyed the patient in serious contemplation. "He's a fighter; I'll say that for him. I would have expected to lose a lesser man by this point."

"Well, I think I'd best go find Mrs. Foster, now that you have things under control. She won't take kindly to being left in the dark about this."

"She won't take kindly to me treating her son," Dr. Clayton declared with a shake of his head. "She won't like that at all."

Mr. Perkins rubbed his finger and thumb over his graying reddish mustache. "Hopefully you've saved the boy's life. She can't fault you for that."

But Deborah knew she would. Mrs. Foster's superstitions would cause her to believe that her son's recovery had been jinxed by Dr. Clayton's interference. She went to the cupboard for more bandages. She would need to stay with Dr. Clayton and explain the good he'd done to Mrs. Foster. The older woman would never listen to the doctor, but she might well be willing to hear Deborah and Mr. Perkins.

Mr. Perkins lingered a moment longer, as if he had something else to say. He shook his head instead and headed for the door. "I'll be back."

"Oh, how I wish this weren't her son." The doctor began to wrap the stump, shaking his head the entire time.

"Dr. Clayton," Deborah began. He didn't seem to hear her, so she broke with protocol. "Christopher." He looked at her. "You've done good work here. He would have died by now if you hadn't interceded. Mrs. Foster will have to realize that sooner or later. She might resent the fact that she wasn't allowed to care for Butch immediately, but in time she'll understand that this was for the best."

"If he lives," he replied. "The man is barely alive. The shock alone may kill him."

"I know." Evidence of the blood and trauma surrounded them.

From Dr. Clayton's earlier instructions, Deborah knew that she'd find warm water in the stove receptacle in his kitchen. "I'm going to clean him up a little."

Dr. Clayton met her gaze and nodded after a moment. "Thank you. That's a good idea. There are towels in the cupboard over there," he said and pointed. "I'll wrap up the dismembered arm before Mrs. Foster arrives."

Deborah nodded and hurried to see to her tasks. Once Mr. Perkins found Mrs. Foster, it wouldn't take any time at all for her to make her way to the office. Deborah returned with the water and retrieved two towels before going to work to remove the blood that had matted on the man's chest and neck. She had just managed to clean Butch's face and neck when Mrs. Foster came screaming into the house.

With something akin to a wounded animal's cry, she crossed the room and all but threw herself upon her son's bloodied chest.

"Git away from him. Git, I say!"

Backing away, Deborah put the towel aside. "Mrs. Foster, Dr. Clayton has managed to stop the bleeding."

"Bah! Git away from him. You have no right. No right at all." She straightened and noted the missing arm. "You done cut off his arm." It was more accusation than declaration. Her face screwed up and she began to wail. "Oh, you done took away his manhood."

"Mrs. Foster, the accident at the mill did that," Deborah interjected before Dr. Clayton could speak. "Didn't Mr. Perkins tell you what happened?"

Margaret Foster rocked back and forth, hugging Butch's good arm to her breast. "Oh, my boy. My boy."

Dr. Clayton exchanged a glance with Deborah. She could see his growing frustration. Just then Mrs. Foster let go of Butch's arm and pointed a gnarled finger at Dr. Clayton. "You've done your worst, but I'll save him yet. He ain't stayin' here. I'll be back to take him home."

"You can't move him, Mrs. Foster. He's lost too much blood already. If you move him, he'll start bleeding again," Dr. Clayton argued.

She fixed him with an angry stare. "I know what I'm doin'. You just want him here so you can finish him off. The devil is using you to try to hurt me, but I won't let him. I'll fix you with a spell that you'll never throw off." She stormed out the door, leaving Deborah and Dr. Clayton in stunned silence.

The silence didn't last, however. Dr. Clayton had clearly reached his limit of patience with the old woman's nonsense. "Of all the ridiculous, absolutely stupid . . . argh." He turned away, muttering.

"I've spent half my life learning medicine, studying and working to be the best doctor possible, and now this backwoods witch comes to undo everything. She'll be the death of this man."

"You've performed to the best of your abilities," Deborah reminded him. "Whatever she chooses to do and whatever happens to Butch—it won't be your fault."

"That hardly matters!" His voice grew louder in his anger. "A reasonable person would understand the danger of the situation. If this were your brother, I could make your mother understand the need to leave him here."

"You certainly could, but she would be just as upset as Mrs. Foster. You cannot change a mother's desperation to save her child. Mrs. Foster might calm down by the time she returns."

Dr. Clayton looked at her in disbelief. "Neither one of us believes that. She won't listen to reason. It's impossible to imagine that woman calming for any reason, but especially in a situation like this. She hates me. She's made my life a nightmare. She's maligned me and spoken against me." He began to pace, flailing his arms as he walked. "She thinks her ways are the only way. She doesn't believe in book-learned medicine."

"It's hard for—"

"And no matter how I work to prove myself, I have no chance with these people."

His tirade continued, the volume of his voice growing. Without thinking, she went to where the pitcher of clean water stood beside the washbasin. She drew a deep breath.

"She has no desire to understand what I can do for this community. I can't even talk to someone on the street without them fearing it will get back to Mrs. Foster and she'll put a curse on them. A cur—!"

In one smooth move Deborah turned. She didn't say a word, but instead swung the pitcher forward and allowed the contents to hit Christopher Clayton full in the face. He stopped in midstep, his jaw dropping in surprise.

As water trickled down, dampening his bloodstained shirt and coat, Deborah offered him a sheepish smile. Dr. Clayton's shoulders relaxed along with his expression. "I suppose I deserved that. I don't often lose my temper, but when I do . . . Well, I'll just leave it at that."

She shrugged. "I completely understand. You might well have to do the same for me one day."

He grinned. "I'll remember to keep the pitcher handy."

ꕥ

Hours later, Christopher sat in the silence of his bedroom. Mrs. Foster had arrived with a half-dozen male relatives and directed them to take Butch back to his home. He had tried to reason with the woman one more time, but she wouldn't hear any of it. Christopher gave up.

"His blood is on your hands now," he declared. "If your son dies, Mrs. Foster, it will be because of your poor judgment."

But she hadn't heard him, or if she had, she didn't care. No doubt she didn't believe his words. Christopher ran his hand through his hair and sighed. Why could these people not understand the good he could do? He had a great deal to offer, and if he wasn't allowed to do his job, Perkins would have no choice but to get rid of him. Then he would have left his mother and father, his siblings, and his life in Kansas City for nothing.

He shook his head. "God, did I misunderstand your direction? Did I fail to hear correctly?" He sighed. "What am I supposed to do, God? Please . . . show me the way."

Chapter 15

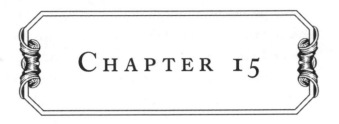

On their third night in the woods, G. W.'s companions seemed only interested in the amount of liquor they had left. Each evening, they had made a habit of sharing what they said was extremely expensive, smooth whiskey. They'd offered G. W. a drink each time, and each time he had refused. Had he any say on the matter, the men wouldn't have brought liquor into his camp at all. He'd seen the results of alcohol around logging, and it usually resulted in someone getting hurt.

Stuart Albright seemed rather amused by G. W.'s abstinence. He spoke of it several times, but always G. W. maintained his calm and refused to comment. He certainly didn't owe Albright an explanation. What G. W. chose to do with his evening was no one's business.

Taking up a cup of strong coffee, G. W. walked away from the fire to think. He'd been watching Stuart Albright and trying his best to figure out what the man was about. The trio of easterners had discussed a great many ideas regarding logging. Apparently they were all in agreement that it would behoove them to buy up many thousands of acres of prime forest while the prices were still low. The idea grieved G. W.—this was his home, and the idea of eastern businessmen buying up the land really disturbed him.

They wouldn't relocate to Texas; it was the mentality of "cut out and get out," as Wright and Bishop had mentioned more than once. Use the resources until they're gone, and then move on. There was no concern about what would be left behind in their destructive wake. G. W. remembered his father saying years ago that they were guardians of the land. That God had given mankind the earth to tend and care. Stripping the land of trees hardly seemed a good way to do either.

He finished off his coffee and headed back to the center of camp. To his surprise, Stuart Albright seemed to be waiting for him. He was sitting by the fire with a book, and when G. W. approached, he quickly pocketed the thin volume and stood.

"So, Mr. Vandermark, it's my understanding that your family has been in Texas since before the Southern states seceded, causing the war."

G. W. figured the man hoped to goad him into some sort of political argument. "That's true enough."

"Why did they choose to come here?" Albright asked.

"My father believed it was a good place to live," G. W. stated. Albright pulled out a cigar and offered it to G. W., but he shook his head and continued speaking. "There was a mighty push for settlin' this land."

"If you have people living upon the land, it's much harder for someone to come in and take it away." He clipped the end of the cigar and drew a stick from the fire to light it. "It was not that long ago we were fighting Mexico for this very place."

"So are you figurin' to settle in Texas?"

Albright drew on the cigar for a moment. "I hardly think so, although I'm not against the idea of investing. I see the potential, just as Mr. Wright and Mr. Bishop suggest. There is a great amount of virgin forest to be harvested. It could prove advantageous."

"For whom?" G. W. asked. "I don't see that layin' waste to the land is going to help the folks who stay behind."

The man shrugged. "People will find other uses for the land. This seems to be hardy soil. Surely they can plant and raise crops or increase their herds and produce cattle for market. It's a narrow view to believe the land is only good for one thing."

"So you'd cut down all the trees and move on—leave the land to be cleaned up by someone else?"

"Probably." Albright's disinterest in the subject was clear. "So what of you? Will you stay after the logging is finished?"

"If I have any say about it, the loggin' will never be done. I hope to pass this down to my children."

"And you actually believe that is possible?"

"Of course it's possible. My pa passed it to me and my brother." G. W. decided to turn the tables on Albright. "So do you think your father and the president are gonna be impressed with what your friends are seein' here?"

"I can hardly speak for either man. They will consider the profit to be made, and that alone will influence their decision. My father has a knack for such things. He's always been able to see the future potential of a product or industry. He was born into money, but it was nothing like the vast fortune he's created."

"I think my father did the same thing here. When he arrived, he and his brother bought what acreage they could. It wasn't much, but they continued to add to it, takin' in small pieces of land as they became available. It wasn't long before they could buy up bigger ones."

"Was it always their thought to manage the land rather than harvest it?"

G. W. thought back to the days when his father had still been alive. The old sadness seemed to drape him like a wet blanket. How he wished his father were still here. He would be able to set Albright straight.

"My pa was a very wise man," G. W. finally replied. "He couldn't read or write well, but he had wisdom that few can boast. He loved God and his family—this land, too. All he ever wanted was to provide a good place to live for his kin and to honor God with whatever he did."

Albright said nothing for several minutes. When he did speak up, his question took G. W. by surprise. "How old are you?"

"Twenty-six." G. W. couldn't imagine why the man wanted to know, but didn't question him.

"I'm twenty-five. I've been college educated and have worked for my father's business, just as you have worked for yours. The differences between us, however, are great. You are a man of the land. I dare say you probably can't even read."

"I can," G. W. countered in a defensive tone. "Not well, but I can read some."

The younger man considered this a moment and drew several puffs on the cigar. "Well, it's not of any real concern. Andrew Johnson was illiterate when he was a child, and he became president. Anything is possible, I suppose." He flicked the rest of his cigar in the fire as Rob approached them.

G. W. had no idea where Albright had planned to go with

the conversation, but he seemed to be lost in his thoughts as Rob joined them.

"I'm bushed," Rob declared. "Headin' to bed."

"I reckon we all ought to do the same," G. W. replied. "I'm pretty tuckered myself."

Rob nodded and yawned. "See you in the mornin'."

G. W. returned his tin cup to its spot beside the coffee pot, then took up a lantern and lit it before kicking dirt into the fire to put it out. He thought about all the things he would like to ask Albright—things that might explain why he wanted to marry Lizzie. Or why he insisted the marriage was legal. He'd never been one to stick his nose in other folks's business, but this time it really stuck in his craw. He didn't want to see Lizzie hurt by this man.

"It must be hard on your pa, havin' you gone all this time," G. W. threw out.

"Not at all. He has plenty of employees to see to what is necessary. He's far too busy trying to influence the president to worry about my absence."

"What's he tryin' to influence the president about?"

The casual question seemed to take Albright by surprise. "Mostly he's working to get legislation passed that will support the various causes of women's rights. He's a fan of the suffragette movement."

G. W. considered this for a moment. "Must make him popular with Lizzie's ma."

Albright gave a laugh. "Indeed it does. She was quite glad to see her daughter wed to a family who could benefit her beloved cause."

Well, at least that gave Harriet Decker a reason to push the marriage forward. But what was Albright's reasoning? He clearly didn't love Lizzie. In fact, as best G. W. could figure, Lizzie rather annoyed him.

He wanted to ask Albright outright as to why he had really come. Why was it he wanted to impose this sham of a marriage on a woman who clearly wanted nothing to do with him? But instead, he motioned with the lantern. "Guess we'd better turn in."

G. W. didn't wait for Albright's approval. He started walking to where they had set up tents. Wright, Bishop, and Albright shared the larger of four tents while G. W., Uncle Arjan, and Rob shared a smaller tent positioned away from the easterners. The other two tents held the other Vandermark employees. They only spent the night out in the forest like this when they were working on a deadline for extra product.

Pausing by Albright's tent, G. W. waited for the man to say something dismissive, but he simply ducked into the lighted tent without a word. Wright and Bishop welcomed him with the offer of a drink.

G. W. had plans to move his visitors deeper into the Vandermark holdings in the morning. He wanted to show them some of the differences in the trees available for harvest, as well as the hardwoods that were intermingled among the pines. Mostly, however, he wanted to finish this journey and get back home to Lizzie. He missed her and could no longer deny his feelings for her. He wanted to tell her how he felt—to tell her that he didn't care about the mess with Albright, that he'd wait for her. Of course, there was a chance she didn't feel the same way, but he didn't think that was the case.

Rob and Uncle Arjan seemed to be waiting for him when G. W. entered the tent. They looked at him rather expectantly. G. W. secured the tent flap and crawled over to his bedroll.

"Guess we'll be parting company in the morning," G. W. said.

"Saw you talkin' with Albright," Uncle Arjan commented. "Did the man have anything of value to share?"

G. W. nodded. "Said his pa is working to get some laws in place that Mrs. Decker likes. Laws that help her cause."

Uncle Arjan nodded. "So that's why she's come to persuade Lizzie to go back with them."

G. W. unfastened his bedroll. "I figure it that way. But I still cain't understand how Albright stands to benefit. Guess maybe in time that will come clear, too." He crawled on top of the blanket and stretched out. It felt good to lie down and rest. His body ached from the day of work. With a sigh, he closed his eyes and put his thoughts on the pretty little blonde at home.

༄

The night passed much too quickly, and before he knew it, G. W. was being roused by his uncle. "Time to get up."

He yawned and stretched. It was already getting light, and from the wafting aroma in the air, one of the men was already frying up some smoked ham. G. W. gathered his things and considered which direction they would head. He'd just as soon take the men back to Perkinsville, but he knew that Mr. Perkins intended them to see just how far the Vandermark holdings extended. Apparently there was discussion about them buying land just to the east of his family's property line, and Mr. Perkins thought it would be good for the men to see exactly what the lay of the land was and how it could best benefit them.

They ate a quick breakfast, then started packing for the trip just as the train whistle sounded. Most of the men would spend the morning loading logs, while Sissy's husband, George, and son David would continue felling trees.

G. W. secured their provisions on two of the pack mules, while

Rob saddled the horse Stuart Albright was riding. Mr. Wright and Mr. Bishop held true to their word and seemed quite capable. They tended their own mounts, while Stuart Albright waited impatiently for Rob to finish.

"How much longer do you plan for us to stay out here?" Albright asked when G. W. came to saddle his own horse.

"I figure we'll be back next Monday. Why?"

Albright seemed to consider this a moment. "I was thinking I might take the train back to your house. Mrs. Decker and Elizabeth must surely be ready to return to Philadelphia."

G. W. stopped what he was doing and looked hard at Albright. "Lizzie's got no plans to go back to Philadelphia. She's told you that several times. Why do you keep insistin' on it?"

The expression on Albright's face clearly proved he'd been taken by surprise, but his tone bore no hint of such feelings. "She's my wife."

"She don't see it that way."

Annoyance crossed Albright's expression. "It really doesn't matter how she sees it. It's the truth of the matter."

G. W. shrugged, trying his best to hold his temper. "Seems to me a man oughta care about what a woman thinks when it comes to somethin' as important as marriage." He stared Albright in the eye. "Lizzie's got a good head on her shoulders, and I think she can decide for herself what she wants. It's obviously not bein' married to you, so maybe you should just stop tryin' to force the issue."

Albright reddened. "Stay away from her, Vandermark. She's my wife, and she will return to Philadelphia with me."

"If I were a bettin' man," G. W. said, allowing himself the slightest hint of a grin, "I'd take a wager on it that you're wrong."

Rob and Uncle Arjan came up just then, and G. W. left Albright to decide what he'd do next. G. W. hated the thought of the man returning home to harass Lizzie, but there was really nothing he could do to stop him.

"They're settin' up to start loadin' logs," Arjan told his nephew. "I guess we'll see you back to home when you finish your job with these men."

G. W. nodded and was starting to say something when George Jackson came running—waving his arms in the air. "Come quick. David's done cut himself bad."

Gone was any concern about Albright. The men made their way to where David was moaning in pain. Uncle Arjan squatted down to see how bad the wound was. Blood had drenched the young man's trousers.

"We started too low, I reckon. Ax just seemed to bounce back off the trunk and hit David instead."

The lower trunks of the older pines were hardened from resin deposits, making the cutting sometimes perilous. The men hated trying to fell them at a low level for this very reason, but the rule was to cut no higher than the diameter was thick. Arjan motioned to Rob. "Get some help. Let's get him loaded on the train and get him to the doctor."

Rob raced off just as Mr. Wright and Mr. Bishop came to see what the commotion was all about. G. W. straightened. "David's taken a bad blow to his leg. We're gonna get him to town, where the doc can stitch him up and tend him."

"Is there anything we can do?" Mr. Wright asked.

G. W. appreciated the man's concern. "No. Just stay out of the way."

The men nodded as Rob returned with several of the other loggers. Once Arjan had tied off the wound to cut down the bleeding, the men made quick work of lifting David and carrying him to the train.

"George, you go along with him. Sissy should have you there to tell her what happened."

George nodded and wiped his bloody hands against his bibbed overalls. " 'Preciate that, Mr. Arjan. I'll be back soon as I see to him."

"Just take the rest of the day, George. I won't dock your pay," Uncle Arjan assured him. "Now, hurry."

George looked like he wanted to say something more, but instead, he gave a slow nod and made his way to the train. G. W. looked to Wright and Bishop. "We should be headin' out, too."

He left them and went to where the horses waited. Albright stood by his mount, looking bored with the entire matter. He held up his left hand, studying his fingernails for a moment. "I don't suppose I understand all the fuss. The man is a Negro, is he not?"

G. W. stopped in his tracks and looked hard at Albright. "What does that have to do with anything?"

Albright shrugged. "It just seems to me that given it's only a Negro and not a white man, you wouldn't make such an ordeal over the matter."

It was clear by Albright's expression that he was trying to irritate G. W. further. No doubt it was payback for G. W.'s earlier conversation regarding Lizzie. He stepped forward, his nose nearly touching Albright's. "I'm gonna forget you said that."

"Why? I meant every word. There are thousands of freed blacks who could easily take his job. Why expend the money and time on a man who was obviously too stupid to keep himself from harm?"

G. W.'s jaw tightened. He wanted so much to punch the man square in the nose. He forced himself to take a step back. "You can think what you like. But just keep in mind, that man bleeds red, just like you're gonna if you don't keep your thoughts to yourself."

Albright gave G. W. a rather sardonic smile and turned away.

G. W. was glad the man had not replied. It had taken every bit of his self-control to keep from acting upon his anger. He could hear his mother telling him, *"The Bible says 'Be ye angry, and sin not.' "* Those words often helped G. W. keep his actions under control. But would it really be a sin, he wondered, if he hit Albright? The man clearly deserved worse than that. Wasn't there such a thing as righteous anger?

Chapter 16

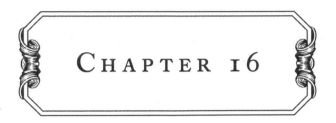

Lizzie found herself constantly thinking of G. W. and Stuart while they were off on the Vandermark property. They'd been gone for a week, and she hoped fervently that when they returned, Stuart would declare that he was mistaken—that they weren't married at all.

She gave a sigh and put away the last of the dried supper dishes. After learning what had happened to David, Lizzie found it hard not to fret about the men. What if some other tragedy had befallen them? What if G. W. were somehow harmed? Lizzie knew she had no claim on G. W. He had appeared kind and considerate of her, and definitely seemed to enjoy her company. But she had no reason to expect more.

"Is there a specific reason for that frown, or is it just life in general?"

Lizzie jumped and snapped her head up as if her neck were a springboard. "I beg your pardon?"

Deborah smiled. "I saw your frown and couldn't help but wonder what caused it. I know you're disappointed that G. W. hasn't returned, but maybe it's something more?"

"There's certainly enough to frown about," Lizzie said. She looked around the kitchen to make certain she'd put everything away.

Deborah came to her and took hold of her hands. Giving Lizzie a squeeze, she lowered her voice. "I know you miss him. I'm sure he misses you, as well."

"Oh, Deborah, am I so obvious with my pining? I feel like a schoolgirl all over again."

"I think you've hidden your feelings well. Although I would be remiss if I didn't tell you that Mother suspects. She has mentioned several times how wonderful it would be to have you in the family. She really likes you." Deborah let go her hold and gave Lizzie a wink. "I suppose I should be jealous."

"Hardly. Look at the mess my life has become. I may or may not be bound in marriage to one man, but I love another."

"Do you truly love him?" Deborah asked. She clapped her hands together. "I had hardly dared to hope!"

Lizzie leaned back against the counter. "For all the good it does me. Oh, why hasn't Father responded to our letter or telegram? I'm starting to fear that something terrible has happened to him. Oh, Deborah, what if he's met with an accident?"

"Stop it. You mustn't worry about your father. He's probably doing what he can to get to the bottom of all of this. You must give him time to work out the details. I'm sure that when he's able to offer you counsel, he will."

"I know you're probably right, but I thought we would have heard something by now. It's so hard to wait."

"At least we haven't had to deal with Mr. Albright or your mother much this week."

"Mother was none too happy with me when I accompanied her back to the boardinghouse." Lizzie drew up her apron hem and wiped perspiration from her forehead. "I know she expected to badger me into submission, but I found the strength to stand my ground. I told her specifically that I would not be forced to return to Philadelphia. She told me I was selfish and needed to consider the feelings of others."

"She should take her own advice," Deborah said, shaking her head. "I mean the woman no disrespect, but she honestly irritates my patience."

Lizzie smiled. "I told you so. Remember all the times I'd return from our visits and rant about Mother's demands?"

Deborah nodded. "I do, and I feel sorry for you." She leaned back against the doorframe. "I'm glad I could share my family with you. Now you can see what I was talking about, as well."

They both heard the back screen door open and turned. "G. W.!" Deborah exclaimed. "Well, aren't you a sight for sore eyes. We thought maybe you'd decided to make the woods your permanent home."

He looked weary but managed a smile and gave Lizzie a nod before addressing his sister. "I wanted to deliver Albright and the other fellas to town before I came home. Took a bit longer than I figured, as Mr. Perkins wanted to jaw a bit about the trip."

"Have you eaten?" Lizzie asked. "I could warm something up for you."

"No, Mrs. Perkins fed me." He patted his stomach. "Ain't near as good as what I get here, but it filled me up. Right now, all I really want is to go to bed."

"What about a warm bath?" Deborah asked. "Lizzie and I will bring you hot water."

He considered that for a moment, then shook his head. "Sounds tempting, but I washed up outside. I'll save that for another night." He crossed the room. "I'll see you both at breakfast."

"You'd best let Mama know you're back. She'll have a fit if you don't."

He nodded at Deborah's comment and kept walking. Lizzie watched him go, wishing she could have had more time with him. She had missed his company—their quiet evenings on the porch together, their occasional walks.

The clock in the dining room chimed the hour. Nine o'clock. Deborah seemed surprised by this. "I guess we all should be getting to bed. Morning will come early enough."

Lizzie nodded and gave another sigh. At least G. W. was home, safe and sound. She might have to contend with her mother and Stuart on the morrow, but worrying over that could wait.

⁂

G. W. stumbled into the kitchen well past breakfast. "Why didn't anybody wake me?" He plopped down at the kitchen table, nearly upsetting a pan of cooling corn bread.

His mother eyed him for a moment, then poured a cup of coffee and placed it in front of him. "Because Arjan said you were to be allowed to sleep. He figured you'd earned a day off since you'd been squiring those men around."

He downed the hot coffee, hardly even noticing the burn, and held the cup out for a refill. "Thanks, it's mighty good. Could I maybe have another?"

His mother grinned. "You know you can have a whole pot if you want." She went to pour more coffee while Lizzie surprised him with a big plate of food.

"We saved breakfast for you. Would you like me to cook you up some eggs to go along with this?"

He looked at the thick ham steak, fried potatoes, and slices of fresh tomato. "I guess a couple of eggs would top this off just right."

She laughed. "Just a couple?"

"Well, maybe half a dozen," he admitted. "Scrambled up fluffy like you made the last time I was home."

Lizzie blushed, and G. W. couldn't help but grin. She was the prettiest gal he'd ever known, and he knew she cared for him. Who would've thought it possible that a city girl all educated like Lizzie could fall for someone like him?

Deborah came into the kitchen and spied G. W. at the table. "I thought I heard you."

"How's the office work coming?" he asked.

"Not too bad. I feel I'm gaining a better understanding of things." She went to pour herself a cup of coffee. "I don't know how Uncle Arjan kept track of it before, but it's all recorded now." She sipped the coffee and smiled. "This is really good."

"Lizzie made it," her mother replied. "She's learned so fast, she'll have me all but replaced in the kitchen."

"Hardly that," Lizzie countered. "I may have mastered coffee, but I still have a great deal to learn. You saw my dinner rolls. They were terrible."

"Well, all things come with practice. We don't use flour as much as cornmeal around here, and yeast breads are always harder to master." She turned to her son. "While Lizzie makes your eggs, maybe you could tell us how the trip went. Are those men going to invest in forested lands nearby?"

G. W. cut a piece of the ham steak. "I believe that's their plan. They marveled at how inexpensive property is around here. Wish I had a bunch of extra money—I'd buy it all up for Vandermark and keep the greedy easterners out."

"Your father said the same thing during the influx of people right after the war. That was the one and only time he borrowed money to buy land. Paid it off as quick as he could, too. But at least we were able to increase the holdings."

"Do you think we should borrow and buy land again?" Deborah asked her brother. "I mean, you did just sign the new contract with Mr. Perkins."

"It's a thought, but we've also got to hire new men. It's all gonna take money. Speaking of men—how's David doing? I feel bad for not askin' last night."

Lizzie placed the eggs in front of him and answered before anyone else could. "Dr. Clayton was just here yesterday. He said David's injury was healing well."

"That's a relief. It looked like a nasty cut."

Mother nodded. "It was bad enough. I suggested Sissy stay home to take care of him until he's able to be up and around. She sent word with George that she figures to be back tomorrow."

"I'm glad you gave her the time off, though I doubt they can afford it," G. W. said, digging in to the eggs.

"Arjan said we could manage to pay her anyway, and David, too. I was glad for that," Mother stated. "They need every bit of money they can get."

"Should I pay them all in cash instead of half company script?" Deborah questioned.

"You certainly could, but Sissy told me that script is just fine. She doesn't like me paying her without her being here to work. She thinks it's charity. I suppose she'd think herself unreasonable to demand cash."

Deborah exchanged a look with her brother. "Like Sissy would ever demand anything."

G. W. shook his head. "Ain't charity. They're good folks. They've been here for this family when others walked away—too busy to help or just didn't care. George and David dug Pa's grave and Sissy prepared his body."

Mother nodded and replenished the coffee in G. W.'s cup once more. "Exactly my thinking." She gathered up several baskets and headed for the back door. "I'll let Lizzie take care of you. I have a garden to tend to."

"Wait, Ma. Is there anything you need me to do for you here at the house?" G. W. questioned. "You know I can't just sit around."

She thought for a moment. "Well, you and Rob have been promising to build me a place to store food, and the lumber is out there waiting. You could sure enough get to work on it, if you absolutely needed something to do."

"I'll get to it after breakfast." He waited until his mother had gone, then addressed Lizzie. "If you don't have anything better to do, you could always keep me company."

She looked hesitant. "Stuart and my mother will no doubt be out here to see me today. Stuart has never been one to wait, if he's of a mind to do something."

"I figured as much, but if you're busy helping me, they can't very well expect you to parlor sit with them."

Deborah put her cup aside. "He's right, you know. Let them come. If you're busy out back helping G. W., they'll either have to wait for you to finish up or come out there to find you. Either way, you won't have to be alone with them."

"I don't know how much help I'll be, but I'd very much like to try," Lizzie said, giving G. W. a shy smile.

"I just hope the two of you will talk about your future and stop this nonsense," Deborah declared, heading for the door. "Honestly, when two people are as gone over each other as you two, they should be planning a wedding—not a food shed."

True to Lizzie's prediction, Stuart Albright and Mrs. Decker showed up just before noon. Deborah heard her mother invite them to lunch. They accepted, though they sounded more irritated than grateful and immediately asked about Lizzie.

"She's working outside," Deborah's mother explained. "She'll be in for lunch, however, so why don't you just make yourselves comfortable? I'll get the meal on the table and let you know when things are ready." She turned at the sound of Deborah coming into the room.

"Ah, Deborah, we have company."

Deborah looked at the well-dressed and now rather tanned Stuart Albright. His blue eyes seemed even more piercing set within the bronzed skin of his face. Mrs. Decker was dressed very properly in a suit of light gray linen and seemed ill at ease. "I trust you had a pleasant journey out here?"

"It was tolerable," Mrs. Decker answered. "The roads leave much to be desired. They certainly aren't the quality of those in the East."

"I'm sure they aren't," Deborah replied and turned to Mother. "Do you need any help in the kitchen?"

"That would be very nice. Mrs. Decker and Mr. Albright

have agreed to stay for lunch, so please set two extra places at the table."

"I'd be happy to." Deborah turned to their guests. "If you'll excuse me."

She was glad to slip away and not have to make small talk. While they both were quite capable of intellectual discussion, Deborah found that she would rather have a long talk with just about any of her neighbors. They might be uneducated, but at least they were genuine.

"Maybe I'm not such a snob after all," she murmured. There were clearly worse things than lacking the ability to read and write.

When Mother could no longer delay dinner, she sent Deborah to retrieve G. W. and Lizzie. Deborah found them out by the summer kitchen laboring over a sufficiently sized A-framed structure. G. W. had smartly positioned it under a thick stand of pines that would shelter it from the sun.

"It's time to eat," she announced. "But be warned. We have dinner guests."

"My mother and Stuart?" Lizzie asked.

"Yes, and as usual, neither seems to be in good spirits."

Lizzie looked from Deborah to G. W. "I'm truly sorry. I have encouraged Mother to go back home, but she will not consider it." She gave G. W. a shy glance. "But I'm going to telegraph Father again. If I don't get a reply, I'll go to wherever I have to in order to see a lawyer."

Deborah put an arm around Lizzie's shoulders. "Hopefully, it won't come to that."

They washed up and walked slowly—almost ceremonially—toward the house. Deborah led the way into the dining room from the kitchen. Lizzie followed and G. W. brought up the rear. It was easy to see that Stuart was less than pleased to see G. W.

"Please be seated," Mother encouraged. G. W. pulled out a chair for Lizzie at the end of the table and took the seat beside her. Albright was clearly annoyed but said nothing as he took his place across from G. W.

Mother offered grace and encouraged everyone to dig in. It was clear that Mrs. Decker was used to being served and still hadn't gotten comfortable with this informal style of eating. She managed the serving spoon rather clumsily, as if to make a special point to everyone of how ill at ease she truly was.

Deborah had to practically bite her tongue to keep from commenting. She was trying hard not to let her anger and frustration get away from her, for she knew she shouldn't disrespect her elders. But what about when those elders didn't deserve respect? What about when those in authority—even parents—chose to do sinful, wrong things? But then, was it a sin for a mother to force her grown daughter to return home with a man she believed was her child's husband?

"How did it go with the A-frame?" Mother asked G. W. She turned to Harriet, explaining, "G. W. is building me a place where I can store food."

"We're pretty much finished. With Lizzie's help, it went quite fast. I just have to pack it with pine straw now."

Stuart looked aghast. "You were helping him?"

Lizzie nodded. "It was great fun. I'd never helped build anything before."

"And well you shouldn't have," Albright countered. "I can hardly believe you would impose men's labor upon a lady of such delicate nature."

G. W. put his fork down and looked hard at the man. "I didn't impose anything on Lizzie. She's the one who insisted on helpin' me."

Albright was unmoved. "That was only because she was being polite. She surely never expected you to take her up on such an outlandish offer."

G. W. turned to Lizzie. "Is that true? Were you just offerin' to be polite?"

"Goodness, no," Lizzie countered. "Stuart, I do wish you would stop trying to determine what I meant by my actions. You really know very little about me. I enjoy hard work. It makes me feel useful. You ought to try it sometime."

Deborah nearly choked on her corn bread. She wanted to burst out laughing but bowed her head as if contemplating her meal.

"Elizabeth!" Mrs. Decker set her napkin down. "That was most uncalled for. Stuart is merely concerned about your well-being. He's trying to protect you, since no one else seems to take such matters into consideration."

"My well-being was never compromised," Lizzie replied. "Furthermore, Stuart has no reason to concern himself with anything at all related to me."

"You are acting disgracefully!" Her mother's face turned red with fury. "As a woman who considers herself a Christian, you would do well to remember what the Bible says about wedded women obeying their husbands."

"Were there any currently wedded women at this table, you might have a valid argument," Deborah interjected. "However, I was under the impression that you did not hold with such beliefs. I remember a discussion we once had about that portion of the Bible. Didn't you tell me that you rejected that belief as something that was reserved only for the times in which it had been written?"

"Deborah, I'm sure you misunderstood Mrs. Decker," her mother said before the other woman could reply. "No one would pretend that the Bible can be picked apart in such a manner. To suggest that some things are true for us while others have no purpose seems quite blasphemous."

"She did not misunderstand me; neither do I misunderstand her now," Harriet Decker replied. She leveled a fierce scowl at Deborah. "My affairs with Elizabeth are not your concern. I would appreciate receiving the respect I deserve. Please stay out of the discussion."

Deborah started to reply, but her mother stepped in. "Mrs. Decker, our daughters are grown women. They have every right to speak up on the issues at hand—especially since this is my home, and I allow for such behavior. I also thought from things Lizzie had told me that you were in support of women speaking their minds."

"Well . . . I never said that . . . I mean . . ." Harriet looked uncomfortably at Stuart and then her daughter.

Lizzie met her mother's gaze. "I suppose this entire situation came about because I was following your instruction. You have told me over and over that a young woman should be allowed to work alongside a man—to earn the same pay—to have the same say. Honestly, Mother, you cannot hold to one set of beliefs for yourself and pin another on me."

Deborah knew it had been hard for Lizzie to stand up for herself, but she was getting better and better at it with each passing day. Her mother was a hypocrite—that could not be denied. The trouble was, Deborah knew there had to be some beneficial reason for Harriet Decker to act in such a manner. The woman had never wanted Lizzie to marry. She had wanted Lizzie to join her cause. She had specifically sent Lizzie to the university hoping she might become a physician or scientific genius—anything that would smack in the faces of polite society's paradigm for the weaker gender.

No, the woman was definitely up to something. There had to be a reason for her actions and attitude. Harriet Decker was not a person to do a thing without it benefiting herself at some point.

If Deborah and Lizzie could just figure out what that advantage was, perhaps they could sway her to their side by offering an even better prize.

It was worth a try.

Chapter 17

As September neared, the temperatures lowered in a surprising manner and summer eased into a gentle, more bearable season. With the change came word that Butch Foster had succumbed to his wounds. His death sent a wave of dissatisfaction and grief throughout the community. Questions began to arise. Was it Dr. Clayton's fault? Had his scientific methods killed Butch? Was Margaret Foster right about the doctor's inability to help them?

Deborah heard the rumors while shopping in the commissary and was frustrated that people should blame Dr. Clayton. Butch's wounds had been massive; to lose a limb and bleed out as much as he had were reason enough to die. Throwing caution and protocol to the wind, Deborah left her shopping basket with the promise to return and went in search of Dr. Clayton. No doubt he'd already heard the news and the awful things that were being said about him.

"I figured he wouldn't survive," the doctor told Deborah. "But to tell the truth, I don't know that he would have made it had he remained here with me."

Deborah's voice was barely a whisper. "You should be aware that Mrs. Foster is blaming you."

He frowned and toyed with a bottle of carbolic acid. "I figured as much."

Deborah immediately regretted bringing it up. "I'm sorry. I know it hasn't been easy for you here." She sighed. "It hasn't been easy for me, either, and I love this place and the people."

He looked at her oddly for a moment. "How is it that you love it so? You're an educated woman who loves learning. You seem completely out of place here."

She smiled. "I am. I miss attending school. For me, it was like having my eyes opened for the first time. Life here . . . well, it just is. And for most of my life, I've been content."

"But not now?"

Deborah considered his question for a moment. "I'm content with knowing that I'm doing what is required of me." She shook her head. "I should reword that. It was never required, nor even expected. Unless of course you count the fact that I expected it of myself."

"How so?"

"I've always felt my family needed me to gain as much knowledge as possible. The world is changing so fast, and the days of a handshake agreement are rapidly fading. Mr. Perkins is even requiring a contract from my family. Without the skill I've learned, I fear Vandermark Logging would be victim to all manner of scheming."

"I suppose I can understand that. You're good to help your family in such a way."

She shrugged. "I suppose so, but it still grieves me to see things as they are. I wish my brothers valued education more. I wish my father had valued it for them. Perhaps they would have been the ones to attend school instead of me."

"That would have been a grave injustice for you."

She met his smile and nodded. "I think so, too. But on the other hand, perhaps it would not have awakened such desires within me."

Dr. Clayton put down the bottle and crossed his arms. "What do you mean?"

Deborah hadn't meant to get into such a conversation, but now she found herself baring all of her secrets with ease. "I feel like a hypocrite—like a society snob."

He laughed, taking her by surprise. "I find that hard to believe. There isn't anything in the leastwise snobbish about you."

She moved to the window. "Yes there is. I'm sorry to say it, but it's true. I look at the people here differently now. When I first went away to school, it was after I'd completed eighth grade. Mother arranged for me to attend a ladies finishing school in Houston. I was quite excited. It was there that I learned French and fine sewing. I learned how to properly instruct household staff and arrange a dinner party." She turned and faced him. "All the things a proper young lady should know. I came back here wondering how in the world I would ever find use for such things, but I felt confident that I would. I even imagined marrying one of the young men I'd grown up around. Then I heard about some of the colleges and universities back East allowing women to attend. The very thought stirred something inside my mind."

"How did your folks feel about it?"

"I think at first they were worried about my going so far away, but when I reminded them that my aunt would be less than a mile away, it calmed them. Then, after attending a year of classes, I found myself awakening to another world. I knew that I could help my family with the business. I stayed in school, learning all that I could, always knowing that I would one day return here and do what I could to help my loved ones."

"And how do you feel about it now?"

Deborah considered the question for a moment. "I know I'm doing the right thing. They were very much in need of my abilities. You should have seen the mess." She laughed, remembering all the scraps of scribbled notes her uncle had given her. "It's in order now, and they have a new contract that will ensure they have work for years to come. I think things are looking up."

At that there was a knock on the front door and a man called out. "Doc? You in here?"

It was Zed Perkins. Deborah recognized his voice and frowned. Had there been another accident? She followed Dr. Clayton into the front waiting area.

Mr. Perkins nodded at her but turned his attention to Dr. Clayton. "I was hoping to have a word with you."

Deborah pushed down a feeling of uneasiness. She could see by the look on Mr. Perkins's face that something wasn't right. "If you don't mind, I'll pick out a couple of your journals to read and be on my way."

Dr. Clayton nodded and Deborah smiled at Mr. Perkins. "I hope your family is well."

"They are, Miss Deborah. Thanks for asking. How about your family?"

"They, too, are doing well, thank you." She turned and without another word slipped into the doctor's office. She could hear Mr.

Perkins begin to speak, and although she picked up a journal to glance through, it was his words she focused on.

"I'm sorry to come here, Doc, but there's been some trouble. As you've probably heard, Miz Foster's son died."

"I had heard," Dr. Clayton replied.

"Well, it's got folks riled up."

Deborah had feared it would be like this. She had hoped Dr. Clayton could escape the ire of her community.

"My guess is that Mrs. Foster is behind the rumors I've heard."

"True enough, Doc, but the fact is, there's talk about me getting rid of you."

Deborah stiffened and forgot about the journal. The very idea of the townspeople listening to Mrs. Foster rather than accepting the truth was more than she could stand. She could barely refrain from rushing back into the waiting room to speak her mind.

"Butch Foster most likely died from loss of blood and infection," Dr. Clayton replied. "I honestly didn't expect him to survive. Wounds of that nature are life-threatening. Still, Mrs. Foster should never have moved him. I'm sure she wasn't overly worried about cleanliness, and it would have acerbated his condition."

"I don't doubt that, Doc, but . . . well, folks are easily swayed in this community. Especially by one like Miz Foster."

"With her superstitious nonsense, no doubt."

"Doesn't much matter, Doc. I'm not at all sure what should be done. Folks aren't comin' to see you like I'd hoped. It seems they only come for care if there's no other choice. Still, I know it's not your fault."

"What is it you want me to do? I can leave, if that's what you've come to suggest."

Deborah leaned closer to hear the response. For a moment, she wasn't sure if Mr. Perkins would answer. Finally, he spoke in a slow, even tone. "I suppose I was hoping you might have a suggestion."

Silence hung in the air and Deborah wanted nothing more than to interject her own thoughts on the matter. She was ready to rejoin the men when Dr. Clayton replied.

"I guess the best thing we can do is pray about it."

Pray? When people were spreading lies and speaking ill of a good man? Surely there was something more. They should call a town meeting or send someone to reprimand Mrs. Foster. Of course, the poor woman was suffering the loss of her son, but that still didn't give a person the right to lie about someone else.

"I think you're right, Doc. God has His hand on the situation. I tend to react too quickly and not spend enough time considering what the Lord would have me do."

"It's easy enough to forget to seek Him first."

"Well, I need to get back to the mill. I don't plan to let folks dictate decisions to me, but I want you to know that it probably won't be easy for you in the days to come."

Deborah heard Dr. Clayton chuckle. "It hasn't been easy yet—might as well not expect it to change now."

She waited until she heard Mr. Perkins leave before marching into the waiting room. "Pray?" she asked, her voice a little louder than necessary. "You want to *pray* about it?"

He shrugged. "Seemed like the right thing to say and do. I can hardly change people's minds by myself."

"But that woman is out there spreading lies about you. You can't just sit idly by and allow for that. She's made enough trouble already."

He looked at her for a moment, then headed toward the office. "I can't force people to like me. Nor can I force them to believe me."

Deborah followed on his heels. "This is utterly ridiculous. Mrs.

Foster is maligning your name and reputation. You've done nothing but serve this community in an admirable and professional manner. It's not your fault that she's full of ignorance."

Dr. Clayton made his way into the examination room, and she marched right behind him. When he said nothing, she continued. Her anger was getting the best of her, but it didn't matter. "You have a right to defend yourself."

"It would hardly change people's minds if I did."

"It might," she declared. "You don't know what might convince them."

"That's true, but more important, I do know that losing my temper won't help."

Deborah couldn't believe his calm. She wanted to shake him. "Mrs. Foster will turn this entire town against you, Dr. Clayton. She will poison the minds of the people and scare them with her threat of curses. It's not right, and I intend to see that it stops," she said, waving her arms in the air for emphasis. "This challenge should not go unmet."

Dr. Clayton turned away from her and walked to the washstand. Without warning, he picked up the pitcher and turned to face her. "Do you need my help?"

Deborah looked at the pitcher and then to Christopher Clayton's face. She immediately felt foolish for her outrage. A sense of embarrassment washed over her.

"I'm sorry. I suppose I am rather out of line."

He grinned. "I appreciate your defense of me. I doubt anyone else would offer me such support. You are a formidable opponent, Miss Vandermark, and if any one person could rectify the situation, I believe it would be you. However, I am coming to see more and more the value of prayer."

She nodded. "You humble me, Doctor. I do apologize for losing my temper. I hate ignorance."

"As do I," he agreed. He replaced the pitcher on the washstand. "More than you will ever know."

ꙮ

Later Deborah accompanied her mother to the Foster residence. The run-down, unpainted house seemed dark and ominous, and the yard was nothing but dirt and dried-out herb patches. It was an appropriate setting for viewing the dead. Deborah was convinced little of life had existed in this place for some time. Mrs. Foster lived her life steeped in superstitions. The living water of Christ had no place among her elixirs and potions.

"I don't imagine Mrs. Foster will be too happy to see me," Deborah whispered to her mother. "I was there when Dr. Clayton worked on Butch."

"I know, but I think it's good that you've come. By staying away, you would only give her reason to believe herself right," Mother replied. "This way, you will come face-to-face with her accusations and dispel them."

"I can hardly raise a fuss in the middle of the viewing."

"I didn't expect you to raise a fuss," Mother said with a hint of a smile. "I think your very presence will offer an attitude of innocence."

They approached the front step and encountered Sadie Foster, wife of Mrs. Foster's oldest son, Matthew. Mother reached out to take hold of Sadie's hands. "I'm sorry for your family's loss."

Sadie nodded. "Thank ya kindly. Ma Foster will appreciate your comin'."

"We brought a corn bread casserole—two in fact," Deborah's mother told the young woman. "They're in the wagon if you want to send someone to fetch them."

"I'll do that. Thanks again."

Deborah followed her mother into the darkened house. Candles had been lit throughout to reveal the somber setting. Butch had been laid out in the front room, coins on his eyes and a cloth tied around his face to keep his mouth from falling open. The air was heavy—putrid from death and decay.

Dressed in patched trousers and a too-small coat, Butch scarcely resembled the robust man he'd once been. Deborah noticed the clock on the wall had been stopped, in keeping with the superstitious traditions. The family believed that it was important to stop all of the clocks in the household lest they stop on their own, foreshadowing another death in the family.

Likewise, the mirrors were covered and the stairs were roped off. If a step were to squeak under the weight of any person while the dead body was still in the house, the Fosters believed that someone in the family would die within the year.

Mrs. Foster caught sight of them and approached with a look of displeasure. Deborah told herself it was just her state of grief that caused such an expression.

"Margaret, I am so very sorry for your loss. I know your grief is great, and I've been praying for you," Euphanel said.

"It's true," Mrs. Foster replied. "I ain't hardly myself, and the loss of Butch is more than I can bear."

"Deborah and I want you to know that if there's anything we can do to help, we are here for you."

The older woman looked at Deborah and scowled. "Ain't nothing that one can do to help. She was with that butcher when he cut away my boy's arm."

Her mother squeezed Deborah's arm but looked at Margaret Foster. "Sawmills are such dangerous places. No one could have known that blade would break loose and sever poor Butch's arm. The loss is great, and he will be missed."

Deborah admired the way her mother chose to respond. Mrs. Foster was clearly at a loss for words. She nodded and turned to look at her son's displayed body.

"The loss," she finally murmured, "is one that should be avenged."

Chapter 18

September 1885

Lizzie knew the time to confront Stuart could no longer be delayed. G. W. had shared what he'd learned from Stuart on their trip through the Vandermark forests, and Lizzie felt she finally had some idea of why her mother so adamantly accepted the marriage. If Stuart's father had a way to help further her mother's suffragette cause, she would push for Lizzie to do whatever was needed. Never mind whether or not Lizzie loved the man.

I've been so foolish, Lizzie thought. *It was childish to act out against Mother, and I've only managed to create a mess for myself.* She sighed. The sooner she talked to Stuart, the better.

Making her way to the front room after supper, Lizzie braced herself for the job at hand. She had already told G. W. of her plans—Deborah, too. Now, she just needed the gumption to see it through.

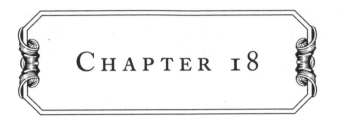

"We'd like to leave tomorrow," her mother was telling Mrs. Vandermark as Lizzie entered the room. She looked up. "That is, if Elizabeth will stop this nonsense and pack her things."

Rather than confront her mother's comment, Lizzie fixed her gaze on Stuart. "I'd like to have a word with you. Would you join me outside?"

He smiled and his blue eyes seemed to spark to life. "Of course."

"Finally," Lizzie's mother grumbled. "Now perhaps we will be able to go home."

Lizzie frowned as she made her way to the porch. The warm glow of light spilled out from the open living room windows. Having no desire to be overheard by the people in the house, Lizzie stepped to the opposite side. It was a little darker there, but she would still be able to see Stuart's face. That was important to her right now. If he lied to her, she hoped she'd see it in his expression.

"I want to know the truth," she began. "No more of this nonsense. I do not intend to return with you and Mother. I want to know what you stand to gain by imposing this marriage on me."

Stuart looked stunned. He put a hand to his chest. "You wound me. You were the one who accepted my proposal. You planned the wedding quite enthusiastically, as I recall."

"I was wrong to do so," Lizzie replied. "I was wrong to agree to marry you. I could never love you, and a marriage without love would be a nightmare for both of us."

"What convinces you that you can't learn to love me? Is it that Vandermark man? Do you fancy yourself in love with him?" His words were edged with a tone of sarcasm. Instead of a jealous sweetheart, he sounded like a displeased father.

"This isn't about G. W. I decided not to marry you before ever meeting the man. This is about us."

"Well, it should be, but it isn't." He stepped toward her, lowering his voice. "Elizabeth, I have watched you these last few days. You are clearly infatuated with G. W. Vandermark. I've tried to be patient about it, but no more. You are my wife, and you must return home with me."

Lizzie narrowed her eyes and cocked her head ever so slightly to the right. "Why? Tell me now what you stand to gain. Why is it that you need me to return with you as your wife?"

Stuart looked surprised and then turned his head aside rather quickly, and Lizzie knew he was preparing to concoct some sort of story. "I want the truth, Stuart. If you lie to me, I'll know it."

"Oh? And what makes you so sure?"

"God." She gave him a look of confidence that she didn't quite feel. "I have come to believe He will give me an understanding of whether you speak truth or lies."

He laughed, but his expression revealed that Stuart wasn't quite sure of the situation. For a moment, she feared he might turn for the house, but he held himself fast. She waited for him to speak, praying he would just drop the façade and speak openly. The silence became an unbearable discomfort. Lizzie knew this was his way of controlling the situation, but she wasn't about to let him have the upper hand.

"Very well. You will not speak honestly to me, so I will bid you good night—and good-bye. I am going to ask Mrs. Vandermark to refuse you and Mother as further company in this house." With that, she pushed past him and headed for the door.

He reached out with one quick move to take hold of her arm. "Wait."

She stopped in midstep. "Release me, and I will stay."

Stuart let go of her, and Lizzie quickly maneuvered away from him. She backed against the porch railing and waited for him to speak. He seemed to consider his words carefully.

"You are correct. I stand to gain from this union, but so do you. You will have everything a woman could want. I will lavish you with gowns and jewelry. I will buy you a large house in the most fashionable district of Philadelphia. And if not Philadelphia, then New York. You will be free to do as you please. You will have a carriage at your disposal and servants to see to your every need. You may entertain and hold parties, spend your days shopping and visiting your friends—whatever you like." He paused and took a step toward her. "Elizabeth, I know you do not love me, but in time you might come to a measure of affection for me."

"And you would want this kind of marriage? A loveless one, built only on the hope that I might come to have affection for you one day?"

"I need this marriage," he answered, clearly more quickly than he'd intended. His discomfort was obvious.

Lizzie pounced on his error in judgment. "Why?"

"It's enough that you know I do," he replied.

"No, it's not." She folded her arms. "It's not nearly enough. I need the truth, Stuart."

He made a sound that reminded Lizzie of an animal in pain. "You are the most infuriating woman."

"Be that as it may, I require the truth."

He studied her for several minutes. His shoulders seemed to slump a bit. "Very well. My father has required I marry in order to receive money left to me by my grandfather. There, are you happy?"

"I did not expect to be happy with your answer, Stuart. I knew you were using me; I just couldn't imagine what you stood to gain. Now I understand. But why . . . me?"

"Your beauty, your education, your social skills—they all fit perfectly into what my father mandates my wife should be. To gain my fortune, he must approve. And he's chosen you, Elizabeth."

"But what of my mother? What is her part in this? Have you promised her some vast fortune?"

"No. She's been promised something entirely different."

"And that would be . . . ?" She let her voice trail off and waited while he shifted his weight and looked away.

"She will get political help."

It was just as G. W. had told her. "You mean her cause will get political support, don't you?"

"Yes. Now that you have the truth, just as you required, it's time to put this nonsense behind us and return to Philadelphia."

"I have no intention of returning to Philadelphia. I plan to obtain an annulment."

"No!" He stepped forward. "You have no grounds."

"I believe we both have grounds. We were false with each other—that alone seems worthy of a judge's willingness to end this fraudulent relationship."

"I won't stand for it. My father won't, either. Remember, you're dealing with men of power."

Lizzie shook her head. "I'm not afraid of you or your father. And, for once in my life, I'm not afraid of my mother, either. I have people here who love me. I will not be forced to do as you say, simply because it's your desire."

Stuart stepped forward and roughly grabbed her shoulders. Giving her a slight shake, he scowled. "You'll do exactly as I say. I have your signature, and that is enough. I will lie or cheat to see that this marriage remains intact. Do you understand?"

Lizzie felt the old sensation of helplessness return. What if Stuart had the power necessary to keep her in the marriage?

"In time, you'll come to see that I'm right—that this is the best way for both of us. You'll see that the life I'm offering you is all that a woman could want. I will deny you nothing."

"Only love," she whispered.

"What?" He looked as if she'd hit him in the face.

"You say you'll deny me nothing, but you are denying me the thing that matters most. You're denying me love."

"I can give you love, Elizabeth. I promise you that." He crushed her lips with his own. Lizzie fought against his hold but knew she was no match for his strength. She tried to cry out, but his mouth against hers muffled the sound.

Just as quickly as he had begun, Stuart pulled away. It was then that she saw G. W. had taken hold of the man. In one fluid motion, he twisted Stuart around and punched him square in the nose. Stuart lost his balance and fell backward with a loud thump.

Lizzie wanted to cheer. Instead, she came to G. W.'s side as Stuart picked himself up off the porch floor. She took hold of G. W.'s arm just in case he had thoughts of continuing the fight.

"I think it's time for you and Mother to leave," she said in a soft, but firm, tone. She looked to G. W. "Would you mind getting the door?"

He quickly complied, leading her into the house. Lizzie noted the stunned expression of her mother and addressed her immediately.

"Mother, Stuart has explained your arrangements with him regarding our marriage. I realize your cause is more important to you than I am, but I refuse to be used in this manner."

Her mother stared back at her with openmouthed surprise. For a moment, she was struck speechless, but then her wits returned. Getting to her feet, she pointed a finger at Lizzie.

"You are an ungrateful wretch of a child. No doubt this is the influence of your new friends, but I will not tolerate the selfishness.

You will do as you're told. I will not see my cause suffer because of your unwillingness to aid us."

"Aid you?" Lizzie exchanged a glance with G. W. "You mean sacrifice my life and happiness for you. This is far more than simply 'aiding.' You require my entire being—my all."

"And what if I do? It's no more or less than I've given."

"But you forget, Mother—this is your cause, not mine."

"Women's rights should be the issue of every female in this country," Harriet countered. "How can we hope to convince the men who run this country if we cannot even rally our sisters to the cause?"

Lizzie shrugged. "I have no idea, nor am I overly concerned about it. I will not sacrifice my happiness for a political scheme." By this time, Stuart had come to stand only a few feet away. She turned to him. "Nor will I sacrifice for the sake of your inheritance."

"This is completely unreasonable," her mother said. "You have no idea the harm you are causing."

Shaking her head, Lizzie looked at them with great sadness in her heart. She was nothing more than a pawn in their game. "You have no idea the harm you've already caused."

"I'm proud of you," Deborah declared when Lizzie finished revealing the evening's conversation. "And I would have dearly loved to have seen G. W. put Stuart Albright in his place."

"It wasn't as satisfying as you might have imagined."

Deborah could hear the sadness in her friend's tone. "Look, it will be all right. We'll go see the lawyer in Lufkin, and if he can't help, then we'll go to Houston. We'll get your annulment and that will be the end of it."

Lizzie shook her head. "I know I threatened Stuart I'd do so, but the truth is, I have very little money left. And without Father's help, I have no way to get any more."

"You leave that to us," Deborah replied. "I'm certain everyone in this family will want to give you whatever you need."

"I can't take advantage of you in that way. I need to find work that will pay me."

"Nonsense. Don't let your pride stand in the way. Besides, I can easily train you to assist me. As we add more employees and more expenses, I'll need the help."

"I suppose I could try it," Lizzie said with a shrug, "but if it doesn't work out, then I'll have to search for something else."

Deborah smiled. "It will work out. You'll see."

Chapter 19

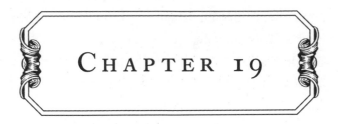

Deborah looked at the town constable the next day and then to the sign posted on a barricade in the middle of the dirt road. The entry into Perkinsville was clearly blocked by the crudely constructed warning: *Quarantine*. She applied the wagon brake and questioned the man standing at its base.

"Ralph, what in the world has happened here?"

He tipped his hat in greeting, then announced, "It's typhoid, Miss Deborah. I can't let anyone in or out. Dr. Clayton's orders."

She looked to her mother. "I suppose we aren't going to be able to trade at the commissary."

"Ralph, is there much sickness?" Euphanel asked.

"The Fosters came down with it first, and most everyone who

lives near them." The younger man pushed his hat back. "Looks to be bad."

"And your family, Ralph? Caroline, the boys?" Mother asked.

"They're fine . . . for now. Thanks for askin', Miz Vandermark."

Deborah thought of Dr. Clayton. He would be overwhelmed with work. "Is there anything we can do to help? I could stay here and assist Dr. Clayton."

"No, Miss Deborah, I cain't let you in. Dr. Clayton said you might suggest such a thing, but I was to turn you away."

She felt her cheeks flush. Dr. Clayton had presumed to know how she would respond. Worse still, he'd told Ralph about it. Her mother seemed to sense her embarrassment and moved the conversation on.

"What about supplies, Ralph? Does the doctor have everything he needs? We can always bring things to you and leave them here."

"Right now everything seems to be under control. Doc says we need to see how far this has spread before we'll really know what's needed."

Deborah suddenly remembered Lizzie's mother. "What of Mrs. Decker and Mr. Albright? Did they leave on the morning train?"

"No one was allowed to board the train. They're still here, quarantined with the rest of the folks."

"Oh dear," Mother said, shaking her head. "That will not bode well with them."

"No, ma'am," Ralph agreed. "They tried earlier to head out your way, and I had to turn them back. That Mr. Albright wasn't at all happy."

"I'm sure he wasn't," Deborah muttered.

"Well, I suppose you'd best turn the wagon around, Deborah.

Ralph, you let the doctor know that we'll check back. If he needs anything—or if you need anything—we'd be happy to help."

"I'd appreciate it if you'd send word to my family. Tell Caroline to hold up at the house and not let anyone in or out. No sense in risking it."

"We'll stop by there on our way home," Mother assured. "Take care of yourself, Ralph."

"You, too, Miz Vandermark, Miss Deborah." He tipped his hat again.

Deborah released the brake and turned the horses in a tight circle.

"I do hope this will pass quickly."

Deborah saw the worry in her mother's expression. "Dr. Clayton is a good doctor, Mama."

"Yes, but typhoid is quite dangerous. I've seen these epidemics before."

She wished she had words to comfort her mother. Deborah knew something about typhoid. William Wood Gerhard of Philadelphia had established typhoid as a specific disease in 1837. She had attended a lecture at the university dealing with various diseases, and Gerhard had been mentioned with great pride.

Typhoid was now known to be spread through fecal-contaminated water and milk, as well as a general lack of cleanliness from person to person. Deborah remembered that the prominent markers of the disease were fever and diarrhea. There were four main stages of the illness, and each one had its miseries.

"You are worried, aren't you?"

Deborah turned to face her mother. "I remember hearing a lecture about typhoid and the many dangers for those stricken."

Her mother nodded. "It will be weeks before we know the full effect."

"I was just thinking on that. At least four weeks are needed to let the disease run its course, right?"

"Yes, at least."

"The people have been so afraid to use Dr. Clayton's services," Deborah said thoughtfully. "I suppose they will have to let him help them now."

"Perhaps this is the very thing necessary to bring the people to their senses," Mother replied. "Although it's a hard lesson to endure, people often have to come to the end of their own self-sufficiency in order to trust someone else."

"Just like we sometimes have to come to our lowest point in order to trust God."

"Exactly like that. We are very stubborn children at times, and acknowledging our need of God is difficult. It makes us feel helpless—out of control. Little do folks realize that when we put God in charge, only then do we find true confidence and liberty from worry. Maybe the townsfolk will see the same thing with Dr. Clayton. They will come to trust him when they come to the end of their own abilities."

Deborah knew her mother was right. "So long as they don't blame him for the typhoid. I've seen folks do that, as well. Blame their caregivers for the very ailment they help them with. Still, Dr. Clayton has often mentioned Mrs. Foster's lack of hand washing and keeping wounds clean. I suppose it's possible that she's the cause of this epidemic."

"There's no real way of knowing, so there's no sense in accusing her. It won't change the situation now."

"Perhaps not, but if she could understand that it was her unwillingness to listen to Dr. Clayton's advice that caused this sickness, maybe she would gain a desire to change. I don't doubt at all that Mrs.

Foster knows a good deal about healing, but with the discovery of bacteria and the cause of diseases, her methods are antiquated."

"I'm sure you're right, but I'd say nothing about it for now. It would serve Dr. Clayton better to simply treat the sick and prove himself capable of helping turn this situation to good."

"He'll have no one to help him," Deborah murmured, not really meaning to speak the words aloud.

Mother patted her leg. "He'll have God, Deborah. You told me he's a man who fears the Lord and prays. God will not abandon him to face this on his own."

"I know, but I fear that with so many folks suffering, he'll have to work alone. He will risk his own health, and that could leave us without a doctor."

"Then we must pray for him more than ever," her mother suggested.

"That's the hardest part," Deborah said, shaking her head. "It seems so little."

"But it's not. You are petitioning the King of all things for help." Mother smiled. "God knows what Dr. Clayton faces physically and spiritually."

"But Mrs. Foster is responsible for turning the people against Dr. Clayton."

"And God is able to change that, as well." Euphanel grasped Deborah's hand. "God is in control, Deborah. Let Him change hearts, for you cannot."

Lizzie was anxious for G. W. and the other men to return from logging. Word had been sent by Mr. Perkins that the mill was running at a very limited capacity, since more and more of the men had fallen ill. So far the Vandermark employees and family were faring well, and Arjan wanted to use the time to work ahead on cutting trees. The logs could sit and wait until they were needed—a sort of insurance against problems that might yet befall them.

Everyday activities went on much as they always had, with exception to their weekly trips into town. Lizzie thought of her mother and Stuart. Had they succumbed to typhoid? For all of her frustration with the duo, she could not wish them ill and found herself praying for their health and safety frequently throughout the day.

Putting another kettle of water to boil, Lizzie checked the clock again. G. W. should be home within the half hour. She hurried to pour a cooled pan of water into a pitcher for use. Deborah had insisted that they boil all water and milk—apparently it helped to kill any typhoid bacteria. It seemed a lot of fuss since none of them were showing signs of the illness, but Lizzie knew Deborah was far more learned about such things and complied without complaining. If it kept them well, it would be worth the extra work. She would be devastated if G. W. took ill.

It amazed her that she'd grown to love this man so dearly. He was nothing like the man she'd imagined herself marrying, yet he understood her as no one had before—not even Deborah. He admired her artistic abilities but also encouraged her to learn new skills. He also offered her laughter and joy, things that had been sorely missing in her life until now.

"Have the men returned?" Deborah asked as she strode into the kitchen.

"I don't think so. Since the train isn't running, I can't always hear them when they get in. I suppose they should be back soon, however." Lizzie turned her attention to the oven and pulled out a large pan of creamed ham and potatoes. "Supper's ready."

"It smells wonderful," Deborah said, going to the back door.

She looked outside for a moment, then turned back to her friend. "I wish I knew how things were going in town."

"I know. I do, too. I was just wondering if Mother or Stuart had taken sick."

Deborah nodded. "I know. I thought of them, too. Hopefully, Dr. Clayton will have warned everyone to boil their water and wash thoroughly."

"Is there nothing else that can be done?"

"Not that I'm aware." Deborah took down plates from the cupboard. "Even amongst scientists, there are arguments and debates on how best to manage sickness. I suppose Mother is right in saying that it's all in God's hands. We can only watch and wait."

The unmistakable sound of the men drifted through the windows. They were bringing the mules in, and it would only be a short time before they'd come to the house, expecting their supper.

"I guess we'd best get a move on," Lizzie said. "Gracious, just listen to me. I'm sounding more and more like a Texan."

Deborah laughed and headed to the dining room while Lizzie began cutting the corn bread. She found a great sense of satisfaction in her routine here, and hopefully tonight she would find herself sitting beside G. W. on the porch after supper. She shivered slightly at the thought. She hoped he would ask her to marry him soon. They both knew it was an implied desire, but the question had never been posed.

She frowned as a thought came to mind. Perhaps G. W. wouldn't ask for her hand until the annulment was secured. She supposed that was only right. He was a gentleman, and a good Christian man. He wouldn't want to besmirch her reputation.

Putting such matters aside, Lizzie squared her shoulders and stacked the corn bread on a plate. No matter what happened, things were better here than they'd ever been in Philadelphia. God would see her through. She had to trust that He had made a way through for all of them.

ꕥ

G. W. finished washing his face and hands. He took the towel and dried off, then drew a comb from his pocket and smoothed back his damp hair.

"You sure are gone over Miss Lizzie," Rob teased him. "I ain't never known you to worry overmuch about your looks."

"No one could ever fuss as much as you do," his brother countered.

Rob shrugged. "I have my reputation to uphold, don't ya know. The ladies expect me to look my best."

G. W. laughed and put the comb back in his pocket. "You're gonna have to pick just one of 'em and settle down soon. Ain't good for a man to be alone—God himself said as much."

"I'm hardly alone, big brother. 'Cept for now, maybe. What with the quarantine, I can hardly head to town for my usual sparkin'." He frowned. "Sure hope things are going good for folks."

"I do, too," G. W. replied, heading to the house. "But right now, I'm hopin' even more that supper's hot and waitin' on the table."

He bounded up the steps and into the house. The pleasant aroma of coffee and ham filled the air. Much to his satisfaction, he found Lizzie watching him from the corner of the kitchen.

"You look like the cat that stole the cream," she teased.

G. W. shrugged. "I feel more like the cat whose stomach is so empty it's pressin' against his backbone."

"Mercy, that can't be good. We'll have to see to that. Can't be having you suffer such misery."

He fixed her with a wicked grin. "Feedin' me won't put me out of my misery, but I don't guess it will hurt me, neither."

Her cheeks flushed, but she didn't look away. "Hopefully, we can ease your suffering in every way—one of these days. Soon."

"That's what I'm a-countin' on," he replied. "And what I'm prayin' on."

Sooner or later, he was going to make this woman his wife. He'd wait for as long as it took.

Chapter 20

Christopher looked down at the ailing Mrs. Foster. He put a hand to her head and could feel that the fever had not yet abated. She was still desperately ill, and worse yet, she knew it. That was the trouble of having knowledge of sickness and disease. Mrs. Foster knew the seriousness of her ailments, and by the looks of it, she was not only in misery and pain but also gravely afraid.

He listened for a moment to her heartbeat. The woman opened her eyes and focused her dazed expression on him. "I'm dyin', ain't I?"

"Nonsense. You just rest, Mrs. Foster. You're doing a bit better, but this is going to have to run its course. Can you take some water?"

She gave a weak nod. He lifted her shoulders and brought a glass to her parched lips. "Not too much at a time. Just sip it."

To his surprise, she did exactly as he told her. "I figure God is punishin' me for my pride," she said as he placed her back on the pillow.

"How is that, Mrs. Foster?"

She put a hand to her stomach and moaned softly. "My pride," she finally continued, "ain't no excuse for how I acted toward you."

He smiled. The third week of the disease was often marked by delirium—perhaps her confession was nothing more than that. "You just need to rest. Soon you'll be back on your feet."

Christopher realized with great relief that he held this woman no malice. For all her ill treatment toward him, she was a suffering soul who needed his help. Whether her change in attitude was due to the illness or a contrite heart, Christopher wanted only to see her recover.

"Is the whole town sick with the typhoid?"

"Quite a few of them are. Some seem to have escaped the worst of it." He blotted her forehead with a damp cloth, then straightened. "I need to go see to the rest of your family, but I'll be back to check on you tonight."

She nodded weakly. Christopher gathered his medical bag and went into the next room to check on Sadie and Matthew. Both were quite ill and into their second week of the sickness. Marked by a rosy rash on their abdomens and bearing high fevers, neither was able to get up from bed without help. Two girls, no more than twelve or thirteen, had been called upon to assist with chamber pots and give water and medicine. Children seemed to have easier cases of the disease or often escaped it altogether. No one knew why. Still more confusing was why some took the disease and died, while others bore the misery and recovered with few complications.

But mysteries such as this had drawn Christopher to medicine in the first place. Treating symptoms and searching for new remedies were always a challenge. But losing lives was a price Christopher refused to pay.

He finished tending the Fosters and moved on to the next family. One by one, Christopher made the rounds to all of the cabins, finishing just after two in the afternoon. He had been forced to expand the quarantine area to include the black town across the railroad tracks. Thankfully, the train was still running, although it couldn't stop in the restricted area. Supplies were brought in on the train and set beside the tracks, just outside of town. Once this was done, the train had to move on before Dr. Clayton could send men to retrieve the goods. At least this way, they continued receiving medical supplies and food.

Walking toward the depot, Christopher suppressed a yawn. His muscles ached and he longed for a good night's sleep. The epidemic was far from over, however, and rest would have to wait.

"Dr. Clayton!"

He looked up and focused his bleary gaze toward the sound. Deborah Vandermark stood just beyond the makeshift quarantine fence. He gave a wave and smiled. He was greatly relieved to see that she'd not succumbed to the disease. He ambled toward the roped boundary, stopping about fifteen feet from the line.

"How are you doing?" she asked.

"Not as bad as I could be. There are still some folks who haven't come down sick."

Deborah frowned. "I wish I could come and help you. You look awful."

He chuckled. "Well, thanks for the compliment."

"You know I meant no insult. It's just that you need help, and no one is qualified to give it."

"The risk is too big. Besides, God is seeing me through."

Deborah glanced toward the boardinghouse. "Have you seen Mrs. Decker and Mr. Albright? Are they sick?"

"They seem fine. Folks at the boardinghouse haven't come down ill. They're nearly a quarantine unto themselves."

"Mrs. O'Neal is a very capable housekeeper. I'm sure she's heeded all the warnings and suggestions you've offered."

"So far, it would appear that way. The few residents who are there seem healthy," Christopher replied. "Although none are too happy about having to be imprisoned."

"They'd like it a whole lot less if they came down sick."

"That's true enough. So how's your family?"

"We're all fine. I've been boiling the water and milk and making everyone wash until their fingers are pruned." She smiled. "I've never seen the boys with such clean hands."

He could well imagine Deborah standing over her brothers with a threatening glare. "And your mother is fine?"

"Yes, she's always been the healthiest of us all." Deborah looked past him to the town. "We heard there were a couple of deaths."

Christopher nodded. "Sadly enough, we lost Mr. Downs and one of the Foster cousins. Amelia."

"Do you think there will be additional deaths?"

He shrugged. "It's hard to say. Some folks are recovering. Mrs. Foster has been terribly ill, but I believe she's turned the corner. I think another day or two will show her greatly improved."

"Perhaps this will take some of the bitterness from her."

"She did tell me this morning that she thought this was punishment for her pride," Christopher replied. "I suppose only time will tell as to whether she changes her ways. Her son Matthew and his wife are very sick. I worry that Sadie might not make it."

Deborah looked as though she wanted to say something more, but she remained silent. He knew she was frustrated she couldn't assist him, and he would have loved to have had her help. But he was simply unwilling to risk exposing her to this dreadful disease.

"Well, I need to get on over to the depot, Miss Vandermark. They've brought in a new shipment of supplies."

"Do you have everything you need? Is there anything we can make for you?"

He considered the matter for a moment. "No, I think at this point I have all I need. Mrs. Perkins sends over food for me to eat—when I get a chance."

"You must take care of yourself, Dr. Clayton. We'd be in a dire situation without your healing care."

He smiled. "A few weeks back, I couldn't beg patients to come see me."

"Mother said it often takes a situation like this to change the hearts and minds of a community. It's sad, but maybe now folks can see how important a doctor is to this town."

"Yes, perhaps you're right . . . but then I must hold myself partially responsible for this epidemic."

She frowned and shook her head. "How can that be?"

"I prayed for God to cause the people to put aside their fears and prejudices and allow me to help them. I suppose I should have been more careful with my request, as I didn't stipulate how I would like to see that change accomplished."

Deborah shrugged. "God's ways are often a mystery. You need to trust that He has heard your prayers and answered them by His design—not so much with typhoid, but with your ability to be the one who can help these folks."

"I suppose you're right." Christopher took out his pocket watch and noted the time. "I need to go. Please give my regards to your family and send word if anyone falls ill."

"I will. And Dr. Clayton, I will be praying for you—for your safety in the midst of this work."

She sounded so concerned that he couldn't help but smile. "Never fear, I will wash my hands and wipe down everything . . . twice."

༄

Deborah returned home, feeling only marginally better. She was relieved to finally see Dr. Clayton, but it did little to allay her fears. He looked terribly tired. How long could he go on like this?

"Oh, Lord," she prayed as she sat down to attend the logging books, "please send someone to help him with this sickness. Don't leave him to face this on his own. There are so many to care for." She considered the possibility of sneaking back to town. Perhaps if she crossed the quarantine line by coming through the back side of town through the woods, Dr. Clayton would have no choice but to accept her help. "Once I'm in there, he can hardly send me away. Oh, show me what to do, Lord."

"Deborah? Did you say something?" Her mother came to the office door. "I thought I heard you call."

"I was just praying. I saw Dr. Clayton in town. He looks exhausted, and I was asking God to send someone to help. The doctor won't allow me to assist him, for fear I'd take ill."

"I'm glad for that." Her mother looked at her sternly. "There's nothing to be gained by even one more person getting sick."

"But I know about the precautions. The things I've read and heard about avoiding typhoid are quite simple: Bacteria are spread because of a lack of cleanliness. I would pay attention to such things whether here or in town."

Her mother smiled sadly. "I know you care about Dr. Clayton, but I'm sure the Lord will watch over him. Please promise me you won't put yourself at risk."

Deborah looked up in surprise. "What do you mean?"

"I know you well enough, Deborah. Do not think to slip into town unnoticed. We need you here. Promise me you'll do as the doctor asked."

How did her mother know her heart so well? Deborah might have laughed had the situation not been so serious. "You always know exactly what I'm thinking. I can't fool you at all."

Mother shook her head. "That's no promise."

Deborah drew a deep breath. "But what if that's where God wants me, Mother?"

"If God wanted you there, He would have had you in town when the quarantine was set in place. Remember—this hardly took Him by surprise."

It was a reasonable argument, and Deborah knew that her mother desired only to keep her from harm. She offered her mother a smile. "I promise I won't sneak into town and cross the quarantine line." She thought for a moment and then added, "Unless Dr. Clayton specifically requests me to come."

"Thank you. I'm sure if he asks for your help that I can rest assured the worst is passed and you will not be at risk."

Deborah waited until her mother left the room, then glanced heavenward. "So if you cannot send me to help him, please send someone else. Someone who understands medicine and who will be willing to listen to Dr. Clayton's instruction."

Chapter 21

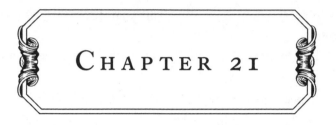

"I have a surprise for everyone," G. W. announced days later as he bounded into the dining room, leather suitcase in hand.

"You're back!" Deborah exclaimed, looking up from the table, as did the others.

"You're late for supper," Mother said with a look of concern. "Did you have trouble in Lufkin? Is something wrong?"

Lizzie eyed him carefully, then let her gaze settle on the leather case. "You took a suitcase just to buy saw blades?"

He laughed and placed the baggage against the wall. "Nothing is wrong. In fact, I would say things are finally lookin' up." He stepped aside, and Brian Decker entered the room, hat in hand.

"Hello, Daughter."

Lizzie gave a squeal and jumped to her feet. "Father!" She ran to him and wrapped herself in his arms. "I can't believe you're here." The hat fell to the floor as he embraced her.

"He was in Lufkin, where I was buying supplies." G. W. explained. "He was fixin' to find you when he overheard my name while I was talking with the storekeeper. God worked it all together for good."

"Oh, indeed He did." Lizzie pulled back. "Why have I not heard from you before now?"

"I've been quite busy. You gave me an assignment, as you'll remember." He kissed her on the head. "And I could hardly come to you or even write until I had accomplished the task."

"Accomplished? Do you mean you have an answer for me?" Lizzie's voice was so hopeful, and G. W. found himself feeling much the same.

"Goodness, Lizzie, let your poor father join us at the table," Mother declared. She motioned for the man to take the seat to her left. "I'm Euphanel Vandermark."

"It's a pleasure to meet you, Mrs. Vandermark. I presume you're Deborah's mother."

"Yes, and you've met my son G. W. This is my younger son, Rob, and my brother-in-law, Arjan Vandermark."

"Good to meet you all." He shook hands with Rob and Arjan before taking a chair.

Euphanel passed him a plate of greens. "We've already prayed, so please dig in."

"But first tell us the news," Lizzie said, slipping into the seat beside her father. "I cannot bear not knowing what you've learned."

"Then let me put your mind at ease." He pulled some papers from inside his coat. "When I received your telegram, I went immediately to Philadelphia to visit a good friend there who happens to be a judge."

"And?" Lizzie leaned forward in anticipation.

"You, my dear, are a free woman. The marriage was not completed."

Lizzie fell back against her chair with a heavy sigh. "Oh, thank you. Thank the Lord."

"The judge said that it wasn't a concern, but he thought it might relieve your mind if we went ahead and arranged an annulment. So we did. These are the papers that will confirm it." He handed them to Lizzie. "Now your mother and Mr. Albright will be no further threat to you."

Lizzie looked to G. W. His heart swelled. She was his. Well, she would be. He picked up the platter of ham steaks and gave himself a double portion.

"I never expected you to come here, Father," Lizzie said gratefully. "Not only because of the distance and expense, but the typhoid outbreak."

"Yes, G. W. told me about the quarantine, but since we weren't going into Perkinsville, we had no difficulty getting here. I was relieved to know you were all unharmed. Typhoid is a terrible disease."

"It is, indeed. We've already lost eight people," G. W.'s mother said sadly. "But we've got a wonderful doctor in town, and hopefully most of the folks are on the mend. Thankfully, no one's taken sick at the boardinghouse where Mrs. Decker and Mr. Albright are staying."

Mr. Decker nodded and took a bowl of grits from his daughter's hand. "That is good news. I'm sure the delay in returning east has been a hardship on Lizzie's mother. There is to be a big suffragette rally in New York City. I know she had planned to attend."

"That's right—she was supposed to speak at one of the affairs. She will be greatly dismayed." Lizzie sighed.

"I think given your father's news," Deborah said, picking up her coffee cup, "the rally will be the least of her concerns."

Lizzie nodded. "Especially in light of what she stood to gain."

"What are you talking about?" Lizzie's father asked.

"Stuart told me he needed to marry me in order to receive an inheritance from his grandfather. Mother, in turn, was promised a helpful vote for her cause if she helped to ensure I honored the marriage."

Her father shook his head in disgust. "I am sorry for that. Your mother has forgotten the importance of love and honor."

Lizzie reached over and squeezed her father's hand. "But you never have."

G. W. was moved by Lizzie's tenderness. Although she had spent more time in her mother's company, he sensed her relationship with her father was much closer.

The rest of the meal passed in catching up on news from the East and sharing about life in Texas. G. W. had already spent a good deal of time talking with Mr. Decker and found the man's company quite enjoyable. Now, however, he longed for time alone with Lizzie. He had an important question to ask her, and now that everything was settled regarding her questionable marriage to Mr. Albright, he wanted to waste no time.

"Miss Lizzie," he said, putting his napkin on the table, "I was wonderin' if you'd take a little walk with me?"

She smiled at G. W. and nodded. "I'd like that very much." She got to her feet. "Let me fetch my shawl." She hurried from the room.

G. W. met his mother's smile as she began to clear the table. Mr. Decker eyed him with a knowing grin. "I suppose," he said as G. W. headed for the front door, "you'll be discussing that matter we talked about in Lufkin."

G. W. returned his grin. "Yes, sir."

Mr. Decker seemed more than pleased. "Good luck."

G. W. knew he'd not rely on luck. His love for Lizzie would be all he needed. He found her waiting by the front door. "Ready?"

She nodded and fixed her gaze on his face. "I've been ready for a long time."

He linked arms with her and opened the door. "Me too."

Lizzie pulled her shawl closer. The air was slightly chilled. The dampness made things cooler and also seemed to enhance the noises of the night. They didn't walk far from the house before G. W. turned to face her. Taking hold of her arms, he pulled her close.

"I don't want to waste any time," he murmured before capturing her lips in a long and passionate kiss.

Lizzie melted against him and wrapped her arms around his neck. He drew her even closer, and she felt her heart skip a beat. *This is what it feels like to truly lose your heart to someone,* she thought. Not only was he physically attractive and a wonderful kisser, but she loved G. W.'s sense of humor, his concern for family and community, his integrity.

"I know I'm rushing things here," he said, "but Deborah is right. I need a wife."

"Just any wife?" Lizzie asked with a teasing frown.

"Hardly," he replied, his lazy grin spreading. "I want you."

She felt a tremor go through her entire frame. "And I want you," she managed to whisper.

"So will you marry me?"

She simply nodded, unable to find the words. Tears came unbidden and slid down her cheeks. She hoped it was too dark for G. W. to see them, but he seemed to know instinctively that they were there. Reaching up, he gently drew his finger across her cheek.

"Don't cry."

"I'm . . . it's just . . . I'm happy. When I think of all I could have lost—knowing true happiness and love . . . well, I can't even speak the thoughts that come to mind."

He took her face in his hands. "Lizzie, life here in Texas won't be easy, as you've already seen for yourself. It ain't gonna be like the life you had back East."

"I know, but I don't care. I like working alongside your mother and sister. I know I have a lot to learn, but I will endeavor to make you a good wife."

"You're already perfect for me." He brushed his lips upon hers in a brief kiss. "I told your father on the trip from Lufkin that I couldn't ever love another woman as much as I love you."

"You spoke to my father about this?" She couldn't contain her surprise. "What did he have to say about it?" They walked back toward the house. From the light glowing from the windows, Lizzie could see the happiness on G. W.'s face.

"I asked him for his blessing, and he gave it. He could tell that my love for you was real."

Lizzie smiled, imagining her father's thoughts as he sat through dinner, knowing what G. W. intended to ask her. Her smile faded, however, as she thought of her mother and Stuart. No doubt they would do whatever they could to stop the wedding.

"Can we marry right away?" she asked. "I mean, could we marry tomorrow?"

He laughed heartily and twirled her in circle. "You are a bold one—exactly what I need."

She felt her cheeks grow hot. She realized too late how forward—almost risqué—her comment sounded. "I . . . well, it's just that . . ." Lizzie knew there was no sense in trying to explain and lowered her head.

"Darlin', don't you go gettin' all red-faced and shy. We can marry right this minute, if you can find us a preacher. You won't get any argument out of me. It's been sheer torture to spend all this time so close to you and not be able to . . . well . . ." It was his turn to look embarrassed.

Lizzie could only giggle. She put her hand to her mouth as he threw her a questioning look.

"So you think this is funny, do you?"

She nodded and giggled all the more. G. W. smiled and took hold of her once again. Pulling her tight against him, he locked her in an iron embrace. "I'll give you something to giggle about. I've been wantin' to tickle you since you first showed up. First it was because you never smiled—you always seemed so serious. Then I just wanted your smile to be because of me."

Lizzie tried to twist in his arms, but he held her fast. When he ran his fingers lightly under her chin and down the side of her neck, it wasn't giggling that Lizzie thought of. She sighed and her knees nearly buckled.

"So do you suppose," she whispered, "there might be a preacher nearby?"

G. W. halted and gazed deep into her eyes before roaring with laughter. In one quick move, he threw her over his shoulder and marched toward the house. "You go pack. We'll take the train to Lufkin tomorra."

"Put me down before someone sees us," Lizzie protested, pounding against G. W.'s back with her fist. "G. W.!"

He only laughed all the more. "I like a gal with some fight in her. Lizzie Decker, you're gonna be the joy of my life."

She relaxed against him and smiled to herself. G. W. pulled her from his shoulder and cradled her in his arms as he climbed the steps to the porch. When he reached the top, he put her down. Shaking his head, he put her at arm's length.

His voice was a hoarse whisper. "You'd best go along now before I kiss you again."

ꕥ

Deborah awaited Lizzie's return to their room. She was hoping that G. W. would propose to her friend, and when Lizzie walked, or rather floated, into the room, Deborah was certain the question had been asked and approved.

"So when's the wedding?"

Lizzie gave a sigh. "Tomorrow we're going to take the train to Lufkin."

"Leave it to G. W. to waste no time."

Her friend flushed. "It was a mutually agreed upon idea."

Deborah couldn't help but laugh. "Spoken like a true daughter of a suffragette. Stand up for your rights, and all that."

Lizzie plopped down on the side of her bed. "Oh, Deborah, I've never been so happy. G. W. is everything I could ever want in a husband. He's perfect. So kind. So smart. So gentle."

"Goodness, but you sound completely daft over him." Deborah shook her head. "Well, I suppose it's a good thing you brought your own wedding gown."

"Oh, I don't plan to get married to him in that dress," Lizzie said. "I'm a simple Texas woman now—not an eastern socialite."

"That doesn't mean you can't dress beautifully for your wedding day." Deborah smiled. "Although I'm sure G. W. won't care what you wear so long as you say 'I do' when the preacher asks if you'll pledge your life to him."

Lizzie smiled and nodded. "I'm so happy, Deborah. I want to cry and laugh all at the same time. It's like all of my dreams came true in a single moment." She looked to her friend. "I even get to be your sister and be a part of a real family who loves each other. I've wanted brothers and sisters all of my life, and now I'll have them."

Deborah laughed and threw a pillow at the dreamy-eyed girl. "And you'll see just how ornery siblings can be. All of this time I've just been being nice to you because you were a guest."

"Well, so long as I get to marry G. W., you can treat me any way you like."

Deborah rolled her eyes and got to her feet. "Guess we'd better get packed."

"We?"

"Of course. Do you think I'm going to send you off to Lufkin without a maid of honor? Goodness, you'll probably have the whole lot of us. Mother would never want to miss seeing her son get married, and Rob and Uncle Arjan will enjoy a day in the big city . . . well, as big as it comes this close to Perkinsville."

"Oh, do you really think they'll join us? That will be wonderful!"

"Wild pigs couldn't keep them from coming." Deborah paused and looked at Lizzie. "Who could have imagined when we ran away from your sham wedding in Philadelphia that you were actually running away to find true love?"

Lizzie met her gaze and a sob caught in her throat as she began to speak. "You told me . . . God would work out all of the details. And now He has." She started to cry and Deborah immediately came to her side.

"He always will," she told her friend. "He is always faithful." She thought of Dr. Clayton just then and realized that God would be faithful to him, as well. She needn't worry about whether or not the doctor would have help. God could and would provide whatever was necessary to get the job done.

"Come on," she said, pulling away from Lizzie. "We've got work to do."

Chapter 22

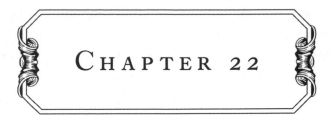

The wedding was a rushed affair, but everyone involved enjoyed the event. The bride vacillated between looking as though she might faint and nervously giggling through most of the ceremony. The groom, on the other hand, grinned like the cat that had found his way into the cream crock.

Deborah couldn't have been more pleased for her dear friend and brother. She found that the very idea of Lizzie being with her in Texas made the life she'd chosen more bearable. It wasn't that she didn't want to be there with her family; she'd just grown accustomed to spending her days reading and learning while at the university. Now that part of her life was over.

"The train is finally coming into the station," G. W. announced. "Guess the Rabbit didn't jump the tracks this time."

Deborah smiled and nodded. She made her way to Lizzie and hugged her close. "I'll see you in a few days."

Lizzie and G. W. had opted to remain in Lufkin for a few days of privacy, while the others would journey through the night to reach home. Deborah released her friend and turned to go as the train conductor approached them.

"Word's come that there's a bad storm brewing just off the coast," he announced. "Looks to be a hurricane comin' in."

Deborah frowned, while her uncle pressed the inquiry. "When did you get word?"

"Just came over the telegraph. One of the ships brought news to Houston, and they've sent out wires along the track."

Uncle Arjan looked at Deborah's mother and shook his head. "Might be we should stay put. No tellin' how fast that storm's movin' in or which direction it'll take." He turned to the other men. "I've seen them come on fast and furious. You don't want to be on the Rabbit when it hits."

"I agree," G. W. said. "Why don't you take rooms at the hotel? I know it's an added expense, but it'll be for the best."

"That seems wise." Mother looked quite grim. "Sissy will know what's happened if she gets word about the storm. She won't fret, and she'll see to the animals."

Lizzie was wringing her hands, so Deborah went to her side to reassure her. "Don't look so worried. These storms occur from time to time—especially in the late summer and fall. There's nothing you can do to keep them from coming, so we simply prepare for them the best we can."

"I've never been in a hurricane, but I've read about the destruction they can cause."

Deborah could remember some very bad storms in the past but certainly didn't want to give her friend undue fright. She believed they were far enough inland that any damage would be lessened considerably—at least she hoped so. "The best thing is to use good judgment. Traveling home just now would not be prudent to say the least." She thought of the folks in Perkinsville. Deborah excused herself. "Lizzie, I'll be right back."

She hurried over to where the engineer was just starting to climb back aboard. "Excuse me. Do you know if the folks in Perkinsville were warned?"

He stepped back down and turned to face her. "Yes, miss. We've left word at every town on our way. Of course, Perkinsville is in quarantine, but they got the message. I blasted the train whistle until the depot master came to see what the trouble was." He smiled from behind a thick mustache. "They'd been wired and were already making preparations."

She nodded, relieved. Her mother came to stand beside her. "Is something wrong, Deborah? I saw you hurry over here."

She met Mother's gentle expression. "No. I wanted to make sure the folks in Perkinsville had been warned about the storm. The engineer assured me he told the depot master and said plans were already being made to assure their safety."

Mother put her arm around Deborah and hugged her close. "Don't worry. Folks there know what to do. I'm sure they'll keep Dr. Clayton apprised."

She looked at her mother rather surprised. "I care about everyone there, not just Dr. Clayton."

"I know that, but I also realize you have a special . . . fondness for him."

Deborah didn't want her mother to think there was something more between her and the doctor than there was. "Dr. Clayton is just a good friend, Mother. I appreciate his intellect, and he doesn't seem to mind that as a woman, I like to expand my knowledge. Don't believe there to be anything more than that."

Her mother laughed. "You are such a goose sometimes. Come along. The fellas are taking our things over to the hotel. Hopefully they've got room for all of us."

She wasn't sure what her mother had meant. Was she implying that Deborah's worries were unfounded—that of course she knew the doctor was only a friend? Or was she suggesting that Deborah was a goose for trying to make her believe something other than the truth?

But that is *the truth.* Deborah rejoined Lizzie and together they walked to where Uncle Arjan waited for them. *What in the world did Mother mean? But if I ask, she's only going to know that I'm troubled by her statement and that, in turn, might lead her to believe that I do feel something more for Dr. Clayton.* Mother and Lizzie took hold of Uncle Arjan's arms, while Deborah followed rather absentmindedly behind.

Surely Mother didn't suspect that there were romantic feelings between her and Dr. Clayton. He was a nice man—quite handsome and very intelligent. She did enjoy the time she spent with him, but she wasn't sweet on him. Or was she? *Oh, grief and nonsense, what should I do?*

Her concern was quickly dismissed when a powerful grip took hold of her arm and pulled her violently to the side of the road. Deborah felt herself falling just as a freight wagon barreled around the corner behind her. She landed with a thud against the firm, lean frame of the man who'd rescued her, then quickly scrambled up to regain her legs.

"I am so sorry," she said, dusting off her skirt.

"Deborah, are you all right?" her mother's frantic voice sounded from behind. "Oh goodness, look at your gloves."

She saw how dirty her gloves were and quickly tucked them into the folds of her skirt. *Funny that we should worry about gloves at a time like this*, she thought.

Looking up, Deborah caught sight of her hero. He was tall—probably about G. W.'s height—and dressed in the unmistakable style of a ranch hand. Throwing her a lazy smile, he shrugged.

"Afternoon, miss."

Deborah laughed as Uncle Arjan extended a hand toward the cowboy. "Thank you, son. We're very grateful for what you just did."

"Did you not see the wagon, Deborah?" her mother questioned.

"I'm afraid I was daydreaming." She smiled at the stranger. "I'm Deborah Vandermark. Thank you for your assistance . . . and the soft landing."

He grinned and slapped his leg. "You're certainly welcome. I hope you're no worse for the venture."

Deborah tested her weight on each foot and flexed her arms. "I seem to be completely unscathed."

"Are you sure, Deborah?" Lizzie asked, her expression one of grave concern. "I thought for certain that wagon would knock you to the ground. I was just looking back to say something to you when I saw him come bearing toward you."

"I'm fine, truly I am. Thanks to Mr. . . ." Deborah looked at the man. "I do not know your name."

"Jacob Francis Wythe. Though my friends just call me Slim."

"Thank you, Mr. Wythe, for saving my daughter. Would you care to join us for supper tonight so that we can thank you properly? We're hoping to take rooms at the hotel and would be happy to have you dine with us this evening," Mother said.

The man's dusty face lit up, although his expression sobered. "I'd be honored, ma'am. But you know, it's not necessary."

Something in the way he added the latter didn't sound quite as sincere. Perhaps he was afraid of missing a good meal.

"I know it isn't necessary, but it's exactly what I'd like to do. I know Deborah's brothers will want to meet you and thank you, as well."

Mr. Wythe picked up his hat and slapped it against his leg, causing a cloud of dust to rise. "I'd be happy to join you, ma'am."

"Let's say about five-thirty; would that be all right?"

"Yes, Miz Vandermark. I'll be there." Casting a quick glance at Deborah, he planted the hat on his head, then tipped it to her and to the other two women. "Thank you kindly."

Deborah watched him saunter off as though he'd just taken first place at the county fair. She couldn't help but giggle.

Mother looked at her and shook her head. "What in the world is so funny? You could have been killed! You know a town this size is no place to lose your thoughts."

Taking the admonition in stride, Deborah nodded and looped her arm with her mother's. "I know. It was pure foolishness. I won't do it again, but . . . it did introduce us to that nice cowboy."

Mother rolled her eyes while Lizzie laughed out loud. Uncle Arjan shook his head. "There are easier ways to meet suitors, Niece. If I were you, I'd try a church social next time or maybe a house raisin'."

"I wasn't thinking of courtship, Uncle. I thought perhaps we could buy some beef—that's all."

At the hotel, they found the men had secured rooms for everyone. Rob and Arjan would share a room, as would Lizzie and G. W. Mother and Deborah would be together, and Mr. Decker would have a room of his own.

"Your room is upstairs and just to the left. There's a washroom across the hall," G. W. said, handing Mother the key. "We'll bring up the bags."

Mother nodded and led the way. "After all that excitement, I'm ready to rest for a bit."

"Excitement?" G. W. asked.

Deborah shook her head. "I'm sure Lizzie will tell you all about it. It starts out rather bad but ends with the possibility of negotiating the purchase of beef." She gave her brother a wink. "Who knows what might happen next?"

ꕥ

The bad weather pushed in with frightening speed. Thick, heavy rain clouds built to the southeast and seemed to boil and churn with great fury as they made their way north. Deborah prayed that the damage would be minimal, then altered the prayer to ask that there be no damage at all. Hurricanes generally played out most of their strength on the coast, and she was determined not to ruin the evening fretting over what might or might not come.

Supper was a rather somber affair, dominated by talk of the upcoming storm. Deborah toyed with her fried chicken. The meal was delicious, but she couldn't help but be intrigued by the man sitting opposite her. There was something about Mr. Wythe that captured her attention.

"So where are you from, Mr. Wythe?" Mother asked.

"Please, ma'am, could you not call me that? If you don't like Slim, how about Jake?"

She smiled. "Very well. Jake."

"I'm from up Dallas way, ma'am. My father has a spread up there."

"And what brings you to Lufkin?" Uncle Arjan asked.

"My aunt. She was up visiting my mama—her sister. I escorted her home and was planning to head back tomorrow. I guess I'll see what's happening with the storm before I get too devoted to the idea."

Arjan nodded. "That would be wise. So you'll stay with your aunt?"

"Yes, sir. She's by herself, so having me here during the storm could be useful."

Mother exchanged a look with Deborah. "I wish we'd known about your aunt. I would happily have had her join us here tonight."

"She was much too tired, ma'am. The trip was hard on her. Wore her out."

"I can understand that," Mother replied. "The trip up here this morning had me dreading the ride home. Our little narrow gauge to Perkinsville isn't exactly a smooth ride."

"That's understating it considerably," G. W. said with a grin.

"So what brought you folks to Lufkin?"

"G. W. and Lizzie were married this afternoon," Deborah said before anyone else could reply. She liked it when he fixed his blue eyes on her.

"A wedding, eh? So tonight we should give them a shivaree."

"I think the storm will provide all the wedding night interference needed," G. W. replied. Lizzie was turning three shades of red, and Deborah couldn't help but grin. She looked down at the table so that Lizzie couldn't see her response.

"Have you lived in Texas long?" Mother asked.

"All my life. I was born on the ranch." Jake fixed a smile on Lizzie and then on Deborah before looking back at Euphanel. "But I don't reckon the ladies are nearly as pretty up there as they are down this way."

"You are sweet to say so." Mother shook her head as if amused.

"Have you lived on the ranch all of your life?" Lizzie questioned.

He nodded. "For most of it. I was a few years at the Agricultural and Mechanical College of Texas."

"You attended college?" Deborah asked in surprise. Everyone looked at her as though she'd insulted the young man, and indeed, it was starting to sound that way to Deborah, as well. "I would have thought the ranch would have kept you much too busy to go away to school," she quickly added.

"My folks wanted me to be the first in the family to have a college education," he said proudly.

"I find that admirable," Mother interjected. "I'm sure your studies have benefited you, even in ranch life."

"Yes, ma'am. I learned a lot of mathematics. Got some military training, too."

"Military?" G. W. questioned.

"Yup. They require all the students to participate in the Corps of Cadets. My pa fought in the War Between the States and figured it would do me well to have some experience. My ma would just as soon there be no more wars."

Mother glanced at G. W. and Rob before replying, "I feel the same way. So tell us about your folks. Were they born here, as well?"

"Yes, ma'am. My granddaddy came to Texas in 1840. My pa was born the next year. We're Texan, through and through."

They heard the first drops of rain hit the small window behind the table. Deborah glanced over her shoulder and wondered again how bad the storm might be. The upstairs windows had all been shuttered against the weather, but a few of the downstairs windows were open to let in the night air. The hotel manager now moved through the dining room, closing these down.

"Sorry, folks, but the wind is pickin' up and will soon have the place drenched."

Most diners appeared unconcerned. They noted the situation, then went back to their conversation and food.

Deborah braved a glance at Jake and found him watching her. He smiled in a sympathetic manner. "Are you worried, Miss Deborah?"

"Concerned, but not overly worried. How about you?"

"Not for myself, but for my aunt. I should probably excuse myself." He got up and pulled the linen napkin free from where he'd tucked it into his shirt.

"Please give your aunt our best," Mother said. "I hope she'll forgive the oversight of not inviting her to join us. Perhaps another time."

He nodded. "I'll let her know." He started to leave, then paused. Looking directly at Deborah, he asked, "Will you be stayin' in town long?"

"It's doubtful," Uncle Arjan replied before Deborah could answer. "We have a loggin' business to get back to, and this storm could be wreakin' havoc on our livelihood. We'll head out as soon as it's safe to go."

"Well then, if I don't see you again, it was a pleasure." He smiled at each person then looked back to Deborah and winked. "Watch out for freight wagons."

She smiled. "I assure you, I won't make that mistake again. I'm normally quite capable of taking care of myself."

He headed to the door but called over his shoulder, "I don't doubt that for a minute."

ꕥ

That night, as the rain fell hard against the windows, Deborah enjoyed her mother's attention and conversation. With long determined strokes, Mother brushed Deborah's thick dark hair, just as she had long ago. There was something so very comforting in the action.

"He was certainly a charming young man," Mother began. "I think he was quite smitten with you."

"Oh, I hope not," Deborah admitted. "Although he was very kind. I certainly owe him my life. That wagon wasn't slowing for anyone."

"And he's educated. Perhaps there might be a future with him. I wouldn't be surprised at all if he makes it down to Perkinsville for a visit."

Deborah hadn't expected this from her mother. "First you talk of Dr. Clayton and me, and now Mr. Wythe. Goodness, but you sound as though you're trying to get rid of me, and I've only just returned."

Mother stopped and came around to face her. "I would never want to get rid of you, but you will find someone and fall in love one day. I think either of those men might be suitable choices."

Deborah shook her head and got to her feet. "I don't. Neither would be willing to remain in Perkinsville. I know for a fact that Dr. Clayton is only doing this to help his family. As for Mr. Wythe—well, he no doubt wishes to continue with the family ranch, and that's near Dallas."

"What are you saying, exactly?" Mother looked at her oddly. "You surely don't mean to suggest that you have to remain in Perkinsville for the rest of your life."

"Well, coming home only proved to me how much my skills were needed. Mother, you have no idea what a mess I found in the books. People owed us money and we owed them, and it was completely mixed up as to who was to receive what. Proper billings hadn't gone out. The only person who knew for sure what was going on was Uncle Arjan, and he kept most of the information in his head. That wasn't useful to anyone."

"He knew very well how to run this business, and don't you suggest otherwise."

Mother's stern response surprised Deborah. "I didn't mean to say he didn't. It was just that . . . well, while he knows what he's doing, no one else really had an understanding of it. What would happen if he died . . . like Father?"

Her mother frowned. "I don't think I could survive that."

Deborah hadn't expected that response but continued. "Exactly. None of us could have survived it easily. We would have had to talk to nearly everyone who'd done business with us to discover what we owed them and what they owed us. And we could only hope they didn't cheat us."

Mother reached out to touch Deborah's face. "I know you've always wanted to help, but I will not stand by and let you tie yourself to the business, forsaking happiness. I couldn't bear it if you fell in love and turned it away because you felt obligated to the family. We can always hire a bookkeeper, Deborah. True love is more difficult to find."

She considered her mother's remark for a moment. The idea of being needed by her family had always driven Deborah to learn—to excel in her studies. For certain, she loved knowledge, but there had always been that desire to better her family's situation. She had convinced herself over the years that she might somehow be able to guide them into a better life.

"I don't know what to say, Mother. I won't lie to you and tell you that I haven't believed it necessary to return and help you all. It was Papa's hope that I could attend school and help Vandermark Logging."

"Where did you get that idea, Deborah?" her mother asked.

"Your father wanted only for you to have the things you desired. He never wanted you to work or labor over anything."

"What are you saying?" Deborah whispered.

Mother looked at her oddly. "Did you only go to school because you thought your father wanted you to?"

Deborah felt an unwelcomed sensation run through her body. It was like suddenly realizing she'd been taken for a fool. "I thought I was needed."

"You are, darling," her mother replied. "But not at the price of your own happiness. You weren't made to be alone in this world." She smiled. "Not with a face like yours. Not with a heart like yours. Your aunt Alva sacrificed love for her family, and I won't see you do the same. Your father always used to say that there was a very lucky man out there somewhere who was going to be quite blessed to take you as his wife."

Deborah forced a smile. Her mother couldn't possibly understand her confusion, and to press for further answers might only serve to upset her. "I can just hear him saying that." Thoughts of her father were bittersweet. "I miss him . . . especially at times like this, with the storm. He always used to make me feel so safe when I was little. I would curl up on his lap and he'd wrap those big arms around me and hold me close. Nothing scared me then. I knew any harmful thing would have to come through him to get me."

Her mother smiled sadly. "He loved you—loved all of us dearly. He was taken from us too soon, but I know he's in a better place."

Deborah wrapped her arms around her mother. "I'm sorry if I made you sad or caused you to worry about me. Let's forget it for now. I'm happy to be right where I am. I don't want to think about leaving again. Not for a long, long while."

ഗ്ദ

Lizzie knocked on her father's door and hoped he wouldn't mind the disturbance. She'd had so little time alone with him and wanted to talk to him before he returned home to his other family.

He opened the door and looked confused. "Is something wrong, Lizzie?"

"Not at all. I just wanted to speak to you for a few minutes."

He nodded. "Come in, but I have to tell you, a bride should be with her groom on their wedding night."

She entered the small room and smiled. "I'll have the rest of my life with G. W. I just wanted a few moments with you. I can't bear that you'll be leaving so soon."

"Well, I know I've only arrived here, but I've already been gone from home for over a month. First with my time in Philadelphia—then my travel here." He smiled. "I've missed you, Lizzie. I missed all of what might have been."

She swallowed down her grief. "I know that, Father. Mother always said you were much too busy to be bothered, but I always hoped that wasn't true."

"It was never true." He reached out to touch her face. "You were my pride and joy then and you remain so now. I only wanted the best for you, and I'm sorry that I didn't work harder to keep you with me. I was convinced it would be better for you in the long run if you stayed with your mother. Convinced, too, that a strife-filled house was no home. That's the reason I left as easily as I did."

"I know," Lizzie said, placing her hand atop his. "I always knew."

He nodded very slowly. "I prayed you would. Just as I pray now that you will never know such pain and separation. You have a good man in G. W. He loves you and he will move mountains to see you happy."

She smiled. "You've moved the only mountain in our way. I'm very blessed." She leaned up on tiptoe and kissed his cheek. "I love you, Father."

Chapter 23

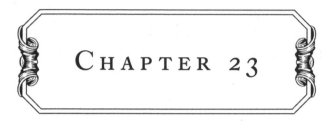

Looks like the house and barns bore the storm well," G. W. announced, sizing up the scene as they disembarked the train. The dogs caught sight of them and came running and howling.

"I do hope there wasn't any damage to the logging site," Deborah heard her mother tell Uncle Arjan amidst the baying of the dogs.

"Nothing we cain't handle, I'm sure," he replied. "The boys and I will get right over there and see what the situation looks like. Don't hold supper for us." Arjan looked to Rob and G. W. "Boys, fetch the horses." G. W. nodded, then gave Lizzie a quick kiss despite his brother's teasing.

"You two are upsettin' the dogs." Rob reached down to scratch the nearest hound behind the ears. "There now, don't be frettin', Decatur. They'll soon grow tired of each other."

"Hardly," G. W. said, winking at his wife. Lizzie blushed and looked away.

Sissy greeted them at the door with a big smile on her face. "Shore glad to see ya'll back safe. Blowed up quite a bit 'round here, but we held on tight."

"And how's David?" Mother asked.

"He be doin' fine, jest fine. 'Nother few days, and he be back to work."

Deborah waited until the men had gone to announce she was heading to town. "I want to see how things are going with the quarantine."

"Oh, quarantine done been lifted, Miss Deborah."

"That's wonderful news!" Deborah turned to Lizzie. "Do you want to come with me?"

"No, I'm weary from the train and have no desire to see Mother and Stuart just yet. You go ahead. If you don't mind, I'm going to go upstairs and move my things."

Mother nodded and turned to Deborah. "I don't like you driving into town by yourself."

"Iffen you like, Miz Euphanel, I ken ride into town with Miss Deborah."

Mother smiled and cast a quick glance at Deborah. "I would like that very much. Let me prepare a grocery list, and you can fetch what we need."

"I already done started one," Sissy said, laughing. "It be all up here." She tapped her head.

Deborah hurried upstairs to retrieve Dr. Clayton's medical journals. She was quite anxious to know how he was faring now that the quarantine had been lifted. Surely it meant that most everyone was on the mend.

She noticed that Lizzie was packing her things and felt a

momentary sense of loss. Mother had insisted Lizzie and G. W. take the big downstairs bedroom that had once been hers to share with Father.

"I'm going to miss you," Deborah said, clutching the journals. "It won't be the same without you. Still, I suppose G. W. would be rather unwilling to let you stay here."

Lizzie gave a little laugh. "G. W. wouldn't be the only one. You make a great friend, but I prefer rooming with my husband."

"You both seem so happy."

"Oh, we are. I never imagined it could be like this, Deborah." She seemed to glow with the joy that bubbled from within. "I'll happily live here the rest of my life."

"You won't miss Philadelphia?"

Lizzie looked at her as if she'd lost her mind. "There is nothing there to miss. You were one of the only friends I had. Mother certainly will have no use for me now." She sat down on the bed. "But you know . . . she never did. I was only a pawn in her chess game for women's rights. It makes me so sad, especially now that I'm a part of your family and know how it could have been." She paused. "It must have been hard to leave them and go away to school."

"I suppose it was at first, but of course, I was doing it for them. I knew I'd be back here one day."

Lizzie frowned. "What do you mean? I thought you went to school because you loved learning."

"Oh, I do. Don't get me wrong." Deborah held up the journals as if for proof. "I love to study, even now. Medicine is particularly fascinating."

"Or is it the doctor who fascinates you?"

Deborah found she couldn't reply. When she found her voice she simply mumbled, "Sissy's waiting on me. I'll be back before you know it."

She hurried from the room before Lizzie could comment further. Why would her best friend assume something was going on between her and Dr. Clayton? Was it possible for feelings to develop without a person realizing it?

If she lost her heart to someone like Dr. Clayton, it would interfere with her plans to help her family. He'd already encouraged her to study medicine, and while Deborah liked the idea, she still felt she couldn't let it take her away from the family's logging business.

There was no other choice. She would have to distance herself from Dr. Clayton . . . and from reading his medical journals.

On the ride into town she contemplated how best to handle the matter. Perhaps she'd just tell Dr. Clayton that with the increase of work the logging company had taken on, there would be no time for reading. She frowned.

I can't lie to him. It wouldn't be right. I've been able to talk to him about most everything. I'll just tell him the truth.

Sissy looked at Deborah and narrowed her dark eyes. "You shore look upset about somethin'. You comin' down sick?"

"No, I was just thinking about the work that needs to be done." At least that wasn't a lie. "I'm fine, honestly."

"Uh-huh."

Deborah had never been able to fool the older woman, so with a sigh, Deborah gave Sissy a hint of a smile. "I guess I'm just trying to figure out where life is taking me. I want to do what's pleasing to God, but I'm starting to wonder exactly what it is He wants me to do."

Sissy nodded. "Jest ask Him, child. He's faithful."

"I guess part of the problem is, I thought I knew what He wanted. All of my life, I've seen the lack of education keep Father and the boys from making a better way for themselves. So many people around here can't read—they have so little. I just wanted to help my family. Maybe I was wrong."

"Helpin' folks is good—ain't never knowed it to be wrong. You folks always done well enough, Miss Deborah."

"But I want so much more for them."

"Mebbe they didn't want more. Could be they were jest happy with life like it was."

Deborah thought about that for a few minutes. Perhaps Sissy was right. It was possible that Deborah, in her travels and education, had imposed her own dreams over those of her parents. But didn't everyone want a better life?

The question warred within her. Her father had always seemed happy enough. Rutger Vandermark was not known for complaining. Maybe that was because he had little to complain about.

Still, as good as that thought was, Deborah felt a sense of confusion. Since becoming old enough to think about others before herself, she had been driven to help her family find better success. She had thought it was up to her to learn whatever was necessary to help them further the business. Was it possible she had wasted her life seeking the wrong thing?

Sissy hummed an old hymn and kept the horse moving down the road. She seemed quite content, yet Deborah considered the woman's life difficult. Most white folks looked down on the people of color. The war had scarred and damaged the country. Even for the slaves who had been freed, Deborah saw fear and desperation. Everything they'd known for generations had been stripped from them. It wasn't so different from when they had been captured and forced into slavery to begin with.

The slaves had been set free, but it wasn't a true freedom. Even Sissy chose to come west to continue working for the Vandermarks. It was a comfort, Deborah had heard the older woman say. A comfort to have an understanding of the folks you were working with. Life had changed so little for Sissy, as was true of many blacks.

Deborah shook her head, but Sissy didn't seem to notice. "Are you happy, Sissy?"

"Gracious—I'm blessed through and through, Miss Deborah. Why you ask?"

Deborah shrugged. "I just wondered. You always seem happy." She smiled. "It encourages me."

Sissy laughed. "It be the joy of the Lord. Never forget God's joy, Miss Deborah."

Nodding, Deborah found herself longing for the confidence and happiness that Sissy had found in God. She supposed that Sissy's situation had left her with few choices. She could forsake God, thinking Him cruel for allowing her oppression, or she could turn to God for strength.

Sissy began humming again and then broke into song. " 'There is a balm in Gilead, to make the wounded whole; there is a balm in Gilead, to heal the sin sick soul. Sometimes I feels discouraged, and think my work's in vain, but then the Holy Spirit revives my soul again. Oh, there is a balm in Gilead . . .' "

She stopped and gave Deborah a big smile. "God always knows what dis old woman needs. Hard times or good," she said, as if reading Deborah's questioning mind, "He be a balm to my soul."

"But do you find yourself longing for more?"

Sissy chuckled. "Folks can always be longin' for more, Miss Deborah. It's the learnin' to be content what gets the soul through. Whether there be more or less—the Lord is my strength."

Ten minutes later, they arrived at the edge of town. It was good to see the bustling activity that suggested Perkinsville was very nearly back to normal. Deborah climbed down from the wagon almost before Sissy had brought it to a stop.

"I'll meet you back here shortly. I promise I won't be long." Sissy nodded and set the brake.

Deborah hurried down the still-muddy road and made her way to Dr. Clayton's. There were several people waiting outside the establishment, and a half dozen more greeted her when she entered.

Deborah greeted each person before approaching the office door. She peered inside but found no one. Slipping into the room, she closed the door behind her. No doubt Dr. Clayton was busy with a patient. She'd just write him a note and leave the journals.

Sitting at the desk, Deborah quickly located some paper and took up the ink pen. She thought for a moment on what she'd say, then began to write. She'd gotten no further than "Dear Dr. Clayton" when the examination room door opened and the man himself accompanied Sally Stevens from the room. In her arms was a small infant.

Dr. Clayton's face lit up when he spied her. "Miss Vandermark. This is a pleasant surprise."

Sally turned and smiled at Deborah. She held the sleeping baby up for Deborah to see. "Come meet my daughter Matilda. Doc says she's perfect."

Deborah got up from the desk and came to where Sally stood. "Oh, she's beautiful. I'm so happy for you."

"I was afraid John might be disappointed that she wasn't a boy, but he said he's mighty pleased."

"And how could he not be?" Dr. Clayton said. "Now, Sally, you remember what I told you about keeping things clean."

"I will. You can count on that." She looked to Deborah. "You'll let your mama know 'bout Matilda, won'tcha?"

"Of course." Deborah knew it wouldn't have taken any longer than attending church on Sunday for everyone to be caught up on the happenings of this small community, but she'd share the news just the same.

Sally left the office and Dr. Clayton turned to Deborah. "What brings you here?"

"I brought back your journals. I was just leaving you a note."

"Do you want to look through the stack and see what's there that you haven't already read?"

"No thank you. I've decided to put medicine aside and focus on my job." As he opened his mouth to respond, she hurried to change the subject. "What happened with the typhoid epidemic? Did we lose more folks?"

His expression revealed he wished to return to the subject of her decision, but he addressed her question instead. "We had two more deaths, for a total of ten. Everyone is on the mend now, and hopefully there won't be another outbreak. Folks have started following my instructions on cleanliness and boiling water."

"Good. I'm so glad to hear that. I don't suppose you'll ever convince Mrs. Foster, but at least others can see the good of it."

"On the contrary." He opened the examination room door and revealed Margaret Foster wiping down the exam table. "Mrs. Foster has become a great asset. Once she recovered, she began to work with me."

Deborah tried not to look too surprised, but she couldn't imagine the two people working together. "Hello, Mrs. Foster," she managed to say when the older woman made her way over.

"Afternoon. Your family escape the typhoid?"

"Yes, ma'am. We're all doing just fine. I must say, I never expected to find you working with Dr. Clayton."

The woman nodded. "God done a work in me, to be sure. My pride nearly cost me my life—other folks, too. Now I've mended my ways. Helpin' here is my way of makin' it up to the doctor."

"Like I told you before, Mrs. Foster, your apology was enough. Please call the next patient." Dr. Clayton turned to Deborah. "So as you can see, I'm doing much better than the last time we spoke."

"I've been praying that God would send someone to assist you." Deborah held further comments about never imagining it would be Margaret Foster who'd answer that need.

"Well, He certainly did that. Now, however, I'd best get back to work. As you saw out front, folks are making up for lost time." He grinned and escorted her to the side door. "It'll be easier to go this way."

Deborah turned to meet his gaze. She felt a strange emptiness at his dismissal. He obviously didn't need her—not that she'd expected that he did. "I'm glad folks have come around to seeing the good you have to offer."

He smiled. "Me too. I hated sitting around, taking Mr. Perkins's money without earning it. Guess those days are behind me."

As Mrs. Foster brought in another patient, Deborah knew there would be no opportunity to speak her mind. She supposed it wasn't really necessary that Dr. Clayton understand her situation. After all, he seemed perfectly content to work on without her.

She bid him farewell and made her way back to the commissary without so much as a backward glance. *I'm doing the right thing,* she told herself. *The necessary thing.* Then why did it leave her feeling so uncomfortable?

Sissy was already waiting in the wagon when Deborah climbed up. Neither made a comment as Sissy guided the horses toward the road home.

"Wait! Deborah Vandermark, don't you even think to leave without first speaking to me."

It was Harriet Decker. The woman was positively huffing and puffing like a steam engine as she bounded out from the boardinghouse. She came to a stop on Deborah's side of the wagon.

"Come down here immediately," the woman ordered.

Deborah looked at Sissy. "Excuse me." Climbing down, Deborah wondered exactly what she should say to the woman. She didn't have long to contemplate, however.

"I've heard the most appalling rumor—that my Elizabeth ran off and married your brother. Is it true?"

"It is." Deborah said nothing more, feeling the need to guard her words.

"She's already married to Mr. Albright! She cannot give herself to another." The woman's voice seemed edged with hysteria.

"She is not married to Mr. Albright," Deborah replied. "Mr. Decker arrived a short time back. He announced that he'd checked into the matter, and there was no real marriage. He secured Lizzie an annulment, just to satisfy any further protests, and that left her free to marry my brother."

"This is preposterous!" Harriet waggled a finger in Deborah's face. "This will not be tolerated."

Deborah shrugged. "Lizzie and G. W. are man and wife. The ceremony was legally completed in Lufkin and witnessed by the family. Your ex-husband even gave Lizzie away, so you see it was all done properly . . . this time."

Something between a moan and a wail broke from Mrs. Decker's lips. "I cannot believe how he goes out of his way to do me harm. You have no idea what you've done."

"Lizzie is the one who has stood up for herself and made her own way—just as you've always suggested she should. Now if you'll excuse me, I need to make my way home before the light is gone." Deborah stepped up and seated herself in the wagon.

"This isn't the end of the matter," Harriet Decker called out. "Mr. Albright will never allow for this."

"Mr. Albright will need to take it up with Lizzie's husband, then. Good day, Mrs. Decker."

Sissy snapped the lines and the horses continued past the boardinghouse. Deborah shook her head. Mrs. Decker wasn't known to back down from a fight, and this time would surely be no exception.

Chapter 24

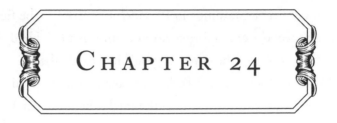

Lizzie had known her mother would waste little time before making a scene at the Vandermark house. After Deborah reported their encounter in Perkinsville, Lizzie had steeled herself for what was sure to come next. When her mother and Stuart arrived the next day, Lizzie invited them into the front room as if nothing were amiss. She allowed her mother to be the one to bring up the topic. Which, of course, she did.

"I want to hear the truth from your own lips," her mother began.

"The truth of what?" Lizzie questioned, as if genuinely taken off guard.

Her mother's face turned several shades of red before she very nearly exploded her declaration. "You know perfectly well what I'm talking about. The matter of you marrying the Vandermark man while already being married to Mr. Albright."

"Oh. Well, the truth of that is quite simple. Stuart and I were never legally bound. Father checked into it and discussed it with some of the best legal minds in Philadelphia. Even so, he figured you might feel better if a formal annulment was filed. He did just that. I have copies of the papers, if you'd like to see them."

"Where is your father? I'd like to take this up with him. No doubt this is all part of some underhanded scheme of his. Legalities are never resolved so easily, and certainly not in a manner to benefit a woman."

"We parted in Lufkin after the storm passed through. He needed to get back to his family. He said you could contact him once you returned home if you had questions."

"You are a selfish girl. You have no idea what harm you've caused." Lizzie's mother turned to Stuart. "What of your father? Can he come to our aid? Can this situation be reversed?"

Stuart narrowed his eyes as he looked hard at Lizzie. "I would not have it reversed, madam. I do not want the leavings of another man."

Lizzie felt her cheeks grow hot, but she held her tongue. She was glad G. W. was away working; otherwise Stuart might well have suffered a broken jaw.

"Oh, this is most outrageous. You had no thought except for yourself. I cannot believe you would cause so much suffering, Elizabeth Cady Decker."

"Vandermark."

Her mother's eyes narrowed. "I don't care what you call yourself; you had a marriage first to Mr. Albright."

"And he clearly does not want me. He said so himself. Not that he has a choice in the matter." She smiled and got to her feet. "I suppose now you will want to return home?"

Mother stood, as did Stuart. "Stuart, I am sorry that you had to come all this way and lose important time with your business dealings. I know you needed to marry in order to receive your inheritance. Perhaps you will find another suitable prospect—someone who does not care about love. As for me, I could not marry for anything less."

"You'll have a lot less when I get done with you and your beloved Mr. Vandermark," Stuart stated matter-of-factly. "You think this to be over and done, but I assure you, I'm not one to stand for such treatment. You gave your word to me—accepted my proposal and planned a wedding with me. I will not forgive you for making me the fool." He picked up his hat and headed for the door.

Fear washed over Lizzie as Stuart's threat began to sink in. Her mother only gave her a smug look.

"You should have known better than to insult a man of means," her mother said. "You have sown the wind, and now you will surely reap the whirlwind."

❧

Deborah sat beside her mother, while Rob and G. W. sat to the left with Lizzie. Uncle Arjan had said that it was important they all be at the gathering and give their honest opinions, but as of yet, Deborah wasn't at all sure what this was about.

"After careful consideration," Uncle Arjan began, "I decided to call this meetin'. I already talked to your mother about this, and we're in agreement. However, we won't move forward if there are any objections from you."

"Objections about what?" G. W. asked. "This isn't makin' a whole lot of sense."

Arjan gave a small chuckle. "I s'pose I am backin' into this rather than just going headlong. This is the situation: In order to build the company and expand the business to meet Mr. Perkins's contract, I'm of a mind to take out a loan. It's not somethin' I've considered lightly, but I think it's necessary. We need new equipment, extra mules, and workers. We'll need to work fast, too. My thought is to secure the loan, usin' the land as collateral. The risk is minimal to us, given that we have the contract with Perkins. However, should something happen to Perkins, I believe we'll have little trouble selling the wood to other mills."

G. W. nodded and looked to Rob. "Makes sense to me. What about you?"

"Sounds good."

Mother took that moment to speak up. "I believe this is what your father would have wanted. He had hopes of expandin' the business."

Uncle Arjan nodded. "There are other considerations, too. The house could use some repairs and expandin'. We'll have to work those things in as time allows or hire someone to help."

"I think it sounds like a good idea," Deborah offered. This expansion would keep her working harder than ever.

G. W. leaned back in his chair and crossed his arms. "Seems we're all in agreement. So what's next?"

"I'm thinkin' to go to Houston. I've already had word from a bank there. We shouldn't have any trouble gettin' the loan."

"When will you go?" Deborah asked.

"I figured to leave on Saturday. I can meet with the bank folks on Monday and set home that night if everything is worked out."

"They'll probably want to see a copy of our contract with Mr. Perkins," Deborah said thoughtfully. "I'll have that ready for you."

"They'll want the deed to the land, too," G. W. added.

"Your mother has already provided it," Uncle Arjan replied.

"Will you bring some new workers back with you? We've had a hard time with David not well enough to work, and like you said, when we go to cuttin' even more trees, we're gonna need extra help," G. W. said.

"I 'spect to bring at least five men back with me. They'll need a place to live, and your mother suggested we could bunk 'em at my cabin temporarily. It'll be a bit snug, but I think it will work out until we can help 'em get another place to stay. If they're family men, I'll speak to Zed about what's available in town."

"I prefer family men," Mother interjected. "They're more reliable—not so likely to go drink away their wages."

"If the weather holds and don't get too cold, they could use the tents," G. W. suggested.

"That's a good idea," Uncle Arjan said, nodding. "The other issue at hand is the growing problems we're having with the rooters. The razorbacks are startin' to be a real nuisance, eatin' the young trees and destroying any new growth."

"We've been thinkin' about ways to stop them, but it just ain't that easy," G. W. added. "Can't lay traps or somebody's livestock is likely to walk right into them."

"Can't fence, neither," Rob added. "You know how folks feel about that 'round here."

"Still, we have to find a way to protect the new growth," Deborah said, giving it serious thought. "When I was in school, I attended several lectures that discussed the idea of replanting. I realize most logging companies like to clear the land and move on, but we've always thought differently. This is our home."

"Our living, too," Mother agreed. "Your father always said it was important to be a good steward of the land."

"Are there other options for getting rid of the rooters?" Lizzie asked. "I mean, what about just shooting them and using the meat to feed the crew?"

"That's a good idea, but the rooters are mostly out at night. It would be tricky to have someone hunt them," Uncle Arjan replied.

"I think we should ask around and see what other folks are doin'," G. W. suggested.

"Dinner's on the table," Sissy announced from the hall.

Mother rose. "Thank you, Sissy. I suggest we head in to lunch."

Deborah got to her feet and the others followed suit. "Uncle Arjan could easily explore the matter while he's in Houston. Other logging industries must be dealing with the same problem. There might already be a ready solution."

"It's worth tryin'," her uncle agreed.

ꕤ

Christopher Clayton took a seat toward the back of the church and suppressed a yawn. He'd been called to deliver a baby in the middle of the night and this, added to the busy week he'd already endured, had left him exhausted.

Brother Shattuck stepped to the front of the church with a troubled expression. "Brothers and sisters, I've had some sad news come to me this morning. Apparently a group of troublemakers attacked a black man last night down by the mill pond. No one knows who the men were, but I suppose we can imagine why they felt the need to do this man harm. It comes as no surprise to anyone here that many whites hold a great deal of animosity toward those of a differing color."

Christopher wondered why he hadn't been informed or called upon to help the man. He had often been summoned across the tracks to treat the people of color. With Brother Shattuck's next statement, however, it became clear as to why the doctor had been unnecessary.

"The man died as a result of his injuries. He wasn't even discovered until an hour ago. He was a good man—a man with a family, just like many of the men in this congregation—but others decided he didn't deserve to live."

He moved down from the pulpit and came to stand directly in front of the pews. "I can hardly believe that civilized men would act in such a manner. There's not a man in this community who doesn't know sorrow and death, and in knowing such miseries, should not willingly give them to another. I'm more saddened than I can say."

There was a low murmuring in the congregation and the man beside Christopher elbowed him sharply. "Preacher ought to mind his own business and talk about the Scriptures." The woman beside him nodded in agreement.

The man to Christopher's left leaned forward. "Somebody ought to teach that preacher some manners."

Suddenly, Christopher felt wide awake.

"This country suffered a terrible division over slavery, among other issues," the preacher continued. "Like a family at odds with one another, this nation fought a war that left many without their fathers, sons, husbands, and brothers. They're mourning in the black church today, and our community faces dealing with the murder of Mr. Samuel Davis."

"Samuel?" Mrs. Vandermark stood in shock. "He used to work for us. Who would do such a thing?" She buried her face in her hands and began to weep.

Deborah came to her side and put an arm around her mother. "Brother Shattuck, is there something we can do to get justice for this man?"

"Justice?" someone questioned from behind Christopher. He turned to find an older man scowling. "Justice was probably already done served. Folks don't put others to death for no reason."

"That's right!" the man beside Christopher bellowed. "Sins of the fathers revisited on the children. That's in the Good Book."

Brother Shattuck's sorrow turned to disbelief. "Listen to yourself! That isn't what's happening here."

"My guess is that man committed a crime." This came from the man at Christopher's left.

"Then the law should have been summoned to deal with the situation," the pastor replied.

In a matter of moments, the entire church erupted in conflicting opinions. Christopher saw Deborah lead her mother from the church and followed after them. They'd barely stepped outside when Deborah's mother collapsed. Christopher stepped forward quickly and caught her before she fainted to the ground.

"Mother!" Deborah reached for her mother's hand.

"She'll be all right. She's had a bit of a shock. Where's your wagon?"

"Just over there," Deborah said as she pointed. "I'll lead the way."

Christopher followed her and gently eased Mrs. Vandermark onto the wagon bed. She rallied as Deborah tapped her hand.

"Mother, are you all right?"

"Oh, what's happened?" She struggled to sit up, but Christopher held her back.

"Take it easy. You fainted."

She looked up at him and shook her head. "How embarrassing." Her expression changed as she appeared to remember the reason. "Oh, poor Samuel. His wife must be beside herself. Two little children and no father. What in the world caused those men to kill him?"

Christopher met her tear-filled eyes. "I couldn't say."

"Hate," Deborah whispered. "That's what made them kill."

Christopher felt a chill run down his spine. No doubt she was right. He'd seen such things before and had hoped to never see them again. For a moment an unpleasant memory came to mind. Hate had been at the very heart of that horrendous moment from his past. Hate had very nearly taken a life then . . . just as it had taken Samuel Davis.

Chapter 25

October 1885

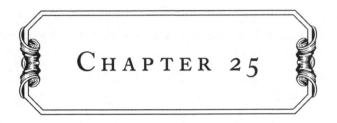

Deborah wasn't surprised that her mother insisted on helping Miriam Davis and her two young sons. Mother's compassion extended to everyone, but especially to those who had no means to help themselves. Not only was it fitting to help the widow and orphans as the Bible commanded, but Mother viewed former employees as extended family—even if their skin was the color of ebony.

"Did you remember the green beans?" Mother asked. Deborah helped her mother get up into the wagon.

"Yes, ma'am. Ten quarts, just like you said." Deborah hiked the skirt of her dark blue gingham dress and climbed up beside her mother. The early morning air had a hint of chill to it, but Deborah didn't expect it to last for long. The afternoons were still warm and sunny, sometimes hot. She loved this time of year. The hardwoods were starting to turn colors; the promise of things to come.

Sadly, she couldn't help but wonder if Samuel's death was also foretelling the future. Back East, she had seen ugliness directed toward many people—not only those whose skin was a different color. There had been many problems with hatred and prejudice toward the Irish and Jews, just to name two groups. Here in Texas, there was more than just a disliking of the Negroes—whites were quite negative toward the Mexicans, as well. In fact, Mr. Perkins wouldn't even hire those of Mexican or Indian blood. His grandparents had suffered under the Mexican government and Comanches had killed other members of his family years earlier.

"Do you suppose we'll see more killings?" Deborah asked as they drove to the Davis home. "A great many people around here seem to feel free to overlook what's happened."

"I hope there won't be further conflict. Arjan plans to speak to Zed about puttin' some additional men out to guard the area. Some old hatreds have stirred up since he hired new people to work at the sawmill. Sometimes it seems the war took place just yesterday."

Deborah focused on the road ahead. "I don't suppose folks will ever be willing to completely forget."

"And maybe they shouldn't, lest we repeat the wrongs. However, forgiving the past is important. My parents held slaves, and so did their folks before them. It's not something I'm proud of, but it's a fact. When Mr. Lincoln called for an end to slavery, my family complied. They believed that the law of the land was to be obeyed. They didn't agree with secession, but it caused them to face much ridicule and anger from their neighbors."

"But that war was about so much more than just slavery," Deborah countered. "I heard an esteemed statesman in Philadelphia. He spoke of the war as if it were really the final steps of our country's battle to become a nation. Until the war, we were simply a collection of individual states without a cohesiveness to join together as one. States' rights were always considered more important than that of the nation as a whole. The fight was also about bringing us together as one."

"Sometimes you have to tear down to build up," Mother replied. "But I don't like seein' where the bitterness has taken us. There will always be those who consider themselves better than their brothers, but the very idea of takin' a life because a person looks different—has a different manner of speaking or religion—that's just wrong. How can good Christian people act like that?"

Deborah shrugged. "Maybe because we aren't really as good as we'd like to think. Being a Christian doesn't mean we are perfect. Besides, don't forget slavery is discussed in the Bible. Many people used that as an argument to support and defend it."

"But now a woman is without a husband and her children without a father—and for what reason?"

Mother brought the wagon to a stop in front of the Davis home. There were several older women gathered near the open front door, while small children played in the dirt. Deborah helped her mother from the wagon, then went to the back to unload the goods they'd brought.

"Afternoon, Miz Vandermark," one of the women greeted.

Deborah heard her mother respond and ask after Miriam Davis. She was surprised when Dr. Clayton came from the house. He spoke momentarily to one of the women before spying her. He gave a brief wave and made his way to where she stood.

"Is someone ill?"

He nodded. "Mrs. Davis. She was expecting another baby, but sadly, she lost it. Poor woman was hysterical. I gave her something to make her sleep."

"First Samuel, and then a child." Deborah looked toward the house and thought of the family that lived there. She knew what it was to lose a father—the void could never be filled. She turned back to find Dr. Clayton watching her with such intensity that it caused her to tremble. "We . . . ah . . ." She waved her hand over the end of the wagon. "Mother wanted to bring the family some supplies."

"I'll help you carry them inside," he said.

Mother joined them. "Dr. Clayton, how good to see you. I hear that Miriam has suffered a miscarriage. Is she going to be all right?"

The doctor lifted a box of canned goods. "I believe she'll make a physical recovery, but she is devastated over the losses she's suffered. I was just telling Miss Vandermark that I gave Miriam something to help her sleep."

"That's for the best, I'm sure," Mother replied. "Is it all right if I go inside and speak with her sister?"

"Of course."

Mother led the way, while Deborah and Dr. Clayton followed behind with their loads. Inside, the cabin smelled of pork grease, tobacco, and death. In the corner, an old black woman sat and puffed on a pipe while keeping watch over Samuel Davis's body. Deborah nodded to the woman as they passed by.

Placing the box on the rickety dining table, Deborah took a moment to look around the cabin. It was terribly small—hardly big enough for one, much less four. The furnishings were mostly homemade and poorly constructed.

Miriam's sister Ruby came from the back room. Her eyes were red-rimmed, and she bowed her head as Deborah's mother took hold of her arm and spoke in a low, comforting voice.

"Ruby, we've brought some canned goods, cornmeal, sugar, and a couple of hams. I wanted to make sure the family had plenty to eat during this sad time."

"Oh, Miz Vandermark, what we gonna do without Samuel?"

"Don't fret. Now isn't the time. Miriam needs you to be strong for her." The younger woman nodded and began to sob as Mother embraced her.

"Why don't you take me to Miriam," Mother said, drawing Ruby with her toward the bedroom. "I know she's sleepin', but I just want to look in on her."

"I'll get the other boxes," Dr. Clayton told Deborah in a whisper.

Several of the women who'd been outside came in and gathered round the old woman. Deborah felt uneasy, almost like an intruder as a couple of the women began to wail. "I'll go with you."

He nodded and allowed her to go through the door first. Once outside, Deborah drew a deep breath of the fresh air and looked to Dr. Clayton. "Thank you for your help. If you need to get back, however, I can manage."

"Nonsense. I don't mind at all. In fact, I can get these last two boxes. Why don't you just wait here." It was more a command than a question. He hoisted one box on top of the other and headed back into the house.

Deborah leaned against the wagon bed and cast a quick glance around the yard. The children were still playing in the dirt, avoiding the awkward sorrow inside. The two Davis children, Jonathan and Saul, were among them. She thought to go and speak with them, but Dr. Clayton was returning.

"Thanks again," she told him. He smiled and she felt her stomach give a flip. The feeling took her by surprise. *What in the world is wrong with me?* She struggled for a moment to think of something to say.

Blurting out the first thing that came to mind, Deborah tried hard to push aside her discomfort. "Do you have any idea how we might trap wild hogs?"

Dr. Clayton looked at her oddly for a moment, stroking his chin as if truly considering the question. "I can't say that I've ever had to deal with wild hogs." His brows rose as he cocked his head to one side. "I don't think I've ever known anyone who wanted to trap a wild hog . . . until now."

Deborah looked to the ground. "I suppose it's just been on my mind. We're having trouble with the razorbacks eating the young pines. We were just talking about it and looking for ways to deal with them."

"What about fencing off your land?"

"No, that won't work. It's too expensive for one thing, but for another, folks around here despise fences. They want their cattle to graze freely. Fencing the land would only make enemies, and in time, folks would simply pull the fences down."

"I see. And I suppose you couldn't just fence small areas of these young trees? Maybe even around each small tree?"

"I suppose it's a thought," Deborah replied. "Very labor intensive, but possible. We talked about traps, but of course, with other animals moving through the area, it's too dangerous."

"That makes sense, but what of creating some sort of trap that would allow only something the size of the rooters to enter? Fix it in such a way that they couldn't get back out once they were inside. It would only contain them, not harm them."

"Is there such a trap?"

"I believe so. Your brothers are handy with tools—they might even build one of their own."

Deborah heard her mother's voice and turned to see her coming from the house. Mother reached out to take Dr. Clayton's hand. "Thank you for helping Deborah with the boxes."

Dr. Clayton put his hand over Mother's. "It wasn't a problem at all. Are you doing well? You look a bit tired."

"I am. This grief has kept me from sleeping at night."

"I could give you something to help," he offered.

She shook her head. "No, I use the time to pray. I figure if the good Lord wants me to sleep, He'll bring it about." She smiled and patted his arm. "I hoped that we might meet up with you while in town. I wanted to invite you to join us for supper tonight. Can you make it?"

"I believe I can." He looked at Deborah. "Perhaps we can talk to your brothers about building those pens."

Mother glanced to Deborah and then back to Dr. Clayton. "Pens?"

"For the rooters," Deborah explained. "Dr. Clayton has an idea of trapping them in a pen—something only big enough for them."

"And even if it caught other animals, it wouldn't harm them. Of course, the rooters might if they got inside with them. It's not without its dangers."

"We can discuss it over supper," Mother said. "I think Arjan would like to hear your ideas."

∞

Christopher eased back from the Vandermark table and patted his stomach. "I must say, of all the folks who've blessed me with a meal, you offer the best. Just don't let it get around, or I might have to go back to cooking for myself."

"No, we'd simply have to have you here for supper every night," Mrs. Vandermark declared.

Christopher glanced across the table at Deborah. She was

beginning to captivate his thoughts in a most unexpected way. Several times a day, she would come to mind. He tried to tell himself that it was only because of her interest in medicine and how he thought she should be trained as a physician. But he knew better. It wouldn't be hard to lose his heart to her. Perhaps he already had.

"Doctor?"

He looked at Mrs. Vandermark in surprise. "I'm sorry. I was just thinking of other things. The meal was incredible. I've never had such delicious pecan pie. I'd love to send my mother the recipe. It's not as heavily sweet as the one she makes. I actually prefer it."

"I'd be happy to send her the recipe. It's one I brought with me when I moved to Texas. It goes way back in our family. Speaking of which, I don't believe I know much about your family. You came here from Kansas City, is that correct?"

Christopher drew a deep breath and nodded. "I did. My mother and father live there still with five of the children at home."

"That's right. I seem to recall there were fifteen children in your family."

"Yes. I'm the oldest."

"Goodness, but I can't imagine how your mother could even get through the day."

Laughing, Christopher easily remembered those times. "She is extremely efficient—much like you, Mrs. Vandermark. I have no doubt you'd handle it in easy order."

"You are sweet to say so," she replied. "Why don't you and the boys go discuss buildin' the pens now? Deborah can bring you more coffee."

Rob got to his feet. "I think Dr. Clayton's idea is a good one. I already have some ideas about how we can do it."

Christopher thought to excuse himself from the gathering, but a part of him didn't want to leave. He had come to enjoy this family.

They reminded him of home and of all that he was working for. His gaze settled on Deborah once again. He was treading dangerous waters. He'd come here with one purpose—to make money for his family. He needed to keep to his plan.

Chapter 26

November 1885

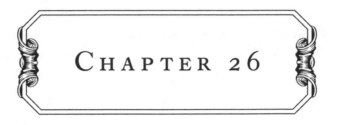

I hope these traps work," Rob told G. W. as they secured the last of the makeshift pens. They pounded stakes to fix it to the ground, then adjusted the door.

"Should do just fine, long as the rooters go for the bait."

Rob pulled out a bucket of slop and poured it inside the pen. "Can't imagine them passing up a treat like this." He laughed and threw the bucket into the back of the wagon. "That makes six pens. Guess we'll see what happens in the mornin'."

Decatur and Jasper looked up from where they'd been lazing under a tall pine. At the sight of the boys loading their tools into the wagon, the two hounds got to their feet and stretched. The sun had dropped below the trees, and the damp air took on a chill that made everyone long for the warmth of home.

"So who you gonna take to the Christmas dance?" G. W. asked his brother. They climbed onto the wagon seat, and G. W. picked up the reins.

"Haven't decided if I'm takin' anybody. You take someone, then you gotta dance with them most of the night. I ain't got my fix on one gal just yet, so I may not ask anyone."

"That's gonna break many a heart," G. W. said, laughing. He reached for the brake as Decatur got wind of something and bounded off in the opposite direction, barking. Jasper followed suit.

"Guess they got the scent of a rabbit," Rob suggested.

"Rabbit stew would be a nice change of pace. What say we put off headin' home for a bit and follow after 'em?"

Rob nodded and grabbed his rifle. "Sounds good to me."

G. W. secured the reins, grabbed his own rifle, and jumped from the wagon. He couldn't think of anything he liked quite as much as his mother's baked rabbit stew. Just the thought made his stomach rumble.

The two men took off in the direction of the dogs, following the baying as Decatur and Jasper led them deeper into the woods. Just as they neared a freshly cleared area, the baying changed to more of a bellowing bark.

"I don't think it's a rabbit they're after," G. W. said as they slowed. "Maybe they've treed a cougar."

"Most of 'em have gone west—at least that's what Uncle Arjan says."

"I know, but it ain't impossible for them to still be around. One was spotted north of here just a couple months back."

Rob nodded, and G. W. pointed. "There they are."

They saw the two dogs had something backed up against the steep creek bank. Without warning, the animal charged, and the brothers could now see it was a razorback—by the look of its size, a male. Jasper quickly jumped out of the way, but Decatur wasn't so lucky. The hog took him by surprise and dragged the dog to the ground in a vicious attack. Blood spurted from Decatur's neck as the tusks dug in.

G. W. and Rob closed the distance to the ruckus. Rob fired his gun over the hog's head but found it did nothing to deter the beast. Jasper tried to join in the fight, but the hog simply knocked him out of the way. Yipping in pain, Jasper got up and charged again.

Rob yelled and fired the rifle, while G. W. called to Jasper and Decatur. Jasper came, although reluctantly, while Decatur was still locked in combat. Rob took careful aim and fired at the rooter. The animal moved, however, and the bullet just glanced off the thick shoulder hide. Even so, it caught the hog's attention, and it quickly abandoned its attack and ran for a brushy thicket upstream.

G. W. rushed to Decatur, while Rob chased after the rooter for a short distance. G.W could see that while the dog was still alive, he was mortally wounded. They would have to finish him off; otherwise, he'd suffer.

"Sorry, boy," G. W. said, reaching down to stroke the hound's bloody face. "You've been a good friend." Decatur whimpered in pain, and G. W. lost little time putting a bullet in the animal. It brought tears to his eyes to kill such a good companion. Jasper began to howl mournfully.

Rob walked back, shoulders slumped. "I lost track of him. I heard the shot and figured you had to put Decatur down."

"Yeah," G. W. said, shaking his head.

Rob handed him his rifle. "I'll carry him back to the wagon. We can bury him at home. If we leave him here, that rooter will just dig him up."

G. W. nodded. "You're right. Let's go."

ꕥ

After a week, the traps proved to be a good investment. They had captured more than ten rooters, and the family shared the meat among the Vandermark workers. Deborah was deeply sorrowed at the loss of Decatur but certainly no more than Jasper and Lula. They seemed to mope around, seeking far more attention than they had before the death.

"I suppose animals mourn as do we humans," Deborah told Lizzie as they sat together on the porch. "Still, it seems so sad. They can't understand or be comforted by mere words."

"I think they're comforted, just the same," Lizzie said as she stroked Jasper's long silky ears. He placed his head in her lap and rested there while the ladies conversed.

"I wish the train would come. I'm so excited about going to Houston, I can hardly stand the wait," Deborah said, getting up again to look down the tracks. They were waiting for the southbound log train in order to catch the Houston East and West Texas line in Perkinsville. It had been determined that since Arjan had secured the loan for the Vandermark expansion, G. W. and Rob would escort Lizzie and Deborah to Houston, where they could buy extensive supplies for the business. If the Rabbit kept any kind of schedule, they'd be bound for Houston before nightfall and hopefully settling into their hotel sometime the next morning.

For Deborah's part, she hoped to buy a crate of books to keep her busy during long evenings. She didn't know how she could feel so lonely in a house full of people, but she often did.

"I hear the whistle," Lizzie declared, jumping to her feet. "G. W., the train is coming!"

She went inside the house and called again. Deborah could

hear her brothers respond and reached down to pick up her valise. Mother came from the house to bid her good-bye.

"Are you sure you won't come with us?" Deborah asked. "We'll have a great time."

Mother smiled and shook her head. "No, Arjan and I have a lot to do. We need to get that pork smoked, and I have to make sausage and soap."

Deborah frowned. "Maybe I should stay."

"Nonsense. I've hired Miriam and Ruby to help Sissy and me. They need the money, and the work will help keep their minds occupied."

Reaching out, Deborah hugged her mother close. "I know they'll appreciate your kindness."

The train chugged slowly to a stop aside the Vandermark property. The small siding train wasn't all that powerful, but it got the job of hauling logs to Perkinsville done in good order. Jack waved from the engine compartment.

"Come on, boys! Train's a-waitin'," Mother called.

G. W. and Rob came from the house carrying the rest of the suitcases. Two trunks were already by the rails. They made quick work of loading the bags, then assisted Lizzie and Deborah into the engine before they climbed atop one of the log cars.

"Let's go!" G. W. called out. They all waved to Mother. "We'll be back as soon as possible."

"Be careful. I love you all." Mother returned their waves.

In Perkinsville, Lizzie found a letter waiting for her. She held it up to Deborah. "It's from Mother."

"Well, open it and see what she has to say," Deborah encouraged. "Perhaps she's accepted the idea of you marrying G. W."

"I seriously doubt that." Lizzie opened the missive and scanned the lines of script. "It's just as I thought. She's telling me how I have solely managed to undermine the suffragette cause—delaying the vote for years, maybe even decades."

"You are such a powerful foe," Deborah said, smiling.

Lizzie continued. "She said that Stuart's father was giving serious consideration to pursuing the matter of my annulment, but . . ." She stopped speaking and looked up in surprise, "Stuart has married."

"Oh, that is good news." Deborah leaned closer and glanced down at the letter. "Does she say who he wed?"

Lizzie nodded in surprise. "Yes. He married Jael."

"Our Jael?" She was the only other real friend that Lizzie and Deborah had known in Philadelphia.

"Yes. Listen." Lizzie turned her attention to the letter. "Mother says, 'He returned home a heartbroken man, and when Jael learned of your treachery, she eagerly sought to offer him comfort. The two were quietly married a short time later. Stuart's father not only welcomed the match, he praised his son for the union. I hope you realize what you've lost.'"

Lizzie looked up. "I cannot believe Jael would marry such a man. She never cared all that much for Stuart."

"I thought, in fact," Deborah said, putting her finger to the side of her temple, "she was in love with Ernest Remington."

"I did, too. She told me the night before my wedding to Stuart that she fully intended that theirs would be the next wedding to take place. She seemed quite convinced."

"Apparently things have changed."

Deborah shook her head slowly. "This will certainly complicate our friendship with her."

"To say the least."

ꕥ

Houston had grown at a rapid rate and looked nothing like Deborah remembered. Now boasting nearly ten thousand residents, the town had blossomed into a bustling city to rival some of those back East. Of course, it had a long way to go to match Philadelphia, but it was well on its way.

The foursome settled into a small but elegantly appointed hotel. It was determined that in order to save money, the ladies would share a room and the brothers would take another. G. W. looked less than pleased at the arrangement but said nothing.

The train trip had been anything but restful, so rather than strike out for the day, everyone in the party decided a brief nap might serve them well. G. W. and Rob, however, changed their minds and came to tell the girls their plans.

"We're goin' over to the bank," G. W. said. "I need to make sure there are no problems with our credit so we can get started right away in buyin' the equipment."

Deborah barely suppressed a yawn. "When will you return?"

"Before evenin'. You and Lizzie sit tight," G. W. instructed. "This is no place for you to go off gallivantin'. We'll be back in time to take you to supper. If you get hungry before then, you can get a meal downstairs."

"Very well," Deborah said, though she already had in mind that after she and Lizzie rested, they might visit some of the nearby shops. She appreciated G. W.'s protective nature, but honestly, she saw nothing to fear. There were hundreds of people walking about on the street. A person would have to be a fool to accost another, for surely half of those present would come to the aid of the afflicted person.

G. W. kissed Lizzie quite soundly before giving Deborah a questioning look. "Are you sure you don't want to bunk in with Rob?"

Deborah laughed, much to Lizzie's apparent embarrassment. "He snores. Lizzie doesn't."

G. W. nodded. "Don't I know it."

After the men had gone, Deborah and Lizzie stretched out in the bed. They dozed comfortably for nearly two hours, and when Deborah rose, she found Lizzie standing at the window.

"Is something wrong?"

Lizzie turned and smiled. "No, silly. I just wanted to see what was out there. You know, for as large as Houston is, it still seems rather primitive."

Deborah straightened the covers and sat on the end of the bed in order to secure her boots. "I'm sure the shops will still have a better selection than we can get at home."

Lizzie came to her. "You aren't thinking of going out, are you? G. W. said—"

"I know what he said, but I'm a grown woman. I fared for myself just fine in Philadelphia, and I will fare for myself fine in Houston. Remember—I once attended finishing school here. Of course, that was quite a few years ago and the town has changed a great deal, but I can't imagine there being a problem. You will come with me, won't you?"

"I shouldn't," Lizzie said. "G. W. wouldn't like it at all."

"He's too protective of you."

Lizzie looked at Deborah for a moment, then sat down beside her. "I've been longing to tell you something."

"What is it?"

Lizzie's cheeks reddened. "I believe I'm with child."

Deborah let out a squeal of joy and grabbed Lizzie to hug her. "Oh, what happy news! No wonder G. W. doesn't want you to go out on your own."

"G. W. doesn't know yet. I wanted to surprise him at supper.

Hopefully, he'll forgive me for telling you first, but I wanted you to help me surprise him."

Deborah nodded. "To be sure, I will. We should talk to the hotel manager and ask about a suitable restaurant. Tonight must be very special. Come on. We can go shopping tomorrow. For now, we need to prepare. We'll probably need a long-handled broom."

Lizzie looked at Deborah in confusion. "Whatever for?"

"To sweep G. W. off the ceiling after he hears the news." They giggled, pressing their heads together like two little girls with a secret. Then Deborah straightened and sobered just a bit. "Of course, we might also take smelling salts with us . . . just in case."

Chapter 27

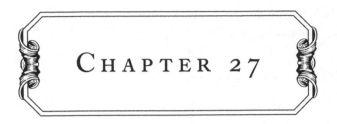

With the arrangements made for a special supper, Deborah found that they still had plenty of time to explore the shops near the hotel. She convinced Lizzie to join her but knew her friend was feeling uncomfortable as they ventured outside.

"G. W. isn't going to like this, Deborah."

"Once he sees that we've returned unscathed, everything will be fine. He should have seen us in Philadelphia."

Lizzie shook her head. "No. No, he would never have approved of that. We were rather . . . reckless at times."

Deborah grinned. "I suppose so, but we weren't as wild as some. Oh look, the shop across the street carries fabric. Let's go explore."

They maneuvered across the busy street narrowly avoiding

several carriages before reaching the other side. Deborah pulled Lizzie into the shop.

"Welcome, my dears," an older woman greeted them. "Are you looking for anything particular today?"

"We need some material for making diapers and baby clothes," Deborah announced.

The woman nodded and led them to a stack of flannel. "This is the best for making diapers."

"How much do you suppose we should purchase?" Lizzie asked.

"Well, ten yards will make you a little more than a dozen diapers," the woman told them. "You'll want at least two dozen diapers available to you, and if you can afford it, I highly recommend three dozen."

"That sounds good. We'll take enough for three dozen," Deborah said, then looked to Lizzie. "Does that sound good to you?"

"I can't imagine a baby ever needing so many diapers, but if you say so," she replied, looking at the woman as if for confirmation.

"Believe me, you'll be glad for them," the saleswoman assured her. "Now, come this way, and I'll show you some wonderful fabric for little gowns."

They spent half an hour picking out material and another twenty minutes in choosing buttons and trims. They ordered the things to be delivered to the hotel and then continued down the street, glancing in store windows as they went. Turning onto one of the side streets, Deborah pointed to a millinery shop.

"Oh, look there—just beyond that small alleyway." She led the way. "Let's go inside. That little straw hat would be perfect for Mother."

"We've already been gone for some time," Lizzie said, glancing back down the street in the direction they'd just come. "Don't you suppose we should go back?"

"It's just now four o'clock. We can take another half hour, at least." Deborah entered the shop and quickly forgot about the time.

By the time they exited, the sun was beginning to set in the west. "I suppose we'd better go back," Deborah said, shifting the hatbox to her left hand. She looped her arm through Lizzie's. "After all, we want to get you all dressed up for dinner. No sense in making such a wonderful announcement looking all shoddy."

"I look shoddy?" Lizzie questioned in horror. She looked down at her gown.

"No, silly. You look just fine. I was only teasing you. Come on."

They had reached the alley when a man dressed in a sorry-looking black suit came hurrying out. He plunged between them as though trying to get past. Without warning he turned and slammed Lizzie backward. She stumbled into the wall of the building, while the man reached for Deborah. Realizing he meant no good, she swung the hatbox hard against his arm. Her action momentarily stunned the man.

"Unhand me," Deborah demanded. Perhaps the man was drunk. Perhaps he was a thief. Either way, she wasn't going to stand for him molesting them. She went to Lizzie and took hold of her arm.

The man rushed at them and grabbed at Deborah's waist for her chatelaine. "Give me your money!"

Lizzie screamed for help, but Deborah knew she would have to defend them as best she could until help arrived. She tried again to knock the man out of the way with the hatbox, but this time he was ready for her. He ripped the parcel from her and tossed it to the ground.

In one motion, Deborah hiked her skirts and kicked the man

hard in the shins. She then turned and pushed Lizzie toward the street. "Get help!"

The ruffian took hold of Deborah and swung her back against the hard brick wall. The action infuriated Deborah, and she kicked him again, but this time her skirts wrapped around her legs, deflecting the blow. Doubling her fist, she sent a punch into the man's face with all the force she could muster. Pain coursed through her hand and up her arm. Hitting someone wasn't nearly as easy as her brothers made it look.

"I'll teach you a lesson you won't soon forget." The man gave a growl and reached out to twist Deborah's right arm to her side.

Frantic to maintain some sort of control, Deborah screamed and pummeled the man with her left hand. He took the first blow in the shoulder and grunted, but still refused to let her go. She doubled her efforts with the second attack, but this time he ducked. To Deborah's surprise, however, her fist connected with another man—her would-be rescuer.

The man let go of Deborah and whirled around to face this new adversary. Deborah hurried to the opening of the alley, where Lizzie awaited her. By now a couple of cowhands had come to their rescue, as well, with a police officer following close behind. The thief didn't stand a chance to escape.

Once the man was manacled and taken away, Deborah turned to thank her original rescuer. To her surprise, it was none other than Mr. Wythe. He beamed her a smile and pointed to his reddened eye.

"You pack quite a wallop, Miss Vandermark."

"Mr. Wythe! What are you doing here?"

"I'm in Houston selling bulls for breeding. I recognized your sister-in-law and was crossin' the street to say hello when she started hollerin' for help."

"Oh, am I ever glad you were here," Deborah replied. "Imagine—someone trying to rob us in broad daylight!"

"Well, it's not exactly that," he said, waving a hand to the twilight skies. "Can I escort you ladies somewhere?"

"We're at the hotel just around the corner and down a block." Deborah looked to Lizzie. "You weren't hurt, were you?"

"No, just scared."

Deborah nodded. "Me too."

Jake laughed. "You didn't look scared. You looked mad."

"I was that, too. I tend to get angry when I'm afraid."

He took hold of Lizzie's arm and then reached for Deborah. "I'll keep that in mind for the future."

He led them toward the hotel, talking all the while about his new purchases and the affairs of the ranch since he'd last encountered them.

"I never figured to see you two here. I did, however, give some thought to stopping off in Perkinsville on the way back north." He threw Deborah a grin.

The comment took her off guard. She wasn't at all certain what to say, so she changed the subject. "Seems you've become my guardian angel once again, Mr. Wythe. I thank you for the help."

"No problem. What, if you don't mind my askin', were you two doing out unescorted anyways? Houston can be kinda rough."

Deborah tried not to sound offended. "I hadn't expected trouble. I attended finishing school here some years ago and . . . I was remiss in considering the changes."

He nodded, looking as though he were pondering a great mystery. "I suppose you were well protected back then."

Deborah couldn't deny that fact. She was never allowed to go anywhere without the escort of someone from the finishing school. "So how long will you be in Houston?"

"I leave tomorrow. I've been here for a week already. I found a prime bull and some great heifers. I plan to strengthen our herd when I get back home."

By now, they'd reached the hotel and Deborah motioned Lizzie inside. Her friend paused, however. "Mr. Wythe, would you care to join us for supper?"

Deborah held her breath. She had hoped they could get by without having to explain their trouble to G. W. and Rob. Neither would be happy with her.

"It would be a pleasure, ma'am, but I'm afraid I can't." He looked to Deborah and boldly gave her a wink. "Although I'm mighty tempted."

Deborah looked away quickly. She tugged on Lizzie's arm. "That is a pity, Mr. Wythe, but we do understand. We'll bid you good day, and thank you once again."

He gave a little bow and chuckled. "You are welcome, Miss Vandermark, and don't be surprised if I don't turn up for a visit one of these days."

She nodded uncomfortably and hurried Lizzie up the steps to the hotel. Inside, she finally let out the breath she'd been holding. "Lizzie, what were you thinking inviting him to supper? We can't let G. W. and Rob know what happened. If they saw Mr. Wythe and he mentioned the situation he found us in—why, we'd never hear the end of it."

"I don't imagine we deserve to hear the end of it," Lizzie said. Deborah continued pulling her up the stairs. "G. W. would want to know."

"Well, as my mama used to say, 'Wantin' and gettin' are two entirely different things.'"

They reached their room without further mishap. Deborah unlocked the door and all but pushed Lizzie into the room. It wasn't until they were inside with the lock secured that Deborah let down her guard.

"I was afraid G. W. and Rob might return and find us out there. Now we can just pretend that nothing happened."

"They're going to know we went out. The fabric will be delivered in the morning."

Deborah looked around the room. "Oh bother—I forgot about the hat I purchased. I suppose it's lost forever." She frowned and began taking the pins from her own hat. "It was such a lovely hat, too. I suppose it's a small price to pay." She looked at Lizzie's doubtful expression. "I don't mind them knowing about our outing, as much as what beset us during that time. Still, if it doesn't come up, there's no sense causing them to worry. Now, let's put it aside and talk about what you're going to wear tonight. You have a big announcement to make."

༄༅

G. W. had never seen his wife looking more radiant unless it was the day they'd married. Tonight she seemed to even outshine that glorious event. She and Deborah kept their heads together through a good portion of the meal, but finally as dessert was served, they seemed less preoccupied.

"This chocolate cake is delicious," Deborah said casually. "I think I would very much like the recipe. Do you suppose the cook would let us have it?"

Her brothers shrugged. Rob stuffed another bite into his mouth and nodded. "It is mighty fine."

"Don't speak with your mouth full," Deborah chided.

"She's startin' to sound more like Ma every day," Rob said with a frown.

"Speaking of mothers . . ." Deborah let the words trail off and looked to Lizzie.

"What about them?" G. W. looked perplexed.

Deborah elbowed Lizzie. "Go ahead."

G. W. frowned. "Does this have to do with that letter your ma sent?"

Lizzie shook her head. "No. Not in the least. I . . . well . . ." She looked at Deborah before turning back to her husband. "We're going to have a baby."

Nothing could have surprised him more. G. W. looked at Lizzie and then Deborah. Maybe he'd misunderstood. He glanced at Rob, who by this time was grinning from ear to ear. He punched G. W.'s arm.

"Well, if that ain't something. Congratulations there, big brother."

G. W.'s gaze was locked with Lizzie's. She smiled ever so slightly—almost shyly. "A baby? For sure?"

She nodded. "I've been pretty certain for a while now, but I wanted to wait. I hope you aren't displeased. It is rather soon."

"I couldn't be happier." G. W. leaned over toward Lizzie and kissed her gently on the cheek. "A baby."

"Why, hello there."

G. W. looked up to see Mr. Wythe. He was grinning and holding a battered hatbox. "Mr. Wythe. It's a surprise to see you."

"I just dropped by to bring this to Miss Vandermark. The clerk at the desk said you were in here havin' supper, so I thought instead of leave it with him, I'd deliver it personally."

G. W. was confused. "How did you know we were staying here?" Just then he noticed the younger man's black eye. "What in the world happened to you?"

Wythe put his hand to his face. "Your little sister packs a wallop. That's what happened to me."

A feeling of dread washed over G. W. He looked to Deborah for an explanation. "You have something to say?"

She clamped her lips together and shook her head. G. W. then looked to Lizzie. "What's this all about?"

"You mean you didn't tell your brothers what happened?" Mr. Wythe asked Deborah.

"I didn't see the need," she said in a rather curt manner. "After all, no harm was done."

"Except for Mr. Wythe's eye," Rob threw out. "That's quite a shiner."

"It was an accident," Deborah declared.

"Yeah, the man she intended to hit ducked. I just happened to be behind him."

"I guess you'd better have a seat, Mr. Wythe, and tell us the whole story. I'm not likely to get it out of my sister anytime soon."

The man laughed. "Wish I could stay, but fact is, I've got other business to tend to. Like I said earlier, I just wanted to drop this off." He handed the hatbox to G. W. "I hope you'll excuse me now."

G. W. got to his feet. "Thank you for your . . . Well, I'm sure you were probably very helpful. Knowing my sister, I can only imagine what mighta happened. Of course, she was supposed to be safely asleep here at the hotel, but somehow I get the feelin' that wasn't how she spent her afternoon."

Mr. Wythe gave a chuckle. "I'll leave it to her to tell. Evenin' to y'all."

G. W. didn't even wait until Wythe had departed the dining room. He turned to Deborah and Lizzie. "Somebody better start talkin'."

Deborah shrugged. "We went shopping."

"We? You mean Lizzie went, too?"

She glanced at the now-empty dessert plate. "I did."

"I thought we had an agreement." G. W. shook his head. "What happened?"

"It wasn't our fault," Deborah began. "We were walking back to the hotel when a man tried to get my money."

"Deborah hit him and actually was faring pretty well when Mr. Wythe came along," Lizzie added.

G. W. shook his head. "It ain't safe for a lady to walk around unescorted down here. Please promise me you won't go out alone again."

Lizzie put her hand atop his forearm and nodded. "I promise."

As they walked back to their rooms, Deborah took G. W. aside. "I'm really sorry. I know you're mad at me, but I'm asking you to forgive me."

G. W. eyed her for a moment. "I don't know what I would do if something happened to one of you. You're the smartest one of us, yet sometimes you don't use the sense the good Lord gave you."

"You're absolutely right," Deborah agreed. "I suppose I get in my mind that I can do a thing without the help of anyone else. I'm sorry. It won't happen again. I promise." She squeezed his arm. "Please forgive me."

"Of course I forgive you." He smiled and led her to the room. "We'll knock on your door in the mornin' when it's time to go down for breakfast. Then we'll take you out shoppin'."

Deborah stretched up on tiptoe and G. W. bent down for her to kiss his cheek. "Good night, brother of mine."

G. W. waited as she opened the door. He peaked in at Lizzie and motioned her to the door. Lizzie stepped into the hallway with him, and after a quick glance down the hallway, she wrapped her arms around him. G. W. pulled her close and lifted her face to meet his. He felt her melt against him as he kissed her.

"I'm so happy," he declared.

"I was worried that you'd think it too soon," Lizzie said, pulling back just a bit.

"God's timing is never too soon or too late. This baby will be right on time." He grinned and kissed her once more on the forehead. "I'm gonna miss you tonight."

He released his hold on her and she stepped back. "No more than I'll miss you." She opened the hotel room door and paused. "Maybe I can convince Deborah to share Rob's room. I'll start working on her tonight."

G. W. laughed and waited until she'd closed the door. Maybe they should just splurge on an extra room.

Chapter 28

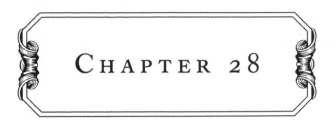

Christopher was surprised and concerned to find Euphanel Vandermark sitting in his waiting room when he finished with one of his patients. He reached out to help her up from her chair.

"Are you ill?"

She shifted her basket to her left hand and reached in with her right. "Not at all, Dr. Clayton. I've come with a plate of cookies and an invitation."

He eyed the gift and couldn't suppress a smile. "What a pleasant surprise. Now, what is it you're inviting me to?"

"Thanksgiving dinner. I hope you haven't already made other arrangements."

"Not at all. I would love to share your table. Is there something I can bring?"

"Just yourself," Euphanel replied. "I know the family will be delighted to see you. Especially Deborah."

He considered her comment for a moment. Deborah had been on his mind a great deal lately, almost against his will.

"I understand she's in Houston."

She nodded. "They're due back the day before Thanksgiving. Sissy and I have already started workin' on the arrangements. She'll be with her own family and friends for the day, but we'll get much of the work out of the way the day before. I wanted to arrange it so that Deborah and Lizzie didn't feel obligated to jump right in and work."

He smiled and reached under the cloth to sample a cookie. "I'm sure they'll want to help, no matter how much you've managed to set in place." He bit into the cookie and found a wealth of spices and nuts. "Mmm, this is wonderful."

"I'm glad you like them. They go well with coffee. They're a pumpkin nut cookie that Sissy created. Our family is quite fond of them."

"I can see why."

"Well, I should let you get back to work," Euphanel said, turning for the door.

"I'm not exactly overwhelmed at the moment."

She stopped and looked at him over her shoulder. "Is there somethin' on your mind?"

He was taken by surprise. "Why do you ask?"

Euphanel turned and her expression reminded him very much of his own mother. "You just seem to . . . well, you seem deep in thought."

Christopher acknowledged her perception, but he wasn't all that comfortable in sharing the truth. "I just appreciate your kindness. I miss my family, and you've helped to fill that void by allowing me to be a part of yours."

"And, of course, there's Deborah."

He looked at her and shook his head. "What do you mean?"

Euphanel looked thoughtful. "I suppose I shouldn't say anything. After all, I've only got my own intuition to go on." She shrugged. "But in my opinion, it's obvious the two of you were meant for each other."

Stunned, he felt his eyes widen. "I . . . well . . . Deborah is a wonderful young woman."

"She is that, and I believe she thinks you a wonderful man. You have a great deal in common."

Christopher didn't know what to say. How could he explain to Deborah's mother that he had lost his heart to her daughter but intended to do nothing about it?

"You know, Dr. Clayton, if you don't put your claim to her, someone else will."

He frowned. "It isn't that easy."

"And why not? Have I misunderstood how you feel about her?" She fixed him with a puzzled look. "Do you plan to go through life alone?"

"Not at all. But there is the matter of my family. My father is unable to work. My mother cannot earn enough to properly care for the family. There are a lot of mouths to feed and bodies to clothe. Without my help, they wouldn't be able to make it very well."

"And you think this would be a problem for Deborah? Why, she would fully support you in such a matter. She's doin' much the same for her own family—only we aren't in as great a need."

"But without a wife and children of my own, all of my extra money can go back to them. A wife would eventually want and need things of her own. Children would most certainly come along, and they, too, would have needs."

"Still, it would be a shame to let true love pass you by. There has to be a way to have both. My guess is that you could probably ask Deborah to wait for you, and she would."

He couldn't help but grin. "You truly think she cares for me that much?"

"I do, but like you, she has it in her mind that she must sacrifice herself for us. It's nonsense, but still, it's her belief. You see, she went away to school to help the family. Had I realized what her deepest heartfelt thoughts were on the matter, I might have refused her."

"But why?" Mrs. Vandermark's comment truly confused him.

"Because she's wrong. Her efforts have benefited us, no doubt about it. I greatly appreciate her desire to improve our business arrangements and handle them efficiently. However, in speaking with her recently, she left me with the impression that she believes she can't marry and risk leavin' us. I told her she was wrong. Perhaps if you give her something more to consider, her opinions will change."

"But it might be years before I could actually wed," he replied.

"All the more reason to secure her hand." Euphanel smiled and resumed her walk toward the door. "Pray about it, Dr. Clayton. I think you'd make a wonderful son-in-law."

ꙮ

Deborah felt a sense of peace and happiness wash over her as her family gathered to celebrate all that God had done for them. Thanksgiving was not taken lightly in this family. Not only was it a time to celebrate a good year of harvest, but it had always been a celebration of God's goodness. For as long as Deborah had memory, she had shared in the family tradition of naming the thing or things she was most grateful for. Each member of the family would tell about the blessings of the year and how God had answered prayers. Mother even encouraged them to keep a journal about it and then share the biggest blessings at the table.

This year was certainly no exception. With the table nearly bowing from the plates heaped high with food, Mother turned to Arjan and nodded. He stood and cleared his throat. "As you know, your father started this time of sharing on Thanksgivin'. I have been blessed to be a part of this family and carry on that tradition."

Deborah glanced at Lizzie. She'd not yet told Mother and Uncle Arjan about the baby. G. W. had suggested she wait and deliver the news during their dinner. Deborah felt almost giddy with delight. They'd had such a wonderful time in Houston, shopping for the baby's needs, as well as Lizzie's. Deborah couldn't help but wish she might also bear a child one day.

Of course, I would need a husband first, she told herself. She glanced across the table to where Dr. Clayton sat. He seemed to be watching her and offered a bit of a smile before turning his attention back to Arjan.

Deborah felt her heart skip a beat. *Goodness, but what is wrong with me? I find myself unnerved by the silliest things.*

She looked up and found Mother getting to her feet as Arjan took a seat.

"I'm so thankful for all of you. My children have always been a delight to me, but now I have the joy of adding another daughter to the family. What a blessing Lizzie has been to me. Deborah, you have also blessed me with your love and care for this family. Even though it's never been your burden to take on, I want you to know that I appreciate and understand your efforts. That said, however, you must also know that I will never stand by and allow for you to let life pass you by."

Surprise must have clearly registered on Deborah's face, because Mother paused. Reaching out, she gently touched Deborah's shoulder. "Don't be so shocked by my words. It's not like I'm sendin' you away." She gave Deborah a squeeze, then went back to reciting her list of blessings.

Deborah could scarcely concentrate on the words. She couldn't imagine what had caused Mother to say those things. It hardly seemed appropriate. What must Dr. Clayton think?

"I have so much to be thankful for, and perhaps one of the sweetest gifts is that God has clearly mended my heart. I was devastated to lose your father, but over the years, I have felt release from that pain. I believe part of it came in G. W. learnin' to forgive himself for what he saw as his role in Rutger's death." She looked at her elder son. "You have to know how hard it was for me to watch you suffer. Seein' you now, having learned to let go of the past and move forward, has been a healing to me."

G. W. bowed his head. "I didn't know how it hurt you. I'm sorry, Mama."

"Don't be. You were simply dealin' with your own grief. How can I fault you for that?" She turned to Rob. "You have always been a bit of a wild one, but I find your love of life has helped to pull me along through my mourning."

He smiled, but Deborah was taken aback to see tears in Rob's eyes. It wasn't often that either of her brothers showed their emotions.

"Dr. Clayton, I'm thankful for you, as well. This community desperately needed a real doctor. You came at just the right time. You are precious to this family, and I hope you will be around for years and years to come."

She turned to Arjan. "Last, but definitely not least—Arjan,

I'm very thankful for you. You have honored me by joinin' with my children to ensure my safety, protection, and well-being."

"You all are my family," Arjan said. "You won't never be without a home or meal, so long as I have anything to say about it."

Mother nodded and took her seat. It was Deborah's turn. Getting to her feet, she thought of all the things that had blessed her.

"I'm thankful for so much. I love . . . all . . . of you." She stumbled over the words, realizing she'd included Dr. Clayton. Hoping no one would make too much of the matter, she quickly hurried on with her statement. "I have been blessed by each one of you in so many ways. I am grateful to have a sister in Lizzie. We have long been friends, but now we are family. I'm blessed by my brothers, who, although they can be a bit bossy and overbearing, love me and only want the best for me. I'm blessed by my education and the life experiences I've had. I am completely thankful for you, Uncle Arjan. Your love and kindness to this family have truly sustained us all."

She paused and turned to her mother. For a moment, her mother looked years younger. Perhaps it was the veil of grief being lifted from her. Maybe it was just the presence of the Lord and the blessing of fellowship. Deborah reached out to take her mother's hand and kiss it.

"I am more thankful for you, Mother, than I have words to say. You have been a constant in my life—an inspiration to me. I thank God for you every day."

She turned back to the table of people. "I, too, am grateful for Dr. Clayton. I'm thankful for his friendship and the way he has shared his knowledge with me." She continued at a rapid pace. "I'm thankful to be home again. I love this place—I love Texas. I'm blessed to be back where I belong."

Taking her seat, she tried not to think about the man sitting opposite her. She tried not to think about his broad shoulders and gentle face. She tried not to remember the times when he'd caused her to feel weak in the knees. She tried . . . but wasn't really making much progress. It wasn't until Lizzie took her turn and announced her pregnancy that pandemonium set upon them, and Deborah could actually consider something besides Dr. Clayton.

When Christopher's moment to speak arrived, he wasn't quite sure what to say. There was a great deal he was thankful for, but speaking it aloud was hard. "I love my family," he began, "and I'm grateful for them. Like Deborah, I'm thankful for my education and also for the friendship you all have shown me since my arrival. I am thankful for this meal, to be sure, and figure you'll be thankful if I keep my comments to a minimum so that we can eat."

Everyone laughed and Christopher took his seat, fearing he might embarrass himself if he remained standing to say more.

G. W. was quick and to the point when he declared his greatest blessings were his wife and unborn child. He spoke of his happiness and the knowledge that God had truly brought it all about. Then Rob stood and told them he was glad they had avoided the typhoid. Everyone nodded, knowing that this alone had been a huge blessing for them.

"I'm thankful, too, that I've never been punched in the eye by Deborah. I've seen what that can do."

Mother cocked a brow. "What are you talkin' about?"

Deborah looked as though she'd like to melt under the table. Christopher waited for Rob's explanation with great curiosity.

"When we were in Houston, it seems little sister decided to go out on her own. She met with trouble, and Mr. Wythe . . ." He paused and looked directly at his mother. "You remember Mr. Wythe, the man who pulled Deborah out of the path of the freighter?"

Mother nodded. "I remember him well." She looked at Deborah while Rob continued.

"Anyway, Mr. Wythe showed up to rescue her once again when a man accosted her and Lizzie."

"Oh my! Is this true?"

Deborah nodded. "It wasn't my best decision."

"Well, she was wallopin' the guy when Mr. Wythe showed up to help her. But it seems the robber ducked and Mr. Wythe took Deborah's blow to the face. Anyway, I wouldn't be surprised if Mr. Wythe don't show up for a visit. I think he's rather sweet on Deborah."

"I hope you won't take another chance like that again," Uncle Arjan declared.

Deborah gave a quick look in Christopher's direction. She blushed and nodded. "No, sir. I don't intend to."

Christopher found himself almost more troubled by Rob's comments about Mr. Wythe than the assault. After all, though Deborah was safe from the man who would have hurt her, she apparently wasn't free from this Mr. Wythe.

He remembered Euphanel's warning about someone else making a claim on Deborah. It seemed there was already a potential suitor. He didn't like the way this news made him feel. It was stealing his Thanksgiving joy and peace. Maybe he should have a talk with Deborah about his feelings. At least that way, he could be the first one to bring up the subject.

Frowning, he shook his head. But what subject was he going to bring up, exactly? Courtship? Marriage? The very thought left him struggling to concentrate.

Chapter 29

December 1885

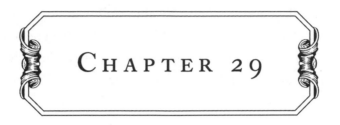

The Christmas dance was only a week away, and Deborah couldn't help but feel uncomfortable. She had been asked to accompany no fewer than five different would-be suitors and had turned them all down. At this point, she wasn't sure she even wanted to attend the dance. Not to mention that Dr. Clayton wasn't among the five who'd asked her to attend. Not that it mattered. Or did it?

"It shouldn't," she told herself. But lately, Deborah wasn't convinced that her heart was listening to her.

"Brought the mail," Rob announced, striding into the room. He gave the stack a toss to her desk. "It looks like Vandermark Logging is startin' to exchange lots of letters with folks. I ain't never seen so much mail."

"Hopefully it won't just be a bunch of bills," Deborah said, glancing through the missives. It took her by surprise to see the decidedly feminine script of her friend Jael Longstreet.

"No, she's an Albright now," Deborah remembered.

Rob raised a brow. "What did you say?"

Deborah opened the letter. "Nothing of importance. I was just noticing a letter from a friend." She glanced at the opening line and smiled. Jael was worried she had somehow broken the most important rule of friendship—never steal a girlfriend's man.

"I'm heading out to the logging site. I'm sure the boys are missing me," Rob said with a grin. "After all, I do more work than any of 'em."

"It's a surprise, then, that Uncle Arjan sent you to town for the new saw blades and axes."

Rob just laughed. "He knows I'm the best at gettin' a good price, too. I can barter better'n anyone."

"Well, get on with you now. It won't stay light forever."

Once Rob closed the office door, she began to read the letter.

> *I never imagined myself married to Stuart, but there are circumstances that brought about this arrangement. One day I will explain. I hope that Lizzie isn't angry with me. I took it upon myself to believe that since she rejected Stuart at the altar, and then again in Texas, she couldn't possibly remain attached. I pray this is so. I would never have wanted to hurt her.*

Perhaps the biggest surprise came toward the end of the letter. Jael wrote of her father's desire to come west and check into the Texas lumber industry. If he did make a trip to Texas, she intended to accompany him. She was certain that Stuart wouldn't mind, and she would simply love to see Deborah and Lizzie.

Deborah finished reading the letter and pondered the situation.

Jael never spoke of loving Stuart. Never once mentioned anything that suggested the two had enjoyed a whirlwind romance. Jael also never said a word about Ernest Remington, her previous beau. It was all very curious.

A knock sounded on the office door and Lizzie came in. "I thought I'd come and see what I could do to help you. Your mother and Sissy seem to have the kitchen under control."

"I was hoping you'd stop by," Deborah said, motioning to a straight-back chair. "Come sit here and read this letter from Jael."

"Jael? Goodness, I never expected to hear from her." Lizzie swept into the room, wearing a simple gown of dark pumpkin. Orange wasn't a color Deborah had ever cared for in clothes, but with Lizzie's coloring, the dress looked quite lovely.

"So what does she have to say?" Lizzie asked as she took her place beside Deborah.

"Here. I'll let you read it for yourself. The news is rather interesting."

Lizzie took the single sheet of paper and scanned it quickly. She looked up and met Deborah's gaze. "I can't imagine what kind of circumstances could come about to cause Jael to give up her interest in Mr. Remington for Stuart."

"I couldn't either. I thought maybe it was something his father wanted, but she also hints that things are not good between the Albright men."

Lizzie nodded and handed the letter back to Deborah. "It doesn't surprise me."

"It would be nice to see her here in Texas, however." Deborah tucked the letter into her desk drawer. "I'm surprised by the entire matter, however. I thought perhaps your mother had erred in reporting the marriage, but obviously that's not the case. I simply cannot imagine the two of them together."

"Nor can I. I thought about the situation for quite some time, and it makes little sense on Jael's part. I can well understand why Stuart did it—he was desperate to get his inheritance. But Jael always had more sense than that. I don't know what could have happened to make her do this." Lizzie's expression was one of worry. "I hope her father didn't force her to marry him."

"Maybe since Jael was the only child still at home and with her mother's passing, her father felt it necessary to see her wed." Deborah began to thumb through the other letters. "If she does come for a visit, we shall have to clarify the matter."

"I agree."

Seeing nothing that couldn't wait, Deborah set aside the mail to take up the balance sheet she'd been working on earlier. "I guess we can begin with this," she told Lizzie. "Although I don't know why you're even bothering with office work now that you're expecting. You have more than enough to occupy yourself in making baby clothes and preparing for this wondrous event."

Lizzie looked rather embarrassed. "I'm afraid I know very little about childbirth. Remember—while you were studying biology, I was learning about European art."

"I know the medical information—at least the portion I could find in books; but you would do better to talk to Mother about the experience. She's done this three times; I'm sure she'll have all the answers you need."

"I feel silly being a grown woman and not knowing. My mother was so remiss in teaching me much of anything that had to do with being a wife and mother. If left to her example for guidance, I'm sure poor G. W. would never have wanted me."

Deborah laughed. "That's hardly possible. G. W. would have loved you no matter. I've never seen two people more smitten."

"And what of you, Deborah?" Lizzie's expression turned quite serious. "When do you plan to open your heart to someone?"

"I . . . I hardly know how to reply." Deborah abandoned her place at the desk and moved to close the office door. Rather than return to her seat, however, she strode to the window and gazed out at the overcast December day.

"What's the matter?" Lizzie questioned. "You've never had any trouble speaking your mind before."

"I know. I've always been able to talk to you or Mother, but this time I feel a bit tongue-tied." She turned and met Lizzie's inquiring expression. "I had honestly figured to stay here—remain single and help my family. Mother is totally opposed to that idea, but all of these years, I thought it was what she and Father wanted. Having me handle the office freed up the men to take their needed places in the forest. Mother and Sissy were then able to handle the animals and the kitchen, and of course now that you're here, they certainly don't need me for household chores. Well, at least not as much." Deborah smiled for a brief moment, then frowned.

"I suppose I'm uncertain as to what I should do. I've planned for one thing all of my life and now that thing seems . . . well . . ."

"To have disappeared?" Lizzie asked.

"No. It's more like it never existed at all. It's as if I invented something in my mind that had no physical substance. Like a child creating an imaginary friend."

She sat down beside Lizzie and gave a sigh. "I feel confused by the entire matter. Mother wants me to marry and start a family. She says she's not, but it's like she's trying to get rid of me."

"Oh, Deborah, that isn't even possible. Your mother has always held a special place in her heart for you. However, I know she's concerned that you would let life and love pass you by, in favor of what you consider duty."

"She said that?"

Lizzie nodded and reached out to take hold of Deborah's hand. "You must understand: She only wants good things for you. She is proud of your intelligence. Proud of the things you've accomplished. She wants you to live life in a way that pleases God, of course. But she also wants it to please you."

"And she believes marriage would be pleasing to me?"

"Who can say? I know she sees the interest young men are taking, and she wants you to feel the liberty of sharing your heart."

Deborah started to reply when they heard a commotion outside. It sounded like Rob calling for help. Getting to her feet, Deborah headed for the office door. "I hope no one is hurt."

She made her way outside as the driver pulled back hard to bring the team to a stop and Rob rose up from the wagon seat. Lizzie came to her side, and it wasn't long before Mother and Sissy were there, as well.

"Come quick!" Rob yelled. "It's G. W.!"

Lizzie swayed and reached for the porch post. "No!" She started for the wagon, but Deborah grabbed hold of her. "You wait here and let me see how bad it is."

Mother and Sissy were already at the wagon. Deborah heard them ask if anyone had gone for the doctor and knew it must be very bad. Lizzie seemed to sense this, too.

"I'll wait," she said, "but please hurry."

Deborah nodded and ran to the wagon. The sight there was not one she had anticipated. For a moment, she thought she might very well swoon. She steadied herself against the edge of the wagon and noted the blood that had soaked through to the wagon bed.

"Rob, what happened?" Mother asked, staring down at her unconscious son.

"He climbed up to top a tree. Somethin' went wrong and the

tree snapped and G. W. fell. A branch impaled his leg. I was just heading out to join them when I spied Klem here driving the wagon like there was no tomorra."

Deborah didn't wait for her mother to comment. She took charge without even thinking. "We need to get him inside. Mother, it would be best to lay him out on the dining room table."

Mother looked at her for only a moment and nodded. "Rob, can you and Klem manage him?"

"We'll do it," Rob assured her. "You just hold the door for us."

"I'll fetch an oilcloth for the table," Sissy said. She was gone before Deborah could so much as comment. She looked to the porch and could see that Lizzie was crying.

"Lizzie, go help Sissy. We're going to need clean towels, bandages, and hot water—lots of it."

Deborah didn't wait to see if Lizzie did as she bid. She turned to her mother as Rob and Klem worked to move G. W. "Mother, this isn't good. He may well bleed to death. I'll do what I can if you'll allow me to. I've observed several procedures and assisted Dr. Clayton. Hopefully, I can do the preliminary things before he gets here."

Her mother took hold of her arm. "Do whatever you can to save him, Deborah. Tell me how I can help."

Deborah drew her mother toward the house. "I'll need your good sewing shears and some tweezers." She noted the piece of tree branch protruding from G. W.'s leg along with bone. It wasn't a simple fracture. Fortunately, someone had strapped a belt around his upper thigh. "We may need some pliers, and get some of the soft soap and melt it in a pan of hot water. After it's melted, cut it with half again as much cold water so as not to burn the skin. We're going to have to clean that wound and see just how bad things really are." She began rolling up her sleeves as she walked toward the house. She could only pray that something she'd learned could now benefit her brother.

By the time the men had G. W. laid out on the table the way Deborah thought most beneficial, her brother had still not regained consciousness. It wasn't a good sign. Neither was the shallowness of his breathing. It was entirely possible he'd broken some ribs and punctured his lung.

The women worked together to cut away G. W.'s trousers. They were hopelessly caked with blood and mud, with numerous jagged tears. Deborah motioned to Rob. He came without hesitation.

"I don't know if the doctor will be able to save his leg. He's got a bad break and he's lost a lot of blood. The wounds are multiple and severe. You may need to lend support to Lizzie. She needs to be careful in her condition."

"You can count on me, Sis. I'll try to keep watch over her. Is there anything I can do to help G. W.?" His worried gaze never left G. W.'s lifeless body. "I shouldn'ta been so slow gettin' back. This might not have happened if I'd been there."

"Stop it. We don't have time for such thoughts. It might not only have happened, but it could have involved both of you," Mother declared.

Lizzie seemed in a daze as she reached out to touch G. W.'s brow. "Please don't leave me," she whispered against his ear.

"He's not going anywhere, if I have anything to say about it. Mother, is the soap and water ready?"

"Just about. Sissy said she'd bring it."

Deborah nodded. "We need to clean the debris from the wound, but in a way that minimizes the bleeding. We won't remove the larger pieces. Dr. Clayton will see to that."

Sissy arrived with the soap concoction and helped Deborah to pour part of it over the leg. G. W. didn't stir or even moan, furthering

Deborah's concern. But she was glad he didn't have to consciously endure the pain.

"We're going to need more light. Please bring several lamps so that we can see better." She hadn't issued the order to anyone in particular, but Mother and Sissy hurried to get them.

Deborah bent over her brother's leg and soaked up some of the dirt and blood with a towel. She then poured additional water over the wound and repeated the process. The flow of blood was stymied by the belt around G. W.'s thigh. The only problem, however, was that cutting off the blood flow for too long would only lead to killing the limb. She toyed with the idea of releasing the belt a bit to allow the blood to circulate through the undamaged vessels. It would also show her whether or not the artery had been severed. If it had, there wasn't much hope of G. W. keeping his leg.

When the lamps were in place, Deborah looked at her mother. "I'm going to loosen the belt to see how bad the bleeding is. Hopefully I'll be able to tell if the artery is pierced. Meanwhile, can you and Sissy strip off his shirt? We need to see what damage was done to his ribs. He's not breathing well."

Everyone went into motion at once. Deborah handled the belt and was relieved when no bright red blood spurted from the wound. Blood oozed from the wounds, but to her surprise it wasn't all that bad. She tried not to think about the fact that G. W. might very well not have much blood left. She opted instead to get back to cleaning the debris. She would leave the belt loosened so long as the bleeding didn't increase.

"Mother," she said suddenly, having a great idea, "do you still have that magnifying glass of Father's?"

"I do." She nodded and headed off without Deborah saying another word. When she returned, Deborah instructed her to hold it over the wounds so she could see better to clean the lacerations.

With meticulous care, she began pulling splintered wood and bits of rock and dirt from the wound. She had worked for maybe thirty minutes when Uncle Arjan rushed into the room.

"Doctor's here."

Deborah straightened. "I've been doing what I could to clean out the debris. I've left the bigger pieces in place for you, in case they caused the bleeding to increase. He seems to be breathing in a shallow manner."

Dr. Clayton nodded and immediately opened his medical bag. Deborah saw that he'd brought a much larger case than he usually carried.

"You keep picking out the small pieces while I listen to his lungs."

Deborah focused back in on her work. She put aside the fact that this was her brother. Such reminders wouldn't serve her well. If anything, it would only cause her to lose her focus.

Dr. Clayton listened to G. W.'s breathing for several moments. "Perhaps a small collapse, but air is moving well." He continued to check G. W. for further wounds. "Arjan told me what happened," he said to Deborah. "Has he regained consciousness since the fall?"

"No, not since they brought him here," she answered.

They both looked to Rob, who shook his head. He turned to Klem. "What about it?"

"Ain't come awake since he fell," Klem told them. "Not so much as a grunt."

Dr. Clayton pulled a large bottle of carbolic acid from his bag. "Hopefully the bleeding helped to clear away some of the fragments."

Deborah pointed to the pan of soapy water. "I used that to clean away the dirt and some of the caked blood. It's Mother's soft soap and warm water."

He nodded while pouring the soapy liquid over the site. Straightening, he then used a liberal amount of the carbolic acid over his scalpel and probes. "Deborah, hold his legs steady, and Arjan, grab his shoulders. I don't expect him to move, but you can never tell."

He noted the belt. "It was good thinking to control the blood flow. I'm going to check the break and situation of the tree piece, and then we'll get to work on seeing if we can save the leg." He looked at Deborah and smiled. "Ready to assist me?"

She nodded. "Just tell me what to do."

Chapter 30

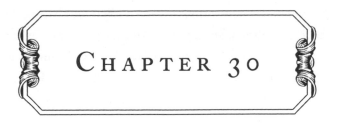

G. W.'s recovery was doubtful the first few hours. His fever soared and his unconscious state was broken only by an occasional moan. Further examination revealed several broken ribs and concern that his back may have been damaged in the fall. The discoloration and bruising were of grave concern.

Deborah remained at G. W.'s side as much as possible as the hours moved into days. Mother and Lizzie were there, as well. The three women took turns cooling G. W.'s feverish body with wet rags. In addition, Deborah helped Dr. Clayton tend to the leg wounds. A makeshift splint was fashioned to hold the bone in place. It was far from ideal, but with the need to watch the wounds for infection, it was the best they could do at the present.

When G. W. finally showed signs of response, Dr. Clayton

started to worry about the degree of injury he'd sustained. "His neurological reactions are slow. However, I'm not overly worried at this point. I think there may be a great deal of swelling along the spinal column, and hopefully that will reduce in time."

Deborah knew how serious the situation might be. Her brother could be left paralyzed. She doubted Mother and Lizzie understood the matter's gravity. Exchanging a look with Dr. Clayton, his expression told her that it was best they kept such thoughts between the two of them. Sometimes knowledge could be the enemy—especially where emotions were concerned. They would know soon enough if G. W. had the ability to move his legs.

"When do you suppose he'll awaken?" Mother asked hopefully.

"I can't really say. We'll know more with each passing day. We need to keep hoping and praying. The fever is down, and the leg looks good. I'm not seeing any infection, but he could still have trouble. We'll just keep watching it closely."

"I'll come again in the morning," Dr. Clayton said as he gathered his things.

"Thank you so much for all you've done," Mother told him. She handed him an envelope. "Tuck this away for later. Maybe it will help your family." He glanced at it for a minute, then put it in his coat pocket. "Deborah," her mother continued, "why don't you take Dr. Clayton to the kitchen and get him a plate of food to take home with him?"

"I will, Mother." She looked to Dr. Clayton, wondering if this would be to his liking. He smiled and opened the door for her.

Deborah made her way through the house knowing that the good doctor wouldn't be far behind. She picked up one of the oil lamps from the front room and carried it to the kitchen as they went.

"Sissy's gone home for the evening, but she kept a plate warming for you on the stove. If you'd rather just sit down and eat it here, I can get you some hot coffee, as well."

He smiled. "Can you sit with me?"

She felt taken aback for a moment. Nevertheless, she nodded and motioned to the small kitchen table. "I've already eaten, but I'll share your company. Why don't we just stay in here rather than go into the dining room?"

"I'd like that." He took a seat while Deborah gathered a cup and the coffee pot. "This is most likely strong. It's been sitting there since supper." She poured a cup and put it in front of him.

Returning the pot to the stove, Deborah next grabbed the towel-covered plate that Sissy had left for the doctor. She removed the cloth and placed the food in front of Dr. Clayton. "I'll bring the silver."

"This looks delicious," he commented.

"It was," Deborah replied, laughing. "Sissy made the most delicious ham loaf with black grape glaze. I think you're going to like it."

She returned with the silverware and a linen cloth, then took the seat opposite him. "I know you're worried about G. W."

"I am, but it serves your family no good to say so. His unconscious state is a mixed blessing and curse. The longer he remains asleep, the more rest his body will get. If he has broken his back or caused grave injury to the spine, such rest will be best. On the other hand, his unconscious state doesn't bode well for injury that may have been done to the brain."

Deborah nodded. "I wish I could have done more for him."

"You helped him a great deal, as did the men at the logging camp. Stopping the blood flow and getting him help as soon as possible were the best things they could have done. You were wise to start cleaning the wound and get him set out on the table. It made a good surgery room."

"There is so much I don't know. So much I wish I did."

"So why not learn?"

She looked at him and shook her head. "Women doctors are hardly tolerated down here. Healers are one thing, and midwives are obviously expected to be women. However, there is little acceptance of women getting an education in any field. Certainly not medicine."

His right brow rose. "And this would stop you?"

"Well, I certainly can't go traipsing off to the university again. Philadelphia allows for women doctors, but the time away from here would be difficult for my family. Especially now." She shook her head. "Goodness, but now G. W. is incapacitated and Lizzie is expecting a baby. There are just too many responsibilities."

"So why leave? Why not stay here and train with me?"

She looked at him in surprise. "I . . . uh . . . don't know what to say."

He laughed and reached for a piece of corn bread. "You could say yes. You could even say that the idea fills you with great joy, because the company would be so agreeable."

Deborah could hardly draw a breath. She felt an overwhelming rush of emotions. Dr. Clayton became quite serious—all hint of humor fading from his expression. He watched her face intently, leaving Deborah unable to look away.

"I'm the only one around here who truly knows the potential you display. I'm one of the very few who recognize your intelligence as something special—something valuable. Others tell you how astounded they are with your ability to think, when what they really mean is that you confuse them. I tell you I'm impressed because I am. I can appreciate what you have to give—what you can yet learn."

Deborah tucked her hands under the table to keep Dr. Clayton from seeing how they were trembling. The very thought of spending hours each day with him caused her to feel rather dizzy. Was this what love was all about? Had she fallen in love with Dr. Clayton?

Maybe I'm just infatuated with the idea of becoming a doctor. She frowned. Maybe that's all it was for him, as well. She knew he had concerns about helping his family, just as she had. Maybe he was actually hoping to train a replacement.

She opened her mouth to comment when Mother came rushing into the room. "Oh, I'm so glad you're still here. It's G. W." Tears were streaming down her face.

Deborah jumped to her feet. "What's wrong?"

Her mother laughed and wiped at her tears. "He's awake."

ꕥ

There was no talk of the missed Christmas dance. Deborah hadn't truly cared about the event to begin with, and now that G. W. was painfully recovering, she had even less interest. Nothing more was said about her learning to become a doctor under Christopher Clayton's tutelage. She began to think perhaps his comments had simply been offered to give her something to concentrate on besides her brother's uncertain future.

As the holidays approached, the atmosphere in the house lightened and cheered. Mother wasn't decorating in her usual holiday fashion, but Sissy still worked to bake many of their favorite treats. The delicate aroma of warm yeast breads and fruitcake filled the air, and visitors were on hand daily to sample the fare. Most came to see how G. W. was doing and even to bring an occasional Christmas gift. Lizzie spent her days nursing her husband and quietly making baby clothes. She seemed almost hesitant to discuss G. W.'s condition with Deborah, for fear of somehow calling disaster upon them.

Mother invited Dr. Clayton to join them for Christmas dinner, but an unexpected baby delivery kept him in Perkinsville. Deborah regretted that he couldn't join them, but she enjoyed her family nevertheless.

As the New Year came and went, Deborah found herself growing more and more restless. Everyone was busy with their own interests and duties; Sissy was very nearly managing all of the chores while Mother helped Lizzie to tend to G. W. when needed. Otherwise, Mother was often off visiting Miriam or speaking to Mr. Perkins on behalf of the townsfolk. The acts of violence against the black folks had increased, and Mother felt quite passionate about helping put an end to such things.

Rains affected production in the logging camp as January progressed. Rob and Arjan were often found in discussion at the kitchen table. Uncle Arjan had hired five men prior to Christmas, and now he was considering arranging for at least two more employees. Added to this, the turpentine company in Beaumont had come to negotiate a deal to harvest resin from the pines prior to their cutting. It was a fascinating turn of events that promised more money for nothing more than allowing their workers to come in and set up their process in forested areas that were not scheduled to be cut for months.

Deborah tried to keep herself busy with the logging books. She faithfully recorded the information of each new employee and arranged their pay in script and cash as Uncle Arjan dictated. In the back of her mind, however, she continued to think of what Dr. Clayton had said. Could it be possible for her to learn medicine and use it to benefit her community?

Deciding to check on G. W. and give Lizzie a break, Deborah left her office work and went to the couple's bedroom. The door was open, and she could see that G. W. had just finished lunch. She smiled and gave him a wave.

"May I come in and visit?"

G. W. grunted a reply, but Deborah wasn't at all sure whether it was in the affirmative or negative. She decided to take it as an invitation, however. Lizzie removed his dinner tray and smiled.

"His leg is aching something fierce today."

"So why are you smiling?"

Tears came unbidden to Lizzie's eyes. "He's able to feel it."

Deborah immediately understood. The swelling to his spine was lessening. "I'm not glad he's hurting, just glad he's feeling." She looked at her brother. "You are quite fortunate, you know."

"So folks keep tellin' me." He sounded less than convinced.

"Why don't you go take a rest, Lizzie? You can lie down in my bedroom. Your old bed is still there. I'll sit with G. W. for a time."

"Yes, go on. I want to sleep anyway, so after I get rid of Deborah I'll take a bit of a rest myself," G. W. declared.

Lizzie hesitated only a moment. "I think I will. I'm sure G. W. will enjoy talking to you. Just come fetch me if he needs somethin'."

Deborah laughed. "There you go again, sounding like a Texan. Next thing you know you'll be drawlin'."

They both laughed at this. Deborah took a seat beside her brother's bed and studied his face for a moment. He was healing on the outside, but he still seemed troubled. Perhaps it was nothing more than his boredom with recuperation.

"So you seem rather . . . well, unhappy?" Deborah half commented, half asked.

"You'd be unhappy, too, if you were facing an uncertain future." His tone was harsh, but Deborah didn't take offense.

"Even the doc can't tell me how long I'll be laid up or if I'll ever recover enough to go back to workin'. If I can't work, how in the world can I support my family? It ain't like there's a lot of jobs for cripples."

Deborah nodded but refused to pity him. "I suppose you're right. I can't see you climbing trees again. Certainly no time soon."

"Exactly. I tried to explain that to Uncle Arjan, and he just kept saying, 'You'll be back in time.'" G. W.'s hard façade seemed to soften just a bit. "We both know that ain't true, but he can't bring himself to say it."

"So what if you had another job to do—one you could even do while you were sick in bed?"

He looked at her as if she'd gone crazy. "And what would that be?"

"What if I trained you to take over the office?"

"I can't read and write well enough for that. I'm not so bad with figures, but even there I don't have the same kind of learnin' you have."

"And I suppose you aren't willing to be taught?" She looked at him quizzically and shrugged. "Maybe you think such things are a waste of time?"

"Hardly. But I'm not so smart as you."

Deborah shook her head. "That's nonsense. You aren't as formally educated as I am, but you are definitely as smart—if not smarter. I could teach you to read and write, as well as keep the books. G. W., it would give you something to fall back on if the worst is realized."

He considered this for several long minutes. Deborah said nothing, allowing him to ponder his words. He was a proud man, but hopefully not too proud to allow himself to be taught.

"I guess I never thought about learnin' anything more. Didn't seem practical."

She could understand that and nodded. "There wasn't time. Father needed you and Rob to join him in the camp. That's why I thought I could best serve the family by going to school and learning all that I could to benefit the business. I always thought that's what Father wanted me to do. Now I realize he was just giving in to my desires. He thought it was what I wanted."

G. W. met her gaze. "But it ain't?"

She drew a deep breath and let it out slowly. "I don't think it is. G. W., I convinced myself that this was what was expected of me. So I gave up any other thought and turned my mind to it."

"And now?"

"Now I see that this could be the perfect answer to your situation. The office and books have to be kept in order. The business end of logging is just as critical as the physical labor, especially now with the turpentine arrangement."

"I reckon I can see that well enough." He frowned and fixed her with an intent expression. "And you really think you could teach me?"

Deborah wanted to shout for joy. The question assured her that G. W. was willing to put his mind to this new venture. "I know I can. You have a quick ability to reason and learn. You figure things out on your own all the time. Now you'll simply have me to help you understand what's what. Not to mention you already have a strong foundation. You can read some, and you know your letters and numbers. I think the rest will come quite easily."

"You sure about this?"

She nodded and got to her feet. "Why don't we get started?"

"I was going to take a nap," he protested.

Deborah laughed. "You can take a nap in twenty minutes."

❧

Christopher didn't know quite what to think when Deborah showed up at his office. It had been nearly a week since he'd been to the Vandermark house, and he worried that perhaps G. W. had taken an unexpected turn.

"Is something wrong?" he asked when she knocked on his open door.

"I suppose you are the only one who can help me determine the answer to that."

He looked at her for a moment, then motioned to the chair. "Have a seat. What can I do for you? Are you ill?" She certainly didn't look sick. She looked radiant, the rich dark green of her gown reminiscent of the surrounding forests.

"I want a straight answer, Dr. Clayton. I don't want you worrying about hurting my feelings or causing me pain. Just a simple yes or no will do."

"I will happily give it, if you will just ask the question." He sat down. "I'm still not very good at figuring out a person's unspoken thoughts. Especially those of a woman."

She folded her hands precisely and nodded. "Very well. Were you serious about training me to assist you?"

Christopher couldn't have been more pleased. He knew the matter was quite complicated, given his family situation and all, but at least this way . . . this way he could spend time with her. If not every day, then at least every week. Looking up, he found her staring at him—waiting for his response. She looked almost like a patient preparing for bad news. He couldn't resist making her wait for an answer as she had done with him.

"No. I cannot say that I was at all serious about training an assistant."

Her eyes widened and her cheeks reddened. She lowered her gaze and seemed to consider this for a moment. "I thought perhaps as much." She looked up, trying hard to appear as though she had her emotions under control. "Very well." Getting to her feet, she headed for the door.

"Don't you want to know my reasons?"

She turned and shook her head. "I think I know well enough. You were simply trying to take my mind off of G. W.'s serious condition."

"Not at all." He got to his feet and came to stand just inches from her. Without asking permission, he took hold of her hand. "I can't train you to simply be my assistant. You are much too intelligent for that. I want to teach you to be a doctor in your own right."

Her mouth dropped open and her eyes widened. *My, but she has the loveliest dark eyes*. She was speechless, which only managed to elicit a chuckle from Christopher.

"So . . . let me . . . let me get this straight. You are willing to train me to be a physician?"

"I am."

"And what will you expect in return?"

The question surprised him. He grinned. "I hadn't really thought of that, but I suppose you can work here to earn your training. That is, if you can spare the time from home."

"And that's all?"

He looked at her and dropped hold of her hand. "Did you expect there to be something more? Perhaps you thought I'd force you to court me? I'm really not that kind of man at all."

Her face flushed scarlet again. "I . . . well, not exactly." She turned her gaze to the floor.

Christopher couldn't help himself. He reached out to touch her sleeve. "I would want to court you only if you truly desired it. I wouldn't want you to spend your time doing such a serious thing unless you could honestly see yourself one day becoming my wife."

Her head snapped up. "You would marry a woman doctor?"

He tilted back his head and roared with laughter. "That's all that you're concerned about? I mention marrying me, and you're only worried about being a woman doctor?"

She shook her head and looked befuddled. "I suppose I didn't think about it that way. Goodness, but you have a way of setting me off balance. A part of me feels like laughing and another part like crying."

"Should I get the water pitcher?" he asked quite seriously.

Deborah immediately calmed and began to smile. "So let me get this straight: You want to teach me to become a doctor *and* you want to court me?"

"That sounds about right. Of course, there is something you need to know, something that might change your mind on the entire matter."

She frowned. "And what would that be?"

"My family. They need me, Miss Vandermark. My father cannot work and my mother can barely earn enough for food. I am sending very nearly every penny I make back to them. Until my siblings are able to help or the younger ones grow up, I cannot think of marrying anyone." He again saw her surprise and added, "Not that I'm proposing. I'm simply asking you to . . . well, commit to waiting?"

She considered his words for a moment. "I think that very wise of you, Dr. Clayton. Your family is obviously in need of your help." She smiled. "It only serves to make me fonder of the idea. I will bide my time."

"But you must agree to stop calling me Dr. Clayton. It makes me feel very old."

She giggled. "But you are old. And your years have made you oh so wise."

He rolled his eyes. "I'm not that old. I'm only thirty."

"Hmm, I suppose that isn't so very old." She cocked her head slightly and smiled. "Christopher Clayton, I would be happy to learn all that I can from you."

He felt the embers of love that had been smoldering within him spark a flame. This woman was simple and complex, all at the same time. How was that even possible?

He gently took hold of her face. Her dark eyes seemed to drink him in. "And I shall be very happy to teach you all that I can."

Turn the page to enjoy

a family recipe from Tracie Peterson,

featured in this book!

Black Grape Tarts

4 cups black grapes
2 Tablespoons cornstarch
1 teaspoon of lemon juice
¾ cup brown sugar
2 Tablespoons butter

Cut grapes in half and pull out seeds. (Or for the old fashioned way: push hulls from skins and set skins aside. Cook hulls until mushy and seeds come free, then strain to get rid of seeds and add pulp and skins back and cook until the skins are tender.) Cook grapes over medium heat until the skins are tender.

Take off the heat and add brown sugar, cornstarch, butter, and lemon juice. Pour into tart crusts. Bake for 20 minutes at 365° F or until the crust is brown.

Sweet Dough Pie Crust

(for tarts—do this ahead of time in order to chill)

4 cups of all-purpose flour
½ cup butter
¼ cup sugar
⅔ cup cold water

Mix dry ingredients, then add butter and mix. It will be crumbly. Add water until dough sticks together.

Divide dough and shape in a flattened ball. Wrap and chill 3–4 hours.

Roll out and use large drinking glass to cut circle that will fit into cupcake pans or mini-muffin pan. Form your tart crust in the cupcake pans. Poke a few holes into the raw dough with a fork to vent and prevent puffing.